A SEASON OF PURE LIGHT

CJ Erick

In memory of my father,
who allowed the universe to exist only on *his* terms.

Acknowledgements

Thanks to everyone who provided early feedback: Travis, and his "agent" Kim N.; Jay, Nelson, Clyde, and John P. Special thanks to Kate for her dead-on word-smithing and reality checks. Thanks to all my children for letting me steal some of their energy. And especially thanks to my wife, Cee, for her faith and support for this obsessive flight of fancy (and fantasy).

Prologue

"Timmistria needs people."

And so Cara cowered with Shawn, standing in line in the rain with all the others, drab and bent like bedraggled pigeons, there despite the weather, the rain — always the rain. And tonight it rolled down her cheeks like warm tears.

What passed for the emigration checkpoint was a tall metal desk under a cantilever awning, dimly lit, foreboding, intentionally stark and intimidating, backed against the ten-meter-high fence that separated them from where they all longed to go. The line of hopefuls moved with the speed of a well-fed snake. Cara tried to calm her heart beating against her breastbone. She clutched the portfolio of transit papers to her chest.

Timmistria, a primitive frontier planet, needed people. Weeks earlier, Cara's emigration officer had read the press bulletin to her: "The beautiful golden world of Timmistria offers pristine landscapes and endless opportunities for adventure and prosperity." She'd tried to learn more about the place as she and Shawn petitioned for passage on the next outbound vessel, but information was sketchy at best. The emigration fees for Timmistria were small, enough that even she and Shawn could find the money.

Unlike Principia, which consumed and digested its human occupants with casual distaste, this world needed people. And it could never be worse than the hell that was Principia. Could it?

There were six people in line ahead of them, and nearly twenty behind, in groups of two and three and four, all milling and uneasy with the same nervous energy of fearful expectation that she felt. Shawn, her younger brother by two years, slouched under his gray-green trench coat and hood, protection from the relentless acidic drizzle. His coat was worn, just like everything they owned, what there was of it. He stared downward, only his nose and chin visible under his hood, and rocked metronomically between heels and toes.

Two people ahead of them presented their papers to the checkpoint agent, a dour, putty-faced man seated behind the chin-high desk. Under the protection of the slanted metal roof and out of the everlasting drizzle, the agent wore only a crinkled black leather jacket over his gray uniform. At his gesture, the two would-be emigrants pulled their hoods back to reveal themselves. The tall one was a woman of dark complexion and wiry dark hair, her features, which suggested Old-Earth-African origin, dimmed by the wan lighting of the checkpoint. The other person was a lighter-skinned man with pock-marked skin and splotches of bleached hair, common marks of a post-gene-war farm worker.

At the agent's nod, they quickly pulled their hoods back over their heads. He waved them past, and Cara's heart skipped and then beat harder with newfound hope. One of four bear-like guards, clad in the red and black leather of the Izio Home Guard, touched a control panel and the gate swung open. The guard shoved the couple through, then stepped in front to block it until it closed. Without looking back, the two lucky emigrants began running, out of the circle of light that illuminated the checkpoint and into the darkness beyond.

Two hundred meters past the gate and electrified fence that held it, in its own pool of light, lay the goal for all of them — the surface-to-space shuttle. The small craft would carry the lucky few to the departing interstellar transport vessel CS Pleasant Princess, headed for several worlds on the Fringe frontier.

Next in line was a group of four, by appearance and demeanor a couple in their 50s and the woman's parents. As the younger man and woman presented their papers, the woman spoke in a strong northern accent of slurred vowels and hissed "s" sounds. The whole clan bowed repeatedly, like a circle of conversing pigeons. Cara's hope at the first couple's success collapsed when the agent barely glanced at the foursome's documents, tossed them back across the tall desk so they struck the younger man in the face, and then waved them all away.

The man protested, which brought the guards from the shadows. They grabbed the emigrants by the arms and necks and hustled them away from the desk, out of the light circle like drunken dance couples. In the eerie calm that followed, the night seemed suddenly darker and the rain colder. Cara felt the fire within her die. She felt the water in her boots, the mucus threatening to drip from her nose, the sores on her arms, the bruises on her legs. If it was possible to age by standing in one place, she grew years older in the next few seconds.

"Papers."

She was drawn back to the high desk, which seemed a sheer merciless promontory as she stepped forward. This was the fourth portfolio of transit documents that she and Shawn had presented at this gate, and these papers, like all the others, had been procured with payments several times more than the official regulation fees. Cara had done other things to get them, memories that kept her awake and shivering at night, things neither Shawn nor anyone else would ever know about.

She laid the documents gingerly in front of the agent, as one might a beautiful broken butterfly. She held no expectation that these would be accepted where all the others had not. And yet she and Shawn had come again, when it seemed they'd been drained of the strength, rinsed of persistence and hope.

Each time they'd come, there was a different agent presiding, another surrogate St. Peter. She wondered by what criteria or cronyism they were chosen, what questions they were asked during their interviews, to find the desired mix of cold-hearted, random judgment. And where did they move to after this occupation, to what other soul-crushing government authority?

The agent yanked the papers from under Cara's fingers with a bored glance. Like those parchment documents, he was an anachronism, serving a function ripped from a lost age.

"Shawn and Cara McElroy, brother and sister." He chewed his words with both contempt and overt suspicion. "Drop your hoods," he croaked, flapping his fingers at them. Cara and Shawn complied. As they stood under the agent's intense but somehow disinterested examination, the guards returned to their stations on each side of the gate, curling their mongrel lips at Shawn as wolves might at a smaller domestic dog. They eyed Cara like a morsel to fight over, leaving little mystery what they would do to her if given the opportunity. And a rejection by this agent could be that opportunity. It had happened to her once before.

She tried to ignore the guards, but they baited her by hooting softly like mourning doves. Determined to keep her poise, she focused on the agent's face and caught him staring at her, not like a hungry dog as the guards were, but like a bird of prey, eyes gray and soulless like glass marbles. She returned the gaze, not knowing what expression would serve best, having failed at this three times before. She must not appear weak, or defiant, or worst, defeated. But how should she carry herself after paying her dues many times over, submitting in ways she couldn't bear to remember but could never forget?

From the corner of her eye, she could see the nearest guard licking between his extended fingers, slurping as if sucking a wet fruit. The others moaned suggestively and snickered. Hearing it, the agent's face turned dark, and he glared down at Cara. Her body chilled as if her own trench coat had been ripped from her, exposing her. When he turned his attention to the guards, her heart stopped beating.

"Shut up, you baboons." He slid the papers back across the desk at her and nodded toward the gate behind him. "Go."

Cara was stunned for an instant but gathered the papers and grabbed Shawn's arm. He stood rigid, like one waiting for a blow to fall on him. She pulled his arm close and tugged him toward the gate. It seemed the guard would refuse to open it, but at the last instant he reached for the panel behind him and the gate swung open slowly.

She whispered, "Just keep moving," not sure if the words were meant for Shawn or her or the gate.

She didn't breathe until they had crossed the threshold and had reached the other side of the fence. Cara fell into a trance then and could do little more than put one foot ahead of the other. She clutched the blessed papers close to her so they wouldn't get soaked and led her stunned brother toward the lights of the waiting shuttle, sitting an impossible distance across the wet pavement. A tall person in a gray or pale green uniform stood at the bottom of the loading ramp, the lights from the open doorway casting an aura above them in the drizzling darkness.

Cara paused so she and Shawn could don their hoods against the poisonous rain. While she covered herself, she caught a glimpse of the person in line behind them, a young woman perhaps four or five years older than Cara, guiding a small boy about five years old. Cara had learned the woman's name on the bus from the terminal. Cristina and her son Paolo were bound for Herpetia, an Old-Earth-sized world about 100 parsecs from Timmistria. She was widowed, her husband having been burned and buried in a mining accident. When she told the story, Cara's throat had clenched at the memory of her own family's similar tragedies. Cristina was trying to join a sister who'd been able to emigrate two years earlier.

Cara stopped to watch, nervous for the young mother and son. Cristina presented her own papers. After a long examination, the agent said in a barely audible voice, "These papers appear forged. Step aside."

Immediately the head baboon lurched forward. The young mother stood her ground at the desk, hands outstretched in protest. The guard grabbed her arm, as he'd done with one of the four prior emigrants. Her hood fell back, revealing her thin face and hollow eyes.

The guard growled, "This way. We need to talk to you in private."

Cara glanced back over to the shuttle. The attendant, now revealed as a tall woman in a simple double-breasted uniform, waved Cara and Shawn forward, but Cara stopped her brother with a hand on his chest.

"We have to help her, Shawn."

Shawn seemed to awaken from his stupor, and together they trotted back to the gate, kicking up water from rain-spattered puddles. The gate had clamped shut, electro-locked against the heavy fortified framework that held it.

Cristina struggled against the guard's grip, reaching for her child, who stood frozen and crying near the desk, his hood down, his dark hair growing wet and slick.

Cara shouted through the gate, so that both the guard and the agent could hear her, "Let them go! You know those papers are real!"

The guard paused to regard Cara, while still gripping Cristina's wrist firmly enough to make her writhe in pain. "Zark off! Get to the shuttle. Unless you want back over here."

"Mamãe!"

Cristina's voice cracked when she called him. "Paolo, come, bebê!"

The agent roared, "Somebody get this kid outta here." To the next people in line, he shouted, "You people step up, or I'll send you all back to your slums."

Cara rattled the gate. "Let her go. I have money." She was lying. Most of their money had been sacrificed on their documents and other illegal fees, and the small amount she carried would surely not buy the woman's freedom.

The guard ignored her and began dragging the struggling woman from her son, who cried and stamped his feet.

The sky suddenly tore open with a sky-spanning streak of white light and a roar that lasted far too long to be thunder. Immediately afterward, sirens began wailing from all around them, and for a brief nonsensical instant Cara thought she'd triggered an alarm. A second streak of light and roar ripped across the heavy overcast.

The guard who'd held Cristina released her, and she fled back to her son. The guards gathered, apparently not certain what was happening.

The agent's voice pierced the siren wails. "Access closed! Clear the field!" The others in line stood for a moment as if stunned but made no move to leave. They gathered in front of the desk, their protests rising in volume and pitch. The guards drew their shock wands and advanced on the emigrants in a human wedge, the air around sizzling with the flash and snap of the electric prods.

Cristina had fallen to her knees and clutched Paolo to her chest. The boy cried and jabbered in emotional Portuguese. The head guard returned to seize her by the arm again. He jerked her to her feet so that she was forced to release the child.

"Come on, you. Not done with you yet."

Cristina fought against the painful grip, then bit his hand. He yelped and backhanded her hard enough to crumple her to the ground.

Cara threw her body into the gate, hoping the impact would jar it open, but it held firm against the heavy magnetic threshold. She looked for a door switch on their side of the fence. "Shawn, help me!"

Ground vehicles and aircraft were coming to life all around them, the whine of fuel-cell engines and turbo-plasma drives adding to the general din assaulting Cara's ears. Behind her, she heard the sound she feared, the shuttle's drives beginning to cycle up.

Part of her brain screamed for her to give up and run to the shuttle, but the sight of the vulnerable young woman being manhandled birthed an upswell of anger and frustration. Shawn found an emergency gate release and palmed it. The gate swung inward, and Cara fell through the threshold, landing painfully on one knee. Shawn helped her to her feet, and they charged through.

The guard held Cristina by the arm and slapped her hard. Shawn pushed past Cara before she could stop him and slammed his entire body into the guard. The effect was like a lemon thrown against a rock. Shawn collapsed against the guard's body and then rebounded and staggered backward. The guard lashed out with his free hand, gripped Shawn by the neck, and flung him to the ground.

Cara joined the struggle. She grabbed the guard's arm and tried to pry his fingers from their grip on Cristina's wrist. But his hold merely tightened, evoking a squeal from the woman. Then he grabbed Cara's arm with his other hand and crushed her against his chest, so that he glared downward into her eyes and breathed cheap alcohol into her face.

"I knew you wanted some of this. You even came back for it."

Cara's wrist held a small pouch of skin she'd grafted on after a brutal street attack. In it was a cocktail of noxious chemicals sealed in a polymer lozenge. She slapped the guard to burst the packet, and the chemicals sprayed into his face and eyes.

"Augggh!" He released both of the women and swung wildly, striking Cara on the side of the head. The blow snapped her jaw around and knocked her sideways, but she staggered several steps and stayed on her feet.

The guard bellowed and clawed at his eyes and face with both hands. Shawn had recovered from his fall and jumped at the guard again, pummeling his massive leather-covered back and shoulders in a barrage of balled fists. He looked like a preteen child against a much larger bully, his blows ineffectual against the guard's armor.

Beyond where Cristina knelt next to Paolo, the other three guards were occupied with their grim blockade, steering the group of protesting emigrant petitioners away from the open gate. The agent stood in his high seat with a hand weapon raised above his head.

"Get back, you scum!" He fired at the ground near the tussling emigrants. An energy bolt struck the wet plasti-crete and spawned a geyser of sparks and a swirling puff of steam.

Cristina resisted when Cara tried to pull her to her feet. She clung to her son and refused to release her grip around his shoulders.

"Shawn! Hurry! Carry the boy!"

Cara's brother had beaten himself weak-limbed against the guard's bowed back and shoulders. His head snapped around at her voice, and he joined her in trying to lift the terrified and shaking woman.

Cara glanced behind him and said, "Hurry, the gate's closing!"

Shawn took the woman's face in his hands, forcing her to meet his eyes. "I will carry him, but you must let go."

She searched his face, then slowly opened her hands and allowed him to pick up the boy. He cradled Paolo to his chest and lunged toward the gate. He slammed it with his hip just before it settled into its frame and pushed through, the boy now a kicking bundle held tightly in his arms.

Cara guided the woman after them. Cristina shivered, either from the electric shocks or from the cold rain. More light streaks crossed the sky, followed by sounds like rushing water that echoed over the field, momentarily drowning out the bellowing of the agent and guards and the cries of the emigrants grappling with them.

Just as Cara and Cristina approached the gate, the head guard leaped from the shadows to block them, wiping his face with a damp rag and menacing them with the shock wand. His mouth moved, but Cara could hear only angry barking over the noises of the aircraft.

Cristina broke from Cara's grasp and tried to run past the guard, but he lashed out with the wand, and she fell to the ground shaking. He struck her several times more, then turned his attention to Cara, slashing the weapon in the air toward her like a swordsman. In a brief pause in the aircraft noise, his voice cut through to her, "Come and get it, bitch!"

She had another chemical pouch on her other wrist, but the wand would keep her too far away to use it.

"Shawn!"

She backed away from the advancing guard. She had learned to be quick in too many street fights, and she knew she could lure the guard further from the gate so she could race around him and escape. But she couldn't make it dragging the injured mother.

Cristina had apparently read Cara's thoughts. When the guard stepped around her, she grabbed his leg and clung to it.

To Cara she said, "Please take Paolo. He'll die here if he doesn't get away." Her face held all the tragedy and fear of a million mothers who had sent their children away to save them.

"Cara! We have to go! They're lifting the ramp!" Shawn stood holding the gate open, struggling to hold the child in his arms. Paolo had seen his mother lying on the pavement and fought to reach her.

"Paolo! You must go! Go with them!"

The guard kicked Cristina's arms away, then struck her again and again with the wand. She cried out at each blow, reaching with her hands, quivering and collapsing to the wet pavement, unable to raise her head. Her eyes pleaded as she whispered, "T-take him. Please."

The guard raised the wand toward Cara, like a big dumb street kid with a blade and a bad greasy haircut. Cara nodded, then bolted around him toward the gate.

She ducked when she passed the agent's desk, trying to avoid his attention. He stood up on the chair's leg supports like a horseman standing in the stirrups. He shouted at the tangle of guards and emigrants, then fired the weapon among them, striking an elderly man with thin gray hair who'd lost his rain hat. The man fell to his knees and clutched his arm.

Cara was past the guard then, but instead of breaking for Shawn and the open gate, she doubled back, leaped to the desktop, and slapped the second pouch of chemicals in the agent's face. He bellowed and stabbed at his eyes. Cara grabbed at his weapon, trying to avoid the trigger and the end of the barrel. The agent was forced to struggle between keeping his grip and wiping at his burning eyes and face. They battled for too long, and Cara could almost feel the guard coming to the agent's aid. She bit the hand holding the weapon, and the agent cursed and spit at her. She almost felt sorry for him, since he'd had the decency to grant passage to her and Shawn, but then bit him again and hammered his wrist on the desk.

"Cara!"

"Go, Shawn! I can't leave her!"

In a spasm of inspiration, she grabbed the agent by the armpit and dug her fingers into the nerves there. His grip weakened involuntarily, just enough for her to wrench the weapon from his hand and slide to her feet. The guard was coming at her in a bull run, but he stopped short when she leveled the barrel at his chest.

She advanced on him then, and he gave ground only grudgingly, testing her, bleeding her of valuable time. A quick glance confirmed the other guards were preoccupied and outnumbered by the emigrants. The agent was busy scrubbing at his eyes with the hem of his shirt.

The guard stopped retreating and refused to go further, so she aimed the gun lower and pulled the trigger. A satisfying bolt of phased light split the gap between his legs and exploded on the wet pavement behind him. He stared down at the singed cloth on his pant leg.

"The next one takes your balls off."

His eyes went wide and then narrowed in rage, but he retreated when she pressed him, this time more urgently. She'd never shot anyone before, but after his abuse of the young mother, she begged him silently to try her again. She fired another round at his feet to motivate him to move more quickly.

"Cara! Now!"

She had reached Cristina, who was shaking from the wand's effects and laboring to rise to her hands and knees. Cara grabbed the woman's arm and tried lifting her, while keeping her eyes and gun sight on the guard. Cristina tried to stand, then fell back to the wet ground.

"You can do it," Cara said. "Lean on me."

The guard eyed them, looking for an opening, a chance to take Cara out. She stared him down. Cristina struggled to her feet, and Cara was able to support her and move backward in the direction of the gate. The guard moved with them, preparing to lunge.

Cara pointed the weapon directly at his heart. "Please try it." He glared but held back, and they continued to back away.

At the gate, Shawn supported Cristina, and together they passed through. Before shutting the gate behind them, Cara stared the head guard down one last time, then considered the other guards holding the remaining emigrants at bay. Shawn followed her eyes and shook his head.

"There's too many and no time. We have to go."

Even as she hesitated, a red and black paneled vehicle rolled up, and a half-dozen uniformed officers piled out, weapons drawn. Cara yanked the gate closed, and the three of them limped into the darkness toward the shuttle, Cara carrying the boy and Shawn supporting the mother. Paolo was too light for his age, obviously malnourished. Halfway to the craft, Cara realized she still held the weapon, and skipped it away into the darkness.

The shuttle ramp hadn't lifted yet, but the craft's engines were revving up to a higher-pitched whine. More streaks of light crossed the sky, and loud roars and drumming of airport operations increased around them. Cara guessed that forces of the Carsinos Rebels were threatening the province.

Shawn waved and shouted to the service crew working on the shuttle's final preparations. The attendant met them at the bottom of the ramp, which began to recede into the hull as soon as they passed through the air lock door. The uniformed woman helped them through the narrow opening and down the aisle, saying nothing about their wounds and damaged clothing. The other emigrants were seated and strapped in, fear still fresh on their faces.

The attendant was a willowy, dark-skinned woman with a voice like melted chocolate, professional and silky smooth, unlike any Cara had heard before. "Find seats, please. We must lift in two minutes."

Shawn helped Cristina into an open seat, and he and Cara assisted her and Paolo with strapping in. Cara's hands and arms were bruised from her struggles with the agent, and the side of her head throbbed from the guard's punch.

Cara asked the attendant, "Is it rebels attacking?"

A sense of guarded tension came to the attendant's otherwise professional demeanor. Now that Cara had a chance to examine the woman's face more closely, she realized the tension had been there all along.

"No, ma'am. We're told Thinker hive ships have begun dropping into the system. The captain of the interstellar vessel has given us less than an hour to dock before he pulls out of orbit. The local fleet authority has ordered him to remain in the system, but he's ignoring those orders."

Thinkers? Here in the Principia System? Cara was suddenly terrified. Could they have cleared their last hurdle, only to be captured or destroyed by the marauding aliens?

"Why would Thinkers be here?"

The attendant could only shrug. To the whole group, she said, "Strap tight. The pilot plans to focus all engine power to the drive, so he won't be able to activate the artificial gravity. It's going to be rough. I'm so sorry about that."

Cara wanted to tell her that none of the passengers cared as long as they made it to the jump ship and out of the system.

Seconds later, the shuttle lifted ever so slightly and then leaped forward, pushing Cara back in her seat. There were gasps from the other passengers, and she found it increasingly harder to draw a breath. Gratefully, Paolo had stopped crying. He apparently found the sensation thrilling and began to giggle.

View screens came to life on all sides, as if the craft were made of transparent metal. Dense gray and brown clouds enveloped them, dotted by flashes of green and purple lights — lightning, she supposed, although no rumbles of thunder penetrated the cabin. Once, a bright white streak passed so close Cara was sure they would collide, but the craft passed above them without incident.

The passengers had fallen eerily silent, except the suddenly courageous Paolo, who laughed at every flash and turned his head from side to side to see out all the windows at once. His mother clutched his hand tightly, her head hanging with eyes closed. Her lips moved, and Cara realized she was whispering a prayer. She was shocked to find she envied the woman her faith. There were times when belief in a higher power would be comforting and supportive. But Principia had pried any such convictions from Cara's psyche long ago, and hope was a difficult commodity to nurture alone.

The pressure holding them to their seats continued unabated, and the shuttle rocked and bobbed as the clouds flashed by them faster and faster. And then they burst into bright sunlight, which filled the cabin with a brash brilliance that blinded Cara. She cried out with the others, bedazzled, and realized it had been months since she'd seen even the dingy sunlight that infrequently reached Principia's twisted ground. The view screens dimmed so the sunlight was more tolerable.

She started when Shawn touched the side of her face, where the guard had struck her. She winced.

He said, "You feel OK?"

She was sure he meant to ask how badly she was injured. Gazing out the windows at the blue sky and wispy white flags of clouds, she imagined she could hear them singing to her. The gray poisonous miasma of smoke receded below them. A gauze enveloped her mind, somewhere between waking and dreaming, and she chose despite her fear and fatigue to answer a different question.

"I feel amazing."

weep, children
when darkness falls on the bony hills
like the witherhawk's shadow
o'er the back of the jarin
ne, weep not in fear
but in loss
depthless and deathless
in emptiness of hearts
as the season of hope passes
and its pure light fades
— Sy-Laril, Timmon poet ca. 2570 GSD

Il Ne-Hilin Sil Gon Arin (*One Death Leads to Many*)
— The Blood Litany

Chapter 1

"The time of favorable weather is for stocking the kithin."
— Timmon proverb

Where is Lonin?

Cara stared into the lemon-rind sky, straining her eyes against the glare, shielding her face from the heat and dust. The summer breeze would stiffen as the day progressed. It already swirled around the single-story buildings in the village square, whined in the amber trees, and tugged at her tunic.

What Cara sought was a star appearing in the east, just over the forest; a star that would blossom into a spacecraft, the landing shuttle from the trading ship. And if this star wasn't one of deliverance, the colony's troubles would multiply. At last, a tiny pinhole of light pierced the haze, blooming blue-white, rising over them before falling slowly toward the south. It wavered and pulsed as it fell. The shuttle pilot was battling strong winds, as she'd feared. The ship's captain had refused her request to delay the landing.

Six years I've been here, the last three as colony manager, and still the rocket jocks won't listen to me because I'm a woman.

Helen, Cara's personal assistant, rocked nearby, her arms wrapped around a leather satchel — the outgoing mail. In the 26th century, people still felt the need to send words on paper. Helen and Cara's other assistant, Mary, who was fifteen years younger than Helen, wore tunics similar to Cara's in the fabric's natural dull tan. Cara's tunic had been dyed pure white at Helen's insistence to identify her as the village manager of

Fairdawn. Cara disliked the higher status the special treatment implied.

I'll wear a natural tunic like the others next time.

A small group of about 30 gathered with Cara and her assistants for the landing. There were men and women in faded short-sleeved shirts, weathered pants, and broad-brimmed hats; typical summer dress for the colonists. Other pedestrian traffic weaved along the streets that intersected near the village center: field workers carrying tools and pushing two-wheeled carts, a jarin-led wagon with barrels of water bound for the filtration plant, teen couriers with red armbands running among them. But still no sign of the Timmon liaison, and Cara and the others couldn't wait any longer.

She sighed and nodded at the two women, and together they led the group of townspeople on the long walk to the landing area, nearly two kilometers southeast of the center of Fairdawn. The wagon teams would be there already, carrying loads of outgoing goods. She was embarrassed by the small stock they had for the ship, six wagon loads of field products and fabrics and seeds, and three of basic ores and geologic samples. So little to offer in the months since the last transport. And sending even this small shipment was a strain on their store of commodities.

The group had walked about halfway to the landing pad when Lonin and three other Timmon rangers appeared at last, emerging from a side path and falling in step with the three women. Lonin didn't look at Cara or say anything, as if his lateness was normal. In fact, he had never been late before.

He was tall, a meter taller than she was. His face, nearly human but with a stronger brow and fuller cheeks and lips, was the yellow of prairie grass, his thick mane like spun copper. He wore his own hip-length tunic, white like hers but with the pleats and vents of the native design, woven from the linen-like fibers of the cannon plant, which Shawn had dubbed "pseudo-cotton."

Feeling her eyes on him, he turned at last and spoke. "Greetings." His voice was impossibly deep, like an enormous bassoon.

"You're late."

The native walked slowly, at least for him. With their long legs, the Timmon could cover a meter with each step and run like antelope. In their early days, she and Lonin had hiked through much of the Timmon territories in the vicinity of the settlement. She'd found herself always running to keep up.

"Shik. We Timmon had a meeting. We sense something odd about this space-ship. There is … concern."

"Odd? In what way?"

Lonin flared his elbows in what was a Timmon shrug. His face pinched downward, creases forming at the corners of his eyes. "We do not know. Something feels wrong."

She pressed him, but he would offer nothing further. They walked on in silence.

The point of light grew into a ball of blue fire that fell before them, disappearing below the tree line. The roar of landing jets echoed in the trees. Lonin pulled his jungle knife with its green half-meter blade and hacked away the viper trees that had grown across the path. Humans and Timmon were too large to be ensnared by the vicious plants, but the whipping branches would still leave painful wounds that healed slowly, oozed, and drew sucking flies.

Cara followed Lonin through the tall amber bushes circling the landing area. The ship had landed and was setting its outriggers, long metal legs that extended to widen the craft's support foundation. With its legs outstretched and its hull a prickly mass of jet nozzles and instrument probes, the craft resembled a gigantic, charcoal-colored night spider.

These craft were designed to land on any of the habitable planets, but Timmistria often pushed them to their limits.

Just let the wind hold off for one more hour.

The breeze defied her immediately and stiffened, pelting her with sand and whistling in her ears. Dust swirled across the landing area, temporarily hiding the bunkers on the opposite side. When it cleared, she spotted the unloading party venturing out of the bunkers with the jarin-drawn wagons.

She waved and held her hands out to halt them. "Stop there until the doors are open!"

The wagon handlers finally saw her frantic signals and retreated to the bunkers. She squelched her irritation. These people worked very hard, but enthusiasm would get a person killed without a dose of sound judgment.

The short blast of the alarm horn sounded sooner than expected, and Cara watched the jarin warily. The shuttle door retracted and the loading ramp descended with all the urgency of flowing mud. When the ramp finally reached the ground, the dull bass throb of the "all clear" horn sounded, like a Timmon foghorn. Cara and her party stepped forward, heads bowed into the gale.

The gangway was a gray plastalloy bridge about three meters wide, suspended from the craft by wrist-thick bars of the same material, with round handrails on each side. The ramp's surface was coated with friction grit to provide traction. Although made of a durable granular material, the surface was worn smooth. This gangway had seen a lot of traffic.

In fact, age touched the lander everywhere. Pit marks dotted the metal surfaces, many patched with a lighter filler material. Panels around the legs and jet ducts were scorched and stained with sooty deposits. Small cracks traveled along the rods supporting the legs. The old girl seemed to sag a little where she rested in the yellow dust. She seemed exhausted. Cara could relate.

A young human male strode down the gangway, rigid against the wind. This would be a third- or fourth-in-command on the trading ship, a junior officer required to make first contact. He was clean of face, perhaps Shawn's age or slightly older. But as he got closer, Cara realized he wasn't in his early 20s; he was a puffy-faced boy barely old enough to shave. His dull gray uniform was too baggy on his long, thin frame and was not new by many journeys. With his dark hair and eyes, and pale skin and facial features, he reminded her of her late brother Tomis. She felt her throat tighten.

The young man spoke in an affected baritone. "First Mate Armbois, at your service, ma'am. Captain Zhenik sends his greetings." He pronounced the captain's name with an odd grinding sound.

"Good afternoon, Mr. Armbois. We're awfully happy to see you."

Behind the first mate came a team of four carrier folk, mammalian beings about the size of chimpanzees. Their faces were covered with thin gray hair and sloped downward to long weasel-like snouts. Their bodies were low and bow-backed and covered in the same gray hair, which sprouted from the sleeves and hems of their pale blue work suits. Six limbs projected from the fronts of their torsos like the legs of insects, and they used any of them as hands or feet as needed.

Gymnastic and strong, they could move a mountain of cargo in a fraction of the time it would take as many humans. They were nearly as intelligent as men, mild in manner and therefore great shipmates, and telepathic. Before her transit journey from Principia, she had never spent time with the carrier folk. But since that time, when she befriended the crew of four on the interstellar transport, she found she had become a friend to them all.

This busy group immediately went about the work of exchanging goods, driven by their characteristic abdominal hum, which was like the pleasant buzz of a bee colony. The carriers formed a line and breezed past her party toward the waiting wagons, each with a large box on its back. As they passed, they greeted her in perfect Galactic Standard. Their lips rippled in waves when they spoke.

"Greetings, Manager Cara!"

She moved aside to let them pass. "Greetings to you all!"

The first mate said, "Ma'am, Captain Zhenik regrets that he was naht able to come down in the shuttle and will naht be able to meet with you in person. We are on a very tight shed-yule, and he must chart our next jump route."

Captains rarely missed an opportunity to make landfall after weeks or months in space. Cara suspected his absence was for a different reason. Perhaps he was very alien and unsuited for this planet, or merely disliked humans.

"Thank you, Mr. Armbois. Please pass along my regrets. Perhaps another time. I believe we are ready to receive the new colonists. Please hurry."

"Very well, ma'am."

Armbois turned and shuffled back up the ramp, but not without gawking at the landscape, the yellow dirt, scrub brush, and amber trees. The carrier folk weaved around him and had already replaced much of the colonists' goods with crates and insulated boxes neatly stacked into the wagons by the time he reached the shuttle's door.

The hot wind blew unrelenting, full of forest smells. Cara's eyes and throat would swell from the bombardment of Timmistria's pollen, and the colonists would spend hours sweeping dust from the goods before placing them in storage.

The jarin snorted and stamped their heavy feet. They were more closely related to reptiles than mammals and tended to hunker down in a thicket of vegetation when the wind came up, but the noise and movement of the wind in the forest made them uneasy and unpredictable. She needed to send the teams and the critical new supplies and equipment back to Fairdawn as soon as possible or risk leaving them on the trail overnight.

At last, the first mate reappeared, leading the new colonists. As a group, they looked like most of those who came to Timmistria, weary, expectant, and concerned by the drab surroundings of the landing area. Cara imagined she and Shawn had looked exactly the same when they first arrived.

"Come on down, folks. It gets much better than it looks here." She waved Helen to her and spoke directly in her ear. "Let's skip the orientation and get the new ones back to Fairdawn. We'll make the speeches in the assembly hall." Helen nodded.

Cara took her usual place just at the end of the ramp, leaving room for the carrier folk to pass. There would be 15 colonists, not a large group but certainly not the smallest they'd had in her time here. Lonin stood next to her like a statue. When the Timmon posed motionless like that, they were usually hiding agitation. Was he so concerned about the ship's occupants? He stared unblinking at the new colonists now coming down the ramp. Just behind, his three Timmon comrades stood frozen and staring as well. She joined them in examining the passengers, looking for something but not knowing what.

Thirteen people descended in groups of two and three, four women and nine men, some couples, most wearing casual loose travel clothing. One couple wearing gray tunics embroidered in red and blue held hands as they descended, giving Cara a brief feel-good moment.

As was her custom, Cara greeted each person by name, welcomed them and then allowed Lonin to greet them. She had taught him the traditional handshake, a challenge for him with his huge two-thumbed hand. During his greetings, he gave no indication of unease.

The last two people on the ship were a blond man about Cara's age, dressed in plain brown work trousers and a matching shirt; and just behind him, a robust but paunchy man of below-average height wearing a yellow long-sleeved shirt over brown dress pants. The first man would be Paul Saarinen, in his 30s; a mechanical engineer who Cara hoped could help them. The second was Julius Dench, in his 50s, listed as a mining expert. Cara had high hopes for him as well.

When Saarinen and Dench stepped onto the top of the ramp, Lonin jerked beside her, and the other Timmon hissed and drew back, palming their blade handles. Lonin stepped up closely at Cara's side, his hand on his blade as well.

She whispered, "Lonin, what is it?"

He growled through clenched teeth. "Can you not see that one, the one whose timeril burns with red fire?"

"Which one? The blond fellow?"

"No, the other. The stout one with the face of a geffin. Death burns in his eyes."

Both men walked deliberately down the ramp, eyes narrow as they peered around. There was an assessing quality to the way each of them surveyed the surroundings, the people waiting, the Timmon, and even Cara, that bordered on suspicion.

Lonin hissed, "Send him back, and the other as well. Do not let their feet touch Timmon soil."

Cara was stunned into paralysis for a moment but then shook herself and walked up the ramp to greet the men. "Welcome, Mr. Saarinen and Mr. Dench. Welcome to Timmistria. I am Manager Cara Harvestmoon of Fairdawn, the village at the center of this Co-Op colony."

Mr. Dench took her hand first. His hand was fleshy and large, but his grip weak. His face crinkled into an indulgent smile, like that of a salesperson, and he spoke in a surprisingly pleasant voice. "Manager. I'm pleased to meet you."

Mr. Saarinen nodded as he took her hand, his grip firm but careful. His face was square and strongly boned, with a solid jaw, and his eyes were an unsettling yellow color. When he spoke, Cara was reminded of the quiet voice of a religious leader she'd met during her later years on Principia. "Pleased to meet you, ma'am."

Cara's mind went as numb as her body. She could think of nothing to do but continue her routine. "This is Lonin, our liaison for the Timmon people, who as you know are our sponsors and friends here on Timmistria."

"Greetings." Lonin's voice was anything but welcoming. He blocked the bottom of the ramp, stepping neither forward nor back, and made no attempt to shake their hands.

Saarinen eyed the Timmon without any expression, and Dench regarded Lonin coolly, like a puzzle to be solved.

After a moment of awkward silence, Cara said, "Please, gentlemen, join the others. We need to get you all back to Fairdawn quickly, in case this wind gets worse." She feared Lonin would prevent the men from disembarking, but he stood aside as they stepped off the ramp and walked toward the waiting group. She waved to Helen and Mary, who led the new colonists from the clearing to the pathway back to Fairdawn. Blowing dust soon obscured them in the wan daylight, and they passed out of sight.

The other Timmon stood in a tight huddle, watching the new ones go and hissing between themselves, tension coiled in their legs, arms and hands alive as they spoke. The one called Kinin, Lonin's cousin and usual travel companion, looked to Lonin and raised his hands in a gesture Cara couldn't translate.

Lonin spoke directly into her ear. "This red one must be brought back and sent away. He cannot stay on Timmistria."

"Dench?"

"Yes. A beast has come to your people, and Death follows closely behind."

So earnest were Lonin's words that Cara was almost compelled to chase after the group and summon the man back to the shuttle. "He's odd, but he doesn't seem threatening."

"To your human blindness, perhaps. To me, his light is a burning red fire. Did you not see how the carrier folk avoided him?"

She hadn't noticed, but thinking about it now, it did seem like the folk had taken a wide berth as they passed by the two men on the ramp.

"What about the other man, Mr. Saarinen? The carriers avoided him as well."

Lonin considered this before answering. "No. He was avoided because he was close to the red one. But he may dangerous also. He is like a closed fist — his light is hidden. Why would he hide his timeril so deeply? He is a mystery, but he is not like the other. There is no question that the red one is evil."

Lonin gripped her arm. "The ship is still here. Order the red beast back. Send Death back with him. Save your people."

Again, she was tempted to do as he asked. Why take a chance on one man when they had so many other problems? She didn't understand Lonin's fears, but the other Timmon obviously shared them. If this fear drove a wedge between the colonists and the Timmon, did it matter that it was irrational?

On the other hand, it wasn't fair to deny the man the opportunity for a new beginning that all colonists to Timmistria wanted. If he proved to be a problem, they could send him back on another flight. If she sent him away now, it would look like a witch-hunt and would certainly discredit her among the colonists. How could she prevent someone from immigrating because "his light was bad"?

"Lonin. I respect your opinion and your counsel. But I can't send him away now, not without a fair chance. Your people have had concerns about others, and those colonists have worked out."

"Not like with this one."

"If I send him away, the other humans will not understand."

"The Timmon will understand."

Cara stared upwards directly into his face. His mouth was drawn into a tight line, and his eyes were narrowed into slits.

"In the eyes of my people, everyone who comes here deserves a chance to make a new start. I'm sure you're correct that Mr. Dench has something bad in his history. But he is here now, and his history is part of the past that all colonists leave behind when we come. To us, he has done nothing wrong. All of these people have tragedies and secrets, maybe even crimes they haven't atoned for. But we welcome them, treating the voyage here as a cleansing experience. And we have never had to deport anyone. It wouldn't be fair to Mr. Dench, or to my people, or even to the Timmon, not to give him a chance. I can't punish a man when he has committed no crimes."

Lonin regarded her silently and then tapped the tips of his tongues together, the Timmon equivalent of a sigh. "Very well, Manager. The decision is yours. But this one is guilty of many crimes, and not the stealing or small violence of some of these others. He is a killer of men, and he has brought his crimes with him. He has not been washed clean on his journey."

Lonin released her arm. Cara felt nauseous and shook her head to clear it. The feeling passed after a couple of deep breaths, and she started toward the pathway. There was a light tap on her shoulder, and she turned to find Germain Beaulieu, one of the crew handling cargo transfer.

"Manager Cara, the carrier folk are refusing to unload some of the containers. Personal things for one of the immigrants. They're saying something about the color being wrong. Should a couple of us unload them?"

Cara looked at Lonin, but his countenance had gone stony again.

"Yes, please do, Tom."

"We'll take care of it, ma'am."

The wind chose that moment to find new strength and voice, bringing a cyclone of yellow dust, obscuring the sun and casting the entire landing pad in a veiled tan light, like the view through dirty eyeglasses. It would complicate the lander's launch and chase her team back Fairdawn. Almost on cue, the ship's alarm horn sounded and the craft's gangway began to rise with a mechanical hum. Most of the wagons had already gone, but the last two handlers waved at Cara and turned their beasts up the road to the village. The draft animals needed no coaxing to head toward home and shelter.

Just when Cara thought they might avoid a balky beast, a roar like the shock wave from a missile strike came at them from the west, and a blinding torrent of wind blasted the field, pushing the grasses and bush almost flat to the ground and bending the trees in a violent dance of thrashing limbs. Branches, small rocks, and flying creatures flashed by, all now dangerous projectiles. Cara crouched and covered her head against objects striking her back and neck. She peeked through her fingers and could barely see the shuttle through the dust and debris. To her horror, it was pulling up its outriggers.

She clutched at Lonin, who had moved up behind her to shield her. "They'll never make it!" she yelled, but the wind tore the words from her mouth and she doubted he heard.

He bent down to press his cupped hands against her ear. "I will help the wagons. Go to the shelters."

She nodded, covered her head with her arms, and struggled toward the bunkers. Her eyes threatened to slam shut against the grit, and she coughed from the hot acrid dust biting her nose and throat. It smelled of rotten vegetation and smoldering brush smoke, laced with the sweet odor of ozone. Cara pulled the front of her shirt up over her mouth and carried on.

Just as she reached the bunker, she heard the warning horn of the shuttle over the wind rushing in her ears, and then the roar of the ground-effect engines. The fool pilot was trying to lift off. She prayed Lonin was safely clear.

She had just reached the nearest bunker when from the dust emerged a jarin. Behind it, still hitched, caromed a supply wagon. The jarin's wide face, with his toad-like mouth and two huge curved tusks, bore a look of terror. He was heading straight for the roaring shuttle.

She called for Lonin, but her words were swept away in the wind. He was nowhere in sight. She covered her mouth with her arm and squinted into the wind, seeing no dark shapes that might be returning villagers. She was alone.

Taking a deep breath through her shirt, she leapt from the bunker and sped off at a dead run toward the cart and jarin. The wind immediately lifted her from her feet and tossed her on her hip in the hard dirt, bruising her side and digging soil and rocks into her skin. She rolled clumsily to her hands and knees and pushed off again, this time lower to the ground, taking low, wide steps.

The runaway cart was past her, careening toward the struggling shuttle. Jarin were not fast but were large and lumbering and powerful, able to pull a twin-axle carriage with several men and supplies with little effort. The beast running from her was large even for his species, and he seemed intent on driving directly under the shuttle. She recognized him from his size and striped brown markings. It was Balthar, and his handler was Jean Caillou. Jean lay motionless in the back of the wagon.

Cara could run fast, a relic of her days on Principia, but she struggled to move her legs against the strong wind that pulled at her clothing and limbs. She lowered her body and pumped her arms to pull herself through the heavy air. She gained ground and in a dozen steps was able to cut off the jarin and grab the side of the wagon.

"Whoa, Balthar! Shik! Nisil!" (*Attention! Halt!*)

The poor beast ignored her. He brayed in a deep moan that somehow pierced the shriek of the wind.

"Whoa, Balthar!" She staggered along beside the wagon until she was even with the jarin's head. She grabbed him by a huge curved tusk, dug in her feet, and leaned back with all her weight. Jarins' upturned tusks were normally filed smooth on the leading and trailing edges for safety, but the yellow tooth was still sharp enough to cut into her fingers. She winced and pulled.

"Shik! Nisil! Nisil!"

The jarin turned slightly but continued to run, dragging Cara along with him. She pulled harder despite the pain, but the jarin was too much for her. He shook his head and tossed her away, almost knocking her off her feet again.

The shuttle's roar increased, and through the dust she saw the outriggers lift from the dirt. As soon as the craft was off the ground, the wind shoved it sideways a dozen yards and the ship's hull crashed into the trees on the far side of the clearing. The jarin paid this collision no heed. Instead, he turned to flash her a confused, fearful glance, then clamped his eyes shut and barreled forward toward the struggling craft.

Cara gained her stride again, leaned forward against the wind, and drove her legs with all their strength. She caught the wagon less than 30 meters from the shuttle, managing to grip the side and throw her body aboard. She landed on top of Jean, who moaned and kicked at her, striking and bending her knee painfully. Despite the pain, she was relieved he was still alive. She clambered over him to the driver's bench. The wagon rocked and nearly threw her out before she could jump into the seat and grasp the reins. She planted her feet against the front floorboard and jerked the heavy leather straps.

"Whoa, Balthar! Nisil! Halt!"

The jarin bellowed again but slowed. He shook his head against the reins and nearly pulled them from her hands. They were less than 20 meters from the struggling shuttle when she heard a murmur from behind. The prone man raised his head and eyed her.

"Jean! Help me!" But the driver's eyes rolled backward, and he collapsed again.

Meanwhile, the shuttle had righted itself and was increasing thrust to clear the trees. Heat from the jets warmed her face and arms.

Cara pulled hard on the reins one last time. The wagon bucked, and she was launched forward onto her hands, busting her lip on the front plank. The jarin's bobbing head was just below her.

"Balthar! Halt!" She raised her fist and drove the butt of her hand square down on the spot between the jarin's eyes. It was like striking a rock covered by thin seaweed. Pain burst from her skin through to her bones.

The jarin carried on for three more steps and then dug his feet firmly into the hard dirt, stopping so abruptly that the back end of the cart reared up and threw Cara out over the headboard. She rolled over Balthar's head and onto the ground right in front of him. She scrabbled to her feet, ready to grab his tusks if he tried to run her over.

But the jarin crouched and held his ground. He bleated weakly and looked at her with an expression of both surprise and hurt that broke her heart. She hugged his giant head and covered his curled ears with her hands. She could feel a deep rumble in his throat, and his face settled into a dark sulk.

The engine thrust roared behind her, and she ducked her head as heat burned her back and neck. She peeked over her shoulder in time to see the shuttle angled efficiently into the wind and accelerating upward. It disappeared into the brown ceiling of windblown dust. Seconds later, the main engines fired with man-made thunder. The normally blinding light was barely visible.

Cara ducked against the wind and lay her forehead on the jarin's head. She cooed directly into his ear, "Easy, Balthar. Easy." She petted his leathery head, feeling the coarse skin and spikes of hair irritating her palm, which was bruised and bloody from where she'd grabbed the tusks.

She fell into a coughing fit that wracked her chest. The beast grumbled again and licked her neck. To her relief, Jean stirred and groaned. But the contents of the wagon were now gone, scattered on the trail by Balthar's flight.

Had they lost the other wagons as well, or was Lonin able to secure them? And what about the villagers and new arrivals — all safe? And this man, Dench, with the evil red light — had she made the right decision? And if not, what could she do about it now?

Chapter 2

Cara raised her voice to be heard above the wind rocking the town government building. "Please welcome Lonin, our host."

Applause was not a universal language among human societies, but those gathered in the main assembly hall, the new citizens and those from the village who'd come to meet them, followed Cara's lead and applauded politely in their own ways. Some clapped, a few flipped their fingers against their thumbs, and one man slapped his thigh. Paul Saarinen clapped absently, but his eyes did not rest. They darted among the crowd, meeting Cara's eyes for an instant and then moving on, taking inventory of everything and everyone in the room. Cara shifted her attention to Dench, who did not clap but regarded Lonin with eagle-sharp attention as the Timmon liaison stepped up to dwarf the human-sized wooden lectern.

"Greetings to you, human friends and … colonists. The Timmon people welcome you to the planet Timmistria. We will help you, but your colony will survive only by the work of your hands."

The colonists' eyes widened, and they seemed as a group to sit straighter and pay closer attention. Lonin was large for a Timmon, which made him an imposing giant among the humans. Even the female Timmon, smaller than the males, were inches taller and broader than the largest human man in the colony. The orientation videos could never prepare the newbies for meeting the indigenous people for the first time.

Lonin's sub-basso voice required attention, even when he whispered. His command of Galactic Standard was impressive, and he learned quickly. The Timmon and Delerin shared one language and were baffled to find that the settlers spoke several. His diplomacy had improved in the six years since human contact, but he still spoke in the straightforward, black-and-white manner of his people. To the Timmon, things were as they were. Using language to soften reality puzzled them.

In this setting, in trying to prepare these people for life on this difficult planet, his directness served a purpose.

"Greetings from the Timmon, and welcome to Timmistria. This is our home. It is all we know. If I say it is harsh, that is a word your peoples use. For us, the ways of Timmistria are as they have been always, and we do not call them harsh. Humans do not know Timmistria, and this not knowing is a … peril. Some of you have been hurt or killed by Timmistria's nature. We will teach you the nature of Timmistria, and we hope you will not join your lost ones.

"There are a few things you must know before we begin your teachings about our home.

"One." Lonin held up a long yellow thumb. "Many Timmon will help you, but many will not. Some do not understand why you are here or why the Timmon council allows your presence.

"Two." He held up the other thumb on the same hand. "Our cousins, the Delerin, permit your colony to stay only because we Timmon ask this. In return, we ask that you follow our customs and the laws of your own people.

"Three." He held up the finger closest to his thumbs. This gesture was also a symbol of the trio of the goddess Timmistria's domains: the planet Timmistria, the hell world Dreyaten that circled the planet, and Deleria, the black star at the center of all things. "The Delerin will not help you, ever. If you insult the Timmon, we will not help you.

"Four." Another finger was raised, leaving only the small, multi-jointed pinky folded under. "We will guide and teach you, but we will not treat you as if you are the very young. If you do not learn what we teach, you will join those who have been lost."

The group was now dead quiet and intensely focused on Lonin's words, even those who had heard this speech before. Cara didn't like this part of the orientation, but it was necessary. The new ones needed to understand the challenges and dangers here.

Lonin lowered his arm now and spoke more solemnly, holding his hands uncomfortably in front of him at his waist. His tone had lost the anxious stiffness from their first meetings, and yet even then, his words had been full of profound wisdom that had impressed Cara. Those hands, intimidating and powerful enough to peel the husk from a chatinil nut, could touch the skin with the softness and tenderness of a lover's lips.

"I am told my manner of speaking can be … blunt? If so, I am sorry. We are sad when your people die, as we are sad when we lose one of our own. Sometimes, new humans come to Timmistria and do not respect her, the dangers here, and the Timmistrian peoples. This is always bad for the colonist. Timmistria will give you many things, but she will not protect you from your mistakes.

"As the sentil of my people, I want you to join this kithin and learn from us. And in this learning, you will teach us of your worlds, your peoples, and the place you call the 'galaxy.' We know little of that large place, and we seek to know more. So this is a good trading part-ner-ship between our peoples, and one that will bring good things to each other's tables.

"The Timmon people have a saying about our home, words you will understand. 'Kalam Timmistria

Kalamin Chassis.' In your language, you may say, 'Timmistria grows all what is planted.' We Timmon will gladly teach you how to plant, so that you may grow well."

Lonin yielded the dais unceremoniously, leaving behind an uncomfortable silence among the new group. Cara made her closing statements, and then her helpers began setting up the tables for the welcoming party. As the group mingled and lined up for the food service, Lonin kept close to Cara, a protective presence at her right elbow. Dench stood along the wall, talking with a group of four men, patting sweat from his brow frequently with a red handkerchief.

Cara started a light conversation with Lonin, details of the next day's plans, normal village business, occupations the new colonists might be directed or persuaded to undertake. These were tired subjects, but she found she couldn't bear his silence. His preoccupation and mental distance disturbed her. His tense expression had returned, and it was like a headache to her, as troubling as his occasional aloofness. The aloofness was typical Timmon behavior. But this disturbed energy, like barely restrained violence, was something she had never felt in him, in all the time they had spent together, either in public or in private.

The Timmon were a reserved, even peaceful people, and she had never thought of Lonin as dangerous before. This day was forcing her to think of him differently.

Chapter 3

"As we grow as species, and technology weaves its magical darkness into our lives, we become uneasy with daily living and forget the joy of the small wonders around us. I grieve for you humans. You suffer so from this affliction."
— Lonin, as told to Shawna Harvestmoon-Serak in "Starlight Thoughts: A Memoir"

Shawn found Cara conferring with her assistant, Pao, at the doorway to one of the large storage buildings. Around them, field workers bustled in and out of the building, carrying canvas bags filled with grain stalks and pulling carts with baskets of ripe yellow fruit and orange tubers. The morning breeze was warm and pungent with the smells of overripe fruit and harvested grains, but overnight it had become a whisper of the previous afternoon's gale.

The building was one of the first built with native wood and stone, with considerable muscle work from Cara and Shawn and the other early colonists. The wood siding and roofing looked faded, a little warped, and holey from insect gnawing, but the place had held up quite well against the dry summer winds and torrential spring rains.

Cara didn't see Shawn at first, following Pao's stylus stabbing at his ever-present clipboard. When she did notice him, she smiled and held up a finger, then resumed nodding as the diminutive fellow jabbered and bobbed like an agitated canary.

One of Shawn's duties as the colony's liaison with the Timmon was to visit each new home site every week, to check progress and to ensure the builders weren't making dangerous mistakes. He was overdue to make his rounds and expected to hear about it.

Cara's skin glowed pink in the heat, shiny with tiny beads of sweat. Beneath the blue short-sleeved blouse, her arms were lean and muscled from working the fields and orchards with the other villagers. Looking at her now, healthy, strong, and less underfed than on Principia, it was hard to imagine the young woman with the hollow, caged eyes, barely more than a girl.

At last, she gave Pao final instructions and shooed him away. A delicate smile bloomed on her face, not the toothy one she used to disarm discontented villagers, just the intimate one she'd wielded on him since they were both very young.

"Kearnin and I checked out that geologic formation near the north border," he said. "I grabbed some samples, and I'm pretty sure there are some carbonaceous deposits there."

"And?"

"I think it might be a winner. Maybe oil and natural gas. If we start excavating soon, we might get a second well in before autumn hits."

"Excellent, Shawn. Good work. So get started right away."

"I knew you'd say that. Anyway, I'm finally making sense of the topology maps we've been drawing. It's different from Principia, but I'm starting to get a feel for it."

"Great! Didn't I tell you you'd figure it out?"

"It shouldn't be this difficult, though. Everything's always so tough here. We can't seem to catch a break."

"Patience, brother. We're making progress. It's hard, I know. But there's going to be a break-over point. I can *feel* it. And when it happens, many things are going to fall into place. The reward will be there. We just have to stay patient."

The power in her voice could have run the village for weeks.

"Well, you know me. Patience is my middle name."

"Of course, Shawn Patience Harvestmoon. It has a nice ring."

"Pfft!"

"Hey, follow me to the medical office. I have to fill in for Dr. Lee this afternoon."

Substitute doctor was one of Cara's many roles, but one she relished. She had a way, a manner one couldn't learn. When they were alone after the collapse on Principia, Shawn had developed a severe fever, and she'd cared for him for days. He vaguely remembered her trekking across the entire war-torn city in search of medicine, returning days later with a pouchful of antibiotics that had likely saved his life.

As they walked, Cara was stopped frequently by villagers asking for things, more water for the laundry services and animal husbandry, more fabric for production of field clothing, more help fighting rodent infestation, more electric power for the communications center, more, more, more. He wondered how she shouldered it all, and in truth the answer many times was "Talk to Pao."

They turned out of the bustle of wagons and workers on the main square, and were able to talk. She asked, "Did you have a chance to check with James on the soil moisture?"

"Umm, yes. It's not good. Only 60% for the three areas he tested."

Cara tried to retain her smile, but gravity won and pulled it down. She rubbed her eyes with one hand. "I was hoping for better."

"That's better than last year."

She sighed deeply. "Yes, it's better. Still, with the latest rains, I was hoping. Just another hurdle, and we'll clear it. But we have to push harder on the irrigation system."

"Yes, sister. We're working on it. We just need some patience."

"Mmm."

"Any luck with the synth-machine?"

She shook her head. "No. Too badly damaged when the jarin bolted and we lost the two wagons. I'm still furious with the corporation for ordering the Gibraltar out of the system before they could attempt another landing."

Her attention slipped away, lost in thought again. More and more, she drifted away during their meetings. He worried about her. She was a rock, but even rocks were crushed by enough weight.

He waited for her to come back, waited for her thoughts. He would always wait for her. The breeze carried more smells of ripening fruit, animal wastes, newly cut wood, old dirt. Speckles of dust transited the sun's rays, tiny meteors kicked up by the gale. The motes would crash-land on every surface, forming a fresh grimy layer every morning. The morning ritual here was: Get up. Wash. Have a cup of kava. Sweep the dust.

She said finally, without looking up. "Visited any of the new building sites today?"

"We plan to this afternoon."

"Good. They only have four weeks until we need the new ones free to help with the harvest."

"I'll begin on the south side and swing around. Those had the most work to do during the last visit."

"How many are still living in the temporary housing?"

"Eight as of a week ago."

"Very good. As usual, most of them chose sites as close to Fairdawn as they could get. Definitely pay a visit to Mr. Dench's and Mr. Saarinen's camps. They're farther out than anyone has built, which doesn't surprise me, but we need to stay on top of what they're doing. I don't want them putting themselves in danger or causing any problems with the Timmon."

"As far as what they're doing, Mr. Dench isn't doing much. I don't think I've seen him do anything himself. He's managed to persuade some of the other men to do all the work for him."

"He's not the first to rely on others. Do you have any idea how he's doing that?"

"Not yet, but I'll keep watching. I'll start asking questions."

"What about Paul Saarinen?"

"The opposite. Doesn't seem to want any help. I haven't seen anyone else out there, except when he needed help setting the main beams and rafters, and he was very quick to repay those who helped him, like he didn't want to owe anyone any favors."

"Did you notice anything suspicious about the place during your last visit?"

Shawn ran images of the camp through his mind — how the main cabin was tucked near an outcropping of rock, good protection against the north winds; shade from several large parasol trees on the cabin and main yard; the beginnings of a garden clearing on the south side where the sun would shine most of the day; the nearness of a clear creek, so deeply hidden in the underbrush that even Shawn and Kearnin had not discovered it during their wide-ranging hikes.

Shawn said, "Nothing unusual, except that he's using the terrain really well. He's supposed to be a mechanical guy, right? An engineer? I should ask him to look at the irrigation system."

"Let's stop by my office a minute. I want to check his file."

Shawn followed her into the single-story administration building, which was the second one after the storage barn to be built of local materials. They'd taken more care with the aesthetics here, with stone walls carefully mortared and several different woods and stains on the window frames and overhangs. Baked clay gutters and drain pipes collected the roof water into barrels at each corner. It had the feel of a rustic summer cottage like the one's Shawn's family had rented when he was very young. The memory dug a pang into this stomach, which he tried to ignore. At this time of day, the short hallway to her office was lit by natural light from the office windows.

Cara's office was a model of her brain, what Shawn might call frantic order. Documents were set in neat piles on the wooden table behind her desk, but the desk was completely clear and newly polished. From the table, she flipped through a stack of personnel files, pulled one file folder, opened it, and began reading. "Reason for requesting a move to Timmistria — 'Seeking new opportunities and life experience.' Pretty standard evasive entry." She scanned down the page, shaking her head and clucking her tongue.

"What's the problem?"

She shook her head again and sighed. "His profile is too perfect, like it was written by someone who knew exactly what we needed. Never trust something that looks too good to be true."

Her face knotted in thought, and then she slapped the file closed. "What am I doing? That's almost word for word what I wrote on our applications."

"So?"

"So shame on me for prying. His past is really not our business."

Something about Cara's outburst troubled him. "Maybe, but there's something else bothering you, I can tell."

She flopped the file on her desk and fell into her chair. She rubbed her eyes and pushed back her thick auburn hair, which tended to defy her attempts at restraint.

"It's this 'red beast' business with Mr. Dench and the Timmon. Lonin has me paranoid about everyone. Like this man, Paul Saarinen. He's come here to help us, and I'm going over his profile with a fine-toothed comb." She slumped down, shoulders drawn inward, suddenly a small woman behind a large desk.

"Come on, Sis, stop that."

"Stop what?"

"Stop punishing yourself for checking up on the new people. We've had this conversation before. You have a right to be concerned. We need to know who they are."

"Up to a point, and I can live with that. What I can't live with is spying or being intrusive. It's repressive. Coming from Principia, I should know better."

Shawn counted to ten. "You want to know where these people come from. You're not trying to control them; you're only trying to prevent them from making mistakes, and to steer them so they can be useful to the community. There's no fault in that."

"And to steer them, all we need to know are the things we can find out after they arrive — their skills and their personalities." Her head hung down, hands alternately pressing her hair to her head and opening in a dance of her thoughts. Her voice leaked out between her fingers and hair. "I spend weeks analyzing the settlers' profiles, trying to figure out where we can *use* them. It's all about 'what can they do for us?' How did I let myself sink to this?"

"It isn't wrong to demand that they carry their own weight, just like we did. They all knew what was expected when they signed the immigration agreement, because you pushed hard to make sure it was in there. No one who's come here was more desperate than we were, and we've always done our best. And in our need, we are justified in demanding the same from these others."

"Yes, and once we made landfall, no one pried into our pasts. Lonin wanted me to put Mr. Dench back on the transport because of his 'bad red light' and the things he *might* do. I'm ashamed at how close I came to doing it."

"Fine. So stop looking at the profiles, and start a … uh, 'Capability and Temperament' file on each new colonist. And stop being so hard on yourself and so easy on everyone else."

"Fine! So what are you doing loitering around here when you're supposed to be out checking up on the new cabins?"

"I'm going. Kearnin and I will be back by dinnertime."

"And make sure to check up on Mr. Dench. I want to know his mining plans. If he says one word about uranium or plutonium, I'll personally put his butt on the next transport off this rock."

"Yes, ma'am."

She smiled at him again, fatigue and stress drawing lines on her face. But the smile also brought a glow to her skin and a spark to her eyes.

He winked and took his leave. He passed through the offices, dimly lit by ambient window light, and pushed the heavy wooden door open into the brilliant sun, colored by the haze of yellow dust in the air. He paused by Cara's open window to watch her.

She'd told him once that it was important for the colonists to see her at her desk working, that her window and door were always open to them. She hunched a bit, head bowed and fingertips rubbing lightly over her eyelids. She rose and stretched her neck and shoulders, lifting herself from her chair in a large breath, and then blowing it out fully and slowly.

Would there ever be time for her needs, for the dreams he had for her?

The settlement had become a needy child for too long, and too much depended on her continued care.

Shawn shrunk back from the window and went in search of Kearnin.

Chapter 4

"Timmistria lights the path for all; the wise follow."
— Timmon proverb

The trail was a newer one that Kearnin and Shawn had cleared using one of the mobile brush choppers. Still, the catcher vines and viper trees had grown back, so the two companions, Timmon and human, were forced to swing blades regularly. They moved in a coordinated manner, covering each other's blind sides, a routine engrained by long hours together in the field. These forests were a gauntlet of aggressive vegetation, designed to cling to and drag down any living thing that ventured within its golden light.

Shawn had begun to call this area of the settled lands "The North Suburbs," but Cara had scolded him about it, fearing that the name would stick. It really wasn't a bad name, and if they didn't name the place, someone else certainly would. The villagers had given names to other areas, many of which were derived from their home worlds or districts. They had "The Alders," "The Garden District," and "Elysium Fields." Their name for the planet's large moon, "Dresden," referred to an Old-Earth city, suggested by someone who was a war history buff. It was a natural name for the seething red giant, and very close to its Timmistrian name, Dreyaten. Shawn hoped to study it one day from a low-flying craft. The moon held a mythic place in the Timmistrian religion. It simmered and glowed with its own internal light, like a scarlet dwarf star, a mystery that begged for investigation.

Shawn and Kearnin worked their way through the heavy brush at a measured pace, keeping all their senses alert, their eyes scanning for any movement in the many levels of foliage. Timmon hunting parties were vigilant about clearing large predators from these forests, but occasionally one evaded the hunts. Shawn's heart beat hard and fast, more from the sense of adventure and danger than from the exertion.

They'd visited all the new camps built close to Fairdawn proper, finding nothing seriously out of line. All the new dwellings had seen progress. Of the eight people remaining in temporary housing, four were set to move out in the next week or two, and the remaining two couples could be ready in three to four weeks with a little extra assistance. The last camp they'd visited, the one being built by the new female couple, was looking good except for some drainage and elevation issues. Kearnin was trained in land usage, so Lonin had assigned him to assist Shawn with these inspections. The tall, thin Timmon had instructed the two women in his improving Galactic Standard where they needed to dig a trench to channel rainwater around the foundation of their dwelling. The women had listened attentively and promised to take care of it.

Colonists were never allowed to participate in Timmon hunting parties, lacking jungle skills and speed, but Kearnin had taken Shawn on many small excursions, hunting small game and birds. The young Timmon seemed to be impressed by Shawn's rabid curiosity about the world, its biology, and its history, and filled Shawn's head with as much lore as he could suck up. By necessity, all Timmistrians were very knowledgeable about Timmistria's plant and animal life, and its natural phenomena such as weather and geophysical activity.

In return, Shawn told his Timmon friend about his home world of Principia and as much as he knew about other Co-Op worlds — which was only what he'd seen in documentaries, since he'd never visited any of them.

Kearnin, unlike some of his race, was fascinated by all things extraterrestrial. He attended nearly every interstellar shuttle landing and delighted at seeing the strange beings who worked as crew members on the landing craft. He even became friends with the traveling groups of carrier folk.

Learning Galactic Standard was another story, a source of frustration for Kearnin, even though he was learning quickly. The concept that one word could mean many things astonished him. The Timmistrian language seemed to have been constructed from a well-thought-out master plan. Each word could have only one meaning. "Ratalin" meant "attack with a pointed object," regardless of who or how many were attacking, or what or who was the target.

The Timmistrian language had changed very little over hundreds of years. A jarin was a jarin now as it had been in the earliest days of Timmistrian history, and it was known by no other word. Humans had already given the hairy reptilian mammal several different names, including "ox," "jabber-donkey," and "pack dragon."

But now, hiking through the forest, the pair communicated only through gestures, whistles, and sharp clicks, mimicking the sounds of native plants and animals. The Timmon used this method primarily for stealth, but it was also very efficient.

They worked their way along a hump in the landscape, clearing new brush from the trail as they went. At the bottom of the next swale, they stepped across a narrow creek, keeping alert for snakelike fish that could attack the legs of the unwary. From there, they followed the trail along a broad, flat ridge that lifted out of the little creek valley. Shawn and Kearnin had cut the trail there because it offered an excellent view of the forest floor on each side, and because the rock base was close to the earth's surface here, limiting the thickness of the brush they had to clear away.

They had seen little sign of large predators or dragons while exploring this route. They paused at the termination of the ridge to drag a fallen branch from the trail, carefully avoiding wooden spurs. From there, the trail circumvented a marshy wood where they'd found an excellent patch of delicious edible fungi, the location of which they had kept to themselves. Timmon delighted in a secret mushroom patch or fishing hole as much as humans. The trail then carried them through a labyrinthine passage that pierced the thick brush at the back of the clearing where Dench's camp was located.

Once in the clearing, Shawn announced their arrival with a loud "Hallooo!" They didn't want to surprise the resident or the men working there, for fear of being shot with an arrow. For the humans, Timmistria was a frontier, and surprise visits were not only rude but foolhardy.

Dench was standing in the clearing in front of the nearly complete cabin, watching three workers nail up sheets of siding. The three men, one new settler and two experienced community members whom Shawn knew, stopped briefly to wave at the two hikers before going back to work. Dench stood with arms crossed, watching them approach.

The cabin was a simple design, a rectangular, roofed 10-by-15-meter box, with one window set into each outside wall. The cabin followed the standard two-room design: a small bedroom and bath, and a kitchen and living area. To one side of the cabin, foundation stones had been laid out to mark off the beginnings of a shop or storage shed. The dwelling's location in the center of the grassy clearing would provide a wide-open view from any direction, but it offered very little shade or natural protection from winds or driven rain. As a result, Kearnin had suggested the roof be laid in with extra-heavy wooden shingles and the north and west walls be sided with pressed dragon skin. The siding being hung by the men was the sun-dried skin of the lumbering reptilian brute, the cremin, just as Kearnin had suggested.

"Greetings, Mr. Dench."

"Greetings to you, young man."

The large, pale man shook hands with Shawn and glanced at Kearnin, who had stopped a good distance away.

Two of the workers applied a roll of lizard skin to the cabin wall, tacking it in place at the top with several nails and then driving in additional nails as they unrolled it downward. The skin was extremely tough, and nailing the dried sheets was a chore. But the third worker, who was cutting the skin on a workbench, had an even more difficult task, sectioning and trimming it with a small, green-bladed Timmon knife. He was obviously struggling.

"These men have made a lot of progress." Shawn started to ask Dench what his secret was but bit the thought back.

Dench nodded gravely. "They have indeed. I couldn't have done it without their help. I'm afraid the stasis and cramped quarters on the transport ship caused the arthritis in my shoulders and neck to flare up. They have been most helpful. I'm not sure how I will repay them, but I hope my future contributions to the common cause will constitute a repayment of sorts."

"I'm sure your contributions will be very worthwhile. And that's one reason for our visit today. Your expertise lies in mining, correct?"

"That is correct. Master's degree from the University of New Boston, summa cum laude. Twenty years' experience in various mining pursuits on the home world and several others. I hope to harness those experiences to shed some light on the nature of Timmistria's geology and thus bring some serious value to the community."

"I've spent some time studying the geology here as well, Mr. Dench. What exactly are you hoping to find?"

"Oh, actually, most mining developers look for the same things, Mister…"

"Harvestmoon."

"Yes. Exactly. I'll search for rare metals at first, the very rare ones necessary for high-technology devices — yttrium, Promethium, Scandium. They can be found on only a small percentage of the habitable planets and are always in serious demand. Of course, there are always unusual jewel stones, which can be converted into excellent cash flow for new settlements. They're not usually particularly rare, but nonetheless, gems from a distant and, as may be called uncivilized — primitive, if you understand — planet, are always an interest to the fashion-conscious buyers. I once discovered a pale yellow carbuncle literally scattered among the ash and rocks of a rather large extinct volcano on Sebadia Three, nothing special in properties or appearance. Those common glassy pebbles became an overnight sensation because the Thinkers overran the system and transport ships couldn't reach the colony for months. In the end, the revenue from those tiny rocks allowed the settlement to launch an impressive tourist trade once the Thinkers were driven out. Of course, the planet was very impressive from an aesthetic and climatic perspective, so the adventure tourism angle was a natural market. But it was all made possible by seed money from the cottage gemstone industry."

"And what about the little yellow carbuncles today?"

"Valueless now, young man. Common as quartz. Timing and market are everything."

"So you've had success in those areas in the past. But one thing you and I as geologists must keep in mind is that we mustn't cause environmental damage, and our exploration must be completely reversible. I've been focusing my work on carbonaceous formations, but even those operations will be phased out as we develop renewable sources."

"Yes, exactly. Another valuable point, young man, and I'm glad you mentioned it. The rare-earth components I seek are also needed for solar-energy devices. If we can make a decent-sized discovery, we can begin production of solar panels on this planet and achieve energy richness for the whole settlement. I have seen this sequence of industries played out on other successful fledgling colonies, my young friend, and I see great promise for this settlement as well."

Dench's smile seemed genuine, and Shawn felt himself drawn to the promise of progress. It was an attractive vision for the future, and he had to bring his mind back to the warnings given by the Timmon about the man. If Dench was a charlatan, he was certainly a talented and dangerous one.

Shawn noticed that during Dench's speech, the three workers had more or less stopped working to listen.

"Well, Mr. Dench, I can tell you're very enthusiastic about the future here, and I wish you and all of us great success. As a fellow geologist, I'd like to be involved in your exploring so we can share what we learn and speed up the discovery process. This colony could use a breakthrough."

"Absolutely, Mr. Harvestmoon. Of course, any and all data will be for the benefit of the community, and I will gladly share what I learn. I understand the community enterprise spirit."

"Great. We'll allow you to get back to your work. Cheers."

"Cheers to you, sir."

Shawn nodded to Dench and then to the three men who were still watching and listening. Kearnin, who had lingered at the side of the clearing well away from the cabin and its future inhabitant, joined him, and they began their hike back to Fairdawn.

Dench was certainly an odd one. Shawn had to admit that he couldn't quite relax around the man; something about Dench's manner kept Shawn on his toes. But it could just have been the "red beast" rumor Cara had mentioned.

#

Dench watched the two recede into the woods behind the cabin. After they'd passed from sight, he turned to the three men who were building the cabin for him: Robinson, one of the new arrivals whom he'd befriended on the journey here, and Smith and Johnson, both residents of Timmistria for three years.

"Gentlemen! I think that's quite enough work for one day, don't you? I'll bet you'd love a drink about now."

Smith, the worker at the table who'd been laboring to cut the drab lizard skins, laid his green knife down and slapped his calloused dark brown hands together. Dark ringlets of hair formed a helmet above his broad face. "We've got plenty of water here, Mr. Dench."

"I'm not talking about that kind of drink, Smith, my good man. Didn't I tell you I'd managed to bring a couple of interesting devices with me from Sebadia? Well one of them can turn local grains into a palatable little aperitif that I think you will find very enjoyable."

Johnson, taller, thinner, with sandy brows and hair, beginning to thin on top, patted his hands together and then coughed. His voice was a dusty croak. "Will it make scotch? I ran out of the two bottles they let me bring months ago."

"Mr. Johnson, nothing so crude as scotch. Have a seat at the bench there, and I'll bring out the little marvel."

The three sat with no more encouragement from Dench. Robinson, a bony fellow with ebony skin and gray frosted hair, said, "Hey, Mr. Dench. We were listening to you talk to young Harvestmoon there. Do you really mean all that about gems and rare metals? Are you planning to share everything with the whole colony?"

Dench paused, taking the time to meet each worker's eyes. "Gentlemen, I absolutely plan to share my findings with the colony. I earnestly believe in this colony and all the good works you hardy people have managed on this difficult plot of land you've been given. But remember our conversations when I recruited you to help me with this camp. I plan to make some great finds on this planet, just as I have on other worlds, or I wouldn't have wasted my time coming here. I will support this colony, but I think it's reasonable that the share of the prize the discoverer retains should be somewhat larger than the shares for those who had nothing to do with it. Also — and please catch my drift here, gentlemen — those who help me will have very generous shares of their own."

Johnson said, "What about the Timmon, Mr. Dench? And what about this environment thing Shawn was talking about? Are you going to let him in on the discovery?"

Dench dropped his smile. "Gentlemen, it should be apparent to intelligent men like you what's going on here. The Timmon have kept you bottled up on this rugged little tract of land, not allowing you to spread out into other territories. Why would they do that? To me, it's obvious. They don't want to share the best places, and they're happy to let you scratch out a meager existence. And why are they allowing us to stay? Why not just kill us all off and take the land back? I've seen them sneak around the colony, men, and I've come to understand why. They are watching us, learning from us.

"As the vids said, they lost a great deal of their lands to the other Timmistrian race, the Delerin, in a great war generations ago. They're not so different from ancient men, gentlemen; they want to win back what was once theirs. They were smart enough to figure out that with human technology, including modern weapons, machines, and communications, they could best the Delerin. This colony is being used, gentlemen."

The three men sat very quietly and watched Dench as he paced and talked. Their faces bore looks of uncertainty and perhaps distrust of him.

"But don't take my word for it. You're intelligent men and not easily fooled by uncivilized natives. Observe things around the village for yourselves with this new perspective in mind. You'll begin to see things that you've overlooked. I know I may sound cynical, but I have the advantage of bringing a brand new set of eyes to this situation. And believe me, I don't like what I see. You fine people are nearly starving, and the Timmon seem to be doing quite well."

Robinson said, "I don't know, Mr. Dench. The people at the top, Ms. Cara, and that Pao fellow, and the folks that run the farming, they work hard for this village. They've all seen some tough times."

"Yes, I'm sure they have, Mr. Robinson. And I'm only a casual observer, but the arrangement between the Harvestmoons and the Timmon concerns me. They're very friendly with each other, correct? The young Shawn spends all his days with the one who came today, the quiet one that stood over to the side of the clearing, watching you work. Watching, always watching. If I were to give the Timmon a name, it would be 'the Watchers.' And what about Manager Harvestmoon? She's very cozy with this Lonin fellow. They seem to spend a great deal of time together. Are they lovers? It sounds odd, but I've seen this scenario played out before. The village leaders jumping planet with the big prize, while the poor colonists are left to continue scratching out a living in the dirt.

"And let me bring this tiny bit of wisdom to you, perhaps the only real piece of wisdom I have gained from 30 years in this trade; every planet has a unique, remarkable prize, and those that find it enjoy the profits. A question for you gents: why did Shawn Harvestmoon pay us a visit today with his yellow-skinned friend and bring up the subject of mining? Because he's looking for that prize himself, and he's afraid we're going to beat him to it. Which would make him our competitor, no?"

The men seemed more puzzled now and cast glances among themselves. Dench let them ruminate on the thought before pressing on.

"But gentlemen, I'm just a geologist who talks too much and sometimes says the wrong thing. I'm just asking you to take a look around at how things run in the village. Now, let's get off this subject, shall we, and just enjoy the cool evening and the companionship. And, of course, an excellent drink. Relax there, and I will return in a moment."

Dench walked deliberately from the small group, letting his observations sink in. It struck him as a shame that this type of subterfuge was no longer a challenge for him. He no longer felt much satisfaction in it.

No matter. His objectives, though delayed by the disaster that had landed him on this hellhole, were larger, much larger. And bagging the larger quarry was going to be very satisfying indeed.

Chapter 5

"To use Timmistria's gifts unwisely is to insult her charity."
— Timmon proverb

Leaving Dench's camp, Kearnin and Shawn struck out quickly and worked their way along the overgrown trail to the northwest. The sun was dipping below the treetops, but there were still about three hours before nightfall. The final camp, Paul Saarinen's, lay the farthest out of any of the human habitations and within a kilometer of the settlement boundary. It was half a kilometer from the nearest camp and three kilometers from Fairdawn's center.

Just enough time remained for a quick visit and the hike back to Fairdawn before dark, as Shawn had promised Cara. Kearnin would have a longer trek to his village, his kithin, and he might choose to spend the night in Fairdawn rather than hike alone in the dark. Shawn had accompanied him back to his kithin in the past and had spent several nights at Kearnin's small cottage. But even though he was generally accepted among the Timmon, his overnight stays had been frowned upon by some.

They plied their way through a thicket of broad-leaved trees that resembled a honey-colored variant of the sycamores of Shawn's world. Multicolored web-winged birds, flashing shades of red and orange and teal, hissed through the fronds above them. Without warning, Kearnin froze on the trail in front of Shawn and held up a two-thumbed hand. Shawn stopped, and his heart beat in his ears. He adjusted his grip on the handle of his long bush blade. But Kearnin had not assumed a defensive posture, and instead motioned for Shawn to join him.

There was movement in the tree boughs where Kearnin pointed, but Shawn could not make out what manner of beast was there. He glanced at Kearnin, who nodded toward the movement, urging his patience. Shawn complied, trying to remain as motionless as Kearnin while observing the spot where the yellow-brown branches of the malack trees shook gently.

Tom Simons, one of the biologists, had taught Shawn that the malack was not a true tree, having no chlorophyll and no other photosynthetic capabilities, but was actually a form of fungus, a giant parasite. The interesting question was on what did they feed? Where did they draw the massive sustenance needed to grow and support their great structures? This was just one of many of the planet's mysteries that gnawed at Shawn's brain.

The foliage rattled, and a four-legged penderin, or "flying monkey," pushed through the leaves and padded along the branch like a gymnast on a beam. It appeared to be a small female, and her pale yellow skin and light brown fur provided excellent camouflage. She walked out into the dappled sunlight and perched. Immediately another penderin emerged, larger and darker: a male. His attention was keenly focused on the female. She seemed to be ignoring him, but a brief flash of red along her neck and back revealed her interest. With a shock, Shawn realized he and Kearnin were observing a mating ritual.

The dance of the penderin was similar to that of many creatures on Principia. The female feigned disinterest as she moved away from the male, back and forth along the branch, but her sinuous movements and the flashes of red skin taunted the male, who was entranced. She jumped from branch to branch to avoid him but coyly allowed him to close the gap, until at last he captured her in his front legs, his wings encircling her body. She gripped the branch with all four limbs, her wings slowly flapping above her back. The male enveloped her and they coupled, his front limbs holding her tightly, his back limbs anchoring him on the branch. His wings began to beat in time with hers.

Shawn felt heat rise to his face and a drop of sweat trickle from his temple, and he realized he was embarrassed to be witnessing the intimate act. But true to Timmon culture, Kearnin was not embarrassed, watching until the end, which involved frantic wing thrashing and both penderin disappearing quickly into the brush. Neither had voiced any mating sounds during the act, which seemed odd. But the forest was brutal and dangerous for smaller animals, and loud mating calls would bring predators.

As reserved and stoic as Kearnin seemed at times, he was clearly fascinated by the natural wonders of his home world. During their travels, he frequently stopped along the way, to admire a field of flowering lichens, to sigh at the reflection of the moons Thoran and Dartan on a hillside lake, or to marvel at v-shaped lines of rose-colored pantin birds crossing a rare bluish sky.

At last, Kearnin led Shawn on, once again taking the lead on the trail and pushing harder to make up for the lost time. Shawn ventured a question as they hiked.

"Shik! Kearnin!"

Kearnin stopped in mid-stride, comically frozen as if he were a frame taken from an animated comedy video. He turned his head to look down on Shawn.

"Shik. Yes?"

"Timmon ne pressin penderin. Ne pok?" (*The Timmon do not hunt penderin. Why not?*)

Kearnin's face tightened into an amber mask, with eyes wide and lips pursed. His voice was not deep by Timmon standards, but it was still deep enough to throb against Shawn's eardrums. "Penderin sin kil kilin Timmon." (*The penderin are small child Timmon.*)

He waited for another question, but Shawn was struck dumb. He nodded for the Timmon to continue.

As they pressed forward, Shawn's mind was a torrent. The penderin were small Timmon children? Was Kearnin telling him that the penderin species was related to the Timmon? Ancestral relatives? There were clear similarities. Like the Timmon, the penderin had yellow skin over most of their bodies, with bright orange or copper hair on their backs. Their faces looked Timmistrian, with full features and similar expressions. Could the penderin be like the lemur, a distant prehistoric cousin of men? The small gray and white lemurs of the Principian forests had survived the harsh wilds as well as any other mammal species from Old Earth.

Shawn was now eager to discuss this with the biologists and Mr. Barrett, the xeno-anthropologist now working in the village as a carpenter. But first he needed to question Kearnin, and perhaps Lonin, about the Timmon beliefs about biological evolution. Did they believe that they truly were historically and genetically related to the penderin, or did they merely feel a relationship because of the physical likeness?

Shawn's ruminations had apparently kept his mind fully occupied, because they reached the cleared area around Paul Saarinen's camp and he could remember very little of the hike. Kearnin let Shawn lead from there but did not linger at the clearing's edge as he had at Dench's camp.

"Hallooo, Mr. Saarinen!"

They had walked only a few meters into the clearing when Saarinen appeared on the other side of the cabin, waved, and stepped over the clumpy grass to head toward them. He was of average height at about two meters, fit but not overly muscled, dressed in light blue cotton pants and a light blue shirt with the sleeves rolled up. His face was wide with solid cheek and chin bones, beneath blond hair trimmed to an inch all over. The only exceptions to his average appearance were his striking, starburst-yellow eyes, which seemed more appropriate for a large predatory bird. He sported no body art or piercings, like some of the other colonists did, and there was always a no-nonsense air about him. In his hand was a foot-long green cremin-tooth blade, standard issue for everyone — Timmon or colonial — and used for a multitude of purposes. He carried it carefully by the hemp-wound hilt, blade pointed downward. He stopped near the cabin and waited for them.

"Greetings, Mr. Saarinen."

"Hello, gentlemen."

He and Shawn shook hands, and then Kearnin stepped forward to grasp hands as well. Saarinen expertly mimicked the two-thumbed grip of the Timmon by folding his index and middle fingers together to create a second "thumb." As they shook, their eyes met without blinking, not with hostility, but perhaps with mutual assessment.

After they broke the interchange, Shawn tried to cut the silence. "You're nearly finished. I don't think we'll need to bother you again."

Saarinen hesitated before responding, which Shawn had learned from their infrequent conversations was a habit. "Should be in good shape. I've complied with the codes, I believe. But you're welcome to come by anytime."

He led them around to the front of the cabin, where the shade from the embankment and trees sheltered the home and the front yard from the evening sun. The breeze had diminished and provided just enough movement to keep insects away and to keep the air from hanging sticky with humidity. Sunlight pierced the tree boughs and lit a plot of ground that Saarinen had apparently laid out for a garden, with the stones set around part of the perimeter. On a worktable were several wooden planks colored in different shades from gray to sandstone. Shawn walked over for a closer look.

"You're planning on staining your cabin?"

Saarinen gazed from the table to the cabin, as if lost in thought for a time. He stroked his chin, which had been shaved recently. "Yes. I was told this lumber will season on its own, so I guess the staining is just a pet project."

"Last time we visited, you were thinking about an irrigation system, which leads to my next question. We're having trouble keeping the main crop system running and wondered if you could offer some advice."

Saarinen's eyes had never left the wooden planks on the worktable. He picked up one that was stained chocolate brown and looked at it edge-on. Just as Shawn began to wonder if the man had heard him, he responded. "I'd be glad to take a look at it. I know some hydraulics, as long as you're not expecting miracles. Pumping water is usually straightforward, but the tools here are limited."

"No miracles expected. Anything you can offer will be appreciated."

"Fair enough. When do you need me there?"

"Tomorrow morning would be great. Is 9 o'clock at the shops too early? You have a long hike."

"Let's make it 8. I'll travel quickly. I need the exercise."

Saarinen put the board down and regarded Shawn and Kearnin with his full attention, arms crossed. Shawn couldn't recall an Earth-human with yellow eyes, but they were nearly universal among the Timmon.

"Eight is great. I appreciate you helping us."

"I think that's why I'm here."

Shawn's unspoken question was, "Why *are* you here?" But that was for another day when he'd gotten to know Paul Saarinen better.

Shawn excused himself and Kearnin, and they took a more-traveled trail back to Fairdawn. Kearnin made a game of it, breaking into a lope and challenging Shawn to keep up. Every few minutes, he slowed down and let Shawn nearly catch him before sprinting off again through the brush.

This section of the trail was relatively safe, or Kearnin would not have left him alone. But there was the air of a trial in their game as well. Timmon children, when old enough to wield a blade and bow efficiently, were made to travel alone through the forest at midday and eventually into the more dangerous evening hours. Although the Timmon seldom traveled alone as adults, there would likely be times when they would need to. For the Timmon, it was necessary survival training.

When Shawn reached the northwest entrance of Fairdawn, he was winded and sweating profusely, and his thighs were trembling. He trotted the last 50 meters, struggling to maintain his pace, and found Kearnin leaning casually against one of the gateposts that marked the formal entrance to Fairdawn proper. It wasn't much of a gate, just two wooden beams flanking the trail, with a longer beam nailed across the top. There was a small shed that served as a guard station, although it was seldom occupied. Kearnin's face was a bit flushed, but there was a smirk on his full lips.

Shawn was just perturbed enough to let his irritation show. "Frocking show-off," he muttered, trudging past the smug Timmon. Without looking back, he headed steadily toward his small cottage near

Fairdawn's center, his hair matted down with sweat, dust sticking to his skin. Kearnin's shadow moved with him, a dark orange harlequin dancing beneath his feet, taunting him.

"Frocking Timmon show-off."

Shawn bathed in the public bath, allowing himself a few gallons of luxury, lukewarm water from Fairdawn's wood-fired reservoir tank. He pressed Kearnin to indulge himself in a brief bath, and the Timmon gave in but did not stay in the bath for long. The Timmon were uncomfortable with the custom of bathing, which they felt wasted water and fuel. Kearnin stored extra clothing in a locker in Shawn's cottage, and he went there to change after his bath. Then Shawn led him to the community kitchen for a brief late evening snack of bread, a bit of Timmon cheese, and a clay mug of potent colonial ale, and they sat at a wooden picnic table in one of the outdoor dining areas.

The sun had set below the western horizon by the time they settled into seats, but a few gas streetlights had been lit by the night steward. Washed, fed, resting, and sipping at a glass of the chewy bitter ale brewed from native grains, Shawn felt a comfortable distance from the rugged world outside Fairdawn. Kearnin sipped at his own mug and looked a little uneasy. His legs were too long for bench seats, and he hadn't ducked low enough when they'd entered the dining hall earlier. A small orange bruise marked his forehead just below the hairline, barely visible in the dim light. Shawn tried not to be amused.

Kearnin's face was an expressionless mask, but somehow it was not the carved stone that it appeared most times. Whether by a barely noticeable upturn of his mouth or by a slackening about his eyes, his face now seemed softer, more accessible. Perhaps it was just the drink. But Timmon never seemed to get intoxicated, though they had become as fond of the human ale as they were of their own fermented juices and beer.

"Kearnin, shik. I want to ask you more about the penderin. You called them 'little Timmon children.'"

Kearnin's slow nod was barely visible in the twilight.

"Do you mean you are related to the penderin?"

Kearnin didn't answer and eyed Shawn with a slight tilt of his head.

Shawn tried again. "If the penderin are small Timmon children, why? Because they look a little like you? Or because you come from the same place?"

"They look like us. We come from the same place."

"Do the Timmon believe in evolution?"

"Ev-el-u-shun?"

Shawn launched into what felt like a rambling explanation of the "science of modern temporal advancement," at least what he was able to study at the underground university. Much of the teaching was prohibited by the Small People's Republic of Principia.

Shawn paused to let it sink in. He thought he had used the family tree model pretty well, but he was still gauging the levels at which the Timmon understood the sciences. By necessity, they had a very good knowledge of their biology, weather, seasons, and even folk medicine. They also had a rudimentary knowledge of physics and astronomy, and they learned quickly.

But Kearnin's expression didn't change, and his gaze wandered to the dim streets around them. Perhaps Shawn wasn't getting anywhere after all.

Glittering insects swept in and out of the lights, and larger, fuzzy-skinned gliding things chased them. The village biologists had not confirmed that these bug-eaters used sonar to track their prey, but Shawn was convinced. On each of the known worlds, where there was a biological niche, there was nearly always a creature to fill it. Flying and swimming creatures that used echolocation were found on every planet with complex life-forms, as Shawn had learned in biology classes at the underground high school.

But, as they were further taught, that niche could be filled from nearly any of the resident family trees, including the plant kingdom. Dr. Simons suspected species of the catcher vines used echolocation, as evidenced by their incredible accuracy in plucking small birds from the air.

Kearnin spoke then, pulling Shawn back from his own thoughts. His words resonated from somewhere deep. "I do not know … if the penderin tree meets the Timmon tree. But they are small Timmon children. They come from the same place. Their light is like ours." Kearnin's coin-sized eyes, with their radiating facets, like small yellow flowers set in glass buttons, turned on Shawn in steady penetration.

"The penderin have lights? Timeril?"

Kearnin did not blink as he responded. "Lin." (*Yes.*)

"Do all animals have lights?"

"Lin."

"But the lights are different for each?"

"Some are different. Some are the same."

"The penderin lights are similar. What about…" Shawn pointed toward the bat-like creatures and night insects. "Them, the perin and sestinan? What are their lights like?"

Kearnin swung his gaze toward the nearest streetlight and followed the fluttering movements of the furry, diaphanous flyers and their prey with the same fascination he had given to the mating penderin. "Their lights are … different. Not so bright. Different." Kearnin grew puzzled again. "I do not know how to tell you."

"Do you mean you can't describe the lights? Is it like trying to tell someone how something tastes or smells? There are no words to tell how the lights look to you?"

"Lin. Yes. We say that we 'see' the timeril because your talking does not have the words. We see the timeril around us like we smell the smells and hear the sounds. Timeril are all around. They are given to us by Timmistria. We do not always … 'look' at them, but we see them. The joyful lights are bright; they call us. And we cannot miss harsh, bitter light. It is like a bad smell. It hurts our sense."

"Like Dench."

Kearnin's eyes met Shawn's and narrowed. Was he angry? Then he looked away again, as if ashamed of his own dark thoughts.

"Mr. Dench's light is red, I know," Shawn said. "Does it look like the Timmon lights?"

"Human lights are very close to those of the Timmon."

"Closer than the penderin?"

"Yes. The penderin are like us, but smaller, simpler. Penderin are simple. Humans are not simple."

"To say the least. So Mr. Dench has a red light, and you Timmon think he is a bad person and might do bad things?"

Kearnin sat motionless, not looking at Shawn. His silence lasted for several breaths.

"Kearnin, friend, forget this. I am being rude. Forget I asked you about these things. I want to understand, and I sometimes ask too many questions when silence would be better. Maybe we can talk about something more interesting. Tell me about your last Timmon hunt."

The Timmon remained a statue of yellow stone, unmoving as only the Timmon could be, except his lips, which shaped words now in a voice deep with danger. "Timeril are not like storytellers in the kithin. They do not tell what has passed or what will come. They may speak of the way of a thing, and talk of where it has been or where it might go, and sometimes they tell us which things are good or bad. Most times the timeril are quiet, telling little because there is little to tell. The timeril tell us how a thing sits in its place. If that thing is at peace and sits quiet, the light will be almost nothing, a faint breath of the wind … maybe?"

"And how does my light look to you?"

Kearnin turned to him quickly, his face pinched in reproach. "Shik, Shawn, it is against the Timmon way to tell someone of his light."

"I need to understand. Just this once."

Kearnin breathed deeply. He relaxed a bit. "When I first met you, your light was like a jumping flame, like it knew no home. Now, it is quieter — I barely notice your timeril at all. You are living quietly now."

"And you cannot see your own timeril. Do you know what yours is like?"

Kearnin smiled in a blossom of bright yellow teeth. His flower-button eyes gleamed. "I am told by our village elders that my timeril flows like blue water, never at rest, always seeking to run away from its course."

Shawn could not restrain a laugh. "What about Lonin?"

Kearnin shook his head a little. "Remember, Shawn. Shik! The Timmon do not usually talk about these things, only in quiet, thinking times. Talking about another Timmon's light is dangerous, and I may dishonor Lonin by talking about him."

"I understand. You know I hold him in very high regard and would never dishonor him. I guess this is a 'quiet, thinking time' for me, and my head is full of questions and curiosity. And ale."

Kearnin chuckled quietly in a deep, scratchy laugh. "Quiet to you is a chorus of pantalin to me!" The pantalin was the large, pink wading bird they'd seen migrating, with a raucous cry and a painful, poisonous bite.

"OK, so what about Mr. Saarinen? What is his timeril like?"

"Because you seek only to understand, I will tell you about Lonin. Lonin has a steady yellow light that does not change. He leads us because we can count on him to be true to the Timmon ways and true to his own people. His timeril speaks this, but we know it in our hearts already."

Shawn nodded. "We would say that he is a rock. Dependable and unchanging no matter what happens. What about Mr. Saarinen?"

Kearnin shook his head again. He'd learned to use the gesture the same way humans did. The Timmon gesture for "no" was a light finger tap to the temple. "Yes" was a tap to the lips.

"He is a … pokuk sin kka? (*what is the word?*) He is a … question?"

"Do you mean that his light changes?"

"No. He does not show his light. We do not see it. And we do not know how this is. It makes us wary."

"Then he is like a puzzle, or a mystery. Are there any Timmon who can cover their lights?"

Kearnin shook his head again slowly, eyes distant.

"But you don't detect anything bad with Mr. Saarinen? No bad colors, like the red you see with Mr. Dench?"

Kearnin's face went hard and dark again, and his words came slowly. "We Timmon talk about the colors, but that is a human word. Timeril remind us of lights and colors, but it is only…" He shook his head and raised his hands in frustration.

"A perception? An appearance?"

"Yes. An appearance. The timeril are like water or wind. They are the fire … no, not fire … I do not know your word. We sense the moving inside coming from a thing. That is what a timeril can be. It is the thing that makes hearts beat, or why water rises to the sky to fall again. It is calarin, but not." He raised his hands in frustration again.

Shawn thought about what Kearnin was trying to convey. Calarin? He didn't know that word.

"Do you mean power? Energy?"

"Yes! It is *energy!* Like the calarantin — you call it lightning — that flows across the sky when the calar come."

Timmistria's weather was unpredictable and often violent, even more so than Principia's in the early summer. Storms and rain could be rare for long periods and then could suddenly ravage the land almost daily. Lightning lashed downward in orange and red firestorms, driving people and beasts to cover.

"I understand what you are saying about your people not actually seeing the timeril with your eyes, and that it is like energy, and not like a light with a true color. Yet you describe Mr. Dench as the 'red beast.' 'Kahl melok.' Those are Timmon words, not human."

Kearnin's words were a growl. "His energy burns like blood. He kills with no thoughts, no pain. Death is nothing. He wears it like tillil."

"Tillil. A tunic. And you think he will kill again. Do you understand that we can't do anything about Dench unless he commits a crime? It would go against human laws to banish him because of what he *might* do."

Kearnin slowly nodded at last, but the flash of orange along his forehead and cheeks confirmed the agitation in his words. Gentle, childlike, nature-loving Kearnin, laid-back Kearnin, was deeply troubled. Shawn began to fear what the more hostile Timmon might think. Or do.

"We will keep a close eye on Dench, Kearnin, you and me, and the others. At the first sign of trouble, we'll ship him away from Timmistria. I promise I won't let Dench or anyone like him damage our partnership. We humans owe the Timmon that much."

When Kearnin looked at Shawn, his eyes held an unusual sadness. After a long pause, he said, "I believe your words."

Chapter 6

"Knowledge is not dangerous. How we use knowledge is
where the peril lies."
— Lonin

After Shawn's assurances about Dench, he and
Kearnin sat quietly in the cooling night, talking little, just
watching the few remaining humans walk home. The
night guard extinguished all but one of the streetlights. As
the darkness deepened, forest creatures walked and
slithered and flew into the village, retaking this place
from the aliens whose presence had banished them. The
two humanoids sat at the table, Kearnin eerily motionless
and Shawn trying to be. Despite their inaction, most
creatures on wings or feet or belly eventually noticed
them, and then, after careful regard, deemed them
harmless and went about the sober business of trying to
mate with or eat each other.

A small pack of pig-like raree surged into the
street crossing, invading the green patches on the
adjacent corner. They rooted up the flowering tomato-like
plants that some of the colonists were trying to cultivate,
thus solving the mystery of the plants' frequent
destruction. Afterward, a large flock of bat-like perin flew
around the square, temporarily clearing the night air of
buzzing insects.

As Shawn felt himself nodding off, Kearnin raised
his head and slid his hand over the tabletop to grasp the
hilt of his blade. He looked toward the silent darkness at
the end of the street. Shawn jerked awake and reached for
his own blade. From the darkness where Kearnin stared, a
subdued growl vibrated the air, followed by harsh
snuffling.

Shawn mimicked Kearnin's lead, remaining motionless but poised to act. His body twitched with the pulsing of his blood, and sweat collected at his temples and armpits. But the snuffling soon faded, and Kearnin released the blade and turned robotically back to his original position, his attention again on the small creatures that slowly returned to the street from their own refuge.

Shortly after that, the two of them, native Timmon and alien human, retired to Shawn's bungalow, with Kearnin choosing to sleep on a coarse blanket in the corner of the living room. Shawn's slumber was slow coming, shallow, and tormented by broken water pipes and phantom beasts with large emerald teeth.

#

Morning light and colony activity banished the nocturnal beasts to their burrows, and Shawn led Kearnin along the well-worn path to the irrigation station. Golden fog shrouded the trees like spider silk. Kearnin's mood seemed less somber. They hiked quickly along the dirt lane flanked by ale-colored grass, flattened and splayed out by cart traffic. The snarls of penderin fighting in the tree boughs above them reminded Shawn of the growling unknown that had invaded the village. He proceeded more cautiously and made a mental note to tell Cara about the growling noise when he got back to Fairdawn.

They found the irrigation system as they'd left it two days earlier. Two pumps were partially reassembled following repairs, and much of the piping was disconnected, with several sections of the translucent, deep-amber pipe stacked haphazardly about the yard. They began sorting through the damaged sections of pipe, until Kearnin tapped Shawn's arm and pointed toward the path from Fairdawn. He didn't pull his blade.

Soon Paul Saarinen appeared, hacking at new vines, stepping insistently through the tall grass. Tanned since landing on Timmistria, he was a man of brown skin wrapped in brown clothing. He joined them and silently looked over the equipment and piping.

"Good morning," Shawn said.

"Morning."

"We need some help here."

Saarinen glanced around at the carnage of the irrigation equipment. "Tell me what's working." He tapped a ruptured piece of pipe with his toe. "And what's not."

Shawn spent the next hour walking him through the irrigation system. The new colonist followed as Shawn explained the system, described the problems and limitations, and discussed their fabrication techniques. Saarinen asked questions as they went, then more questions. If he had seemed quiet and reserved during their previous encounters, he was certainly not shy.

After that, he insisted on seeing the upstream piping all the way to the creek, and downstream all the way to the main irrigation field. This required a long hike and generous climb up a 60-degree bluff of rust-colored rock. His questions left Shawn slack-jawed and struggling for answers. They hiked to the creek, then back along every foot of piping to the pumps and then to the higher fields, examining each joint and branch and valve. Shawn caught Kearnin staring at Saarinen, turning his head one way and then another, as if trying to locate the source of a faint sound.

After a final walk-down, they picked their way down the rock-jumbled bluff to the creek basin and back to the pump station. Saarinen spent several silent minutes, with Shawn and Kearnin watching him, examining the pumps and the damaged piping. Shawn fought the urge to make small talk and just waited. Kearnin was much better at waiting silently, still turning his head from side to side as he watched the man stooping over the pumps.

The fog dissipated but remained as an uncomfortable weight in the creek bottom. It was by then early afternoon, and Shawn's stomach was beginning to protest. He swatted a biting fly on the back of his shoulder, and the movement and sound snapped Saarinen from his thoughts. He rose from his crouch and joined them. "I have a few ideas that may help."

"Good. I think we're willing to try anything at this point."

"This varnish you use to build the piping comes from local tree sap, right?"

"Yes. The malack."

"It seems to be a good resin material."

"But not for pipes?"

"Actually, I think it's very suitable for pipes."

"Then it's our technique. We're not curing it properly."

"No. I think your curing technique is effective. I think all that's lacking, Shawn, is some structural material. Do you have something like mesh that you could wrap around the pipe?"

Shawn looked at Kearnin with raised eyebrows.

Saarinen clarified, "Some type of heavy cloth with a wide weave would work, I think."

Kearnin asked, "What is … 'mesh'?"

Saarinen spread the fingers of both hands in straight lines and laid them across each other at right angles in a crosshatch pattern. "Like this, but smaller. Like a net."

Kearnin grunted. He motioned for Shawn to follow and walked toward the creek in long strides. When Shawn caught up, Kearnin eased into the mud and hacked at the bases of the reedy stalks that grew waist-high in spikes from the creek bed. Shawn pulled his blade, and he and Saarinen stood watch. Shortly, Kearnin stepped from the weeds, dragging an armful of the stalks with him. He laid down the stalks, knelt and drew his short blade, and slit a stalk down the length of the stem. His long fingers deftly peeled away the tough outer shell, revealing a tubular network of tan fibers. He pulled patches of the material from the exposed stem, each about a foot long and three to four inches wide, and held one up for Shawn to inspect.

He said, "Pril. We use it to bind wounds and to make nets for small fish and birds."

Shawn took a patchy section, held it up and looked at the daylight through it, then handed it to Saarinen. "Is this something you can use?"

Saarinen turned the delicate plant material over in his hands, then held it with both hands and pulled. The mesh stretched and then snapped back without unraveling. He tugged at it twice more, and then frowned in thought. "If you could harvest this in larger sheets, it would be perfect. But even in this size, it should work."

Shawn said, "Really? How do we use it?"

Saarinen stood up from his crouch, holding the mesh up in the sunlight. "I think it'll act like the steel mesh used in concrete. It should give your pipe better strength and reduce the cracking problems."

"That'd be beautiful."

"We'll need several hundred square feet of it."

Shawn glanced at Kearnin. "We?"

Saarinen looked confused. "I assumed you wanted help building the new pipe. My camp's complete, and I need to start contributing to the village."

"No, no! I mean, yes, we can use your help. Absolutely."

The faint trace of a smile touched Saarinen's face. He nodded. "Good. Tomorrow? I foresee several days of gathering reeds and pitch."

"Yes, and we have others who can help. I'll ask the board to draft more. Nine o'clock is good, at the maintenance shop."

"I'll see you there."

"Oh, and Mr. Saarinen, we heard a large predator in Fairdawn last night. It may still be in the area. Please keep your eyes open." Shawn felt stupid with his choice of words. Saarinen struck him as one who might sleep with his eyes open.

But Saarinen showed no offense and just nodded. "Like your videos said, we must always be careful. The unknown hazards are more dangerous than the known ones, aren't they?"

"Yes. I can't argue with that."

With a nod to each of them, Saarinen unsheathed his blades and took off at a steady run through the brush. He passed out of sight nearly as silently as a Timmon.

Kearnin followed the man's retreating form, even after he'd disappeared.

Shawn asked, "Did you see anything? His timeril?"

"Shik. Ne."

Chapter 7

"We see as we are. Timmistria sees all things as they are."
— Timmistrian proverb

"The humans have brought peril to our people since their arrival. We've tolerated them at Lonin's insistence. But now they bring a melok and harbor it in their kithin, and we are expected to tolerate this as well. Lonin trusts the humans too much. And you, Lajin, ask us to trust you too much."

Gagarin, given the floor of the council meeting, had wasted no time in becoming inflammatory. His barking voice echoed off the chamber's six walls, despite the heavy woven rugs hung there to soften the noise. The rugs depicted images designed to ease tension, some of workers in the field, some of pastoral landscapes. The makers avoided places the Timmon had ceded to the Delerin and images of conflict.

Lajin, the Timmon leader, responded with no warmth. "Be careful, Gagarin. Your skin glows red like moonlight. If you continue, you may be mistaken for the melok."

Gagarin pressed on, undaunted. "The Timmon are becoming more dissatisfied with the situation, Lajin, and they hold you responsible. Those who never agreed with letting the humans stay on Timmistria have louder voices and will no longer go unheard."

"They've always had their chance to speak, Gagarin, and your voice on the subject has always been clear."

Gagarin held the important position of terrigin, which translated to "voice of the lesser tribe." The terrigin was responsible for supporting minority political positions. Gagarin had been elected terrigin because of his impressive speaking voice and his staunch opposition to the human colony.

Lonin sat at Lajin's left hand. Gagarin sat directly opposite, with his strongest allies, Jakin and Yelletin, at his sides. All three were strong traditionalist tribesmen. The other twelve council members sat on each side, completing the circle around the council table. No other Timmon were allowed at these special meetings, and the heavy wooden door was barred from the inside and guarded from the outside.

The regular council meetings were open to the people, but Timmon history had shown that private meetings were also needed so council members could speak without inhibition. A special meeting such as this could be called at any time by any council member, with the approval of any four others. Gagarin had little trouble finding four supporters. Lonin was surprised this meeting wasn't called weeks before, shortly after Dench's arrival. The delay had given Lajin and Lonin more time to prepare.

"Yes, you and Lonin won the vote, but beliefs are changing. Many seek another vote, and the result may be different this time."

The original treaty with the humans granted them indefinite access to the lands they had been given. By application of old Timmon law, a tribal treaty was a powerful document, and although this was the first treaty with an off-world "tribe," the same rules applied. Dissolving the human treaty would require a vote of 13-4, which was not likely. But only a simple majority was required to stop all Timmon assistance. Without Timmon aid, the humans had little chance of surviving longer than a season or two.

Lonin glanced around the room, trying to judge where each member might sit on the issue should a vote be required. He knew Gagarin and his two supporters were lost votes. Among the other twelve, there were perhaps two who would side with Gagarin. The others were at worst undecided.

Lonin still held influence over nearly all of them. But fear was a gray shadow that dimmed the lights of many here. Fear was a powerful tool in the hands of the passionate — and a friend of Gagarin.

The political situation involving the acceptance of the humans had always been like the swinging of the sun gauge's shadow. Time was both a gift and an enemy: the passage of time had brought no calamity, invasion, or punishment from Timmistria, but not much good had come from the human settlement. There were no mechanical wonders, no improved foodstuffs, no other advances or gifts, and all the visionary ideas that Lonin, Lajin, and the human sponsors had offered were becoming tired, unrealized promises.

The Timmon had donated their labor, resources, and knowledge, and the fruits of that cultivation had been meager. Even before Dench's arrival, the sentiment had been growing among even the most progressive Timmon that this was a lost crop that should no longer be nurtured. Now, even Lonin found it hard to justify the colony and harder to deny the threat the humans represented.

Gagarin was free to use this meeting as a personal speaking stone. He was a talented speaker, a concise thinker, and a worthy terrigin. He had long ago earned Lonin's respect for his work ethic and fairness of action, although Lonin seldom agreed with him. Now, they sat at opposite sides of both the table and the human debate. Lonin expected no quarter from Gagarin and was prepared to give none.

"A new vote must be called if eight council members request it."

"I'm aware of council rules and Timmon law, Gagarin. All rules will be followed as firmly as the roots of the malack."

"We hear you, Lajin. You tell us that you'll follow the rules and that a vote will be taken if the rules require it. What you're not telling us is why you're hiding behind the rules and not volunteering to call a vote immediately. You know that the people want a vote now. They want to know why we continue to harbor the invaders and why we are not acting to remove the red beast!"

Lajin remained calm, but his face darkened. "Great thought went into the writing of the treaty with the humans. One of the important parts of the agreement was to make sure the humans have the same protections that the Timmon enjoy in our treaty with the Delerin. Those protections require that we allow the human settlement to be governed by human law. They are bound by the same restrictions we Timmon are. They must build only within the lands they were given. In these five years, the humans have abided by the treaty's rules and have lived by their own laws, and time has shown that this arrangement has worked well. There is no cause to change the way we've lived together because of unrealized fear."

Gagarin shook his head. "I agree there've been no major catastrophes with the humans, at least up to this point. But I cannot agree that the arrangement has worked well. They've never presented us with a threat of this magnitude before. Many among the Timmon see the coming of the beast as the first step of a greater plan, and that plan could be an invasion."

"The red one is a problem to be addressed, but calling it the sign of an invasion isn't reasonable."

"Is that so? We know they have greater knowledge of machines than we, which means they have greater knowledge of weapons. We can guess that they greatly outnumber us, since they reside on many worlds, not just one, as we do and as they once did. Is it not reasonable to conclude that they moved from this 'Earth' to other worlds through aggression? With their weapons and machines, what could stop them?"

Gagarin paused, sweeping a glare around the room. "And how would we know what a human invasion looks like? A small colony may be the way they always begin, and it may already be too late for the Timmistrian races. I see this as a plan. Establish a small force. Ask for help. Learn the ways of the world and its peoples. Then bring in the real invaders. No, it doesn't seem so unreasonable to me."

"'One Delerin does not a war make,' Gagarin. The same is true of one unpleasant human. As far as we know, the red one has done nothing wrong and has broken no human or Timmon laws. If we Timmon had acted upon every fear or every suspected incursion by the Delerin, we would have violated our treaty with them long ago, probably to our own destruction. To this date, we've held several meetings with the humans. Their leaders are well aware of our concerns, and they have assured us they will watch the red one vigilantly and will remove him from Timmistria if he violates any law. We trust that Timmistria keeps her watchful eyes on this one as well."

"All well, Deminin, but if the humans were to begin building a stockpile of powerful weapons, would we wait until they began using them before we acted? By then, it would be far too late. They accept our food, our help, and our gifts, and for all we know, all the time they may be building and storing weapons. Who among us knows what lies behind the walls and beneath the floors of their buildings? Who has seen for themselves?"

Lonin chose this point to step into the discussion. "I have seen. They are not building weapons. Their tools are crude by human ways, and they struggle with simple machines, like those that thresh their grain and bring water to their fields. As you recall, Gagarin, you gained favor among your tribe as a young council member by insisting the humans be given the driest and least fertile lands we could offer them. They accepted those lands with grace and gratitude. To this day, they struggle to survive. Their young perish at a high rate, and their storage places are never filled with food. They do not have time to build weapons. They spend all their time in the challenge of surviving the dark season."

Gagarin paused, with the look of a fighting cat caught off guard. "Truly, Lonin, your eyes are much sharper than mine, and none here doubt your words, but even you can be fooled. It is well known that the humans are your friends, and sometimes friendship can blind one's eyes. Many in your own kithin believe the humans are a threat. Like most in my tribe, they believe this red beast is the weapon the humans have brought to overrun the Timmon. They also believe that we owe it to our people, our kithin, and our families to strike now before it is too late."

Lajin maintained his legendary calm. "To strike now without provocation would violate Timmon law."

"Sometimes events defy order and the laws serve us badly. And in those times, the laws must be set aside."

"Without laws, we become yellow beasts and no better than a pack of vikin. Choosing a time such as this, and saying that it is 'outside the normal order,' does not excuse unlawful action. Soon, every crisis becomes outside the normal order, and the laws become meaningless. It's in these times that the laws show their true value. We have signed a treaty with the humans, and this time of concern, based on possibly unfounded fear, does not warrant casting our entire system of order to the winds."

"And that treaty with the humans that you are so proud of, written with little input from the kithin I represent, may be our destruction. Can we take a chance that the humans are not a threat? With the eyes of the red beast on our homes, can you guarantee our people that we will be safe?"

At last, Lajin allowed his calm to fall away, and the power of his presence shone out. His face colored in the bright orange of a battle mask, and his ears and nostrils flared in agitation. "By the grace of Timmistria, Gagarin, I was elected Deminin, and as long as I hold that title, we Timmon will abide by the trusted laws of our people, and we *will* abide by our treaty with the humans. If it is our undoing, then I trust Timmistria will damn my light to Dreyaten and convey all the Timmon people to peace circling the black star Deleria. If the humans are to be the cause of our destruction, then this red one is only the messenger, and killing it now will only anger them and hasten our doom. Call me a fool, and call the red one Lajin's Bane if you will, but I have sworn to hold the laws of our people in this hand…" He held up his left hand, dual thumbs and fingers spread in an embrace. "And to defend them by the power of this hand…" He lowered his left hand and raised his right. "And I intend to do just that!"

None moved as Lajin's words echoed around the hall. At last, Gagarin bowed his head in formal deference to the Timmon leader. "Your judgment is wise and learned, Lajin, Deminin. With Timmistria's eyes upon us, we will abide by the treaty, until the time when the Timmon people may change their voice. But it may be that this decision will be taken from our council. The Delerin are not bound by Timmon law or by our treaty with the humans. Those who speak with the Delerin say they fear the red beast as many of us do, and they may act to remove it and all the humans who brought it here. I hope their anger doesn't fall upon us for our part in bringing this danger to Timmistria. And I trust you understand that our treaty with the Delerin takes precedence over our treaty with the humans. If the Delerin act, the Timmon must step aside."

"I haven't heard of any anger or imminent action by the Delerin."

"But if they were to act, you agree that the Timmon would be powerless to stop it?"

"'Powerless' is a poor choice of words, Gagarin. We always have the choice to influence events."

"But in this case, our influence should not include standing between the Delerin and the humans, to the detriment of our people."

"As I said, I have not been told of any action by the Delerin. We will influence those events if they move from speculation to reality."

"I'm afraid that the time of action will come very soon, and the Timmon people want to know what your plan is."

"I will address the concerns of the Timmon people, Gagarin. In the meantime, I trust that none of our people will 'influence' the Delerin to act because of exaggerated fears and self-serving reasons."

Gagarin's face flushed orange in anger, and his timeril flashed. If he had not made overtures to the Delerin, it had at least crossed his mind. "Our people would not incite the anger of the Delerin, Deminin Lajin. But I have been told the humans' act of bringing the red one to Timmistria has Delerin anger brewing like an awakening volcano. May Timmistria protect the Timmon and shield us from their wrath."

"As you say. If there is no other business, I move that this meeting be closed. We all have work awaiting us."

Around the table, the council bowed their heads in closing and silently left the chamber. Shammin, the guard, unbarred the door and followed the last council member out. He pulled the door closed behind him, leaving Lajin and Lonin alone. They sat quietly a moment, letting the voices of the members and guards drift away outside.

Lonin said at last, "The meeting went as expected. No surprises from Gagarin."

Lajin shook himself from deep thoughts. "Ne. Gagarin is consistent and predictable."

"And in this case, correct."

"Shik. Yes. Our own contacts confirm that the Delerin are becoming agitated about the red one. In time, despite any assurances we give them, they will act."

"We must do all we can to prevent an attack."

"'Prevent' is the key word, Lonin. You know as well as Gagarin and I do that by Timmon law, if the Delerin go to war against the humans, we cannot stand in their way."

"Gagarin may also be correct in another way, Lajin. Sometimes the laws serve us badly, and the right course of action may defy the law."

Lajin raised his eyes from his own hands to Lonin's face, his look hard and earnest. "Perhaps, but not in this case. Many of the Delerin suspect we harbor the humans in an effort to gain more power so that we may expand the boundaries of our lands. I don't blame them. I would feel the same way."

"Unfounded. From the humans, we seek better lives for all Timmistrians, to be not as much at the mercy of the seasons, and to open our skies to trade and travel.

The Delerin would benefit, just as the Timmon would. We seek no advantage to be brought to bear on the Delerin."

"Don't we? With human tools, machines, and weapons, and the skies open to us, our boundaries could seem constricting and intolerable. The humans disrupt the natural order of things, Lonin. Because of this, they threaten our peace. By letting them build this colony, we have set many things in motion, and the outcome has always been in doubt. I may have ruled unwisely and brought hard days to my people. We have to walk prudently and quietly now, lest our decisions made five seasons ago lead to our doom."

"Deminin, I have no doubts about our decisions. The possible benefits of friendship with the humans — *these* humans — far outweigh the risks. They speak of a war with another alien race, which they fight across millions of kikkin of space and among the stars. Had we denied the humans sanctuary, I believe this war would have come to our lands in time. Our isolation on Timmistria would not have protected us."

Lajin nodded gravely. "You may be right, and I trust your counsel as much now as I did when we made the treaty. But we must meet with the humans again and urge them to remove the kahl melok before its presence leads us to a war with our cousins. And the time is short, Lonin. The time is very short."

"Agreed, Deminin. I will plead our case again."

"'Timmistria rules in all things,' friend."

"Timmistria rules in all things."

Chapter 8

"The perin that leaves the nest unready to fly falls to the vikin waiting below."
— Timmon proverb

When Shawn saw Saarinen walk into the maintenance shop at 8:45 a.m., the team had already begun work. They'd laid out the best reeds as internal molds for the pipes and had begun to extract thin sheets of the fibrous matting from the water plant stems. Mark, James, and Scott, their latest recruit, had gone to gather more sap, this time with a basket of freshly sharpened drill bits and the larger solar-powered drill. Shawn had several more strong young men in reserve, in case the drilling exhausted his first crew.

He laid down the curved metal knife he was using to strip the mesh material from the water plants and went to meet Saarinen at the door. When they shook hands, Saarinen's grip was firm and insistent, and his eyes met Shawn's directly in a way that seemed easy, automatic, and borne of long habit. Then they stood just inside the doorway, Saarinen with arms crossed, surveying the work in progress. Shawn allowed him to break the silence.

"These men work well together."

Shawn nodded. "Most of the time."

"Did you choose them?"

"I did encourage some of them to join us."

"I think you did well. Why don't you show me what you've done so far?"

They spent the next half-hour walking through the shop, examining the tubular reeds to be used as molds and the growing pile of mesh material extracted from the water plants. Saarinen was critical about selection, asking the crew to clean the reed tubes to a fine smoothness and lending a hand to sort the mesh by thickness, hole size, and even color.

"We don't know which materials will work best, so we need to test them methodically."

He spent a good amount of time explaining to Gregor and two others how slight changes in the pipe's circular shape could lead to weak spots. The two helpers seemed dubious and eyed Shawn to confirm that they needed to continue sanding. Shawn nodded slightly. The men glanced at each other, then bowed their heads and went back to rubbing pieces of dragon skin over the reeds.

Saarinen then turned his penetrating gaze on Shawn. "I think we need gauges to measure the pipe diameter and roundness. Otherwise, the men will have to rely on visual observation, which will affect quality."

"What do you suggest?"

"For diameter, a simple tape measure will work. For roundness, we'll have to find or make several pieces with circular cutouts. Not easy, but I believe it's necessary."

"All right. Let's go to the metal shop and see what's available."

As they walked between buildings, the sun had turned bitter and burnt the parched sky to a reddish-orange. Dresden followed the sun's path, like an annoying smaller brother, defying the yellow Class G-Zero star to outshine its blood-colored light. Shawn's nostrils began to burn in the heat, and his mouth tasted of dust.

"Mr. Saarinen, you know a lot about making pipes."

Saarinen scrunched up his mouth. "Not really. It's just easy for me to come in at this stage and make suggestions. We don't know yet if any of my ideas are going to hold water. No pun intended, I promise."

Shawn chuckled. "I looked at your profile, along with those of the others in your landing party, but that was months ago and I don't remember much. I do remember that you're a materials engineer, from Crest? Where did you study?"

"A small school called Riesen Institute of Technology, just outside Burlington, New Vermont. A well-regarded program in the country I was born in. But I'm afraid I wasn't well-regarded there."

"Why?"

"Not the best student. Other interests. Boredom. A fondness for alcohol. All the usual reasons."

"But you got your degree, and then what?"

Saarinen breathed in and out deeply. "A couple years in industry, then war broke out with another country. All the technical people were drafted into military support roles. After the war, I was discharged. More years in industry, and then a move to Cambiana. Not much else to tell."

"And then Timmistria. Would it offend you if I asked why you came here?"

Saarinen smiled sheepishly and shrugged. "No. I suppose I'd be offended if you didn't ask. Adventure. Opportunity. Running away from something. We all had reasons for coming here, right?"

"Sure. But you seem more talented than most who come. You must have an interesting story."

Saarinen's smile faded. "No. Dull, actually. I'd bet your story is more interesting."

They'd crossed the busy town square; the dirt street was as hard as paving stones under their feet. Shawn led Saarinen to the door of the metal shop and held it open for him. He propped the door open with a wooden wedge the metalworkers kept there for exactly that purpose, and the sunlight flooded the otherwise dim hallway beyond. The walls had been painted eggshell-white the previous autumn, but the dust and humidity had yellowed them. Shawn made a note to add repainting this building to the list of work items, and then led Saarinen to the tool rack along one wall. They began looking through tools and gauges for something with a smooth, even curve, in a diameter near what they needed.

Shawn pulled several pieces of thick scrap metal from a collection bin, and Saarinen began sorting through them. Daylight leaked in from the vent holes in the ceiling. Saarinen looked over from the piece of stained steel he had been holding up to the light. "You and Ms. Harvestmoon came from Principia, correct?"

"Yes."

He nodded. "From what I know about that system, it's not a mystery why you left."

"It was good to leave. Difficult, but we've never looked back."

Saarinen pointed to a place on the piece of scrap he held. "We can cut through the middle of this hole and remove the burrs to make two gauges."

"I can ask the metal shop guys to finish it. I'd like to go check on the gang collecting the malack sap. I think the team here is doing well with the tubes and matting."

"Good. I'd like to come with you, if that's okay."

"Please do. You'll have ideas for improving the sap gathering."

"Ah, maybe. I really just like being in the woods. I'm looking for an excuse. And a guide."

Shawn gave the scraps to two metalworkers who came in shortly afterward. Saarinen followed Shawn back to the maintenance shop, where they looked at the materials the team had prepared while they were gone and left instructions on how to use the new gauges when they were delivered. Then they packed two small backpacks with dried fruits, bread, and water skins and set out.

The villagers they passed greeted Shawn warmly and nodded soberly to Saarinen, probably surprised to see Shawn with the recent immigrant and not Kearnin. The dusty streets soon led them from the knot of one-story rough-cut stone and wooden buildings at the village center to the outer circle, where the buildings were less dense, and then past the final guard post before the main trail heading west. With the sun high and Dresden trailing closely behind, the burning daylight forced them to don the wide-brimmed hats Shawn had packed.

They moved smoothly along the trail, a two-man convoy passing into the trees and leaving behind the rest of the human population. Shawn felt as comfortable with Saarinen covering his back as he did with Kearnin. The overhead canopy thickened, filtering some of the light and turning away some of the oppressive heat. But soon, he felt an inexplicable sense of unease. He paused on the trail a minute to listen.

Behind him, Saarinen stopped and squinted.

Shawn asked him, "Does it seem odd to you? Something different?"

Saarinen nodded, his face tight with concern. "Yes. It's too quiet, with no penderin or small creatures moving around."

"The Timmon haven't located that cat Kearnin and I heard two nights ago."

Saarinen's yellow eyes widened. He gripped his blade and nodded in the direction they were traveling. "Go as fast as you want. I'll keep up."

Shawn nodded and set out at a faster hike. He glanced back once to find Saarinen nearly on his heels and increased his pace, slashing at vines as he went.

The team gathering sap had planned to work in one of three different locations in the woods. The first was the malack woods that Shawn could just begin to see through the orange pine and yellow lichen they were hiking through. He nearly missed the side trail leading to the right and toward the wood, and he had to stop abruptly. He waited an instant to make sure Saarinen was behind him, and then pressed on.

He hacked at the catcher vines that shot out at them from each side of the trail, a sign that the other men had not been through there earlier in the day. He decided to check anyway. The normal clouds of biting insects were there, but none of the bat-like things that usually chased them. Saarinen's blade sang behind him. They made the short hike to the grove of trees in a couple of minutes. Shawn pulled up, with Saarinen halting a few paces away, but as they had expected, there were no signs of the sap-gathering party.

"Mark! James!"

Shawn's voice faded dully into the thick brush. He paused briefly and repeated the calls in the opposite direction. The woods yielded no response. He wanted to kick himself for sending the party out with so few members.

"Let's move on to the next location."

Saarinen nodded, hefting his blade, and they set off again.

The main trail grew gradually narrower and rougher, but there were signs that the other party had been through. Wheel marks in the trail appeared fresh, and some of the scrub brush that had grown in close appeared to have been freshly cut. They pressed on.

After long minutes, they reached the trail entrance to the second stand of trees, a trail not used in some time and thoroughly overgrown. They didn't waste time there, moving on again. The main trail narrowed further, and the brush on each side showed obvious signs of the passage of the cart. Flies swarmed a pile of grassy herbivore dung on the trail. Most of the catcher vines had been cleared, but Shawn and Saarinen were forced at times to slow their pace and swing their blades to hack at the stragglers.

The eerie quiet that had triggered Shawn's sense of danger was more intense here. These trails, so deep in the woods, were normally thick with flying animals and usually rang with the calls of penderin and birds, and sometimes the deep, beating rumble of large lizards. Now there was little to hear but the whining drone of insects.

They soon came upon the four-wheeled cart parked to the side of the trail. Shawn suspected it was too heavy and wide to drag into the third stand of malacks, no doubt grown thick with underbrush. The draft beast had been unhitched and wisely not left alone. With no attention, the jarin would have grown bored or hungry, broken or chewed its bindings, and meandered back to Fairdawn.

The trail was nearly overgrown, but signs of recent passage were obvious — broken branches and slashed vines. Shawn began to doubt his state of alarm and wondered if the whole urgent flight had been for no reason. But as he raised his blade to begin hacking the brush ahead of him, Saarinen halted him with a hand on his shoulder. When Shawn turned, Saarinen touched a finger to his mouth. He listened. The sound that came through the repressive forest made the hair on the back of his neck stand up; the growl of a large predator, possibly the one he and Kearnin had heard in the village, and it was coming from the direction of the malack grove, perhaps 50 meters away.

Shawn and Saarinen eased forward, keeping low and stepping quietly, dodging the catchers, not wanting to alert the beast with the sound of the blades. They heard the growl again, this time closer to the wood. It was taking an eternity to reach the clearing, and Shawn had to fight the urge to break into a run.

At last, they slipped into the shadowy area beneath the trees. From Shawn's memory, this grove had a large clearing beneath the main wood, like most malack forests did, in a jagged circle. He moved forward to the edge of the clearing, where he could peek through the heavy brush that ringed the woods. Saarinen joined him, just to his left.

In the center of the clearing stood the jarin, mumbling loudly and gnawing at the reins binding it to the trunk of a small tree. The three members of the sap-gathering team crouched in a semicircle around the draft animal, foolishly but valiantly guarding it, blades drawn, their eyes darting about the perimeter of the clearing.

Shawn eased into the clearing, and then events broke in a flash of frightening images, during which he had no time to think, only act.

From his right, a nightmare beast of yellow skin and feathers and fangs, much larger than a man, loped into the clearing and charged at the jarin and its defenders. At the same instant, Kearnin and two other Timmon jumped into the open from a point opposite Shawn and bellowed louder than he thought possible.

The beast, equal parts cat, lizard, and bird, turned and charged the Timmon at blinding speed. Kearnin managed a glancing blade stroke at the yellow fury as he dodged, and one of the other Timmon fired an arrow that scattered feathers but did not slow the thing. The third

Timmon was knocked sprawling by a blow from the monster's paw but was able to roll away into the brush.

Shawn, fearing for Kearnin, sprang forward and charged. Still facing away from Shawn, the beast bounced on its haunches as it threatened to attack the Timmon again. It screamed in a high-pitched screech that chilled Shawn's blood and nearly stopped him in his tracks. He was nearly within blade range when it turned suddenly and slashed at him with a dagger-rimmed paw that struck his blade, nearly slapping it from his hand.

Shawn backpedaled clumsily, and his heart pounded as the animal pursued him. To his relief, the three other villagers came forward and flanked him, Mark and James yelling to distract it. They found out like the Timmon that this hellbeast was not spooked easily. It growled menacingly, let loose another painfully loud screech, and then sprang forward and attacked them.

"Look out!"

They tried to hold together while pointing their blades at the monster, but it was too swift and unpredictable. It feinted right toward Mark, then dodged erratically left and lunged at James and Scott, bowling them over with its front limbs, knocking them to the ground and scattering their weapons.

"Yaaaaa!" Shawn yelled and swung his blade wildly as the animal barreled into him next, flattened him, and raised a hideous, snakelike head on a serpentine neck as if to strike him. Before it could, more yells and singing blades drew its attention, and Kearnin and Saarinen were there, hooting and stabbing at the feathered freak, lunging and falling back in turn, trying to draw it away.

It seemed to be working. The beast advanced on Kearnin and Saarinen, who gradually retreated toward the side of the clearing where the Timmon had first appeared.

Shawn gathered himself and turned to the others. "Find your weapons. Let's help them."

The three men were dazed but not seriously injured. But just as the animal appeared to be poised to charge Kearnin and Saarinen, it proved unpredictable again. It spun on its tail and attacked Shawn's group again.

Kearnin yelled and leaped after it, but it ignored the distraction. It jumped ten feet in the air to land among them, standing over them and leaving them defenseless. Its terrifying snake head drew back to strike, so close now that Shawn could smell its breath, sour with the stench of decaying meat. It ignored Kearnin's cries and seemed content to glare at the colonists where they knelt or lay around it.

Then a flash of white struck it on the side of its head and bounced to the ground. The beast grunted and shuddered. It was a Timmon arrow, which hung by its tip for an instant before falling at the creature's feet. Then another arrow struck it in the side, this time sticking an inch or two into its fur.

Its skin flashed in waves of orange and red. It slapped the arrow away and turned to face its attacker — Saarinen, standing ten paces away, with a Timmon bow and another arrow nocked and drawn. He fired, and this arrow struck the beast in the forehead, just above the eye, before bouncing harmlessly away.

This offense was too much for the creature to ignore, and it advanced cautiously on Saarinen, as if puzzled by this bold thing that dared attack it. Saarinen retreated a step and drew another arrow from the Timmon quiver on his back.

Shawn again tried to pull his party together and searched the ground for a blade, intending to join

Kearnin, who was sneaking around to attack the creature's blind side.

Saarinen fired again, this shot finding a soft spot beneath the shoulder, burying inches into the flesh. The monster roared and slapped at the arrow, snapping it so the stick end remained in its fur. At that point, Shawn was able to put his hand on a blade lying on the ground near Mark and tried to muster the strength to attack, finding himself nearly too weak to stand with shaking knees. Kearnin's yell did not turn the creature from its now-relentless pursuit of Saarinen, who continued to retreat slowly. He had another arrow strung, but his quiver looked empty.

Another Timmon bowman appeared from somewhere to stand next to Saarinen, then shot an arrow that struck the beast in the other shoulder. It screeched again, drawing back as if poised to leap at the archers. Saarinen fired, and the creature slashed the arrow from the air. The point stuck briefly in its paw but fell away when the thing shook the paw violently.

Again it readied for a leap, but the steady figures of Saarinen and the Timmon standing silently side by side facing it was enough. With a throaty growl, the same as Shawn remembered from the other night, it drew back on its haunches and leaped away into the forest in three great bounds, clearing the head-high brush with feet to spare.

Almost afraid to move for fear that the devilish thing would surprise them again, Shawn tried to gather himself. The Timmon archer handed Saarinen arrows from his own quiver, and the two stood at the ready. Kearnin joined them, blade drawn. He seemed more interested in Saarinen than the animal, shamelessly looking him up and down.

Saarinen returned Kearnin's look, face tense, and then turned to speak to Shawn. "We'd better gather up quickly. That thing wasn't seriously hurt. It could come back at any time."

Kearnin said, "The crellil will not return."

Saarinen continued as if he had not heard him. "Once we get the injured back to town, we need to put together a hunting party. Shawn, do we have anything besides blades and bows to hunt that thing with?"

Shawn had pulled himself to his feet and had begun to check his companions. They were all stunned, and James and Scott had nasty gashes where the monster's claws had pierced their leather gloves and vests. He didn't know if the claws were venomous, but their wounds would need to be treated to prevent infection.

"Not really. We have long bows, some longer blades, and a few spears and nets. We used up all the pepper bombs years ago on the dragons, and blasters were never allowed."

He pulled a handkerchief from a side pocket in his breeches. He ripped it into two-inch strips and motioned for James to hold his arm out, then wrapped a strip around it to cover a wound. He tied a double knot to secure it. "We need to get these men back to town quickly. I'm not sure we have time to bring the jarin. We should cut it loose, and maybe it'll have a chance to get back to Fairdawn before that monster finds it."

Kearnin said, "The crellil will not return. It might be dead already." He pulled an arrow from the other Timmon's quiver, holding up the point. "Jin."

Saarinen pulled one of the arrows he'd been given and examined the tip. "Jin? Poison?"

"Yes. We track this one since we heard it in the village, two nights ago. I am sorry we moved slow." Kearnin gestured toward the men wrapping their wounds.

Shawn waved off his concern. "No apologies, friend. If you hadn't come, we could all be dead." He bowed forward, hands spread in an open, two-thumbed manner.

"No thanks to we Timmon. It was Mistin Saarinen who shot the crellil."

Saarinen said, "How fast does this jin work?"

Shawn added, "Will it kill a crellil?"

Kearnin had been joined by the third Timmon, who had suffered the first savage attack. Kearnin and the other archer examined his arms and shoulders for injuries, but the heavy animal skins he was wearing had protected him from the marauder's claws and teeth.

"Jin will kill the crellil. Jin kills almost all beasts, but not the cremin … the 'dragon,' so you call it."

"Good. Even if the thing isn't coming back, we have to get these men back to Fairdawn and treat their wounds. Will you be all right? Do any of you need assistance or treatment?"

"Shik. Ne. We will find the crellil where it now lies dead. We will bring it to your village. Your people need to learn it. More may come."

"OK. Mark, please cut the jarin loose and let it follow us back. If that monster is dying, the jarin should be OK. We need to get moving."

James was finding his blade and gingerly putting it in its side sheath. He said, "What about the sap we gathered, and the tools?"

"Leave them. We'll return for them in the morning, if the crellil is found dead and there are no others in the area."

After Kearnin and the other Timmon disappeared silently into the brush, Shawn asked Mark, who was essentially unhurt, to lead the five-man party. They returned to the trail from the clearing and headed east back to town. The two injured men, James and Scott, rode the jarin, which did not flee when they cut its bonds. Mark took its reins. Shawn hoped that keeping the injured men at rest would minimize irritation and swelling around their wounds. They complained about riding at first but discovered that any sweat in their cuts caused burning pain, and from then on they rode in silence.

The jarin, still spooked from the attack, rambled faster as it went. Mark was forced to release the reins and let it trot freely to keep from getting dragged. The driving beast tore along like a slow juggernaut, clearing the trail of brush and any remaining catcher vines, ignoring the stinging plants. Its riders were forced to duck and cover their heads, and the others struggled to keep up.

Shawn wondered why the settlers had never used the jarin for this purpose before. If they tied on some long trace tethers to steer the animal, they could use it to clear a new path in a fraction of the time it took several strong men with blades and the brush cutter. The jarin had become a smaller version of the destructive cremin, the "dragon," which decimated any vegetation, dwellings, or unfortunate animals caught in its path.

Back at Fairdawn, the medical volunteers joined the village doctor to examine and treat the men. Shawn and Saarinen submitted to complete examinations as well. Small wounds that went undetected could quickly become infected. James and Scott were dosed heavily from the meager store of antibiotics, and their wounds were treated with antibacterial and antifungal salves. They ended up spending several days in the clinic under close observation, but no serious infections or allergic reactions developed.

Following his examination, Saarinen excused himself to return to his camp to wash and eat, but he promised to return to the shop in the early morning to help retrieve the sap and tools. Shawn went by the shop to see how far the workers had progressed on the materials, and then headed for Cara's office. On the way, several people stopped him to ask about the jungle attack. News traveled quickly in the small village.

#

He found Cara looking out the window at the fading evening light. When he knocked and entered, she turned, her face tight and pale. He wondered if she'd been in the office all day.

"Shawn, thank god. You're all right?" She crossed the room quickly and hugged him, clutching him close to her. He let her hang on to him. She was shaking.

"I'm fine, Cara, thanks to Kearnin and the others."

After she calmed down, she sat him down in the chair opposite her desk, left the office to fetch him wine and a small meal, and made him tell the story as he ate. In the telling, he was forced to make sense of the blur of images, and he tried to set things firmly in sequence in his mind. It was difficult. Shock and adrenaline had compressed time in his memory. After going over it several times, with Cara asking questions, he guessed the entire attack had taken less than two minutes.

As he finished the bread and cheese, Tommy, one of Fairdawn's three "runners" — Cara disliked that term and strongly requested that the villagers call them "couriers" — rushed into the office and blurted out that a Timmon hunting party had brought a "yellow tiger" to the square. Shawn set down his plate, and he and Cara followed the youth out the door just as he disappeared around the corner on his fleet pre-teenage feet.

When they reached the square, a crowd had already gathered. There were perhaps 30 people there, with more coming. In the center of the crowd were six Timmon rangers, two females and four males, including Kearnin. The body of the crellil lay on a flat wooden litter, and some of the villagers were lifting the head and shoulders and draping them over a wooden sawhorse. The fanged snake head and clawed feet were laid out on the ground for examination. The sheer size and deadly appearance of the crellil made Shawn uncomfortable, and he hoped the Timmon had made sure it was dead.

Kearnin prodded the beast with a long wooden stick as he answered questions from the villagers. The crellil's eyes were dull and lifeless now, with none of the yellow and red flash that had magnified its terrifying appearance. Cara stood about ten feet from the creature. She said nothing.

Kearnin saw them and stepped down from the litter. He wasn't the least intimidated by the scary predator on display, and to Shawn it seemed that his casual attitude was not merely because the monster was dead. He'd obviously seen crellil before, and no doubt other more fearsome things. His coming to meet them didn't shake Cara from her solemn posture.

Shawn asked, "You managed to drag it all the way here? That quickly?"

"It is not heavy. Crellil are large, but they are not heavy. They are jumpers and gliders." To emphasize, he returned to the yellow horror and motioned for one of the female Timmon to help him lift the front leg. A light brown membrane extended from the crellil's forelimb to the sides of its rib cage, like a bat's wing. After confirming that Shawn and Cara had seen the sailing flap, Kearnin laid the limb back down gently and returned, but not before he and the female exchanged looks. Shawn had never seen Kearnin flirting before. His manner was surprisingly human.

Cara broke her silence. "I thought these forests were clear of large predators. We've never seen anything like this. Do they normally live close to here?"

"Shik. Ne. They are of the deep forest. Visits to our lands are not often. They tell each other not to come to Timmon land or they might be killed. But if they choose to come, we cannot keep them out. They move quickly and pass many kikkin. But they choose not to come. We have not seen the crellil in these lands in many years. They do not fear us or the Delerin in their own lands. In their lands, we are food."

Cara said, "Did lack of water or food drive it here? Will more come?"

Kearnin looked at Cara as if asking him more than one question at a time was unfair. "By Timmistria's wisdom and learning, no things happen for no reason. This one is bright-colored and fed well, and its lands are not dry this season. Hunger did not bring it. If one crellil comes, more will come. We bring this one here to teach your people about this danger. Word of this crellil is now spread to the Timmon kithin, and my people guess a reason for this coming."

He stopped speaking suddenly, and his gaze fell on something just behind them. Orange flashed in his eyes.

Shawn followed his gaze. Dench was moving through the crowd, approaching the beast's litter. As Shawn watched, the five Timmon who had gathered nearby drew away, some with hands on blade hilts. One looked toward Kearnin and raised a hand in question. Kearnin nodded once, and the Timmon became gold and brass shadows, vanishing through the crowd, leaving the yellow monster and the red beast to the humans in the square. Kearnin wore a mask of agitation.

Cara said, "You think Dench brought the crellil?"

"Shik." He nodded. "Lin."

Shawn said, "Kearnin, the crellil coming has nothing to do with Dench. It's a coincidence."

"Co-ins…"

"Coincidence. Two things that happen at the same time, but not for the same reason. One thing did not cause the other."

Kearnin frowned, continuing to watch Dench nervously. The fleshy pink man was now at the litter, looking down at the dead creature there, asking questions of the others and nodding. Outwardly, he didn't look threatening.

"Timmon do not believe in … coincidence. All things are bound together." With an effort, he pulled his eyes from Dench. "I will go now."

"OK." Shawn held out his hand to Kearnin, who grasped it too firmly. "Thanks again, friend. You saved lives today. The list of our debts to you and your people grows ever longer."

Kearnin broke his grip and began to leave, then hesitated as if about to speak. He dropped his eyes and walked out of the square. Shawn felt uneasy watching him go.

Cara turned to Shawn and said, "The more I grow to know these people, the less I understand them. This superstitious fear of Mr. Dench seems so out of character." She turned back toward the pudgy, bald man standing near the litter and dabbing sweat from his brow with the ever-present handkerchief. "They don't fear that yellow thing, but they fear him. Look at him. The red beast? He's a geologist, for god's sake."

Shawn had to agree. The doughy man was not someone whose company he enjoyed. Dench was opinionated, asked a lot of pointed questions, and was condescending. But there was nothing threatening or dangerous in his appearance or manner.

Cara went on, "But I can't just disregard this problem. Whatever it is about Dench, his 'red light' or whatever, it's causing a rift in our relationship with the Timmon. And I have no idea what to do about it."

"Well, the easy thing would be to ship him out on the next transport."

"But not the right thing. It would be unfair to Mr. Dench, who upended his life to come here. And we need his skills. You know how hard it has been to get anyone with technical skills to come to Timmistria. What would the corporate sponsors say? 'You shipped a perfectly good geologist off-planet because the natives said his light was bad?' You and I would be the next two shipped off, with one-way tickets back to Principia. Or worse."

Shawn decided to change the subject. "Speaking of skills, I wanted to talk to you about Paul Saarinen."

"Hmm. Yes?"

"You know he's been working with us on the irrigation problems. He's come up with some good ideas for the piping, for making it stronger."

"Yes. So his engineering background is legitimate, and you think he'll help us?"

"Yes, definitely. But that's not what I want to talk about. He killed the crellil."

"I thought Kearnin and his hunting party killed it."

"Kearnin arrived just as the crellil attacked, but before they could shoot it, it pounced on them and then attacked us. Paul picked up a Timmon bow and shot it. It was too fast, and we couldn't keep it away with our blades, but he stood there and calmly shot it with several arrows until it ran off. He didn't know the arrows were poison-tipped. He just stood his ground and fired."

Cara looked again at the huge yellow and orange monster with the tooth-filled reptilian head draped over the sawhorse. She shivered.

Shawn continued, "His first shot hit it in the head and bounced off. His second pierced its shoulder."

"Did he say anything about having used a bow in the past?"

"I haven't asked him yet. But think about it. We walked into a battle with a monster that no humans have ever seen, and that we don't show in the training vids, and he calmly picks up a bow and arrow that he's never handled and pops this thing in the head. You remember how difficult it was for me to learn to shoot. It took me weeks with a Timmon bow before I could hit a three-foot target from 30 feet away, and that was using a child's bow. He picked up a full-sized bow and shot that thing in the head. If I hadn't seen it, I wouldn't believe it now."

Cara looked from Shawn to the crowd still gathered around the crellil, just now beginning to thin out. "Well, it seems the mystery of Mr. Saarinen deepens. Maybe he'll open up to you over time."

"We go back to work on the irrigation system tomorrow."

"OK." Then she suddenly threw her arms around him, squeezed him hard, and spoke quietly into his neck. "You've got to be more careful out there, Shawn. You're all I've got. Remember that."

"I know, Cara. I'll be careful."

She sighed and released him. He had never seen her look so small, almost turned inward on herself. He didn't like seeing her so upset.

"We have to get the sap and cart tomorrow. I'll take a large party."

She nodded, distracted.

"We'll be OK. Promise."

She looked at his face, like she was exploring it. Her eyes were wet. She breathed deeply in and out. Nodding absently, she turned to look at the carcass lying on the pallet. Dench was there still, talking with the others. She stroked her chin, lost in thought.

Chapter 9

"The geminil sleeping is still to be watched."
— Timmon proverb

"There is and can be only one Timmistria."
— Lonin, from "To Walk in an Alien Land"

Paul showed up at the maintenance shop the following morning, ready to work, as if the stunning events of the previous day had never happened. Kearnin had come as well, with three other Timmon archers. He reported that Timmon hunting parties were sweeping the lands around the woods, finding no new evidence of crellil or other large predators, and were expanding the searches to all Timmon lands bordering the colony.

Shawn assigned three people to collect and sort the pipe tubes and materials, and then test them with the new measuring gauges. Shawn, Paul, and Mark led a larger team of seven, and they set out with two wagons and draft beasts. Once outside the human compound, the trail seemed less aggressive than before. After several passages in the previous days, the snares and catcher vines were less numerous, the forest creatures swooped and screed in great abundance, and the party reached the third forest trail without incident.

The battle scene in the clearing beneath the malacks was as they had left it. Scuffed marks in the root-penetrated dirt showed clearly where the crellil had charged the Timmon and then the humans. The jarin stamped nervously and sniffed the ground where the other jarin had gouged the dirt in its effort to break loose from its tether. Two blades were recovered, as well as several Timmon arrows, three of them broken. Shawn warned the team not to touch the arrow points, and one of the Timmon soon collected them.

After one last warning, "More crellil will come," Kearnin left two Timmon archers at a high vantage point in a natural blind of malack branches, and he and the other archer left to catch up on their own duties. Before Kearnin left, Shawn waved him away from the group, who were breaking off in teams to collect the sap from the previous day's efforts and to begin boring new collection holes.

"Kearnin, one last thing before you go. During the battle yesterday, was there any time where you could see Paul Saarinen's light? Did he reveal his timeril?"

Kearnin shook his head in the odd Timmon way of imitating the human gesture, too wide and too slow. "Shik. Ne."

"Damn. I was hoping he'd let his guard down."

"His … guard … is not important. I know all I need to know about Paul Saarinen."

"And what do you know?"

"He is a strong warrior. He risked his life for others."

"Yes, he did, and he was very cool under pressure. But even a bad person can act good to win the respect of others."

Kearnin frowned, nose flaring and large lips pursing. "Timmon do not 'act good.' He faced the crellil and killed it. He did not 'act.' The crellil was wild and would kill us all. He had no time to act, only fight. I do not care about his timeril. I have seen his light."

Kearnin stood silently and motionless then, as if carved from one of the great trees that stood around them, painted in yellow, orange, and tan. He sometimes drew away like this, retreating within himself when there was serious Timmon business waiting on him. He wanted to go. He'd had enough of Shawn's questions.

Shawn said, "Thank you. Shik. Sil ah-hil. Silin ah-hil." (*Go in peace. Fly in peace.*)

"Shik. Lin. Silin ah-hil."

Kearnin left Shawn, not physically at first but spiritually, face hard and eyes surveying the forest, no longer interested in his friend or the other villagers beginning to work. Without moving, he seemed to melt into the forest, and then his body followed him as it slid effortlessly and silently into the yellow woods.

#

Cara, steaming cup in hand, stood by the litter that held the crellil. The native kava was a hot, bitter drink of local Timmistrian berries that resembled Principian coffee. One of her pet projects was selective breeding and hybridization of several strains of the low-growing shrubs that produced the dark purple berries, and the results were beginning to show promise. The drink was still too gummy and bitter, and she and the biologists' efforts to reduce the caffeine content had been mostly unsuccessful, but it was the best they had, and it was getting better.

Lonin had set his cup down on the litter while he examined the crellil's claws and teeth. He pulled the legs out one at a time, stretching the beast out to its full four-meter length. He then spread the bright yellow and tan plumage of the crellil's tail. It was long and kite-shaped, coming to a narrow point. To Cara's surprise, Lonin gripped the tail firmly at its base, drew his long blade, and cleaved it off with one vicious chop.

He laid it next to the litter and then came back to Cara's side, looking over the stunning carcass as if admiring a flowering plant and not a deadly predator that had nearly killed some of his people. He remained silent, gripping his kava mug. It was a game he sometimes played. After a couple minutes, she gave in.

"OK, Lonin. Why did you cut off the tail?"

He looked at her in mock surprise. "Shik. The tail must be awarded to the crellil killer. You have told me it must go to the quiet man who hides his light, Paul Saarinen."

"Yes, that's what Shawn and Kearnin told me last night. He picked up a Timmon bow and shot the crellil with a poisoned arrow."

Lonin nodded and sipped from the mug. "I will take the tail to him."

"You? A sudden interest in the 'quiet man'?"

"Yes."

"Good. Find out all you can. I have concerns."

"As you wish. My concerns are with the red one."

"We have discussed that situation, Lonin. Nothing has changed."

"Nothing has changed for you, but outside the human territory, there are events. The Timmon have met, and suspicion grows. We are closer to a change, and that may mean loss of support for your people."

Cara sighed. "I know, Lonin. Your people have been incredibly supportive and beyond helpful. If you withdrew support tomorrow, we couldn't find fault. But we're so close to the breakthrough we need. And Mr. Dench and his geological surveys may be part of that. Despite your feelings, he may be instrumental in allowing us to repay you and your people."

They stood, sipped, and looked at the crellil, once a terror and now a clownish decoration.

"I can't say that I like him either."

Lonin did not respond immediately, letting her words fade into the dusty daylight. "Perhaps the red one can help your people here, but not without a cost. There are also the Delerin to think about. Their patience wears thin."

"Is there any way we can meet with them? Maybe if we set up a meeting with the Timmon and Delerin leaders, and introduce you to Mr. Dench, we can resolve this misunderstanding."

Lonin rarely looked at her in a condescending way, but this was one of those times. "The Timmon and Delerin will not meet. And we will not sit with the red one. Only your blindness allows you to tolerate that one."

Cara felt her brow tightening. "Fine. I'm sorry I suggested it. But you leave me with few options."

They stood silently for a few more minutes, Lonin sipping loudly from his mug, which no doubt by now had gone lukewarm like hers. At last, he handed her the mug, now empty.

"I will deliver the crellil's tail."

#

Dench found the man, Harrison Thomas, sharpening tools alone in one of the shops. When he looked up and saw Dench standing just inside the doorway, he seemed genuinely happy to see him.

"Well, hey-ya, Mr. Dench! Nice day. You come down to help sharpen the scrapers too?"

"Scrapers? What do they scrape?"

"Dragon skin, Mr. Dench. The season is comin' pert near, and if we can kill a couple of the beasties without having an army of them on top of us, we'll be cleanin' them."

"Hmm. I may have to examine them to see if there is anything that will help with my work. And that's why I came to see you, Thomas. Our early tests have given me excellent insight, but I need to do some in-depth research. To do that, I need to contact some of my sources off-planet. Since you run the ansible, I was wondering if you could arrange some additional time for me."

Thomas continued to hone the scraper blade with a patch of worn dragon skin and did not answer immediately, much to Dench's annoyance. When he did answer, it was not encouraging. "I dunno, Mr. Dench. The ansible time is divided up even, and everybody gets a share. The council watches the log pert close."

"That seems reasonable, Thomas. But let me ask you a question, my friend: of all the colonists who use the ansible, who on Timmistria has a better chance of bringing wealth and prosperity to this colony than I do?"

"Uh, I reckon nobody, Mr. Dench."

"So doesn't it make sense that I should get more access to the tools I need to accomplish my work?"

"I'm not sure. I'd have to get it cleared by the council."

"Well now, my good man. I appreciate your respect for procedures, but we both know what the council will say, don't we? They will deny me the tools because they are afraid they will have to share the profit. If we involve them, we might as well forget about getting our fair share. And I'd hate to see you miss out on the rewards you deserve as part of the core team. Does that make sense, Thomas?"

"You're a hard man to argue with."

"That's because I have the courage to speak the truth. And the truth is I'm a hard man in all ways, Thomas. I reward those who help me accomplish my important work. Those who choose not to help me, I will not reward. And right now, I'm asking for your help."

"Well, you know I been glad to help you so far, Mr. Dench, but giving you extra ansible time is gonna put me in a tight spot when the council looks at the log."

"So don't report it on the log, Thomas. I will make my contacts late in the evening when the system is normally down and prying eyes are not around. I get the time I need, at no risk to you. I help the colony become profitable. People live better, and fewer die, Thomas. Everybody wins. And all it takes is for you to step up and be a visionary like me and the others on my core team. Every adventure and flight of discovery requires a few bold men who refuse to be held back by rules made by so-called leaders to keep the profits in their own hands. We visionaries are the true leaders, Thomas, and I thought you were one of us, one of the bold men who build communities. But I could have been mistaken."

"Now hold it, Mr. Dench. Like I been sayin', I helped you plenty, building your cabin and helpin' with the surveying and all. You can't say I haven't. I just ain't comfy with breakin' the village rules."

Dench looked at Thomas evenly and flatly for a few long seconds, and then sighed. "I see, Thomas. Yes, you have helped me, and I appreciate all you've done so far. But any common laborer can swing a hammer or hold a measuring stick. When I make the important find — and I always do — I will pay you gladly for those hours of manual labor. I suppose I had regarded you as a leader among these common laborers, and as such, I was willing to reward you as a leader should be rewarded. My mistake. Good day, my dear Mr. Thomas, and good luck with the dragon skins."

He turned to leave.

"Now wait up, Mr. Dench. Hold the tomatoes."

Dench took another step away, then paused. Thomas had stopped the honing and was now looking around dimly and stroking his chin, which had not seen a razor in days.

"I'm not sure I'm much of a leader, but I don't like bein' called common either. I've done a lot of hard workin' for this colony, and sometimes I wonder if it was a mistake. There don't ever seem to be much in the way of rewards."

He laid down the dragon skin and turned the scraper blade in his hands, as if really looking at it for the first time. "I don't suppose letting you use the ansible for a few minutes when it's normally shut down is going to hurt anything. Especially if'n it helps your work and brings home some profits."

Dench waited quietly.

"You havin' a meeting again tonight and passing around some of that good liquor you're makin', Mr. Dench?"

"Mr. Thomas, if you get me access to the ansible, then I am having a meeting. And you can have a double snifter of my best."

Thomas nodded. "I'm on shift tomorrow evenin'. Come by about 8:15, and I'll have the system still on and ready."

Dench nodded. "Very good decision, Thomas. A leader's decision. A common man would not recognize when bold action is needed."

"Well, like I said, I'm not sure about bein' a leader, but if helping you with your work will get us some decent tools and plenty of food, I'm willing."

"Good man, Thomas. Welcome to the team."

Chapter 10

The sap gathering progressed much more smoothly, as if they'd finally paid their dues over the last three days and were being rewarded. Shawn led his team, now larger and better armed. The forest offered no new dangers, except for a flock of biting perin that had swooped down as they moved the camp. The men drew blades and slashed several of the flittering winged things from the air, and the flock retreated. No members of the group were bitten, but one of the draft beasts lost a small hunk of tail to the beak-like jaws of the honey-colored flyers. The jarin snarled when bitten and then grumbled like a grumpy old man all the way to the next camp.

As they were preparing to pack up the equipment at the second camp, two tall Timmon males appeared from the path. One was Lonin, and the other his cousin and regular traveling partner, Kinin. Over his shoulder, Lonin carried a feathery yellow headdress, which looked uncomfortably familiar.

Lonin raised his free right hand, thumbs extended outward. "Greetings, Shawn. Greetings, all."

Shawn returned the open-handed salute, joining his index and middle fingers together to imitate the second thumb of the Timmon. "Lonin. Kinin. Great to see you, and a pleasant surprise."

The two Timmon joined Shawn. "Shik. Yes," Lonin said. "I am too much away with Timmon business. We learned from Cara that one of your party killed the crellil yesterday. This is a worthy act. In his honor, we bring the tail of the crellil to give to him. Can we meet him?"

Having gathered together to move to the next site, the entire hunting party had seen Lonin and Kinin approach and had stopped packing to listen to the conversation. Shawn searched around for Paul, who seemed to be hiding behind James near one of the wagons.

"Paul, could you join us?"

After a pause, Paul walked around the half-full wagon and between two men who stepped aside for him. Lonin looked down at Paul but, in that odd respectful way of his, did not look down. His voice was vibrant. "You killed the crellil."

Paul shook his head. "No, sir. We all fought it, and several people hit it with arrows."

Lonin lifted the crellil's tail from his shoulder and held it before Paul. "You display modesty. We were told that you shot the arrow that killed the crellil, a feared and wild beast. In respect and by Timmon tradition, you are given the tail."

Paul looked at Shawn for direction, who nodded. Paul lifted the fluffy feathered skin delicately, cradling it in both hands.

"Few Timmon have earned such a prize, and those events often follow loss of life. The council of Timmon kithin thank you for your actions, and we thank Timmistria for guiding your hand."

"Thank you. I'm humbled and ... embarrassed." Paul looked as uncomfortable as he sounded. He bowed slightly, still cradling the tail. Shawn helped him fold it carefully and led him to one of the wagons, where they stored the tail in one of the backpacks they used to bring food and water.

Lonin said, "Timmon do not share the human emotion of embarrassment. Shik, Shawn, if you and Paul Saarinen have time, we would like you to take us to the place of the battle. We would like to hear the story. There is always something to learn from an event like this."

Shawn said, "I feel guilty leaving the work to everyone else, but we will show you what we can."

He and Paul led Lonin and his companion to the malack stand where they had fought the crellil. The rest of the crew would finish gathering the equipment and head back to Fairdawn to deliver the collected sap to the maintenance shop. The trail was now a trampled passage two arms' widths wide, cleared by the jarin and wagons going in each direction. Shawn led Paul and the Timmon at a good pace, expecting Lonin and Kinin to be at their heels like Kearnin normally would be, but Lonin kept back a comfortable distance. Shawn had spent some time in the field with Lonin, especially in the early days, when few Timmon would interact with the humans. He was a master woodsman who could cover an amazing amount of ground effortlessly and silently.

At the clearing, Shawn tried to recount the sequence of events for the two Timmon from the blur of images in his memory, as he had for Cara. He walked about the clearing trying to mark where the Timmon hunting party had made their stand, and where the humans had been attacked. Paul helped fill in details, recounting his own location and the movement of the Timmon archers after they were waylaid. Shawn was curious about where the second archer had gone between the crellil's charge and the moment he'd reappeared at Paul's side. Paul had seen him run to the clearing's edge and call out into the brush, probably to bring more fighters. Lonin confirmed that a second hunting party had been working in the area but had been out of earshot.

Lonin said, "We have learned again a lesson. Hunting parties must always be close together in case of need. It troubles me that our people must relearn a lesson, but Timmistria has given us only short memories."

Shawn said, "I'm afraid you share that trait with my people. We knew there was a large predator in the area, and yet I sent this group out with only three men and a draft beast. The smell of the jarin alone could have attracted the crellil, not to mention the noise. It was a terrible mistake, and they could have been killed before Kearnin and his party got here."

Lonin nodded. "You did not lead wisely."

"So me and the three men were here, all either still on the ground or kneeling, and the crellil was advancing. I saw something hit the thing in the head and bounce off, and I realized it was an arrow. Paul was standing over there with another arrow already strung up, slowly drawing the bow back. The crellil shook its head and turned that hideous snake face around, and then twisted its whole body around and started advancing on him."

Lonin turned to Paul and said, "You picked up the Timmon bow from the ground, and the … pack of arrows, and then shot the crellil in the head. Why did you choose to shoot it there?"

Shawn expected Paul to say it was just a lucky shot.

"It was intent on finishing off the downed men. It was no longer responding to yelling, and attacking with blades wasn't effective. I wanted to anger it and convince it to attack me instead."

"And then what were you going to do?"

"I didn't think about that. I was just buying time. I hoped the others would be able to gather themselves and escape."

Lonin said nothing more for several long seconds, examining Paul with the same fascination Kearnin had during the previous days. Finally, he said, "You are more skilled with a bow than other humans. Why?"

"On my home world, I sometimes hunted with a bow."

"Your world has wilder-ness like Timmistria, and you hunt for food."

"Not often. We hunted as a hobby. My world was highly populated, and food was mass-produced."

"I have heard of this from other humans, hunting as a 'hobby.' The villagers also sometimes play 'sports.' It always seems to me not a useful thing to do. There is much running and jumping, and sometimes anger and injury. But in this case, I see your hobby has given you useful skills."

"As I said, it took everyone to drive off the crellil. I'm glad I was able to help, but it was your people who had the foresight to bring the weapons."

"Yes. The crellil are a danger known well to the older Timmon, and the young Timmon are taught. I enjoy your modesty. Thank you again for your action." Lonin nodded to his traveling partner. "We have seen all we wanted to see, and now we will escort you back to the village. We have business there as well."

They headed out immediately, Shawn again leading them and trying to set a rapid pace. They soon passed the other malack groves, following the fresh tracks of the jarin and carts. Shawn was relieved when he saw the team weaving through the brush ahead of them. The four of them fell in behind and followed the collection party down the winding trail, past the guard post and into the village, well ahead of the dark and any new frights it might bring to the settlement.

\#

Johnson drained the last of his small glass of liquor, and Dench took his and Smith's glasses back into the cabin to refill them. He adjusted the controls on the processor slightly to increase the level of the narcotic, and then filled the two glasses. He then set the control back to zero before filling his own glass halfway. He carried the three small snifters out of the cabin and back to the table, setting the spiked glasses before his "helpers." He took a small sip of his drink, rolling the silky-smooth liquor around his mouth. The warm machine-made brandy was addictive enough without the narcotic and extremely dangerous with it. He never let the men have more than two glasses. He wanted them controllable and talkative, but he didn't want to affect their day-to-day behavior. Johnson usually became loose in the tongue after a glass of the liquor, and Dench could get the latest news from the village grapevine. The simpleton would have little memory of it in the morning.

"Smith, did ya see the hideous mug on that crell thing? Glad I didn't run into it myself. They showed some ugly brutes on the vids afore we got here, like the dragons, but they didn't show that one. They say one of the new guys killed it. Said he used a Timmon bow. Shot it right in the head. The Timmon cut its tail off and gave it to him as a reward. They say Lonin himself gave it to him."

Dench asked, "Which fellow was that?"

Johnson said, "The quiet one with the odd eyes. Sarin, or somethin' like 'at."

"Saarinen. He used a Timmon bow? I wonder where he got it."

"They say the crell beast jumped on the native huntin' party, and then that … Saarinen fellow picked up one of them's bow and shot it with a poison arrow. Someone said he shot it right in the eye from 50 yards, but the eyes looked OK from where I stood lookin' at it. I didn't want to get too close. I was a'feared it was just knocked out and was going to wake up angry. Ugly thing. Head like a snake."

Smith said, "No. He grazed it in the shoulder. Timmon poison did it in."

Dench said, "It still seems like a daring thing to do, staring down a charging beast like that with a strange weapon."

Smith said, "Sometimes under stress, people have been known to do amazing things. Maybe this was one of them."

"Perhaps. Where is our friend Mr. Thomas tonight?"

"Oh, he said he had to take an extra shift on radio duty this evening. He said someone was sick and it might last a couple days."

"Ah, I see. We must all contribute where we can. And speaking of duties, we have some serious exploration planned for the morning, and we need to turn in."

"Aw, Mr. Dench, how 'bout just one more swallow of that brandy? I still got dust in my throat."

"Mr. Johnson, you know we must never overindulge. But I feel a break is coming soon, and there may be a few drops left in the converter. Now let's remind ourselves about the most important rule; we don't tell anyone else about my little brew. If anyone finds out what we have, they'll expect me to share with others outside of our little team, and then there won't be enough for us. Right, gentlemen?"

"Right-o, Mr. Dench!"

"No argument here, Mr. Dench. They expect us to share everything around here. It's a commune, until it's time to share the workload. Then it becomes 'Johnson and Smith, do all the work.'"

"Hmm. As I've told you, Mr. Smith, you and the others who follow the rules share everything. But you can bet that the council saves a bit of the best for themselves. Our leaders are just biding their time for the big break to come through, and you will learn a bitter lesson on how far this communism will go. Pardon me if I choose to not become a victim again."

"Aye, Mr. Dench. Me and Smith are with you on that one."

The two men nodded vigorously. Dench smiled.

Chapter 11

With eight workers building pipe, Paul helped Shawn organize an assembly line. Two men came in early to begin heating and rendering the first pot of tree sap to thicken it so it would stay where it was painted. Two more took the thickened sap and began painting the first of a series of tubular pipe forms. Paul suggested painting on one layer of sap and letting it set up before applying the matting material. After painting eight pipes, the two workers went back to the first pipe and began applying the second coat.

Wrapping the pril napping evenly around the pipe proved more difficult than they'd expected. The thin mesh stuck to the wet sap upon first contact and then tended to wrinkle and double up. The first pipe was a mess. Shawn stopped the work, and each of the crew took turns trying to apply the thin matting in even, smooth strips. After no one in the group, including Shawn and Paul, proved dexterous enough to handle the material, one of the men jokingly suggested recruiting one of the village seamstresses.

After exchanging a "why didn't we think of that?" look with Paul, Shawn ran to the textile shop and returned with Rita and Carmona. The two women, about 45 years old and less tanned than most of the others, having spent long days inside the shop, picked up thin strips of the mesh and eyed them suspiciously.

Rita said, "You want us to do *what* with this stuff?"

Shawn said, "Wrap it evenly around that pipe. The sap is sticky and will hold it in place, if you can lay it down evenly."

She and Carmona looked from the cloth to the pipe and then eyed Shawn and Paul with disgusted annoyance. But they set about applying the strips, handling the tender mesh material with ease. Holding one side of the cloth to keep it tight, they wrapped it expertly around the pipe so it looked like strips of grip tape on a cricket bat.

With appreciative hoots and applause, the others immediately voted them in as permanent team members.

After getting the process fine-tuned, they worked in waves, passing over the seven remaining pipe spools with alternating layers of sap and mesh. At the end of the first long day, they had seven pipes in various stages of production.

During the second day, several groups came by to visit the workshop. The story of the crellil's attack and the victory over it by the man with the yellow eyes had made the rounds, and the drafting of seamstresses into the team further raised curiosity. Shawn found he had more volunteers than he needed and no longer had to spend valuable time twisting arms to get recruits.

They were just finishing the final mesh wraps on the complete set when Cara entered the shop with Pao Shing-Shing, her secretary and systems manager, in tow. The small Asian man seemed uncomfortable in the shop, but he would know exactly how many man-hours were spent and how much raw material was consumed on this work. Shawn walked them through the production process, where Cara had a bright chat with their seamstresses-turned-pipe-builders, and then led them to where Paul was working with two men at the sap-thickening pot.

Paul was preoccupied with regulating the temperature of the wood-burning stove that the metalworkers had fabricated for the pipe builders. He manipulated a metal rod to adjust air vents on the stove's sides, looking into the stove through a peephole and shaking his head. The only change from this scene an hour ago was that the shop had gotten progressively warmer and Paul had removed his long-sleeved overshirt. His arms and hands were thick and scarred — a worker's build. His previous jobs had apparently involved some kind of hands-on work.

He noticed Shawn and Cara approaching and looked about as if searching for an escape route. But he stood up from his crouch, set down the metal prodding rod, wiped his hands on a small hemp towel hanging from his belt, and waited for them.

Shawn stepped aside for Cara, and she extended her hand. Shawn was needed elsewhere in the shop, but he didn't want to miss the meeting between these two, which would likely be a sparring match.

She said, "Mr. Saarinen, it's good to see you again."

Paul shook her hand lightly and let it drop. "Ms. Harvestmoon. Good to see you as well."

"You've had a busy few days."

He nodded soberly.

"Shawn was showing me this new process you've come up with. It's very impressive."

"Not unless it works, ma'am. Shawn and the others invented the process. I just suggested a few things. We'll find out if I added any value."

"I'm not an engineer, but Shawn's explanation of all this make sense, and it is very promising. You seem thorough and innovative. I wouldn't be surprised if you were successful on your first try."

"I would. But I think we'll find a good combination. It will take time."

"Fair enough. I appreciate you stepping up to help. I'm sure Shawn's told you how important this work is."

"Yes, that's very clear."

"There are many things we need help with, many opportunities. I have to warn you that we'll be keeping you very busy with systems that need attention."

"That's not a problem. That's why I'm here."

Cara's eyes narrowed. "Well, I hope you'll let us know when we overload you. I can get a little too demanding. Right, Shawn?"

Shawn grunted.

"In your position, that's to be expected. I came here to apply my skills wherever they're needed most. I wish they were more applicable, Ms. Harvestmoon."

"Call me Cara, please."

"OK. Please call me Paul."

"Good. Paul, Timmistria's unpredictable and challenging. We never seem to have enough skilled people. I've already warned you that I ask a lot. You may be surprised at what skills are important, and you can do more to help than you think."

Paul nodded.

Shawn said, "I came here with a degree in geology and have seldom had time to make use of it, but I do all kinds of other stuff."

"Shawn's told me about your cool actions in dealing with the crellil, Paul. In your bravery, you probably saved several lives, including his. I really can't come up with words to describe my appreciation."

Paul shifted uneasily. "We all reacted, miss, and others responded more decisively, Shawn included. There was no bravery on my part, just fear. Without Shawn and the Timmon, we would have fallen."

Cara nodded. "I'm sure you're right." She breathed in and out deeply, and her eyes found Shawn's. "But Kearnin confirmed that things played out just like Shawn said, how you calmly shot it with a poisoned arrow. I'm amazed. I really don't want to put you on the spot, but I think it's important that we hold some town meetings about the attack for all the village members. I'd like the whole scouting party to be there to talk about the attack and answer questions. Would you please do that for me?"

Paul looked down. "I think this is where I let you know you're overloading me."

"Ha-ha! Not so! And I know you're up to the task. It's so important. Say yes, you'll do it."

Paul looked to Shawn for support, but he could only shrug and say, "You might as well agree, or she'll keep after you until you give in just to get her off your back."

"OK, I'll be there. I can see now why they elected you village manager."

Cara's eyes gleamed, and Shawn judged that Paul had won this match.

#

Over the next several days, the pipe-building team worked long hours in the stagnant, humid air of the maintenance shop, laying down layers of varnish and mesh, and then burning out the pipe molds. The wiry, translucent pipe sections were less brittle than the old pipe, and somewhat rubbery. At Paul's suggestion, they pressure-tested the pipes by tapping metal caps into each end, filling them as full as they could with water and then pressuring them up with compressed air from their small, solar-powered compressor. By his calculations, the pipe near the pumps would need to handle pressure of about 150 pounds per square inch to supply the fields' needs. The first trial pipe fell far short of this target but was still strong enough for use farther out in the field. After testing, the spools were hustled out to replace failing sections in the farthest fields, where the water pressure would be lowest.

They repeated this sequence methodically, building pipe in controlled conditions, testing it and assigning a pressure rating, and then hauling it to sections of the irrigation system where the pressure would remain slightly below the rating. Paul made the team document everything. Soon they were able to push test pressures to 50 pounds, then 60 and beyond.

After two days of failures to move the upper test pressure above 90 pounds, one of the workers, young D'wi', suggested that the burning technique to remove the core was actually damaging the pipe. His friend, a clownish young man named Cl'nt'n, remarked that they should build pipe out of dragon skin because "e'en a razor blade cain't cut that sheet!" To Shawn, it was another example of useful ideas coming from unexpected people if you were just willing to listen.

So, as Cl'nt'n suggested, they built pipe using strips of cremin skin to strengthen it. During the test of this pipe, the team all gathered around, sweaty and dirty in the hot afternoon. The little air pump chunked along, more and more slowly as the pressure in the pipe crept higher, resisting the pump's small piston. The needle touched and then slowly moved past mark after mark on the dial: 120 pounds, then 130, then 140, and when the tiny needle drew even with the 150-psi mark on the pressure gauge, the group broke into a loud cheer, hugging each other shamelessly and patting each other on the back. Even Paul smiled.

#

Cara had set up the informational meeting for the next afternoon. Shawn washed after spending a long morning in the shop, but he was sweaty and dust-coated again by the time he reached the public speaking area near Cara's office. He was surprised by the huge turnout, especially considering the heat and the still air. Passing his eyes over the crowd as he took the podium, he estimated at least 100 people had come, an expectant crowd that swelled beyond the available space.

He wasn't comfortable with public speaking, so he tried to remember that he knew almost all of these people personally. He also reminded himself that these folks were not here for a performance, only for information. Most of them had been on Timmistria for three years or longer, and another dangerous animal was not enough to rattle them, but they were of course concerned. And he would swallow the lump in his throat and do his best to inform them about what had happened.

Shawn spoke first, followed by the biologist, Tom Simons. Then Cara summarized the dangers of the crellil and opened the floor to questions. A group of four sat to Shawn's right, men who had been there: Paul, Mark, James, and Scott. Questions from the crowd followed, and the answers essentially repeated the information the group had already provided.

The large gathering offered an interesting benefit, providing perspective of the broad diversity of the colony's citizenry. An example was Hai-Hai Yaan, a blue-skinned native of Bintak. Her skin had been dyed the pastel color of a lactan blossom as a child, as was the custom in her society, marking her as a member of a lower caste. Little wonder she'd emigrated. Among the 200-plus colonists on Timmistria, nearly half displayed some kind of tribal or social marking, including skin dyes, tattoos, piercings, and ritual scarring.

"I am Hai-Hai. Textile shop. We go to gather hemp vines tomorrow. What is your plan to protect small women in the field?"

Tom, now seated at Shawn's left, answered her. "Until we assess the danger, all parties working outside Fairdawn must be accompanied by armed guards equipped with bows and poison-tipped arrows. We will also have nightly patrols.

"The Timmon tell us that it has been many Timmistria years since a crellil has been seen in these lands. We hope this appearance is an isolated incident and not the harbinger of a migration. The Timmon do not know. And until we know, we will have to take all available precautions."

A low murmur went through the crowd. Cara stepped up and recognized a large, red-faced man several rows back and to the far left side of the audience.

Glancing over, Shawn saw a flash of red — a handkerchief. Dench was there, standing in the wings.

"Name's Mullin, ma'am. I work in the fields a lot, but I'm in the blacksmiths' guild. May be an unfair question for you all, but do we have enough bows and arrows and people that can use them?"

It was another question that had been covered in the talks, but Shawn didn't mind explaining again. He held up a hand to take the floor and stood to answer. Standing gave him a better view of Dench.

"To be brief and to the point, Mr. Mullin, the answers are 'No' and 'No.' Most of the dangerous plants and animals we face on Timmistria are best defended against with light blades, so those are the weapons we produce in large numbers and train everyone on. Cara and the shop foremen have put together a plan to produce more bows and arrows, in the Timmon design but smaller. With our shortage of shop workers, we're calling on anyone with experience in woodworking or metalworking to help. Any of you with archery experience, we ask that you sign up for a bow fitting and training. There are no doubt others of you, like Mr. Saarinen here, who came to Timmistria with some skill but have not had the time or need to use it. Well, the time has come, and the need is great."

Mullin remained standing during the response and now raised his hand again. "I'm good for that. But another thing: we have heard about another dangerous animal, a red monster, that's been seen in the area. Are bows and arrows good enough to protect against that?"

Shawn glanced at Cara before responding. "Yes, Mr. Mullin, we've heard of this also and have discussed it with the Timmon. It seems this is a legend. They're not aware of any red monster living in the Timmon or Delerin lands. So if you hear talk of a red beast or red monster, there is no such creature, as far as we know."

After another hour of this informal roundtable, Shawn was gratified that the concerns were being addressed and many of the townspeople were leaving. He was surprised to see Dench standing next to Paul at one point, nodding as Paul explained something to a small group gathered around him. It made sense for Dench to be there. His survey and exploration work took him into the field daily, nearly always into the least-frequented parts of the settlement, and at times into the Timmon lands. He would naturally be concerned about newly discovered threats.

Finally, exhausted from talking and mentally drained, Shawn led a tired-looking Paul from the small group of stragglers back to the craft shops, where the pipe builders were finishing up for the day. The work had progressed amazingly well. Three new trial runs had been completed and were drying on sawhorses. Mark and James, both having left the meeting as soon as possible, had organized another trip to gather malack sap for the next morning. James, who was still somewhat uncomfortable interacting with the natives, had even ventured to the Timmon outpost on the west side of town to arrange a Timmon hunting party with archers to accompany them.

Upon hearing this, Paul said, "I need a wash-up and sleep. I'll be here early to guard the sap-gathering team."

"Paul, take a day to rest. We can take care of this."

He agreed and left the shop. Shawn watched him leave, followed his precise movements, his perfect posture, his efficiency of motion. Even after all the events of the last few days, he remained a complete mystery. Shawn knew almost nothing about him: his background, his family, his religious beliefs, his political views. But he had to agree with Kearnin that it didn't really matter anymore where Paul Saarinen had come from. He seemed genuine and was proving more valuable every day. His technical skills and expertise were just what Cara had been praying for. He was almost too good to be true.

#

"This is Dench."

The face on the view screen was humanoid but pale aqua in color, with large liquid eyes. Beautiful, really. "Tapol here. How do you fare, Meetah Dench?"

"I'm stuck on this little yellow rock. It's hot and humid. The food is horrendous. My cabin is a hive for insects. And I'm surrounded by idiots. How do you think I fare?"

There was a pause in the transmission, and Dench wondered if this was a delay in the response time of the ansible or Senior Tapol being caught off guard by Dench's attitude. Tapol was a Serfan, and sometimes his overly pleasant manner pissed Dench off. Like now, when there was important business to take care of.

"Tapol, I've got only a few minutes of unauthorized ansible time, and I need to transmit some things quickly before someone catches me here. Seenk gimly, poota?"

"Gemly."

"Did Johanson get the berth on the next transit?"

"Yeth."

"Good. Is he bringing the list of items I requested?"

"All except the gazing spotter. It was very large and difficult to smuggle."

"How the hell am I going to pinpoint ordnance without the pointer, seemak?!"

"Easy, Seta, we have found a smaller unit that will accommodate. New tech. More power, less size. He will have it."

Dench sniffed and then breathed deeply, remembering a personal motto: *Clarity of thought, clarity of action.*

"Fine. You two make damn sure his documents are correct and that he knows who he's supposed to be. The manager here isn't a fool, and she checks the references. Make sure it doesn't raise any eyebrows. But don't make his papers too sterile — throw in some shit. There needs to be some unspoken dirt in his profile, or the authorities here will be suspicious. And Johanson better have it memorized *before* he gets on the transport."

"Yessir."

"Fine. I have a blurb to send you. I want someone here checked out. Another colonist; came in on the transport with me, so I know our people did a check on him. Uses the name Paul Saarinen. I grabbed a DNA sample from him today at a town meeting. Sending … now. And, by the way, good call sending the Geno-Bite in my pack. Add a 50% bonus on your next credit run."

"Thank you, Meetah Dench."

"Dee naw. I reward those who serve me well, Tapol. And you know the second part of that mantra."

Another pause.

"Yeth, Meetah Dench."

"Very good. I need everything on this guy. I think he's Co-Op Fed, and I'm not sure why he's here. If he's tracking me, I can take care of the problem, but I'll be having a discussion with some of your associates who didn't check him out properly the first time, and it won't be pleasant."

"Yeth, Meetah Dench."

"This guy has skills he didn't learn in engineering school, so find out where he learned them."

"Gemly."

"OK, that's it for now. I'll be getting more ansible time, but it may be at odd hours, so make sure one of your close associates is monitoring this channel. The time for our move is very close now, Tapol, and I must be able to reach you whenever I need to."

"Yeth, Meetah Dench."

"I don't care if you're eating, meeting with the local governor, or in a crim making pleasure with your 17 wives and husbands. If I call, I want you on a secure line in five minutes. Gimly?"

"Gemly. Yeth, Meetah Dench."

"Fine. I'm out."

Dench tripped the call switch and tapped the Bluetooth button embedded below his right jawbone. The ansible set was more advanced than he had expected for such a rustic colony, and he was pleased. It made his work much easier and reduced the risk that his cover would be blown.

He lifted himself from the chair, careful to touch nothing else in the small office. He opened the door to the outside and peered up and down the dark, narrow side street where the electronics room was located. This lightly traveled street was another lucky break, making his coming and going less risky. He stepped out into the dark and took the street toward the shop where he'd meet the two men who would escort him back to his cabin.

Dench had always considered himself somewhat lucky, and that luck seemed to have returned when he was spirited away to this rock. His operation on Sarena had been a complete debacle, and all the extreme planning wasn't sufficient to prevent a spate of unlucky events from laying his operation open. If all had gone well, he would have now been sitting as governor of the largest independent sector of the settled galaxy, with a near stranglehold on the regional stewardship.

But all had not gone well. The unexpected deaths of two of his chief inside men in separate transit accidents had crippled his intelligence for the operation. Then there was an escalation in tensions between two provinces, leading one to casually toss a nuke at the other's capital. The pulse had disrupted subspace communications just as Dench's forces launched. His vessels were blinded and lit up on every detector in the central system.

It was lucky that Dench had escaped that madman governor's assassination squad after the coup attempt had been revealed. His personal transport had evaded military craft as they fled the system, and his people had been able to get him to Nevadas, where he boarded the transport to this jerkwater world, where his enemies were not likely to find him.

But there was another profound stroke of luck here: his finding this system and its strategic jump point. How lucky that the point had remained undetected for this long — improbable that the empirical coalition hadn't set up a base here and that the Thinkers hadn't overrun the system and made slaves of the Timmistrians. A few well-placed bribes from Dench's people and the timely disappearance of the area survey manager had kept the jump route's existence secret.

He reminded himself of the thing about luck: it was great when it ran true, but one was a fool to rely on it.

His window of opportunity ended with the triennial general election, where he planned to wield a great deal of influence. First on the agenda was developing a new base for military operations. He'd been studying the Timmistria system for some time. It was far enough from the central government at Smyth Alter to avoid observation, and the idiots there would hardly notice when he covered the system in a communication blackout.

The other deciding factor had been the discovery of a hyperspace jump route directly from Timmistria into the heart of Smyth's planetary disc. Spy and rebel groups were continuously looking for uncharted free jump space to Smyth or other strategic Co-Op installations, but the costs and odds of success were staggeringly prohibitive. How the underfunded Black Dragon rebels had found the route was beyond him — an insane stroke of luck? Luck for him, as it turned out. His spies within the organization recognized the value of the find, hacked the rebel AI systems, and either kidnapped or killed all those involved with it.

Just like mining, one didn't have to be the one who discovered the mother lode. One just needed to be nearby with a loaded firearm.

The natives were the kicker. He'd lost most of his boots-on-the-ground forces during the debacle that required his rapid escape. The Timmistrians would do nicely as replacements, with the proper indoctrination and training, once they understood the price of resistance.

And then the real fun would begin. He had old scores to settle. And a very long memory.

Chapter 12

hark
hear her voice in the sun-warmed earth
through the running waters
on the night breeze
softly singing and insistent
Timmistria calls you to lead
— Timmon sonnet

Cara leaned on her elbows, chin resting on her hands. She felt the first pangs of a headache between her eyes. "Now the sewer system's malfunctioning?"

Pao shivered in front of her desk with clenched fists, as if he feared she'd physically punish him for bringing bad news.

Was she that hard on people?

He said, "The t-treatment pits are not t-treating. We can't m-move the material, and the odor is becoming an issue."

"Has Chrisof run his tests? The bugs are okay?"

"He said pH and aeration are normal. But the bacteria count is very low and dropping."

"So we may be poisoning them. Try to find the source."

"Yes, Cara."

He hesitated to leave.

"And?"

"The electricians are reporting issues with some of the solar-generation panels."

"Causes?"

"They've been trying to run diagnostics on the bad units, but the power levels are so low they're too weak to power the internal signal transmitters, and the—"

"What's the impact?"

"Our power generation is down about 20% right now. We've pulled all nonessential electrical usage, although ansible consumption is up for some reason, and we've managed to keep all essential usage at full load. Any further loss of generation, and we will have to begin cutting Level 3 usage. Level 3 includes the maintenance shops, office lighting, data recording and—"

"I know what Level 3 includes. I helped make the list."

"Yes, ma'am. Food processing is behind schedule, and John reported finding two new varieties of burrowing worms in the apples that were being inspected before drying."

"Just for fun, any good news today?"

"The irrigation system appears to be performing above average, and field moisture levels are well ahead of last year."

"That's nice. Thanks." She sighed. "Ask the sewer department to meet me at the treatment building in…" She glanced at the pile of Requests for Action forms sitting in her in-box. "…two hours. Please swing by and ask Dr. Wonge to attend."

"Yes, ma'am."

"And Pao?"

"Yes, ma'am."

"Thanks for staying on top of all these things. Thank you." She forced a smile, hoping it looked genuine.

"Yes, ma'am. You're welcome."

Outside Cara's window, the sun lit the greenery lining the street and cast a glow about the workers moving there, pulling small handcarts and leading draft beasts pulling larger wagons. A load of the newly redesigned irrigation piping went past, on a long wagon drawn by one old burly jarin and guided by two of the top shop workers, Mark and James. The irrigation system was one apparent success in the litany of problems.

Many of the colony's systems had been brought in on the first two or three flights to Timmistria and were now five years in the field. With little upgrading, and emergency-only maintenance, the systems were deteriorating. And without a major source of income, the settlement had little to trade or sell in order to purchase replacements or even procure spare parts.

Every one of the people outside the window knew how difficult things were, how close they had come to starvation at times, and how close they were to seeing those times again. Shawn and Cara and the technical people were making progress in understanding this strange world and worked hard to maintain the technology they brought with them, to prevent their community from sinking into stone-age barbarism, but the benefits of those efforts and the technology so far were barely enough to keep Fairdawn alive.

Those people out there had been through tough times, and yet they carried on day after day, ignoring the perils, ignoring the hunger pangs, stiffening their resolve when illness took their friends and family members. How did they manage? Had they been so toughened by their previous lives? Was Timmistria better than where they'd come from? Or was it just something in people that they were able to set aside their fears in order to function?

Once, she had visited the cottage of a young couple who had just lost their three-month-old child to a respiratory ailment that had struck Fairdawn. She found their cottage empty, and, fearing the worst, gathered a search party, only to find them both doing community work in the village. The woman was preparing meals for sick families, and the man was helping to process plant leaves to produce fever-reducing medications. She asked them why they were not taking time off to grieve, and they each gave her the same answer: they couldn't save their child, but perhaps they could help save someone else's, and it was best to stay busy.

Memories of her lost brothers came to mind then, as they often did. Dilind, Michael, Trey, Tomis. She recalled their faces, each in turn, and those of her mother and father. The only family holograph video she'd saved from the collapse was a disjointed chronology of birthdays and holidays, small ones learning to walk, older boys playing sports and coming home from hunting or fishing trips, Cara tagging along always, never one to stay home if the boys were away. And Mother and Father like overwhelmed shepherds watching it all happen.

She hadn't been able to save four of her brothers, only Shawn, and she was committed to keeping him safe. Late at night, over a glass of wine, she would watch the vid again and let herself remember.

But now her emotions seemed buried under the stack of formal requests. She softly cursed her own invention of that document. With a sigh, she leaned forward and pulled the top few forms from the stack, each a sheet of ugly, grainy reed paper. Most of the requests would be unreasonable and impractical. But she needed to stay busy, and now she had a meeting in less than two hours.

#

Shawn had gotten back to his dorm room very late and very tired. With a quick snack and wash-up, he was asleep almost before reaching his bed. Exhaustion made for deep sleep.

And morning made for bright light in his face and pain in his body. Severe leg cramps pushed him out of bed, and he staggered around the tiny room, trying to loosen the knots in his calves and thighs. He'd apparently left the curtains drawn to one side, and full morning light fell across his pillow. His clothes were in a heap in the corner, and his toothbrush and cleanser were thrown on top of them.

There came a light tapping sound at his door. He bent over and rubbed his calves.

The tap came a little louder the second time.

"Mr. Harvestmoon? Are you awake?" The voice was high-pitched and male. Pao.

"No."

Cara's assistant unwisely ignored him. "Mr. Harvestmoon, the Manager has requested that you meet her at the sewage-treatment facility at 9:00 this morning."

Shawn's clock was hidden in sunlight, and his eyes were not focusing very well yet. "What time is it?"

"8:30, Mr. Harvestmoon. She asked that you bring Mr. Saarinen as well."

"So she gave me 30 minutes to eat breakfast, hike out to Paul's cottage to get him, and hike all the way back to the sewage plant?" He took several deep breaths and leaned down into an upper-leg stretch. It hurt, and his stomach grumbled to add insult. Hunger never did help his attitude. "Tell her to go get him herself. I need kava."

"She's meeting with electricians right now, sir."

He sighed. "I'm on it. Tell her I'll be a little late."

"Mr. Harvestmoon, she anticipated your late arrival, but she has another meeting at 10 a.m. and requested that I ask you to be punctual. She said that she would arrange breakfast for you and Mr. Saarinen at the treatment facility."

Nice. Breakfast at the sewage plant.

"Go away!"

He listened to the soft patter of steps retreating down the dormitory hall and nodded in satisfaction. He wasn't going to let some brown-nosing wimp or his sister's unreasonable demands upset him. He wanted kava, food, and a decent stretch. Then he'd be willing to brave a trip to the sewage plant.

He heard light footsteps returning and another tap on the door.

"I thought I told you to go away."

"Pardon, Mr. Harvestmoon, but I came to tell you that Mr. Saarinen is at the pipe shop. He has been told of the meeting at the sewage-treatment facility and has indicated he will arrive promptly at 9 a.m."

"Return to the shop and tell him to meet me at the small dining area in 10 minutes."

He could hear the messenger hesitating, but quiet steps marked his departure.

Shawn rinsed his face in the sink. The coarse flaxen towel scratched his sunburned face and arms. He grabbed a fresh tan shirt and pants from the shelves and began pulling them on. Retrieving his jarin-leather belt from yesterday's pants, he found that the clean pants fit him very loosely. He cinched the belt down to the next hole, the very last one. Long hikes, heavy work, and skipped meals had trimmed him. He looked at his thin frame in the mirror: his arms hung like well-muscled brown ropes, and his face was bony. He was reminded of holo pics of long-distance runners.

He straightened the coarse shirt over his frame, grabbed the last pair of clean socks from the shelf, and retrieved his boots from under the pile of yesterday's clothes. With all the other work to do, pipe building, sewer fixing, and dragon tracking, he also needed to do laundry today.

This administrative role should have come with perks, like a maid.

Dressed, he headed out the door, to food, and then to the sewer. The irony of that was not lost on him.

#

"We increased the aerator rate and raised the number of cycles from four to six. The energy boys have been complaining about the electrical usage, but we think this is on the priority list."

The sewage plant manager's face was broad and ruddy and puffed out more than normal. Cara kept her voice level and calm. "Yes, I have to agree, Chrisof."

"We're checking pH and contaminants around the clock, just to make sure we aren't getting short duration spikes harming the bacteria. It all looks within normal parameters. Nothing out of the ordinary. But we continue to lose bacterial count." He pronounced "bacteria" as "back-tree-uh."

"What was the count this morning?"

"630."

Normal was about 6,000. The smell at the processing area was always putrid, but now it was strange as well as strong and unpleasant.

"What's your plan going forward?"

"I can reverse the air and add some food, but the system is loaded with food already. These things should be growing like monsters, but they're dying off. I've run out of ideas."

He kicked at a tiny weed tumbling across the dirt road. The treatment pits lay to their right, square-shaped dugouts 50 feet on a side and 6 feet deep. Cara knew the exact dimensions, as she had helped to dig them. They were filled above normal level with a sludge that was unusually thick and dark, like peanut-filled ganache.

Chrisof Charl was a large, ruddy man with a quick wit and an equally quick temper. He'd come to Timmistria on the first settler transport as maintenance foreman and had since focused his talented mind on the water and sewer systems. He knew this foul-smelling but necessary facility like his own GI tract, and if he couldn't solve the problem, it was a huge problem.

"OK. Chrisof, let's all go into the office here and start typing what we know and don't know on the whiteboard. Something's been missed, and we need to find it quickly."

Chrisof's face turned red like a Timmon's. "Beg your pardon, Manager, but nothing has been missed. I've gone over and over all the conditions, tested all the inputs, and looked at all the equipment. Everything is normal."

A flat voice came from the rear of the small assembled group, the voice of Paul Saarinen. "Have you considered whether the bacteria have mutated?" Whispered side conversations and quiet rustling stopped.

Cara said, "Mutated? Mr. Saarinen, can you please explain how you came to that conclusion?"

Paul's voice was matter-of-fact, almost disinterested. "He said all the equipment and conditions are normal. He's found no contaminants or chemicals that are known to be toxic to the bacteria. There could be a new strain of native bacteria or fungus in the slurry, but Mr. Charl's team surely would have spotted something like that during the microscope counts. Nothing in the system is different, so I'm guessing the desirable bacteria have themselves changed. They've mutated."

Cara turned to Dr. Wonge, one of the settlement's biologists. "Lance, does that make sense?"

The white-haired lab man pulled at his wispy chin hairs. "Hmm. I think it's unlikely. But it's certainly possible."

"How do we find out?"

"I can run a DNA test — a crude one, as you know, since our equipment is only field-grade and not a full-scale lab unit. And then I can compare it with the original DNA profile. It would have to be a major mutation to show up in such a rudimentary comparison. Do we have any of the original culture, Chrisof?"

"Aye, one starter dose."

"We can run a test on that as well."

Cara said, "Suppose the bugs *have* mutated. What then?"

Chrisof replied, "About all we can do is re-seed with the starter dose. But to do that we'll have to kill off the remainder of the damaged bugs and flush them from the system."

"How long would that take?"

"Too long. A few days to clear the tanks, then a minimum of two weeks to grow the culture up to processing levels. We had hell getting it to go when we first set up the system years ago. Almost lost the whole thing several times." He shook his huge, shaggy head gravely. "That should be considered only as a last resort."

"Well, if the bugs keep dying, we may have no choice." Cara thought about having to do without the sewage system for three weeks or more. It wasn't a pleasant prospect.

Chrisof apparently agreed. "Digging small sanitary pits for 20 people while we started up the sewage system was workable. Trying to teach over 200 villagers how to handle their sewage needs for four to six weeks won't work. We'll have all the usual diseases — dysentery, E. coli. You're going to end up with a lot of sick people, and some of them will die. Especially the small ones."

"I agree with you, Chrisof. So give me options."

Paul interrupted again, quietly. "Set up a series of test vessels with bacteria and sewage samples in each. Treat each one differently. Add more oxygen to some, less to others. Dilute one. Add chemicals to another. The bacteria are different, so the old treatment methods aren't working. Perform controlled tests and find out what works."

Shawn said, "Yes! We can set up a number of trials like we did with the pipe design. Find the best combinations of food, chemicals, ammonia, and oxygen. Run a progression of secondary experiments based on the results."

Cara frowned. "Chrisof, can this be done?"

Chrisof stood silently, eyes raised. The crowd shifted nervously as he rolled his eyes skyward and sighed. "Yes. Not sure if it will work, but it's worth a shot. We should use our old treatment regimen as a control. I'll need some large vessels, 100-gallon tanks or larger. Hmm. We'll need a way to aerate the samples."

He looked around the assembled group. "I'll need manpower to tend and stir samples around the clock and to run bacterial counts. And all my regular people are tied up trying to fix the main plant. The work will be difficult and unpleasant, as you can all imagine."

Paul said, "I'm in."

Shawn smiled and winked at Cara. "Me too."

Cara nodded. "Thank you both. Chrisof, we'll get you all the assistance you need. This is now our highest-priority work area. Give Shawn a list, and we'll pull together to make it happen. OK, right now I need to get back to Fairdawn. I have a number of business items to take care of. Shawn and Mr. Saarinen, may I speak with you for just a moment?"

The smell of untreated sewage and the added odor of the bacteria were difficult to tolerate. The look on Shawn's face as he settled at Cara's side told her he might be regretting his decision to help. As Chrisof and the others went to their tasks, Paul joined Cara, his face empty — not guarded, just blank, as if incapable of expression.

"I don't like having to keep asking you to take on the hard tasks, but…" she shrugged and continued, "…I don't seem to have a lot of choice. Shawn, if you can get a list of Chrisof's needs and take care of them, I will focus on other pressing village issues."

"Right. I'm on it, Manager."

"Mr. Saarinen, you seem to have a knack for these technical puzzles. Can I call on you to oversee the testing? Chrisof is an excellent foreman, but he has a tendency to draw conclusions too quickly and may go off in a direction before the tests are complete. You seem to be both innovative and methodical, and I think we need both of those traits here."

"Yes, ma'am. I will stay with the testing."

Cara caught herself staring at his eyes. "I'm not sure I ever thanked you enough for your work on the water piping and for how you handled yourself during the crellil attack. And now, you've again come up with a possible answer to a serious problem."

If she expected a response, she got none. Paul remained impassive, as stony as a Timmon.

She said, "We've tried to make it a practice never to dig into the pasts of our people. But I am very curious about your experiences, how you came to acquire all of your … knowledge and these skills that have helped this community so much so quickly. I hope one day we have the time to talk about it, if you'd feel comfortable. I'm guessing your life has been fascinating."

Paul showed signs of life, as if coming out of deep thought. He shuffled his feet. "Nothing special, Manager. Probably not much different than anyone else here."

"Maybe so, but I would still enjoy hearing about it. I appreciate you coming. Please take care of things at your camp this afternoon, and be prepared to come back early in the morning. It'll take Chrisof and Shawn the remainder of the day to gather the equipment. I'm afraid these tests you suggested are going to come back to haunt you with long hours and hard work for the next week or two."

Paul nodded. "Thank you. Laundry and cleaning to do. First light tomorrow is OK?"

"Very good. Thank you."

He nodded again and was gone, leaving Cara and Shawn alone. The sewage workers were moving about, and occasionally Chrisof strode by, voice booming and arms waving around, his second-in-command trailing behind like a small moon and writing on a clipboard. Chrisof was brilliant but sometimes tiresome.

"Shawn, who is this guy?"

"Huh?"

"Paul Saarinen. Who is he?"

"I … don't know. He's damn smart, that's for sure."

"Learned anything about his background? He knows chemicals. How does he know piping? And sewage treatment? And how to shoot a bow and arrow?"

"I don't know. He's a closed book. I think he'll open up over time, but so far…" He shrugged.

Cara shook her head, suddenly feeling very weary.

"I would let it go, but curiosity is killing me. My next problem is Mr. Dench. The Timmon aren't changing their tune, and now they're telling me about unrest among the Delerin. It's beyond my grasp how the Delerin can even know that the guy is here."

It was Shawn's turn to shake his head. "I've been busy, but as far as I know, all Dench has done is what he said he would do — look for valuable minerals and hydrocarbons. He's got a regular group that gathers at his cabin most nights, but that's hardly unusual. Card games and social gatherings are pretty common here. He's almost a model citizen, except for his cynical attitude and the fact that he always seems to find a way to be unavailable when the tough work comes around."

"Lack of motivation isn't so unusual. Even so, the Timmon have held council meetings to discuss him, and they fear the Delerin will take action. I can't just ignore this and hope it will go away."

"I almost wish he would do something wrong so we could just ship him out and be done with it. He doesn't realize he's the 'red beast.'"

"If that's going to happen, I hope it happens soon before this issue blows out of control. Gotta run. Check in with me later. Actually, let's have dinner, just you and me. We don't ever seem to do that anymore."

He nodded and smiled wanly, and she left for the village.

#

Paul's first call went to his contact at the foreign ministry, code name Blackburn. The ansible was unsophisticated but serviceable, and he wasn't having any issues getting through to his parties. Once he made a connection, he laid the data blurb disk against the mouthpiece. After several seconds, a female comm officer came on, audio only. The lilt in her voice was clearly Lustran, but that's where the accent ended. Her diction was robotic.

"This is Outbound. Please provide voice confirmation."

He cleared his throat. He was hoarse from two days working with the bugs, which was a real concern, considering the lack of medical treatment.

"Sharren, Paul. 1145-7778-007."

"Confirmed. I'll connect you."

The line went silent for a good five minutes before his contact came on, again voice only. Paul tried to hide his annoyance.

"Blackburn here."

"Sharren, reporting."

"I'm all ears."

"The colony is at Stage 3B, critical. Without intervention, estimated failure rate 70% within two years."

There was a brief pause before Blackburn asked, "Status of relations with indigenous peoples?"

"Stable but possibly escalating toward hostility. Some superstitious crap involving one of the colonists. Typical Indy flakiness."

"What about suitability for the application?"

"No major prohibitions identified. They're flaky, like I said, but they understand conflict and seem to respond to typical humanoid stimuli. Capability assessment, possibly the best I've seen. Intelligence with linear thinking patterns. Hierarchical societal structure. Physical capability is superior among land-based bipeds."

"Very good. Continue with your observations, and identify the individuals we need to work with when our forces move in."

"Already have that. Big yellow Alpha named Lonin. I think there's more to the name, but it's convoluted and lengthy. He's the liaison between the Timmon and the colony, and a big dog with the native tribes. My information says he also has contacts with the second native race, the Delerin."

There was another pause, then, "Good work. Continue observations and report again in 10 days. Blackburn out."

The connection dropped before Paul could ask about his transfer. Annoyance gave way to anger.

His second call was to the only man he could trust, Mark Sparling, a general in charge of the security bureau at Smyth. Mark was five years Paul's senior, and they'd weaved around and through each other's careers on their ways to special ops commands. Mark had beat him by only months, which allowed them both to declare victory, since Mark had years more service time.

Paul punched in a series of codes that got him directly to the desk he wanted. When the call connected, his friend's voice burped from the speaker in a suspicious growl.

"Sparling."

"Sharren here."

Mark hooted, and the screen came alive with his talking head, a big square block of bone and meat with gray bristle on top and blue eyes that no woman could resist. "Where you been, boy? I ain't heard from you in weeks."

"They're keeping me busy here." He gave his friend a brief on the state of the sanitary systems at the colony. "It's the same thing that bit us on Cepheus that first summer. No-brainer here."

Mark laughed. "Twenty years in, and you're back to cleaning the shitters. That's gotta hurt."

"Literally. I don't have the back for it anymore. But we've got it under control. Just cut the feeding back and aerated like hell, and instant bloom. Listen, I didn't get a chance to quiz my Outbound contact about my return date. Can you check on that?"

"Give me a second." Mark looked away from the camera for a moment, a much shorter pause than Blackburn had forced on him. Then he met Paul's eyes and frowned. "Media coverage is still hot. We need another crisis to reset the attention. I can ask one of the squads to rough up the Devonians if you want, to take the heat off you."

"No. But I'm bouncing off the walls here. What's your opinion? Do they plan to bring me back, or are they just letting me rot out here?"

"It's just the media, buddy. Play nice for a couple more months, and they'll drag you back to clean up some of the shit around here. This place needs an enema."

Paul laughed with Mark then, and they signed off, with one last assurance from Paul's friend that he hadn't heard of him being blacklisted.

He left the communication booth for the dirt streets in the village center, now in the sticky heat of mid-afternoon. He navigated around workers, wagons, draft animals, and the tawny Timmistrian goats that had become knee-high nuisances around Fairdawn. A break in the septic system trials allowed him time to walk and think, and this leisure proved a bad thing. Thoughts of Helwin haunted him, and the anguish of losing her felt like a hand squeezing his chest, making it difficult to breathe. The thought that followed was equally daunting, one that had begun to trouble him whenever the boredom of the place settled over him and he ached to be back in the sky.

Even if he was recalled and given another commission, without Helwin ... where the hell was he going to go?

Chapter 13

"It is enough to be who we are. But we must be who we are at all times."
— Deminin Lajin

Something changed in the sounds from the woods around Paul's camp. He stopped hacking at the weeds near his work shed, ready to pull his blade. It was approaching midday, and his sweaty skin was gathering fine dust and pieces of cut grass. Three days had passed since he helped fix the sewage problem. He offered to jump into the harvest, but Shawn had "fired" him and sent him to his camp for "detention." He struggled to tell the young man that idleness was killing him, giving him too much time to think.

Something or someone was approaching from the direction of Fairdawn. The bird calls had altered from the normal clicks and warbles and whistles to edgier warning cries, muffled in the thick foliage. He waited. Soon sounds of movement came to him, the crunching of brush underfoot and the hacking of a blade striking leaf fronds. The intruder was too noisy for a Timmon; someone small and light-footed approached on the main trail.

Why would a human woman, traveling alone, be coming to his camp?

He took two more wide, sweeping cuts with the long-handled scythe and stood leaning on the handle, waiting for his visitor to emerge from the brush.

She did, soon, and Paul was gripped by mixed emotions. Cara Harvestmoon appeared on the trail, wearing her usual khaki linen shirt and pants, carrying her blade and a short-handled container made from wooden strips. A basket. Lunch? Her pants were tucked into brown leather and dragon-skin hiking boots.

He found himself fascinated, watching her stepping carefully, moving in a way that was strong, steady, and decisive, and yet terribly feminine. She was a good leader, which interested him. And, he had to admit, she was attractive to him on other levels. She was also somewhat foolhardy, traveling to his camp alone.

Seeing him, she sheathed her blade and raised a hand in greeting, and her bright smile flashed.

I'm not ready for this.

He fetched his shirt, donned it quickly, and met her where the trail crossed a small rock bridge he'd built over the creek. The bridge was eight feet wide, easily passable with a jarin and wagon. He had used a piece of discarded irrigation pipe as a culvert and installed guards on the edges to prevent dangerous amphibians from climbing over. But it was not completely safe, and Paul stood with hand on blade until Cara crossed to his side.

He offered, "Good morning."

"Good morning, Mr. Saarinen. Making use of your time off, I see."

"Staying busy is always a good idea for me."

"That doesn't surprise me. If you're at a good stopping point, I brought chicken sandwiches, some cooked greens, and fresh fruit pie."

"I think I can find time for that, Ms. Harvestmoon."

"Cara, please."

"Sorry. Cara. And please call me Paul."

"Thank you, Paul. As often as I've called on you recently, I think we can dispense with the formalities, don't you?"

"It's a habit, ma'am."

"Yes, but it makes me feel like I'm taking charge."

She looked about for a place to set the basket down. He pulled his eyes from her face, gestured for the basket, which was surprisingly heavy, and led her to his wooden worktable and bench. At the table, Paul handed the basket back to her and grabbed a reed brush he'd hung from the side of the table. He swept dust and wooden shavings from the tabletop and the single long bench seat. In these dense forests, the wind brought a constant deposit of dirt and pollen. When he'd finished sweeping, she set the basket on the table's edge and began unloading small items wrapped in yellow elephant-ear tree leaves.

"With everything you've done, I thought I owed you lunch. I hope you like these sandwiches. The bread was baked this morning from this year's wheat crop. It's amazing."

The unmistakable scent of fresh yeast bread came to him and mingled pleasantly with the scent of the woman. His heart beat faster.

Stop it, fool. Nothing good can come of it.

"What is the 'chicken,' really?"

"Oh. I hate to admit it's a pandaril, the large flyer. Not bad, really. Funny how we cling to names from the past. On Principia, the birds we called 'chicken' didn't resemble the birds of Old Earth. Earth chickens were large and lived on the ground, I think. Principia's chickens were the size of rats and roosted on roofs."

She stopped and looked around. "Do you have any plates? I'm afraid I didn't bring any."

"Oh, yes. Sorry."

He went to the cabin, returning with two large wooden plates, steel forks and knives, mugs, and a covered gourd jug ¾-filled with filtered creek water. Cara had placed two thin woven place mats uncomfortably close together on the table on the side with the bench. She then took the items Paul had brought and placed them neatly on the mats, one by one. After organizing the two place settings, she held up one of the plates, made of malack wood, sanded smooth and coated with the same lacquer finish the pipe crews used to fabricate the field piping. She turned it over, examining it with a crinkled brow.

"Who made these plates?"

Paul moved around her, pouring water into the mugs, and set the jug to the side. "Uh, I did."

"How?"

"I took some odd-shaped end pieces from the woodshop scrap pile and turned them down on the big lathe."

"When did you find time for that? We've kept you so busy."

"While we were building pipe. There was dead time between trials."

"So instead of resting, you made plates."

"Staying busy…"

"Yes, staying busy is important. Next time you're 'staying busy,' I should like a set of these for the council table."

"Yes, ma'am."

Cara looked up at him quickly, blushed, and returned the plate to its setting. "I'm sorry, you thought that was an order. I guess taking charge has become a habit for me."

"Having someone in charge is important here. You do it well."

"I'll take that as a compliment."

"Please do."

She placed several yellow-wrapped objects on the plates, then a roundish item on the table just beyond.

"OK, please sit, and we'll enjoy this food before the bugs do."

He motioned for her to sit first, and then joined her. They unwrapped the sandwiches, and the smell of roasted poultry made Paul's stomach growl.

"I have to admit, I came today on more than just a social visit. One reason was to see if I could convince you to run for one of the open council seats. The year-end elections are coming up, and I want to see your name on the ballot."

He looked at her around his sandwich, waiting for her to take the first bite. "Why me?"

"We need your leadership and commonsense approach. We have many good people, but not many that I trust to lead during a crisis. You've shown you can keep a cool head, and you have excellent ideas. I have to think you've held leadership roles in the past. We need that here."

She bit into the sandwich, and he followed suit. The bread was firm, wonderfully grainy and nutty, the meat savory, somewhat wild in flavor, and juicy.

She swallowed before going on. "My second reason for coming isn't related to village business — I'll just throw it out there: I'd like to find out more about you. How you learned all the things you seem to know. My curiosity is killing me."

"This sandwich is delicious. My compliments to the chef."

"Thank you."

"You cooked this chicken? It's quite tasty."

"Yes, I did. When I'm in charge, I like to stay busy during my downtime."

He chuckled. "Touché."

"Pardon?"

"Fencing term. It means you scored a hit."

"Fencing? You mean sword fighting? That explains your skill with a blade."

Paul swallowed and took another equally delicious bite.

"You explained that your skill with a bow was from sport hunting. But there's a big difference between hunting rabbits and killing an attacking crellil."

"I didn't hunt small game much. Mostly deer and wild boar."

"Mm-hmm. How are the greens?"

"Delicious. Did you grow them during your downtime?"

She took a bite. "Actually, yes."

"Did you learn to grow things on your home world?"

She shook her head. "Growing things on Principia was difficult."

They ate in silence then for a while. Paul savored every bite and tried to avoid staring at her face. It wasn't easy. Her blemish-free skin and reflective green eyes were very pleasing.

The breeze rustled the brush, bringing the smells of dust and forest to them and keeping the bugs to a manageable nuisance. Cara's face was striking even doing something as mundane as chewing. Paul found it hard to look away, but he desperately needed to.

He broke the mood by talking about his home world, Crest, a heavily industrialized world whose main exports were technology and engineering. "My mother and father were both engineers, and I was an only child. I guess they took a passive interest in gardening, the arts, even raising a family. They tried to expose me to social events and cultural interests, but anything I didn't show much interest in or aptitude for, they dropped. For them, it was always about the work.

"This sandwich is just ... very good. I can't remember ever eating one this good."

"I take it your parents didn't cook much."

Paul chuckled. "I remember Claire, my mother, cooking about five times total. Every time a disaster. We ate a lot of synth-meals. Of course, everyone did. The Crestites are masters at manipulating the carbon atom. That's a guild motto, by the way."

"Where are your parents now?"

Paul's last contact with either of his parents had been months earlier. This discussion was risky, because he wasn't free to reveal that he'd followed both of them into a military career. "At last report, Claire was building a large water-extraction project on a gas giant's moon, in a system well out on the Orion Spur, about 1,000 LYs from Sol. Roger was heading up heavy metals mining on a planet about 500 LYs outward, toward the Sagittarius arm."

"So they separated?"

"Legally? I don't think so. They only signed short-term contracts. No lifetime commitments on Crest — those are extremely rare, and looked down upon, since they could affect someone's career goals. The work just took my parents to different places. They always tried to meet up every year or two, and as far as I know, they still do."

"So after you finished school, you followed the same path?"

He nodded. "Large projects on several worlds. I learned a lot, built a lot of different things. Saw a lot of different places and peoples, and other species, some intelligent."

He paused to look at her face again. "Am I answering your questions? Now that you're finding out how boring I am, am I killing your curiosity?"

"No, you're just feeding it. And nothing about your life sounds boring."

"Maybe it just sounds boring to me."

"And I still don't know why you decided to come to Timmistria."

Paul shrugged. "Every place I've been has been either heavily industrialized or developing rapidly. I guess I was bored and was interested in a more primitive location."

"If that's true, you made a good choice. But I'm not buying it."

"No? I was being honest."

"Oh, I think you were. I'm not questioning anything you said. But when I was a young girl on Principia, before the collapse, when there were still public schools, I had the wild idea I wanted to be a media reporter. My writing teacher told me there was a big difference between reporting the facts and reporting the truth. You, Paul Saarinen, have given me the facts about where you came from, but I don't have the sense that you've told me the truth about who you are. The mystery remains."

Her eyes danced as she teased him. "This sandwich *is* good. I wish I'd made more."

Their eyes met then, and he felt as if she were drawing the truth from him through the wordless air.

"Sorry I seem evasive. But you're just as guilty. You offer a few bits and pieces about life for you and Shawn, but not much beyond that."

"Hmm. That's fair. I make a habit of not talking about my past. It was tough for us, but most of the people here could tell stories that are truly heartrending."

"I know a little about the collapse of Principia and the Thinker incursion. From the occasional news vid."

That wasn't completely true. Paul knew a great deal about Principia, the fall of the sovereign democracy of the planet's largest developed nation, also known as Principia, and the ascension of the whole world dictatorship, led by Zanith and the Small People's Revolution. He doubted any of the other colonists had memories of more brutal oppression and violence than Cara and her brother did. The Thinker attack had been turned back successfully, but it was followed by a deeper militarization.

"Like I said, I was a schoolgirl when it started. There were eight of us then: Mom and Dad, five brothers, and me. Shawn was the youngest, then me, then Dilind, then the twins, Tomis and Trey, and the eldest, Michael. Mom was a doctor; Dad, a manager at the power plant."

Paul stopped her. "Excuse me, but watch it. There's a black biter hovering over your head." Paul stood and swung at it with the swatter he kept at the table. He caught the large black fly full on with a quick wrist flip. Slapped several yards away, it gathered itself and flew off. Its angry buzzing sounded unsettlingly like a Timmon cursing.

"Sorry. Go ahead. What were your parents like?"

"Thanks for taking care of that menace. I got bitten on the shoulder last month, and it was swollen for days." She rubbed her shoulder. "My parents were … serious? About everything. Work, education, raising children. Not cold, but reserved. I knew they loved us, but I can't say they were openly affectionate."

"So your house was very orderly."

"Oh, no! The opposite. The boys were all wild and rambunctious, and I was right in with them. My parents were serious about child-rearing; they just weren't very good at it. I remember Father explaining to Tomis why he shouldn't throw rocks off the apartment balcony, and patiently reasoning with them all to clean their rooms. Mother resorted to bribery to get all the boys to eat healthy foods or do their homework. Little or no discipline. You can imagine how well that worked. Chaos."

"Only you and Shawn came to Timmistria?"

"Yes. We were the only ones to survive and leave Principia. The others — all lost."

"I'm sorry. And I'm sorry I brought it up."

"No, not a problem. I can talk about it now. That wasn't always the case."

"What do you remember about the coup?"

"More than enough. The first sign of trouble was the flyovers — large military craft passing just above the trees. Mother and Father seemed to know very little. We were ordered to stay indoors. And then bombardments — red flashes on the horizon, the rumble of thunder. Father was ordered to the power plant full time. I remember the tenderness in his eyes when he hugged each of us before he left. I'd rarely seen that look, and it scared me more than the flyers or the distant flashes.

"We never saw him again. Two weeks later the facility was hit, and he was never found."

She paused, and her eyes searched for something distant in the forest. When she continued, her voice was very flat. "I remember the fighting stopped then, and the soldiers began collecting people. First Mother, because she was a medical worker. She was allowed to visit twice. Then the first wave of engineered viruses passed through."

She stopped for a moment and gathered herself.

"The virus took her. Then the soldiers came again and took Michael and the twins to work in the mines. There were food and water lines at first, and the three of us who remained made do. The handouts became less frequent and then stopped altogether. The soldiers came again and took Dilind. They promised him food and water for the family if he would come peacefully. We never saw any of it. The next time they came, Shawn and I kept the doors bolted, but the soldiers broke them down. Fortunately, we were too young to be of any use to them, and they left after ransacking the apartment. Older girls were taken. I was very lucky."

Paul remembered an urban campaign early in his career, going from door to door in an apartment complex. His company had been trained to expect a trap behind every door. What they found weren't armed resistance fighters but small broken families cowering in corners, their faces dirty and stricken. He hated himself after that and almost declined his next reenlistment.

"It's a cliché, but all that seems so long ago. I've lived two lifetimes since then, one with Shawn, working to get off Principia, and now, four years here, working to help us all survive."

She took another small bite of the sandwich and sipped at her cup. Her next smile seemed unaffected by the story. "I'll take this life, thank you."

Paul looked down at his own plate, feeling dangerously weak inside. He ate and drank, hoping the feeling would go away and afraid it wouldn't.

He said, "You've done well. There's a great deal of promise here."

"You say that like you don't consider yourself part of it. But I agree. We have an awesome future ahead, if we can just make it to profitability. We're so close. We just need one big break."

"I think you'll find it soon."

"I think you're right!" Her eyes sparkled. For not the first time or the last, the light in her face seemed to come from within. She was the one to look away this time, the breeze blowing wisps of auburn hair away from her ears. "But I'd be lying if I said it wasn't tough now. We're at a very precarious point in our development. For one thing, I'm always concerned about the single men here on Timmistria. There aren't many opportunities for romance, so obviously there's intense competition for the single women who come here."

"That's true of any human frontier, though. Most of the men who come here recognize that."

"You're right, and there is a dangerous set of social ills that result — alcoholism, drug abuse, fighting among the men, prostitution, suicide. So far, we don't seem to have a problem with any of those things. And the council works hard to stay on top of that, evaluating the mental health of our people. We strongly encourage women to come here, but the competition among colonies is fierce. We're not very successful."

Paul shrugged. "Things will improve over time."

"But the wait may be too long. I worry about the men in general, and I worry a lot about Shawn. I want him to have the chance to have a family while he's young. I worry about you as well, Paul."

He swallowed a bit of the flavorful greens, shaking his head, both at Cara's words and at his delight with the well-prepared food.

"There's no reason to worry about me."

"No?" She finished her sandwich with a dainty bite, licking her fingers while swatting at the flies now hovering over her greens and fruit. "You're a complete mystery to me, Paul, and that isn't really a good thing. You've become very important to this colony in such a short time, and we can't afford to let you get away. But if we don't know who you are, how can we know how to keep you?

"I have so many questions, and I'm afraid to ask them. But the one I can't help asking is this — with your skills, you would have been welcome at any colony. Why did you choose this one?"

Paul cleaned the last crumbs and bits of vegetables from his plate. The pie remained, but Cara's question had dulled his appetite. "I think I answered that question on my application."

"Yes, evasively, the same way I did, the same way nearly everyone else here did." She cleared the last of the greens from her plate and turned her haunting eyes back on him. "I'm sorry. You don't have to answer that, and I have no right to ask, really. We find out so little about our people's past lives, and it's probably better that way. But it's funny; we do get some people who'll put real reasons on their apps. One man wrote, 'My wife found out I was spending weekends at the brothels and is trying to kill me.' Another wrote, 'I owe the loan shark two million lentars.'" She shook her head.

He was relieved she pulled the focus off of him, and he tried to keep it steered away. "What about you, Cara? No family plans?"

"Me? No! Not now. Too busy. At some point, when we beat this planet and children have an easier time, maybe. I lost four brothers, Paul. I don't ever want to bury my children."

"I'm sorry. No offense intended."

She leaned back and rubbed her eyes. "None taken. It's just not the right time for me. Maybe it never will be. But Shawn, he'll have a family. A big one, I hope. Getting him off Principia before the place withered us both was really my life's goal. This—" She swept her hand at the forest around them. "This, even with the bugs and the crellil and the Delerin boxing us in, is still

Heaven. And we'll succeed here. My nieces and nephews will flourish here."

She smiled. "I guess that's my second life's work. But right now, Timmistria can be a lonely place for single people."

"Are you concerned about Shawn taking a Timmon lover?"

Her smile slowly collapsed. She looked at her plate. "Like I did, you mean?"

Paul could say nothing.

"How did you find out? Rumors among the men at the shops?"

"No. No one has said anything. I guess it was obvious during the orientation meetings."

"Perceptive. I never tried to hide it. You disapprove, I guess?"

Paul felt his own words squeezing in on him. He shook his head. "None of my business. My observations are that it usually doesn't work out well."

She studied his face. "To answer your question, I do worry about Shawn. He knows about Lonin and me, and I'd rather he stick with human company. He loves the Timmon people, their ways, and their stories. I know he's lonely, and … he's all I've got. I'm not going to lose him, and he will have someone sweet who loves him, and they will have a family."

She continued to watch him. He returned her look without blinking. "Are you xenophobic?" she asked, finally.

He shook his head and went back to his greens. "No. I've had bad experiences with alien races, is all."

"Hmm. You're not very convincing. Something I should tell you — Lonin treated me better than any human male ever has, and I don't regret our relationship at all. We ended it because it was a risk to us and possibly detrimental to the colony."

"Again, none of my business."

Cara sat in silence for a moment. When she spoke, her voice was cool. "Another thing I should tell you, I guess. My third reason for the visit. If things went well at lunch, I was prepared to let you know that I was beginning to find you very … interesting." She set down her fork. "Not so much now."

She stood slowly, began to gather her things, placed them in the basket, and closed the lid.

"I'll leave you the pie. It's fresh Timmon blackberry. Very complex, but a little bittersweet."

She stepped away then, crossing the yard at a deliberate pace, scanning the ground and the sky, hand on blade. She stopped just as she was about to step onto the bridge. "Oh, just a reminder, you're due back in the shops in the morning. Please be on time. I still want you on that council at the first of the year, so I will expect your 'petition to serve' on my desk by noon tomorrow."

She crossed the creek and turned back to toss one last barb. "And I still want a set of those plates!"

She stalked off, the noise of her angry march marking her passage along the trail.

After she left, Paul hacked down all the weeds in the camp. The place had never looked so good.

#

The night wore on. Lonin's arms began to ache. Still he did not move with Cara in his arms, not wanting to awaken her. She had come to him, her face a smooth pink mask covering pain, and her light a bruised moonbeam. Lying motionless now but hardly relaxed, he let the anger rise in him for a time, feeling its sharp edges on his senses.

Anger was not to be taken lightly or used unrighteously, but it was also not to be denied. It was a tool, like the sling or the blade, and it was to be unsheathed and wielded when there was a need. He felt that need now like a strong thirst. The red one was not the only human who threatened this colony, and it was time to reveal the depths of the one known as Paul Saarinen.

Chapter 14

PRINCIPIA – APARTMENT
Winter 2512 GSD

Evening light from the single window lit the apartment, the one Cara and Shawn had occupied for the last two years, a fetid box with cracked plaster and peeling paper, whose plumbing worked sometimes, and electricity hardly at all. He'd been studying at the rickety synth-wood table, trying to ignore the rumbling in his stomach, but his attention was wandering.

Then, without a knock or other warning, the doorknob rattled, and a key searched for and found the lock. She opened the door but held it against the cold draft that threatened to blow it wide open and bang it against the wall. She was carrying a thin sickly green plastic bag into the kitchen. He knew the bag contained a treasure of sorts — food for a day or two. The stiff, bitter breeze chased her inside, a chilling draft that didn't entirely give up its assault after she had closed the door and latched it in three places. She picked up the metal bar leaning against the near wall and dropped it across the entire width of the door into the slots on each side.

She laid the bag on the far edge of the table, which swayed slightly. When she took off her coat, he was shocked by the small, round bruises on her arms and what looked like a burn mark on her left forearm. Her arms, cradling the bag, were thin bands of flesh and bone sticking out from the sleeves of a pale pink frock.

"Brrr! It's a little cold out there. How was school today?" Her eyes seemed hollower and grayer than usual.

"Good."

She moved around the kitchen, filling the larger of their two worn enamel pots with tap water, then setting it down on the counter to add two drops from the small bottle of chelate solution sitting next to the sink. Without the chelate, the heavy metals in the water would take refuge in their body tissues. With the water treatment, the metals would pass in a dark cloud in their urine.

"Where were you last night? I got worried."

Cara hesitated for just an instant, and he immediately regretted asking. She didn't turn to look at him as she spoke. "I'm sorry, Shawn. I found a temp job for a few hours a week and didn't get a chance to come by to tell you."

"You need to let me go work at the mine."

She did turn on him then, and her look made him regret his words even more, a look that said, *Don't make me have this argument again.* She retrieved the bag from the table, not taking her eyes off his, withering him, then returned to the sink to wash vegetables. Her silence was a lingering punishment.

He said, "I got a 910 on the geology exam."

She stopped again and stood for a moment with her hands in the basin. When she turned to look at him this time, her face was that of a woman transformed, his previous comment completely forgotten. A broad smile blossomed on her face. Even with hollow eyes, she was beautiful.

"Shawn! Wonderful! I *told* you you could do it!"

She set down her knife and the potato she'd been cleaning and threw her arms around him in a hug so tight it was almost painful. She hooted as she shook him playfully. He could feel her bones as they hugged, and he promised himself that he would not ever ask her questions that he knew would upset her. He swore he would do what he could to make her smile like that again, always.

She pushed back, grabbed the hair on the back of his head, and smiled at him, face to face, hers pale and lined. There were spots on her skin, probably from toxins in the water supply, but her green eyes twinkled, her teeth were impossibly straight, and she was the most beautiful woman he had ever seen.

"Isn't that what I've been telling you? You're too smart to waste yourself digging up uranium ore. You're meant for bigger things, Shawn. Much bigger."

"But I got a 620 on the written essay in Standard Language."

She pursed her lips and nodded with a wink. "So you have some more work to do there. Just be patient, brother. We have to work hard at everything we do, but it makes us strong. We're learning to overcome anything. We just have to be patient. It's not all going to fall in our laps overnight. But the better times will come. Trust me." She sighed, patted his cheek, and went back to the cooking.

He thought about their future, the visions she'd planted in his head, of a planet with blue skies and green fields, of communities of hardworking people living in peace. He would practice his geology and make great discoveries. She would find work, cooking in a community kitchen or doing clerical work for a small company. He would meet a good woman, and they would start a family, and Cara would be the doting aunt, babysitting his children whenever he'd let her spoil them.

But there, in that tiny, poorly lit kitchen, her vision seemed impossibly far away. He couldn't tell her how he struggled at school. Nightmares wracked his sleep. He was always tired, so tired, and he fell asleep sometimes during class or when he studied. One of his instructors had held him after class and chewed him out for snoring during the lecture. He tried to explain, and in the end, the instructor's face had softened. He'd sent Shawn out, suggesting he try to catch a nap before class.

Shawn wanted to believe in Cara's dreams, but were they kidding themselves? He didn't know anyone who had been able to leave Principia. Why should they be the ones?

But her smile and her energy, and all her sacrifices to keep him from dying like their brothers had. He loved Cara. And dammit, he refused to let her down. If she thought his studies would help them get out from under the darkness of Principia, he would study as hard as he could.

Chapter 15

Paul worked a short day at the shops and was returning early from his shift. He intended to get a bite and change his shirt, and he was to return to supervise the afternoon shift while Mark moved over to help in the South Field. The light fell at an early afternoon angle through the woods, casting dappled shadows on the ground. He focused on gliding silently through the woods, letting the eyes and ears of the animals test him. The goal of this sport was to travel without raising warning calls.

But half a kilometer from his camp, he felt the presence of another on the path behind him like a heaviness in the forest. It wasn't an animal, and he doubted any of the colonists could be as quiet in these woods. He maintained his pace, as if oblivious to the intrusion, but he tested the looseness of his blade sheath, ready to sprint away if the follower charged him. He was still minutes from his camp and its weapons locker.

A lone Timmon following him. He could think of no comforting reasons why.

His follower was content to stay back, but as soon as Paul crossed the bridge, the other closed the distance, no longer interested in stealth. Yards short of the cabin and the weapons, he had no choice now but to turn and stand.

Immediately, the Timmon liaison, Lonin, pushed the brush aside, walked steadily to the bridge, and crossed it. He moved insistently but without haste. He would know Paul was alone and miles from the nearest settlement.

The Timmon was dressed in a short leather loincloth and vest, and his face was painted in lines of red. His bare upper arms were wrapped in gold beads, and red lines were drawn upwards on his legs and body. The muscles in his legs bulged when he walked. Paul waited.

Lonin stopped ten meters away. With thick arms bent and hands flexing at his sides, he was an ominous sight.

"I'm guessing this isn't a social call." Paul waited for Lonin to speak. He let his hands rest on the handles of the two blades sheathed at his sides. He took a deep breath through his nose to slow the beating of his heart.

At last, the Timmon spoke. "You have two choices, human. Reveal your true light, or die here."

Paul guessed a motive and spoke to gather time. "I thought the Timmistrians did not murder."

"Not correct. Killing is sometimes justified. And if it is justified here, I will also take my own life. It is the way."

"And what purpose will that serve? She needs you. And I think these people need me. They're barely surviving now."

"Save your words. It is time for you to show your true self, or stay hidden and die without dignity."

With that, Lonin pulled a wicked green brush blade from his belt and advanced. In their few brief meetings, the Timmon ambassador had always been very reserved. As Paul stepped around to take a position behind the outside eating table, pulling his own blades, he didn't recognize this Timmon. An animal intensity and ferocity had come to the normally placid eyes, and his nostrils flared in red spasms. Paul had known that death could come from any quarter in this colony, but this was not a way he had expected.

He glanced about, seeking sanctuary, and Lonin took this moment to attack. He leaped forward, gripping the edge of the table with his left hand and flipping it backward. Paul dove to the side, toward the open door of his shop. The table edge came down on the back of his heel, but he gained his feet quickly and broke into a run. Lonin would be very fast and would make short work of him in the open. His cabin was farther away and out of reach, so the shop was his best chance.

What did the Timmon want him to reveal?

Lonin followed quickly and was now upon him, his face drawn back in a snarl. He pounced...

...but Paul was not there. He dodged to the right, away from the shed and also away from Lonin's first strike, which bit the earth where Paul had been a split second earlier.

Lonin moved quickly to intercept and took a second swing. Paul thrust upward hard with crossed blades against the downward slash of Lonin's blade. The ringing impact of steel-hard enamel filled Paul's head and sent a shock wave down his arms and through his torso. He pushed the blow to the side and rolled away, immediately countering with blades swung high toward Lonin's trunk-like neck.

Lonin moved easily out of the reach of Paul's scissor cut. As the next slashing swing came at him, Paul had barely enough time to deflect it. He had no chance to counter, allowing Lonin to spin back into an assault position, legs spread wide, squatting into a powerful coiled flex, absolutely deadly. Paul regrouped, falling back into his own combat posture. His body flowed out ahead of his mind, and he launched a reflex-driven spinning attack, bringing his blades in a cyclonic spiral of razor edges aimed at debilitating targets on Lonin's body: shins, knees, forearms, elbows. Few men, or aliens, were not surprised by this unconventional slashing attack, but

Lonin stepped aside. Paul flailed about, wounding only the air.

Even having seen the speed of the Timmon rangers during the crellil attack, he was surprised that his blades had missed so completely. His mind became very calm. He'd taken his best shot, and the Timmon had evaded him. There was little doubt Lonin would kill him and little else Paul might do.

So he attacked, launching a series of pivoting, suicidal blitzes of blade and feet. He was loose and fluid, weight balanced evenly, shifting from foot to foot, each feint or parry followed by killing thrusts and slashes. Paul's blades mostly struck only the air, except when Lonin chose to parry blows with his own blades as he saw fit, toying with Paul, each counterblow sending spikes up Paul's forearm tendons to his shoulders. The Timmon's face became an emotionless mask.

Paul was expending an incredible amount of energy and could not maintain the exertion level for long, but there was little reason to postpone the end, and there were worse ways to fall. He had imagined his death in a firefight with the Thinkers or one of their converted clans, but this death, on this remote planet, would serve just as well. At last, his body betrayed him, and he faltered. He lost his balance for only an instant, but it was long enough. Lonin stomped on Paul's foot and trapped it briefly before Paul could kick free, and it was all the advantage he needed. He moved on top of Paul now, bringing his blade crashing down with both hands against Paul's desperate parries.

"Stop hiding and show yourself, human!"

Each blow was a machine hammer driving Paul more deeply into a crouch so that his knees were slammed into the ground. He tried to dodge to one side, but Lonin would have none of that, moving and delivering skull-splitting blows relentlessly, with only the tense shock absorbers of Paul's weakening arms to save him, until his muscles could respond no more. With a sweeping blow and a straight-legged kick, Lonin launched Paul into the air. He landed on his side, blades scattered, with Lonin standing astride him. His blade pinned Paul's neck to the dirt. Lonin stopped there, as the echoes of blade on blade died and quiet fell on the clearing.

Paul lay on his side, staring at yellow dirt and yellow grass inches from his eyes. "Do it."

The blade leaned into his neck, and sharp pain bit.

But then the pressure eased, the nipping bite of the sharp edge ceased. Lonin's shadow moved away, but Paul could only lie where he was, exhausted. His arms and legs had nothing left and quivered uselessly. He couldn't even roll over onto his back.

"You may be a worthy fighter. Maybe your light does not lie to me, and you are truly not an evil man…"

At that, Lonin pushed Paul onto his back, his foot on Paul's chest, and pointed the tip of his blade at Paul's throat.

"…but you are not worthy of her. If you ever hurt her again, I *will* kill you."

For an instant, a hint of the war grimace returned to Lonin's face. Then he stepped away, leaving Paul lying on his back in the dirt.

Eventually Paul summoned the energy to roll to his side, then to his hands and knees. Lonin was walking about the clearing, smoothing torn-up clumps of grass with his booted feet and righting a small pot they'd apparently kicked over during the fight. Paul weakly pulled himself to a sitting position, elbows on knees. The yard was a wreck, tools scattered, plants hacked and limp, garden borders ravaged. He couldn't remember causing the wreckage.

"Get up now. We will put your kithin back in order." Lonin looked over at Paul sitting in the dirt, eyeing him up and down. "After you wash."

They rinsed off, standing side by side, from two of Paul's water buckets, which were hung from hooks on the side of the shop. They didn't speak. Paul felt empty, diminished, exhausted, not like an athlete but like a flame. Talking was too much effort, and all the energy he could muster was consumed by washing the dirt and sweat from his arms and clothing. His hands still shaking, he stripped to his underclothes, rinsing himself completely from head to toe. Lonin washed the streaks of paint from his face and ears.

Paul's neck was marked by a sticky, cracked line of blood. Another scar, another story not to be told.

Dressed only in pants, belts, and scabbards for short blades, they repaired the damage they'd done to Paul's yard. They set the table upright, repaired rock borders, and moved dirt and shorn greenery with shovels. Communicating only with nonverbal signals and gestures, they quickly replaced everything, save the items that were broken. These were piled near the shop. When they finished, Lonin stood in front of the table and surveyed the yard. Paul stood a few feet away, pretending to look around as well but really watching only the yellow giant.

Lonin turned to Paul and nodded, which apparently meant the same thing to him as it did to Paul. Then he motioned for Paul to follow him. They gathered their long blades from the table, and he led Paul into the shop. Inside, Paul pushed open the window coverings, thin amphibian skins stretched in wooden frames. Dusk was falling rapidly now, and the light through the windows was dim. The work shed was still hot, with very little evening breeze to carry the heat away.

Lonin laid his scabbards on the flat workbench. He raised his long blade to look at its edge against the light in the window. The Timmon ratan-i looked as if they were shaved from pieces of translucent lime-colored glass or quartz. Paul took a cue from Lonin and began examining his own blades, checking them from tip to hilt for cracks or other damage. Besides a couple of light nicks, he could find nothing seriously wrong. The ratan-i were certainly not brittle like a crystalline mineral. It was an interesting chemistry that made the material hard but not brittle like a glass would normally be. Lonin laid down his long blade and was now examining his shorter work blade. He didn't look happy.

"We have work to do. But not tonight. It will be dark soon, and there is not enough light to repair the cremin teeth. But they must be sharpened and sealed again soon, or the dry air will weaken them and they will turn to dust. Tomorrow, I will show you the way."

He donned his belt, latching it at his side, and pushed his blades into their sheaths. He walked out of the shop. Paul followed. Lonin crossed the yard to where they'd hung their clothes to dry and began getting dressed. Paul's clothes were still a little damp, but the moisture made them cool and refreshing. Now fully clothed and belted, Lonin stood and regarded Paul silently. Still somewhat worn from the fight, Paul felt very small.

"I will meet you at your work tomorrow morning when my duties are completed, and we will treat our ratan-i."

And with that, the tall yellow man walked from the camp, as if he had not just tried to kill Paul. Paul shook his head, his thoughts a turmoil.

What had Lonin wanted Paul to reveal, and what had he seen? Was the Timmon disappointed that he hadn't felt the need to kill him?

Was Paul disappointed?

Chapter 16

"Things sought are seldom worth the seeking. Unless they are."
— Timmistrian proverb

"It is there." Lonin pointed ahead and to his right. Paul stepped up closer behind Shawn and strained to see through the dense foliage at the side of the rough trail. They'd been hiking for nearly an hour. He saw open sky through the clumps of multihued yellow and brown leaves, and the green of a cremin blade below that, and a flash of brightness.

Ten days had passed since Lonin attacked him. Paul had arrived at the workshop that morning, ready to begin molding some critical pieces of the water supply manifold. There he was met by Shawn and three Timmon — Lonin, Kearnin, and the Timmon archer who'd also shot at the crellil. The archer was introduced as Crellin, which Paul found somehow fitting, and the three Timmon shook his hand warmly.

Then Paul's plans changed. They wanted him to join them on a day hike into Timmon territory, with the main objective of scouting the areas to the northwest in preparation for the imminent "dragon" invasion. They hoped to develop new tactics to route the destructive beasts, the cremin, around the human and Timmon settlements. But more exciting to Shawn was an excursion to Shill Wellin, a large fertile valley several klicks west of where they would be scouting. According to Shawn, none of the colonists had seen this valley, but Kearnin had told him it was magnificent.

In reality, the pipe work had been challenging for a time, but all the difficult work had been done, and

Paul's mind was beginning to wander back to Helwin and Delos. Some new kind of work was welcome.

The country was very rough, with thick underbrush and canopy in the typical colors of this planet — oranges, browns, a few reds, and the pervasive ruling yellow. Paul had found Timmistria's landscape to be striking at first, but the planet's ever-present color scheme, seemingly without seasons, had become tiresome. It did bring up memories of childhood trips into the country, of grain fields and corn stalks in late autumn, when the verdant greens of spring were bleached out by the sun's brutal summer rays.

They stopped briefly in a small clearing, formed by a huge ocher fungus and surrounded by aggressive catcher vines. Here Lonin paused to explain that the ambling trek of the cremin through these forests was difficult to predict. For hundreds of generations, the Timmon had tried to divert the huge reptiles around their fields and kithin, with fire, smoke, rock walls, and even odorous plants, and all had proved only minimally effective. During cremin migration, the creatures walked through Timmon lands, destroying fields and homes by the sheer inertia of their haphazard passage. They were slow and of low intelligence, so they seldom claimed Timmon lives, but they would kill and eat any animal that came within reach of their heavy forelegs and mouths.

They were difficult to kill, with thick hides and hard scales over their heads and vital areas. But the Timmon killed several of the brutes every migration and used various body parts for tools and building supplies. The siding that adorned many of the structures in the Co-Op colony and the Timmon kithin was cremin skin. The green ratan-i that all Timmon and villagers carried were made from cremin teeth, already razor-sharp and wickedly curved when pulled from the reptiles' mouths.

Cremin were killed only when alone and far from others of their kind. The beasts led solitary lives and tended to avoid each other. In fact, during the migration, they tracked each other by smell and avoided each other's paths. But the beasts were ravenous carrion eaters, and killing one during the migration would draw many more of them. They would gather and fight over the carcass, creating a much more destructive and dangerous situation.

After crossing the territory for most of the morning, when they had stopped for a brief water break, Shawn asked Paul if he had any ideas on rerouting the cremin away from the occupied areas.

"Some vague thoughts, maybe. Do they have any maps of the area?"

Shawn coughed and glanced furtively at Lonin. "The Timmon don't make maps."

Paul said, "No? Every civilization I know of draws maps. That's usually the second type of recorded information, after pictures of animals."

Lonin's voice interrupted. "We Timmon do not need maps."

Paul asked, "How do you remember the locations of remote camps or hunting grounds? Or small watering holes? How do you show others where important places are?"

"We know where things arc. We see the places."

Paul looked at Shawn, who shrugged, then asked, "When you build a large building, do you make drawings and plans of it before you begin?"

Lonin nodded. "No. We talk. We understand. We see it … in our minds … how the building must look. Then we begin."

"I see. Unfortunately, I am not so gifted. It would help me to see this land on a piece of paper."

Shawn said, "I guess we need to spend some time drawing more maps."

Paul frowned. "It sure would be nice to have a copter or hummer available."

Shawn gave Paul a strange look. "Yes. It would." He turned to their guide. "Lonin, can your people build a model of this land? Something that looks exactly like this place, only very small?"

"A ... model? Is that like the places you build for your human plays?"

Shawn shook his head. "No. Those are stage settings. Stages are full-size and are more like a cutaway view of a place we make up in our heads. Like a cabin with the front wall removed. A model is a small replica of a real place. Here, let me show you."

He walked to a patch of dirt and rocks near several fernlike trees, where there was no undergrowth. "Lonin, Kearnin, look at this."

He began moving rocks and scraping dirt with his feet, then gouged indentations into the tough, dried clay with a flat stone and a stick. He then took the stick and scratched three ragged parallel lines across the small patch he'd cleared.

"We tried drawing maps, and that was not a success. Taking the three-dimensional images in your heads and trying to draw them in two dimensions on a piece of paper didn't work. But what if we ask you to build a model that looks like the real thing? Like this."

He pointed at the small stones he had piled at one end of the clearing. "Here are some hills. These scratches are creeks and rivers. And these weeds — let me take the tops off and plant them here — these are trees. Just tiny trees. Now, if we built something that looked exactly like this area, except very small, we could use it to track the dragons and make the most of our diversionary tactics."

He searched around again and picked up a stubby, rectangular rock about two inches long, placing it between two creeks. "This could be a dragon." Kneeling down, he held the rock with his fingers and moved it downstream.

Lonin stroked his chin. "This model is a place you know on your world? Principia?"

Shawn stood, slapping dirt from his hands and pants. "No. This is just a place I made up. A real model would look like this, but it would be a small copy of this whole area, with hills, rocky points, rivers, creeks, and valleys." He moved his hand in a wave, as if following a rolling hill. He bent and picked up his dragon stone.

"Every day we would move the rock to show where the dragons are. Then we could plan our ambushes based on their movements."

The three Timmon stood looking down at Shawn's scratches in the dirt. Kearnin stooped and began moving rocks around. He placed stones together into a tighter pile, then found a larger rock and placed it to one side. With a flat stone, he graded over one of the gouges that had represented a creek, used the edge of the stone to cut the far left creek deeper, then turned it and connected it with the far right creek.

"This is Denil Denlin. The creek Denillalin. This one Denlival. This is Denn."

Shawn nodded. "Denn gets hit hard by cremin, doesn't it? From this model, you can see why. Any beasts that come down the hills between the creeks get funneled right to Fairdawn." Shawn crossed his arms in satisfaction. "We need a way to force them to cross one of the creeks, like a high wall with a shallow ford nearby that they would take instead."

Lonin stared down at Kearnin and his model, and his exaggerated features settled into an expression akin to a frown. The skin around his cheeks and neck darkened.

He said, "The Timmon will not build models."

Shawn's jaw dropped, and his arms fell to his sides. "Why not?"

"We will build no models. Kearnin, the Timmon will build no more models."

He walked away from the group, leaving the two colonists stunned, and stood near the entrance to the clearing. "Come. The day gets long. We must go now if we are going to the valley and back before dark. Shik, Kearnin. Sil shinil. You and Crellin go now to your duties, but go quietly. We three will go from here. Your work is important, and our work is other."

Kearnin stood from his model, rising tall, more than two feet taller than Shawn or Paul. "Lin, Lonin. Ah-hil."

"Ah-hil. Go with care. Mind the crellil."

After the strange end to their discussion in the clearing, Lonin led Shawn and Paul on a fast hike through the difficult, constantly changing trail. At times it climbed onto ridges, rocky and dry, and at others it dropped into thick vegetation-choked valleys, foggy and wet with drizzle. Conversation was sparse, as Lonin's ratan-i swung out at the jungle's vines and birds, dodging flying beasts and always alert to other dangers. Paul fell into an energetic but relaxed rhythm, and his mind remained clear of the past. Lonin's strange behavior at the clearing was a question for another time.

#

"It is there."

Yellow sky and foliage were the background that formed this place, but a patch of green flashed through the brush where Lonin pointed. How odd that it should be there, the first green Paul had seen other than cremin teeth since he'd arrived. Before Paul could ask any questions, Lonin pressed ahead, sweeping his long blade in wide arcs across the trail ahead of them. With each swing, the muscles of his arm and back tensed and bunched, and Paul was reminded of an Old-Earth tennis player. He remembered the strength of that swinging ratan and how it had driven him to the ground. How easily Lonin could have killed him had he intended to.

Farther down the trail, the brush to their right began to thin out, giving them open views of the valley below. Paul caught glimpses of steep wooded slopes giving way to grassland, lit to glowing green by the brilliant sun. The trail then turned back to the left, into heavier brush, and their view was cut off.

They hiked through a stand of catcher vines, thick, ropy, and persistent, and Paul had to focus on cutting and slashing. The woods here were decked in bright yellows and oranges, loud with the calls of creatures, and the air was alive with yellow and brown flying things, some of which flew close enough to threaten the hikers.

Then the trail turned abruptly back to the right, and Paul and Shawn found themselves following Lonin across a wide rock outcrop overlooking a different world. The two stopped dead, stunned. Lonin walked to the edge, put a foot up on a rock, and leaned a sharp elbow on his knee, gazing outward in satisfaction.

On a typical old terran world, the emerald green valley that lay stretched out before them might have been a wilderness park or wildlife sanctuary. Here on

Timmistria, a persistent yellow and brown planet, it was an impossible marvel. Shawn whistled quietly.

The wooded slopes Paul had glimpsed were actually a series of steep ridges, rising in staggered succession to the rocky scarp that formed the valley's rim. The near edge, to their left, rose several hundred feet from the elevation of the outcrop where they stood. The valley was narrow, and the far edge, jagged like black and gray teeth, was no more than ten or twelve klicks away.

The steep slopes below them fell away onto rolling hills, painted in intense green, brightly lit by the sun perched in the cloudless sky. Cleaving the valley was a broad creek or river, which wound down from the highlands to the right. The water was the blue of ocean algae. The white of rapids dotted the flowing stream. The glint of light that Paul had seen through the brush was from the creek's termination point, a narrow lake several kilometers away to their left, which bent around and disappeared behind a sharp rocky point.

Shawn said, "Wow! The Timmon have talked about this place, but words don't do it justice. It's incredible."

Lonin seemed lost in the world below them. A warm breeze blew up the canyon slope, carrying smells both familiar and strange: the bouquet of flowers; the effusive crispness of pines; but also the strong sweetness of ripening fruit, and musky vegetation smells unlike any Paul had come across in his weeks in the human settlement.

Even the sky here was different. The normal pale yellow he'd grown accustomed to was ghostly thin, and a hint of terran blue washed through. The ceiling was dotted with the wheeling shapes of birds, along with some larger winged creatures at higher altitude. Paul realized these flyers were very high, much higher than he had first thought, which meant they were also much larger. As he watched, one of them began to descend. It spiraled lower into the valley, revealing itself at last to be a huge reptilian flyer. It fell steadily from the sky and leveled off just above the grass, before crashing onto something hidden in tall grass on the plain below, likely some herbivore that had just met an unexpected but natural end. Now somewhat uncomfortable, Paul looked back over his shoulder at the sky behind them.

Shawn had not seen the attack and remained transfixed, staring open-mouthed down the valley in the direction of the river mouth and the lake. Lonin, motionless like the rock promontory behind him, gazed out over the valley.

Paul asked, "What do you call the large flyers that hunt in the valley?"

Lonin replied without taking his eyes from the landscape. "That one is called repelin, or 'nap cilo' — father of the sky. It is like the perelin — the small flyer the humans call 'fruit bat' — but many times larger and of more mature spirit. It counts all the birds as its children and herds them patiently in the seasons. Without the repelin, the skies would be ... untamed."

"What do they eat?"

Lonin swung his face around, wearing the equivalent of a smile. "Anything they choose. We Timmon are glad they do not have a taste for us."

Paul chuckled. "Hopefully they will not develop a taste for humans. Lonin, may I ask what this place is? Why is it so different? The green color must be plant-based chlorophyll, like terran worlds, like my home planet."

"This is Shill Wellin, Valley of Birth. The green life rises from Timmistria. It is a gift."

Shawn asked, "Are there other places like it?"

"I have seen two other places like Shill Wellin. One is in the Timmon lands, and the other is in the lands of the Delerin. Those others are not as ... grand? The Timmon elders tell of other green places on Timmistria, but we have not seen those lands in many generations."

"Valley of Birth. Do the Timmon believe you came from a green place like this?"

"Shik! Lin. That is our belief. But humans have taught us we do not ask questions enough. We are not — your word? — scientils? We see what is, and our minds are at peace."

He turned back toward the emerald cleft in the earth, his face no longer serene. "Seeing only what is, and not what was or what will be, is no longer enough."

Shawn's enthusiasm began to boil over. "This is astounding. I'd love to bring our biologists here. We've talked a lot about Timmistria and the lack of green plants that can perform photosynthesis — making food from sunlight. From our studies of other planets, almost all of them have green plants that feed the food chain. There are some others that do not, but their life always remains very primitive, usually bacteria and algae and little creatures that live off other chemistry. But none of those yellow or orange worlds have the rich biology that Timmistria does. I wonder if it's possible that these green places, these wellin, provide the basic carbon-based compounds that are the foundation of the food chain on Timmistria."

Paul nodded. "Excuse me, Lonin, but I am curious about something as well. Shawn and I are from terran-type worlds, where there is abundant water and the world is mostly green and blue. Timmistria is a beautiful planet, but for me, this green valley is soothing to my eyes. When you look at this, you can see that it is a different color here, and you understand that we humans call the color we see 'green.' Do you think you see the same color we do? And is it pleasing to you?"

"I enjoy human questions, but sometimes they are painful to my head. When I look at this wellin, this valley, I see a 'barrin' — a 'color' — that is very different from most of my world. It is … pleasing. But what you ask, is what I would call 'beal' the same as your 'green'? How can I know? Mr. Saarinen, your eyes are yellow like mine, not the color of other human eyes. Does that mean you see things as I do? Is my 'kahl' your 'red'?

"There is a Timmon saying. In your language, it would be, 'It is a gift to look through the eyes of another.' I enjoy human questions because the asking gives me this gift. Do you see?"

"I think I do."

"That is one reason I brought you here. This Shill Wellin, like all of Timmistria, is a gift. We Timmon … cherish it. I know that many of you humans cherish Timmistria's gifts, but not all of you do. Those Timmon and Delerin who opposed the humans remaining here had this fear, that the strange people from the sky would not cherish Timmistria and that they would harm the balance. So far this has not happened. But you are many more now than when you first came, and there is more fear.

"I show you this wellin today because I know that you, Shawn, cherish Timmistria. I do not know you well, Paul, but your actions speak softly for you, and I hope you will also cherish her. As part of this gift, and because of the many gifts that we Timmon have given you, I must ask that you help me to teach all humans who come to our world to cherish her as we Timmon do."

Shawn and Paul exchanged glances, and Shawn spoke first. "Lonin, I hold the many gifts from the Timmon people with the greatest appreciation. I think I speak for the village council and manager and all of those in the colony. We love the gift of new lives here on Timmistria, and we will continue to work very hard to preserve it and to be protective of the land you have given us. Right, Paul?"

"I agree completely."

"Shik. Thank you, friends. Those are strong words. I see you believe them. I fear your belief will be tested in the coming days."

Lonin stood motionless again, a gold and brass statue draped lightly in tan skins and cloths, leaning elbows on one knee, as if fashioned by a sculptor such as Xin Qua or Flores de Seu. His words hung like a shroud over them all. After long quiet moments of taking in the beauty, he broke the spell.

"Shik, enough fearful talk from me and strong words from you. Arm he pressin! As you would say, let's explore!"

He started back to the trail where it broke from the high scarp, but stopped to hold out a hand. "Blades ready, friends. The repelin is not the only predator in Shill Wellin, and most of them are not such picky eaters."

The valley indeed proved a verdant land of fragrant plants, rocky swift streams, and beautiful singing birds, but also of ever-present dangers. Once, Lonin drove away a large catlike beast with flat ears and a weaselly face by raising his blade high over his head and bellowing painfully in a deep, guttural cry. And several times the three adventurers found themselves among huge vines that tried to loop around their arms and legs. One nearly pulled Paul from his feet before he was able to cleave the ropy vine apart.

Lonin told them these vines, called shin shilin, would hold a victim suspended several feet above the ground, out of reach of predators, and then small teeth would burrow into the flesh of the victim's legs and consume it from the inside, all while the victim hung and perished of thirst. Paul had seen a multitude of brutal animal and plant predators during his military campaigns, but the thought of being hung upside down and sucked dry by a vegetable spider made him shudder.

On crisscrossing trails, they worked their way down from the rocky scarp, a jumble of brown and tan stones and small green places with lichens and low scrub bushes, onto the rolling hills below. They found these hills a patchwork of grass, knobs, and woody lowlands, crossed by rivulets and dotted with small algae-choked bogs and ponds. The trail, what there was of it, was a tight animal track with no evidence of recent passage by men or beasts. In places, they were able to walk for a hundred meters or more along high ridges, in relative safety through bright green, shin-high "grass." In other places, they had to carve their way through the heavy vegetation, guarding against attack from all directions.

Lonin led them onward, pausing occasionally to look about, as if listening for a sound that Paul could not hear, and then suddenly plunging on ahead. He stopped here and there to point out an interesting plant or massive insect hive they had not seen, but then he pushed on, seeking a place he seemed to know but had not been to in a long time.

Through one grove, they came upon a creek of clear water flowing noisily over trunk-sized boulders. Lonin paused and stooped low to refill his two water skins from the flowing stream. "Shik. We cross this creek here, before it gets too wide. It is the Shillin Caparin, and we will follow it to its end."

"How far, Lonin?" Shawn wiped sweat from his brow and watched the water pass below his feet.

"Not far. Less than one-half kikkin. Two of your human kilometers. The trail will be easier." He glanced about, searching for and finding the sun. "We will make it back to your village before dark, but we must move quickly. Do you need rest? Do you have water and food?"

Shawn said, "I have some dried fruit and crackers, but we had better filter some water."

Paul had fruit and crackers as well, since they had not stopped to eat. During field missions, he had gone days without food and had lived on a minimum of water. "Yes, I should refill my water skins as well."

He and Shawn stooped and used the portable water filter Shawn had brought to process three liters of water into their skins. They had received vaccinations against the numerous bacteria, viruses, and parasites found in Timmistria's waters, but there was no reason to take chances. As they worked, Lonin watched the stream intently for dangers, blades at the ready.

They found a narrow place in the creek where large stones rose up at regular intervals across the stream to form a series of elevated stepping-stones 15 feet above the water level. The upright rocks separated the stream into a series of parallel rivulets. Lonin was able to step across the fissures from stone to stone, but the men had to jump. It was not particularly difficult or daring, but the stones were wet and coated with green slime and lichens. And to fall between them meant a long drop into the dark water, which was perhaps very deep, or perhaps dangerously shallow, and perhaps inhabited by unknown living dangers. Shawn and Paul judged their leaps carefully.

As Lonin had predicted, the trail downstream was easier travel: wider, flatter, and more worn by the passage of animals. Being on an animal trail meant that animal encounters would be more probable, and they didn't lessen their alertness. At one point, another smaller side trail joined them from the right. In the soft earth were clearly visible large humanlike shoe prints pointing downstream. Lonin paused briefly to examine them.

"Delerin. They went there, the way we go to the stream's end. Two or three days ago. They will be no danger. We are nearly there."

Shawn said, "Well, let's go."

They carried onward, and Paul found himself enjoying the heightened sense of awareness that jungle work always brought him. In these woods, there were no troops from a rebellious regional militia — or worse, Thinkers in mechanized battle suits — but the natural dangers were as severe as any he'd ever encountered, and their weapons were primitive. They came to a place where the stream was much larger and louder. Here the trail veered to the right, rising higher, away from the creek. Lonin stopped.

"Come, gentlemen. We have arrived."

Within 50 meters, the trail changed dramatically, becoming a rocky ridge, worn smooth and slick from eons of rain and wind.

"Step carefully."

As they climbed above the green forest, the place Lonin had sought was clearly visible ahead: a large rock promontory, pushed up from the green forest below like the cone of a tremendous termite mound. The trail soon rose above the green brush, and they scrambled across bare stone toward the summit. They were now completely exposed and out in the open, and Paul instinctively glanced overhead for the dark shapes of the giant flyers.

They scaled several meters of rough limestone rising at about a 45-degree angle. A slip here meant a painful roll into the brush below, as there were no flat places to break a fall. Then they abruptly came up against a granite-like wall, which rose above them and curved out of sight into the pale blue sky.

Lonin began circling the rising stone, looking for a trail that would lead them to the top. They came upon it soon, a crack or vein in the massive stone about two shoulder widths across, leading upward and into the rock at a skewed angle. Lonin paused again before beginning the climb.

"Careful here, my friends. This climb is not easy for Timmon and will be less easy for you. No humans have been brought to this place, and it is not likely that more will come here soon. Are you willing to try?"

With gleaming eyes, Shawn said, "Of course, Lonin. We didn't hike all this way to miss the view. Lead on."

Paul nodded. "I'm ready."

The crevice was a deep cleft in the solid rock, as if the massive stone had been dropped and cracked before being set in its forested resting place. The climb was difficult, sometimes perilous. They moved steadily but not slowly, mindful that the daylight hours were waning. They still had the downward climb and hours of hard hiking back to Fairdawn. Paul's body began to complain about the strenuous exercise, reminding him that he had not worked so hard in many months. They soon pulled themselves from the crevice onto the gently rounded dome of the summit. It was a perfectly egg-smooth platform.

A great place to be plucked from, Paul thought, but the only dark shapes he could see were very high and far to the north.

Having found no airborne dangers, he allowed himself to relax enough to take in the view, which was well worth the hike and climb. It was simply one of the greatest panoramic scenes he had ever encountered.

The rock they stood on fell away on all sides into the damp forest. From this vantage point, they were able to look down on the tops of the trees, constructed in layers of shades of green, colors that Paul struggled to name; kelly, evergreen, jade, lemon-lime, emerald. Insects and birds flew below them, over patches of white, yellow, orange, and red flowers that dusted the tops of the tree boughs.

To the south, the creek tumbled over one last stairstep of large boulders before flowing out into a wide delta. It was joined by another stream, and together the rivers meandered through a grassy bog into the narrow lake the explorers had seen earlier. The wind kicked the lake into white-capped waves, which caught and reflected yellow sunlight. The absence of sailing vessels, large powerboats, and commercial ships seemed very odd. In fact, there were no boats at all, not even a small canoe or fishing boat. Paul imagined the water's depths inhabited by plesiosaur-like monsters, giant coral polyps, or gargantuan fish that would drag down a small boat and its sailors, the stuff of preteen storybooks.

Farther out from the rock, the multi-green forest gave way to the low rolling hills they'd crossed, peppered with small woods, glades, and ponds. Even from this distance, Paul could make out the dark shapes of herbivores wading through the grass, some huge, slow and cowlike, some sweeping like antelope through the grass in leaping herds of 50 or more. Paul imagined doglike pack animals and large predators creeping through the tall brush, picking off the weak and less fleet of foot.

Beyond the grassy slopes rose the rockier and steeper hills, and the canyon walls beyond them, a curtain of browns, tans, and yellow veins splotched with green, rising to the jagged line of the canyon's rim. Above this broken and cracked wall, the pale yellow sky rose for perhaps 30 degrees on the east and west before giving way to the bluish-green sky directly above. The sky was a near identical analog to the southerly lake — the same color and the same absence of man-made craft.

Lonin stood on the rock, feet spread, large arms folded across his chest, looking at nothing in particular. He was a statue, carved from the same smooth stone. "It has been several seasons since I stood here. I hope it will be fewer before I come again."

Shawn asked, "Lonin, where does the lake go from here?"

"Shik. Shill Wellin goes estin — 'south,' you would say — for many kikkin. The Shill Sarin becomes a river at the far end of the valley. It crosses the dry lands and flows into the sea about nearly a … thousand kikkin from here."

"Wow. Have you explored those lands?"

Lonin paused. "The lands belong to the Delerin and are wild and dangerous. They are rarely traveled by the Timmon. Too many who have sought these lands did not return. Those who find them have hard stories to tell."

Shawn turned his gaze from the lake to Lonin. "Hmm. You answered a question, but not the one I asked."

Lonin flashed his yellow teeth. "I learn much from my human friends. When I was young, I traveled. I have seen some of those lands."

"Any places as beautiful as these?"

"There is beauty there, to the Timmon eye. Do humans see beauty the same as Timmon?"

"Ha. Good point. So this valley is within Delerin land. Would they be angered if they knew you brought us here?"

Again, Lonin paused. The sounds of low bellowing and birds chirping came to them on the wind. "Perhaps."

Paul said, "This is a wonderful place, Lonin. I thank you for bringing us here. I have never been in a place so natural and untouched by men. I keep wishing for a flying machine so I could view these wide lands from the air. But Timmistria is probably better off that we don't have one."

Shawn and Lonin exchanged looks, and Shawn said, "We have something to show you, back at the shop."

"Shik, lin. One day we may spend a night in Shill Wellin. The sky is filled with odd lights and falling stars. But it is also dark and dangerous, and we are not prepared this day. We need to begin our travels back. Night comes, and even the Delerin seek shelter when the sun sets on this place."

It was difficult leaving the brilliant monument, especially knowing it might be years before they ever returned — if they ever did. The climb down the rock was more treacherous than the climb up, as they had to find blind footholds and handholds while lowering themselves into the deeper shadows. The sun was racing for the horizon when they returned up the trail that led back north along the creek. Lonin stopped them with a hand gesture and stared into the jungle ahead, his eyes squinting. Paul prepared himself for the attack of another crellil-like creature, but Lonin's warning words defined a higher level of threat.

"Delerin. They wait where the trails come together."

Shawn asked, "Is there another way out of the valley?"

"Yes, but the way would be longer, and the night would catch us." He turned a hard face back to Paul.

"When we meet them, put away your ratan-i and let me talk. They have no quarrel with us, and they must let us pass."

With that, he pressed forward with more urgency, and the two men hastened to keep up. They had cleared the trail earlier and were able to travel quickly, arriving where the trails met in half the time of their previous passage. And that was where the Delerin had chosen to meet them, four native rangers in tan field clothing, all mature males nearly Lonin's height and bulk, blades sheathed but loose in their scabbards. Their faces were leaner and more angular than those of the Timmon, and their hair longer and wirier.

Lonin gestured for Shawn and Paul to wait well back, and he strode forward to the group. Paul begrudgingly holstered his blade, and Shawn followed.

The ensuing discussion was limited to Lonin and one of the Delerin, apparently the leader. Nothing but his speaking role set him apart from the others; he had no insignia, particular manner or dress, or any kind of talisman. Perhaps the natives' abilities to envision the physical world at a telepathic level made outward signs of rank unnecessary.

The conversation went on for some time, a combination of voiced words, hisses, and croaks, interspersed by the imperative word "shik," which was more of a hissed syllable, meaning something like "Attention, important words to follow." The timbre of their voices changed little from start to finish, but small shifts in posture made Paul feel the heat was rising. All the while, the Delerin speaker gestured regularly in Shawn and Paul's direction.

As they talked, the sun continued to speed toward the horizon. There was little chance they would make it back to Fairdawn before complete darkness gripped the forest. Shawn and Paul exchanged glances, and the younger man's deep sigh confirmed his concern.

The discussion ended abruptly, and Lonin returned to them. The Delerin pulled blades and disappeared into the brush, silently and with no sign that they'd been there, except perhaps more footprints in the soft dirt.

"Friends, we must choose now. Night will fall upon our backs. Our choices are to find shelter and wait for light, or to travel and seek the shelter of your kithin."

Shawn asked, "Which would you recommend?"

Lonin paused before answering. "There is danger in either way. Were I alone, I would run and trust Timmistria to guide my way. But you are not fast."

The two exchanged glances again. Shawn seemed a little stricken by the way the incredible journey was turning out.

Paul said, "I vote we go. I'd rather face whatever's ahead while on my feet and moving than holed up in a trap."

Shawn nodded, his face knotting in resignation. "Let's go."

Lonin took the lead and set a brisk pace, with Shawn behind him and Paul guarding the rear. The sun dipped below the far western edge of the valley, and immediately a chilling fog sprang from the grass and threatened to blind them. Jumping the large boulders over the creek narrows was doubly treacherous in the dusky light, the gaps between the huge stones now bottomless shadows. Past the crossing, Lonin took them on a different trail up the side of the canyon, avoiding the large spider vines but forcing them to slow their speed to clear unbroken trail.

Farther on, a pack of pale-haired hog-like raree blocked the trail and challenged them, growling and screeching. Their musky odor hung in the thickening fog. Lonin paused to allow Shawn and Paul to move up close behind him, and then he charged at the beasts, snarling and clashing his blades together. Their fangs glinted in the failing light, but they parted into the brush and let the intruders pass, with Paul running backward for a dozen steps to ensure the raree didn't follow and attack them from the back.

At the top of the valley rim, they climbed 20 meters through tumbled boulders and over the final bluff. The fog had not reached this high in the valley, and the way was less dangerous than the observation stone, but they were forced to holster their blades and climb with both hands. The pale pink light failed just as Lonin pulled the men over the edge and onto the rocky spoils that led away into a wall of lightless forest.

They skirted the outer edge of the woods until Lonin found a trail that had been recently cleared. Stepping into the thick brush and canopy of trees was akin to walking into a cavern. Paul judged that the trail they were on angled north toward the main trail they'd followed outbound. A half kilometer in from the trail junction, they came upon Kearnin and Lonin's cousin, Kinin, who were waiting for them. Lonin seemed unsurprised by their presence.

The way onward became an intense, sweaty endurance test, ten kilometers through rugged trails, with Kearnin and Kinin setting a torrid pace. Shawn and Paul tried to keep up and yet remain mindful of the darkening forest. Lonin followed the humans, and it was reassuring to have him back there.

For the first time in months, Paul felt like himself. Pausing to hack at a catcher vine and dodging a large inky bat that lunged out from the shadows in the filtered moonlight, he imagined them all as ancient tribal hunters, moving through the wild forest with grace and efficiency, the safety of their camp leagues away through hostile territory. Sooner than he expected, and disappointingly so, they reached the first outlying signs of the settlement.

If they'd been tribesmen, home at last from a long hunt, there would have been friends and family waiting for them to return, to hear their tales and enjoy the fresh game they brought. But he was an outsider in this tribe. The one who would have waited for him was gone forever.

Chapter 17

"There are lessons in even the smallest thing."
— Timmon proverb

The shed sat neglected in the brush, out away from the stored farm equipment. Paul had never been to this part of the colony, an undeveloped area a quarter kilometer from the village square.

The wood siding was faded to gray, now only partially shingled with dragon skin. The virulent native vines and brush had enveloped and devoured it. Shawn and Lonin hacked at the brush as they stepped over and through, but they avoided clearing a visible path. Shawn told Paul during the hike that not many knew about the small two-person flyer, and the council had agreed it was best to keep it that way. Resources were very thin in the community; they couldn't spare anyone to work on the flying machine, and they didn't want anyone unauthorized and unskilled damaging it.

Why they felt Paul was the right person was a mystery to him, but he didn't mind the challenge. It was another way to pass the time and keep his mind occupied. Otherwise, he'd end up thinking about Cara and her penetrating gaze, and all those obvious similarities to Helwin. Images of her face had begun to haunt him at night.

Shawn had trouble with the lock but was able to pull it open after some intense fiddling. He lifted it from the rusted steel loop holding the door in place, and then he and Lonin hacked at the sun-colored weeds until they were able to wrestle the door open enough to allow them all to enter. Shawn stepped through, and Lonin signaled for Paul to follow.

Inside, dim light leaked in through cracks in the walls. Shawn, braving poisonous insects and reptiles, felt his way along the wall to his right, finding what appeared to be shutters. He struggled with the latch and eventually swung the wooden doors open. The early morning sunlight seemed to ooze into the ageless gloom of the shed, driving the building's small denizens to the refuge of the shadows. The light illuminated a tall metal rack with weathered glass lab equipment, a stack of old wooden stakes and boards, several rotten wooden buckets, and the item they had come to see — the nodular shape wrapped tightly in a black shroud of heavy-duty shrink-wrap.

Shawn pulled a hand brush from his backpack, carefully dusted the top and sides of the wrapped machine, and then returned the brush to his pack. Paul worked his way over and helped him cut away the plastic chrysalis. The flyer was very close to what Paul had imagined when they'd described it to him the evening before: an open-cockpit, two-person helio, with a fuselage that looked like a stretched bathtub. It was painted white, with two single-file synth-leather seats and a small rear-mounted rotary engine. It looked untouched by time, no doubt sealed with a micro-polymer protectant film, similar to military issue. Paul started to ask about the rotor shaft and blades, but then he noticed a long black-wrapped crate lying against the far wall of the shed.

Shawn said, "Early on, we decided to leave it wrapped up until we had time to set it up properly, and then we delayed until one of the mechanics we were promised made the jump over, and then no one came. That was four years ago." He looked over the machine as if it were a family heirloom or a vintage automobile, lying neglected in the corner of an abandoned garage. "Do you think it can still fly?"

Paul wasn't a mechanic. His training required a basic knowledge of most things mechanical, but most of it was in building materials, munitions, and larger flying craft. With the exception of one desert campaign, he'd never piloted anything smaller than a 12-man lander. But this flyer had been packaged for long-term storage, and the early settlers had had the good sense not to penetrate the oxygen and water barriers.

"It'll fly."

"Can you fly it?"

Paul nodded.

"Sparkin'! How do we get started?" The young man lost his restraint and began prancing about the machine, waving his short blade.

"Shawn! Easy! We need to have a plan before we unpack it any further."

Shawn deflated a little. "A plan?"

"I said it would fly. I didn't say it would fly today. Or even this week."

Lonin's dense voice rolled from where he stood near the shed door. "Shik. This machine is important. It is a thing of wonder and will help my people see the good you humans can bring. Now that we are close to seeing it fly, we should not waste this … opp-ortunity. The time for care is upon us."

Shawn sheathed his blade. "So how do we start?"

"With the manuals."

Shawn nodded but didn't move.

"They're back in the village, aren't they?" Paul asked.

"Yes. In the vault." Shawn stood with arms crossed, rocking on his heels. "I don't suppose we could have a closer look at this thing before we head back?"

Paul smiled. "Be careful with the coating."

They peeled the remainder of the outer wrapping from the fuselage and blades, and then removed the packing that filled the two small seating pods. Shawn was fascinated by the controls, gauges, and instrument panel, and he could hardly refrain from flipping the power switch. Here was sophistication and elegance missing from the small military flyers Paul had operated. More attention was paid to design and decoration. The downside was inferior robustness compared to a military-specification unit. Once the protectant seal was compromised, Timmistria's harsh environment would take a toll.

Shawn and Paul stood back and admired the smooth, lazy curves of the flyer's fuselage and the expanse of the cockpit. Lonin stepped forward to examine the forward cockpit and control panel. Satisfied, he next looked at the small seat of the passenger compartment, a tight fit for even the humans. His shoulders slumped and he frowned pathetically as he gazed down into the tiny space. The men laughed, chuckling at first, then rocking until tears fell. Lonin's surprise at their humor made his discouragement all the funnier.

They spent the next two days reading the manuals, pacing around the untouched flyer drinking kava, and deciding how to proceed, with breaks to take care of other village business. The pipe work required little of their time. James, possessed by the spirit of scientific research, pursued the perfect pipe formulation relentlessly in his position as foreman. Likewise, Chrisof focused on improving the waste system, relieving Shawn and Paul of that duty. Chrisof's renewed and self-destructive abandon prompted Cara to threaten him with detention unless he took time off to sleep, eat, and especially bathe. Paul was not disappointed to leave those two problem areas to other people now that the immediate emergencies had been addressed.

The flyer was a new challenge, not critical to their survival in the short term but important to Fairdawn's relationship with the Timmon. This wasn't a project to jump into headfirst like the other problems, where trial and error was an efficient method. Here, the error part could mean destruction of the craft and death for its occupants. It therefore required a methodical, careful approach. Paul had to curb his own natural drive, but the slow progress was killing Shawn, who paced about the shed like a caged animal. Lonin remained ever patient. To Paul's surprise, he showed up every morning, as if he had infinite time to spend there in that dark shed just to make this "opp-ortunity" happen.

Fairdawn fell into the annual routine of preparations for the harvest and the dragon migration. The next transit arrival was delayed by six weeks, so there was little to do in that area. The break between the recent emergencies and the busy harvest allowed Shawn and Paul to spend days working on the flyer. Some of the work was mentally challenging, such as developing methods to perform the precise measurement of machine tolerances or balancing the rotors without the necessary tools. Other tasks were not strenuous but tedious, such as days spent buffing the protective coating from the engine compartment, fuselage, and rotor blades. During these slow periods, Lonin was reliable and indispensable. He used the time to ask Shawn and Paul myriad questions about their worlds and travels.

On such a day, Paul and Lonin had disassembled the flyer's fuel-injection system and were scrubbing the parts with an oil distillate, using some of the village's store of toothbrushes. Shawn had gone to Fairdawn to attend a planning meeting and to help Cara with some scheduling tasks. Lonin's questions turned to places, people, and machines. And, oddly, physics.

To one question, Paul found himself answering, "Men can't live on very large planets, because the gravity is too high and would crush us. Our bodies are intended for conditions on Old Earth. Stronger gravity weighs on our tissues and reduces a person's life-span."

Lonin's huge hands seemed too large for handling small parts, but the size was more than compensated for by the two thumbs that opposed each other, his multi-jointed smallest finger, and his forefinger's ability to extend into a tapered point, like a cat's claw. If the ability to grasp and manipulate tools was a main driver in the development of a race's intelligence, then the Timmon should all have been Einsteins or Zeelands. Perhaps they were.

Lonin said, "Our people say that Timmistria holds her world to the sun, Semeril Terl, by a strand of her hair, and that Dreyaten is held in her grasp by the threads of a millil worm. Many threads — tayin."

"Tayin? How many is that in Galactic Standard numbers?"

"I believe it would be called 'thousand.'"

Paul nodded. "So many words to learn with a new language."

"You seek to learn our language. I am … pleased."

"When I've traveled, I've always tried to learn local languages. I'm not good at it. Most worlds have many, and I could never attempt common phrases in more than one or two. It's rare for a race of people to have only a few. And I've never seen a world other than Timmistria where there is only one language."

Lonin scrubbed intently at a fuel jet. His questions shifted between subjects, as they often did when they talked.

"This thing, gravity. Where does it come from? Does it do other things?"

"Gravity is a basic force in nature. Where does it come from? If I were a physicist, I could answer that properly. There are other forces, electromagnetism and others. Men have worked for hundreds of years to figure out why these forces exist and how they are related. We'll be working on those questions for hundreds more, I suspect."

"What does gravity do to things?"

"Things?"

"Rock. Fire. Water. Air."

Paul paused. "For rock — gravity crushes it and shapes it round, into a spherical shape, like Timmistria, or like my home world, Crest. On heavy planets, mountains do not grow. But there are very few rocky planets much larger than Old Earth or Timmistria. Most are gas giants, huge balls of hydrogen and helium, like the large blue planets that circle your star. You have names for them? The bright blue stars that change their places in the sky?"

Lonin stopped and pondered again. "You mean Talarin and Melerin."

"Yes. Gas giants. Similar to Spectrus and Oculus in my home system. There's life on those planets, but it's very different from ours. The gas giants I know all have their own smaller satellites — moons — and nearly all of those hold life. Some are similar to us — to humans and Timmon, I mean."

Lonin said, "And some are different, like the cremin and jarin."

Paul remembered the multi-celled bacteria that floated in filamentous colonies in the dense methane clouds above Oculus' fluid interior. He said, "No. I count the cremin and jarin, and the crellil and penderin, as life like us. We're all ... built of carbon ... solid in form, with limbs and internal organs. Some life is ... very strange. So different that it couldn't live on Timmistria. Only in the places where it's found."

Lonin nodded, selecting another part from the table. "Will I be able to ride in the flyer?"

A painful memory came to Paul then, of Helwin sitting in the cockpit of an LH-7 hopper for the first time, intimidated by the controls, her hands — which had wielded laser-sticks, repaired ansible boards, and operated pin-rocket guidance drones — suddenly paralyzed by indecision.

She'd said, "OK, Paul. Run through the start sequence again." And then when he'd run through it for the fifth time, shaking her head, "I'm never going to get this."

In his mind now, her face was replaced by Cara Harvestmoon's, and Hel's blond, cropped bob by Cara's dark auburn shag.

Lonin was watching him, as if whatever light or aura he'd seen during their battle had risen to the surface again. Paul swallowed hard to ease the tightness in his throat.

"Yes. You won't just ride. I'll teach you to fly it." He returned the gaze. After a strained moment, in which he felt as if Lonin were trying to see through him, he laid the throttle body he was scrubbing in its place on the parts board, set the brush aside, and wiped his hands on the rag hanging from his belt. "Come on."

The controls of the flyer were not as robust or simplified as those of an LH-7, but the functions were nearly identical. Paul was back up to speed on the operation after studying the manuals and could have flown the craft immediately. But he had doubts about fitting Lonin into the small cockpit.

"This screen shows all the engine information, just like this one showed the speed and direction. Once we power up, this screen will show engine RPM — revolutions per minute —" Paul spun his finger in a small circle. "Temperature, fuel level. There are alarms for all of those, but you need to check them regularly anytime you're airborne."

"Air born? Is flying like birth?"

Paul thought a moment, surprised by his own choice of words. "Maybe, if you are a butterfly leaving a cocoon. This touch pad controls speed, this one the altitude — how high you are — and this one is the steering. The flyer will take care of adjusting the craft's angle of attack and bank angle."

Paul illustrated these by tilting his flat hand up and down, then side to side. Lonin listened intently and nodded throughout Paul's instruction. Paul expected him to understand very little, but as with most technical issues, the Timmon understood more than he let on.

"This flyer has no wings like a perin, and no rockets like a lander. You say these blades will spin above our heads, pushing air down and lifting the machine."

"Yes."

"The blades are thin. They are strong enough to lift the machine with two humans?"

"Yes. They always design a safety margin into machines like this. The rotor is several times stronger than it must be to lift a full craft. Even so, the controls will tell us if we're too heavy to fly."

Lonin walked around the fuselage, looking in at the controls, then leaning back to take in the whole. But his thoughts did not follow his eyes.

"Why would humans need more than one language? What is the purpose?"

It took Paul a moment to shift gears and catch up. It was as if there were three or four different brains in Lonin's head, simultaneously processing different parts of the conversation. Was this like the swordplay? A way to draw him out?

"I'm not sure there's a purpose. Humans are never satisfied with anything. We always have to change things, try to make them better or just different. There's a religious legend about why there are many languages."

"A ... religious legend?"

"Yes, the Tower of Babel. A group of people decided they wanted to climb to Heaven, the ... kithin of their god. So they tried to build a tower tall enough to reach it. But their god was angry. He cast a spell that made them all speak different languages. Since they could no longer understand each other, they couldn't communicate to build the tower. The legend says that's why men have so many languages and understand each other so poorly. Maybe that's what it would be like if you and your people couldn't all see the same thing when you build."

Lonin paused for an instant to look at Paul, his face unreadable. "The Timmistrians would not try to reach Timmistria's home."

"Perhaps that's why you only need one language." He chuckled, but Lonin didn't get the joke. "Nor would most humans. But we have a history of being very superstitious. When we don't understand things about ourselves or our world, we make up stories and legends to explain them."

Lonin's face grew darker. "You believe Timmistria is a legend."

Paul felt a mental punch to the gut. He was tripping over his own stupidity. "No. Timmistria is very real for you and your people. I'm not a religious man, and I haven't thought much about it."

Lonin nodded. "I now understand why humans have many languages."

The Timmon walked away without further comment and returned to the parts table, leaving Paul standing alone. He selected another fuel jet and began scrubbing. Paul quietly joined him. Lonin's hands cradled the flyer part as if it were a jewel in a ring setting and he a jeweler checking for flaws. It was a while before he spoke again.

"There are those among the Timmon and Delerin who believe the human colony is not an opp-ortunity for us, only a threat. They believe more humans will come, push the Timmistrians from our lands, and take Timmistria by war."

Paul sighed, looked over the injection socket he'd picked up, scrubbed it, set it in its place on the template, and chose another. There were only about a dozen parts left to be cleaned, and then they'd be ready to reassemble the fuel controller. "Your people are wise. That's the history of humans."

"So we should force the colonists to leave?"

"It's too late, I'm afraid. We're here. If you forced these colonists out, humans would be back with greater force and more weapons. The best your people can do now is to learn all you can and move your technology forward rapidly; learn to live with us."

Lonin fell silent again. They scrubbed parts, the sound of their brushes punctuated by the buzzing of insects and scratching of the shed's other inhabitants, which had become bolder over time. Paul touched the blade at his side holster instinctively.

"Do all peoples you meet learn to fly and travel into space?"

Paul shook his head. "No. I don't study civilizations, but from what I know, most do not. Less than half learn to fly. About one out of five launch spacecraft into orbit. Some of those races get no further than launching satellites — small vessels that circle their planets and send communications. The Co-Op has a communication satellite in orbit around Timmistria. But interstellar travel — flying the great distances between stars — has been achieved by only a rare few: humans, the Thinkers, and a few others we know of. There may be others that travel throughout the galaxy, or between galaxies, but humans haven't met them."

"Why does one people learn to fly in space and others do not?"

"That's a question for an exo-anthropologist, one who studies the growth and evolution of intelligent peoples. But technology is usually the result of conflict. People learn to kill each other more efficiently, and they advance their science in the process. Humans are always at war, with ourselves and with others. All of the spacefaring peoples are very aggressive and warlike. Or were at one time." Paul finished one part and began another. "Some have learned to avoid war. Humans have not."

"The … Thinkers … also have not learned to avoid war."

"Thinkers don't *want* to avoid war. If they find your world, they will descend upon it, make slaves of the Timmon, and drain Timmistria of its resources. Any humans would be eaten."

Lonin looked up at Paul, eyes narrowed. "What is their appearance? Do they have many languages?"

"They look like humans, only smaller, with very large heads and eyes. We named them 'Thinkers' as an insult, but the name stuck. They've learned to speak Galactic Standard. I've heard them speak their own language, but I can't tell you if they have more than one."

"You have met the Thinkers? You have fought them?"

"Yes."

Lonin eyed him intently for a moment, then relaxed his shoulders with a humanlike shrug and went back to his scrubbing. "The Timmon and Delerin learned to … avoid war many generations ago. We have lived with each other peacefully since that time. Is this why we have not learned to fly?"

"I don't know, Lonin. From what I know, there are many factors involved in a race's development of technology. It isn't just conflict that drives it. A people need time, and resources, research, and education. Timmistria is a harsh world. Your people have spent most of your time and resources just surviving. Maybe technology is a luxury that the Timmon haven't been able to afford."

Lonin's gaze found the open window, focused far away. "The Timmon have not learned to fly. We are Timmistria's children." His eyes came back to meet Paul's. "We have only one language. And we may be eaten by Thinkers."

A tiny rodent peered over the edge of the table. They both stopped and watched it climb up. It sniffed its way across the tabletop, ignoring them. Lonin hissed at it, and it cowered and glared up at him, then scurried off the table. He went back to working on the part in his hand.

"The shenifil's bite is poisonous to humans."

"Great."

"One woman almost died from an action of aller … aller…"

"An allergic reaction?"

"Shik. Yes. That is a problem for the humans."

Paul nodded. He didn't want to think about poisonous rats any more than he had to, so he changed the subject. "Shawn tells me there's an important legend about the truce between the Timmon and Delerin. I'd be interested in hearing it."

"I do not like that word — legend. Legend means a fiction, like the 'theater' that you humans like to perform."

"Sorry. I won't use the word."

"Thank you. Many generations ago, the Timmon and Delerin fought. The Delerin were many, and they gained the … do you say 'higher hand'?"

"Gained the upper hand. Yes."

"Many died on both sides. To end the dying, the leaders of the Timmon and Delerin met in a fight, one against one, to decide the winner. The Delerin leader was younger and stronger, and he killed the Timmon leader, ending the war."

"There are similar … stories in human history."

"The Delerin leader, Tironin, then acted to end all killing, saying that any who killed another, Timmon or Delerin, should take his own life. Tironin then turned his ratan on himself, signing his command in his blood. Since then, any of our people who kill another is bound to take his own life. Since that day, we do not kill each other." Lonin's eyes explored Paul's face.

Paul struggled to find the right words. "A powerful story, Lonin."

"The bodies of the two leaders lie beneath a stone marker, at a place where our borders meet."

"So this story is not just a legend. It's history."

"Shik. Lin. The two Timmistrian peoples are in this way forever bound by time, by our sacrifice, by the strength of our lights, and by one language. The Delerin also do not fly, and they may also be eaten by Thinkers."

"Well, perhaps protection from the Thinkers is the most important gift humans can give the Timmistrian peoples."

But the price may be high.

"Tell me more about Timmistria, Lonin. Not the planet, but the spiritual being."

"By the words 'spiritual being,' you mean 'legend.'"

"If I promise to keep an open mind, will you promise not to resent my lack of faith?"

"Your mind may be open, but your timeril is closed like the eye of a cayin as it feeds."

Paul quietly set down his part and brush and faced Lonin, fingers suddenly gripping the table in front of him. "How does my light appear?"

"Seldom. I saw it for the first time only at the point of my ratan."

"What color was it?"

"Blue and … what is your word? — light black?"

"Gray?"

"Maybe. Gray. The color of things burned. The color of ash."

"What does that tell you about me?"

"Timeril tell only of your ways. Also, they may show how your past has changed you."

"Why did you attack me?"

"I told you then — to punish you for hurting Cara. And to make you reveal your purpose here."

"But why? Why was that so important?"

Lonin's eyes narrowed. Paul wondered if his expressions were becoming more humanlike. "Cara, as I said."

"Cara?"

"She began to favor you. But then she visited you, and her light was wounded. I needed to learn of you. I needed to know if you are worthy." Lonin's eyes were steady on Paul's, but they held no anger.

"Would you have killed me if you'd found me 'unworthy'?"

"If your timeril had shown me evil, I would have killed you."

"The 'color of things burned' sounds evil enough. So why didn't you kill me?"

"Your timeril told me that you are deep like the ocean and that you have had a hard life, with losses and regrets. It did not speak of evil."

Paul's face felt warm. "Perhaps my light is different from yours. Perhaps what would be evil for you is not evil for me."

"No. Evil is the same among all Timmistria's peoples."

"If you'd killed me, by Timmon law, you would have then killed yourself?"

"Of course, but not by Timmon *law*. Because of the grave lessons learned in our history and to honor those who died to save our people."

"Tell me about Cara's light. Shawn hinted that she is special."

Lonin breathed deeply. "Her timeril is the color of starlight, clear and white, unlike any other. The Timmon saw her from across space as her transport approached. She is the reason the Delerin allowed the human settlers to remain. They feared her, but they feared Timmistria's wrath more if they made the humans leave. Timmistria looks upon Cara and welcomes her with open hands."

"So? She is a special woman, and a good leader, but pure as starlight? Her home world of Principia is a horrid place. I would have guessed you could see that in her timeril."

"Her light is too strong. When joy takes her, it blinds my eyes."

"You're lovers. Are you sure it's not love blinding you?"

"We are lovers no more. It was best for our people to end that. But my vision is clear. Your lack of faith in Timmistria does not bother me. But be careful in your faith in Cara, human. I may find you unworthy yet."

"Would you kill me then?"

"If you harm Cara, I will kill you."

Lonin's eyes still harbored no anger, but Paul also had little doubt that his words were honest.

"I wouldn't intentionally hurt her, or anyone else." Paul picked up his part and brush and began scrubbing. "But I always seem to hurt people anyway."

"Your timeril disagrees."

They worked from then on in silence, not looking at each other. In short order, they finished the last of the parts.

"We will now assemble this … controller?"

"No. I think I've had enough for today. I want Shawn to be here for that anyway, so he will learn how it must be done. I'm ready for something more strenuous. How about we start looking for a place for the landing pad?"

Any landing pad needed to be flat and open for at least three times the width of the helio's rotor blades. They needed a place similar to the transit lander pad but not so far from Fairdawn. After several hours of searching, they realized all the flat terrain near the village had been utilized, and the lander pad proved to be the best option, although it would require them to cart fuel a long way. They'd also need a hangar and a wheeled buggy to move the flyer more easily.

Lonin and Paul spent the remainder of the afternoon marking the location the hangar and then hauling materials for it. Paul's mind mercilessly replayed the last days with Helwin over and over. By the end of the day, he imagined he could see his own light, and it was the color of darkness.

Chapter 18

The air was thick with humidity, like wading through ocean surf. The hunting party worked their way forward through the trees. An acrid odor pervaded the mist, giving Paul a sense of loathing.

He stretched his senses out in the way of the Sikur, silently pushing the envelope of his awareness outward, trying to pinpoint and identify all that moved or stirred or breathed in the space around him. It was a skill he'd spent long hours developing in brutally dull training on Sikirit 5, a steaming forest planet, well out on the galactic arm. He hadn't practiced recently, but the skill returned soon enough, and he was able to locate each Timmon in the party. Lonin was several yards to his right and just forward. He moved steadily and extremely quietly, making it very hard for Paul to detect him. The other Timmon were stealthy and hard to locate as well.

This was an elite, seasoned hunting party, and among the villagers, only Paul had been invited. He'd been told his presence was a first. And he had no doubt that Lonin had everything to do with the invitation. Even the friendlier Timmon had opened their world only grudgingly to the humans, and the hunting ways were still closely guarded secrets. While working on the flyer, Paul had questioned Lonin about why he didn't want Kearnin creating a model of the area. Lonin finally admitted that, although he trusted Cara, Shawn, Paul, and others among the colonists, he didn't trust them all. He didn't want to create tools that could be used against the Timmon by others who might come.

The stifling odor was a reminder that the party didn't seek food. The stench came from the cremin that had begun their late-season march from summer feeding grounds to wintering locations. This section of the forest was directly in their main migratory route through Timmon lands, skirting the human-occupied area.

The purpose of this party was twofold: locate the cremin on the leading edge and try to divert any that were approaching a Timmon or human village. The hulking beasts were incredibly destructive, leaving behind a trail of defecation and acidic, slimy mucus that killed vegetation and fouled water supplies. The Timmon killed a limited number of the creatures for their useful by-products, but these hunts were not without risk. The corpse would draw countless biting flies that could spread diseases from the rotting flesh. The meat was infused with the same acidic poisons as the mucus, and therefore inedible to men and Timmon, but would attract a host of dangerous large carrion eaters. In fact, the Timmon traditionally described an unwanted guest or event as being "as unwelcome as a dead cremin on the land."

Small creatures burst through the group of hunters, flashing through the undergrowth. The creatures ran by so quickly that Paul couldn't get a good look at any of them, seeing only tan-scaled skin and sensing things both mammalian and reptilian, like much of the wildlife on Timmistria. Had the creatures attacked him, Paul would have been hard-pressed to react fast enough, and he was unsettled at his own vulnerability. But these creatures seemed intent only on flight, fleeing that which Lonin and the others sought.

The odor intensified as the party advanced.

Ahead, the sounds of Lonin's movement ceased, and Paul stopped behind him. A grunt from Lonin brought all the others to a halt, and the party became sonically undetectable. Paul took three long, deep breaths to still the rush of his heart in his ears.

Lonin whistled twice: short, high-pitched, birdlike notes. Paul recognized it as his own pre-assigned signal, the one given to him because it was the only Timmon call he could reproduce. He whistled in response and advanced to Lonin's position. Lonin's skin tone and jungle dress blended in so well with the thick brush that Paul was nearly atop the crouching Timmon leader before he could make out his shape.

Lonin waved Paul to his side and spoke in a croaking voice, like a deep-throated bird speaking Galactic Standard.

"The small ones, screenon, flee the lizards. We go quietly not for fear of the cremin, but because of those that hunt the small ones. Be very careful now for large killers."

Paul croaked back, "The odor is strong. Are they close?"

"Not yet. It will smell very bad soon."

Paul wanted to ask him what his idea of "very bad" was, but he just nodded.

Lonin pointed to the ground near his leather-booted feet, where ant-like insects formed streaming columns that followed the same route taken by the small creatures and birds. "Even the masson do not like them."

Several grunts came from ahead of their location, followed by a loud growl of almost subsonic depth. Lonin's face darkened, and his eyes grew wide. A cremin at last? He motioned for Paul to follow, and then plunged quietly but quickly through the brush toward the sounds. Paul went after him but found it difficult to keep up with his low, loping strides. Whatever this new threat, in the space of one brief signal, the hunting party had abandoned all caution. Paul could hear the rapid movements of the others converging on the location from where the signal had come.

The undergrowth was some of the worst he had seen, with vines and roots reaching to drag him from his feet. He strained to follow Lonin's movements, where the Timmon flowed through the heavy forest. Paul moved right to cover his flank. The other Timmon were approaching from positions left and behind, and Paul was Lonin's only support to this side. He pushed himself harder through the foliage, trying to reduce the distance between them.

The low growl came again, this time loud enough to rattle his teeth, going from the same spot Paul had gauged earlier. A deafening animal scream raked the forest and raised the hair on the back of his neck. Lonin didn't falter but sprinted onward, nearly to the source with Paul just behind. The others were still lagging to Lonin's left.

Paul followed Lonin and burst through a small opening in the brush into dazzling sunlight. Lonin was five yards ahead, still running quickly. In the clearing was another Timmon, smaller than Lonin, boldly facing off against a monster from a child's storybook. Dwarfing the crellil, this beast was the size of an elephant, covered in thick fur with yellow and brown stripes. Its gigantic head was crowned with a towering mane like a giant Timmistrian lion.

It crouched as if to spring on the Timmon, who stood his ground with ratan-i drawn, hissing at the great cat. Lonin added his voice, his hiss as loud as a steam turbine, and the beast rose up on its hind legs and brandished huge padded paws. Shiny yellow claws the size of Paul's long blade glinted in the sunlight. The creature roared again. When it stamped its feet, the ground shook.

Lonin never slowed as he charged the animal. He ran ahead directly at the beast, while the other Timmon continued to hiss at it and moved to attack its far flank. It swung a massive paw as wide as a barrel lid at Lonin's head, but he darted aside, slashing. Fur flew from the place where the ratan connected, and Lonin circled left, swinging at the next paw swipe.

Paul didn't slow his own headlong flight, running to the right around the edge of the clearing, trying to avoid the beast's attention. Where could one attack such a thing? Even a poisoned arrow might have little effect on an animal of that mass. He hesitated at the beast's side, frozen for a moment. Other hunters had joined Lonin and the first Timmon, and were all weaving back and forth in front of it, trying to keep it distracted while others darted in and slashed. None were able to get close enough to do any damage. The swinging of the cat's massive paws kept the Timmon away easily.

When the beast leaned forward to strike, Paul saw an opportunity. He sprinted around the rear and ran past each of the treelike hind legs, slashing at the backs of its legs just above the foot, where the major ankle tendons should have been.

The cat bellowed and settled back on its rump, but not before sending Paul flying with the sweep of its thickly coiled cable of a tail. The blow caught him along the back of his neck and shoulders, hard enough to lift him from his feet, launching him past the Timmon who were now attacking the beast's far side. Paul gained his senses quickly enough to tuck his blade and roll twice before coming to his feet and turning for another attack.

But the great cat, now hobbled by Paul's blade work, fell back awkwardly onto its haunches, and the entire party of Timmon swooped in, ducking beneath the wild swinging of its paws. These were quickly severed, as was the tail. Then one bold Timmon youth climbed up its belly and slashed at its throat, sending a spray of bright green blood cascading out over the clearing. The end came quickly, and it lay thrashing on the ground. The Timmon fell back in a circle, avoiding the beast's death throes.

Paul walked forward, working his neck and shoulders against the pain from the tail blow. He felt a dull burn where he'd been struck. Lonin stood near the twitching carcass with a pleased look on his face. Water droplets fell from several tall trees that formed a fence around the clearing, like beads of sweat in the extreme afternoon humidity. The droplets steamed where they fell on the brown hairless skin of the animal's stomach. Paul smelled rotten meat.

Lonin, seeing Paul approach, motioned for him to come closer. "Turn around."

Paul did as he commanded and let the Timmon examine his back. Several of the Timmon standing nearby hissed, which Paul took as a bad sign. The Timmon people hissed a lot. Lonin didn't touch his back but guided him back around with a hand on his shoulder.

"Do not touch where the tail struck. You will push the hairs into your skin and onto your hands."

Lonin spoke to one of the Timmon, a female, judging from her smaller size and white hair stripes. "Tarron. You and Maggon will take Paul back to Manager Cara now. She will treat his wound. You will take him there quick and safe." Lonin spoke to her then in the Timmistrian language, probably repeating his instructions, and she nodded and left them.

"Paul, the tail hairs of the tharnon are poisonous. You will not be happy tomorrow."

Paul would find this to be an understatement. "What about that?" He pointed at the now-dead monster being gutted and quartered by several of the Timmon.

"I am pleased with it. This is our answer. We will drag the body of the tharnon along the path of the cremin. They will follow, thinking there is food. We will lead them away from our homes. This body is a great treasure. But our luck is your misery." The quiet young Timmon woman had returned, bringing with her another, who was stockier and darker of skin and hair.

Lonin said, "Tarron, go quickly. Leave now. Time will make the pain worse."

Tarron, now at Paul's side, touched his arm and nodded in the direction of Fairdawn. Maggon stepped up to join them.

Tarron said, "We go."

She was young and even quieter than Lonin in her movements, swifter and more agile. She set a rapid pace through the jungle, with Paul following as best he could and Maggon trailing him. They stopped occasionally to check his condition. And the fact was he was not doing well. The hairs from the tail irritated his skin, like a mild, itchy sunburn that soon bloomed into a tight pain that made his skin crawl. Tarron urged him to drink plenty of water when they took a break but didn't delay, pushing him to keep moving. Her entire Galactic Standard vocabulary was apparently: "We go."

In addition to the burning, Paul was also feeling weak, dizzy, and a little nauseous. Adrenaline began to kick in, but he fought the accelerated heart rate with long, slow breaths. He focused his vision on Tarron's swift figure in front of him and concentrated on putting one foot in front of the other. He had to trust her to lead him down a safe path. As the pain in his neck grew fiercer and his weakness deepened, he knew he was in no condition to fight a real threat.

They pressed on for several klicks, and Paul still took in the changes in foliage, colors, and sounds. The stench of the cremin lessened, and the air was fresher and less humid. Paul felt they were following a different route than the hunting party had taken on the way out. This way seemed flatter, more solid, and somewhat less rolling and wooded. But his head was beginning to pound, his neck and back were bruised and burning, and he had to dodge an occasional jumping creature or snarling bird. He prayed it would end soon.

And gratefully it did. The brush cleared, paths merged, and with one last backward glance, Tarron led Paul at a slightly less hectic pace through the outlying fields, past the guard post, and toward the village center. She whistled three times very loudly, and almost at once two other young Timmon females fell into step with them.

Paul hadn't known there were so many Timmon in the village. Tarron spoke rapidly in the shik-shikking Timmistrian language. The others looked over at Paul with unreadable expressions. Tarron then pointed ahead and spat out what was undoubtedly Timmistrian for "You go!" One of the others sprinted ahead at full speed, nearly 50 kilometers per hour. The other three fell back with Paul, surrounding but not touching him, apparently ready to catch him if he fell.

Paul soon found himself trudging up the three steps to the office of the human colony's only "doctor." Dr. Lee was of Old-Earth-Asian descent, as he was more than happy to remind everyone, and his amber coloration gave him a certain higher status with the Timmon. In truth, Dr. Lee was not a certified physician but a nurse's aide who had taken the role of doctor through default and necessity. The founding party's only certified doctor had succumbed to a parasite-related illness in the colony's second year, as he'd worked desperately to stop it.

By the time Paul was led into the medic room by
two white-clad human nurses, the burning on his neck
and shoulders was a searing agony. One of the ladies
motioned for him to sit on the exam table. She was a
short, dark-haired woman twice his age who was
apparently hesitant to come closer than about five feet
away. He tried to focus his mind on a pain-management
technique he'd learned in the military. It didn't help
much.

The door opened, and Cara came in, followed by
an older woman in a white frock and his two Timmon
guides. Tarron and Maggon found a place to stand against
one wall, fulfilling the command from Lonin to "stay
with Paul." Cara set a crude leather satchel on the only
desk. She turned to him then, not meeting his eyes. Paul
wondered if this was a sign of anger or concern.

"Mr. Saarinen, can you please stand and turn
around?"

Paul rose and turned slowly, holding his neck and
back straight, as any twisting made the burning worse.
Now facing away from the two women, Paul looked at a
blank off-white wall, dingy with age but otherwise very
clean. He heard no sound from Cara or the Timmon, but
the other woman hissed grimly, very Timmon-esque.

"Helen, I think we have enough of the pitch.
Please bring more of the lotion, and, uh … the deadener.
Need it now."

The door opened and closed, and he heard Cara
scrabbling with something behind him.

"Mr. Saarinen, what we have to do first is clear
the fibers from your skin's surface. Then we have to try
to draw out as much of the fiber material that's penetrated
as we can. The doctor has more experience with this than
I do, but he got called out to an accident in one of the
north fields. He's not likely to get back for a couple

hours, so you're stuck with Helen and me. I did talk to him by radio, and he asked that I look out for signs of shock. So if you feel weak or very nauseous, please let us know. I'd like to tell you this won't be painful, but the truth is it's going to hurt like hell."

"It already does. Please start."

"Very well. Try to sit on the table. We have to be careful not to touch the places you've been hit, to avoid pushing more fibers into your skin or getting infected ourselves."

She moved around behind him, working quickly, all the time keeping up a line of patter. It helped to keep him distracted. He forced himself to concentrate on a single black dot on the wall and on her voice.

"First, I'm going to spread a sticky tree pitch over the areas I can get to. This will grab the loose fibers and hold on to them so they don't penetrate further. I'll start here along your neck and ears and move downward. I'll begin dabbing lightly with a brush at the base of your neck. I'll count to three before starting, so try not to flinch.

"One. Two. Three."

Despite the warning, Paul tensed against the sensation, which felt like a red-hot blade on the back of his neck. It was his turn to hiss.

"Sorry. I can't do anything for the pain until we get this first coating of the pitch on. I'll take a break when you want me to."

"No. Please get on with it."

"Once we clean the pitch off, we can deaden the skin with a pain-killer before applying the solvent. This is a technique taught to us by the Timmon. There are many creatures on Timmistria with poisonous hairs or bristles, and this is the standard treatment. Tarron knows the technique and will make sure we do it correctly. Right, Tarron?"

"Yesss, Miss Cahda."

"After I get your neck, we'll have to cut away the rest of your shirt. Try not to shake out any loose fibers. As bad as the hairs are on the skin, they're worse in the sinuses."

Paul tried to imagine a tharnon tail-slap to the face. He shuddered.

"Tarron told me about the attack of the big cat, and your uh ... unusual fighting technique. She was impressed by your bravery, but not your wisdom. She said it was a large tharnon and that you may have saved one or more of their lives. She also said they are using the carcass to lure the cremin away. That's impressive for your first hunt."

"Unh. Don't tell her I would have run away if I'd known the danger."

"Hmm."

Paul winced as Cara dabbed at the area just above his shirt line. The door opened again, and he heard at least two people enter.

"Oh good, Helen. Please begin mixing the darden root into the oil. Make quite a bit. We're going to need it. Teresa, please get scissors, gloves, and tongs. We need to cut Mr. Saarinen's shirt and gently peel it down. We need to work quickly — the fibers are working themselves in, and we have nearly his entire back to treat."

He heard the sound of rustling and metal clinking behind him, then Cara's face appeared, her head bent over sideways, level with his. She came around and squatted in front of him, examining his eyes one at a time.

"I'm not in shock."

"No, I don't think you are. That's good. Most people would be. We don't treat many cases like this. The spined cats are very rare, thankfully, and the tharnon is the rarest and largest. We know this treatment works. It's just not pleasant. And enough of the fibers have gotten into your skin that you're going to be very sick after we're done — fever, nausea, dehydration. But you will pull through, and other incidents like this have not led to long-term side effects."

"That's good."

"Yes. Yes, it is. Now, Teresa and I are going to cut your shirt along the top and down the sides, and then slowly roll it down your back. As we roll it, I'm going to dribble some of the pitch in it to catch loose fibers. More pain for you, I'm afraid, but there's not much we can give you right now that won't weaken you further and increase your risk. Are you ready?"

"Yes."

"OK. Teresa?" Cara's face disappeared, and her voice came from behind him. "We're going to begin cutting at both shoulders now."

Cool metal slid along the top of Paul's arm at the seam line as the women methodically cut away the heavy linen shirt. Just the weight of the shirt pulling downward created an uncomfortable tug on his back, like a thousand cat claws digging into his skin. When the fabric was lifted away, it was like each little claw gouged out a sliver of flesh. Liquid fire touched his shoulder — the pitch, apparently — and slowly spread down his back where the claws had been. His skin quivered with the pain.

"I'm sorry, Mr. Saarinen." Cara's voice was soft, comforting, something to focus on.

"Please keep talking. Tell me a story. About your first year here, maybe."

He heard a deep inhaling and exhaling.

"OK. We arrived on a transport. It was early summer here. I remember being impressed by the heat and the dryness. We didn't know it was unusually dry that year. We were all so tired. The carrier was an old one, and equipment broke down routinely."

The fabric pulled away slowly, and Paul tried to ignore the sensation that his flesh was being ripped from his bones. He focused on Cara's voice, the words, and the story. He was familiar with pain, the long-term effects of pain, and had fought it head on countless times, directly, arrogantly, belligerently. Distraction was better.

"The colonist groups are always assigned an inventory of supplies — a certain amount of food, water, and gear to set them up for their first few months while they acclimate. How much you bring depends on what you can pay. We were not a wealthy group. Very few who came to Timmistria brought a lot. Our supplies were minimal even when we first set out.

"The equipment failures during the transit didn't help. There was spoilage, even in the dried stores. Some of the water was contaminated by a hydraulic leak — it was nearly a weekly event to have something ruined. Our ship, the Pleasant Princess, was sadly misnamed, I'm afraid. By the end of the voyage, we were calling her the Desperate Duchess, or worse."

The shirt was pulled from the last few inches of Paul's lower back, and the women moved around to his front, which was still fully covered.

"Mr. Saarinen, we're going to repeat the process on the front now. It looks like the welts aren't as bad, but we have to proceed even more carefully. You could breathe in any hairs that become airborne, and it would be dangerous for us too. We really don't know how effective these cloth masks are, and I think you've seen how easily the fine hairs can penetrate cloth. Helen, put one of the masks on Mr. Saarinen."

Helen pressed a round fabric filter to his nose and mouth, held in place by two strings that she tied carefully behind his neck. The mask muffled his voice a little. "So the Princess was unpleasant."

Cara, now standing where Paul could see her, was as focused as a surgeon might have been, pouring a thin amber liquid onto the top of his shoulders, where the fabric that formed the front of his useless shirt started.

"Don't turn your head. We still need to work on your face, scalp, and neck. Does your scalp hurt?"

"No."

"Good. Your hair must be protecting you. But we're going to have to cut it off. We'll never wash all the fibers out. Janks! I wasn't even thinking about your eyes. Helen, soak a couple pads in the pitch. We need to cover his eyes. Mr. Saarinen, you're probably going to lose your eyebrows as well, but we have to take all precautions."

"Paul."

"I'm sorry?"

"Call me Paul. The 'Mr. Saarinen' stuff is wearing me out."

Her eyes met his, and she blushed. She looked away quickly. "Yes, Paul. And no more talking. But one more question, first, *Paul* — do you feel any burning on your tongue, lips, or nostrils?"

"No."

"Good. Now you'll have to be quiet. I wish we could seal your face in a breathing mask."

The pain on his back was now something alive and growing, climbing up his neck to his ears. He shuddered again as a thousand tiny darts stabbed his back in waves.

"Go back to your story, please."

"OK. I'll talk, but now you really need to keep quiet. We'll work quickly on your head and neck. I'm sorry for all this. I've helped in treating the Timmon a couple times, but I'm having to improvise somewhat."

"Sorry for the inconvenience."

Her mouth dropped open a little, until his chuckling told her he was teasing. Her face flushed further, and she caught herself trying to brush a lock of hair from her eyes. Intensity became her.

Cara and the lady she called Teresa worked steadily and methodically over Paul's neck, chest, and back. They trimmed his hair and dabbed his head in the pitch. The musky odor of the stuff added to his nausea, and he fought off vomiting.

As Cara had warned, the burning pain continued to blossom, and Paul found himself gritting his teeth against it, focusing on her voice. She spoke evenly, nearly without emotion, as if talking about someone else. He regretted asking her about the first year, but he found himself too fascinated to change the subject.

"Where was I? Oh, Helen, is the pain deadener ready? Good. As we finish an area, start dabbing it lightly over the cleared skin. Yes, use that lightest brush and put it on very thinly. We want some of the pain to go away, but we don't want it to soak through the skin and knock Mr. Saarinen — Paul — unconscious. Thanks. Yes, the first year. Stores were very low on the Princess when she arrived. The colony here was having a difficult time as well. They had been counting on additional foodstuffs, water-processing equipment, and experienced technicians who would be able to contribute immediately. What they got was a small group of tired, desperate people with few skills and fewer provisions.

"The ship's crew was entitled to all the provisions they needed to make a return voyage. By all rights, Captain Royal could have commandeered everything, including additional supplies from the colony. And with the weapons the ship's crew carried, they could have taken whatever they wanted by force. Thankfully, the captain was an honorable man and spent a few days locating the closest port of call. He even arranged for a supply ship to meet them at their jump-in point so they could take a minimum of supplies with them. Even so, there was very little left behind, and I remember the desperate and disappointed looks on the colonists' faces as the ship lifted off.

"There was help from the Timmon, thanks mostly to Lonin. The colony was not generally popular with our hosts, who had their own problems then. Times were hard, the weather was dry, and food was hard to grow and find. The colony wasn't understood. Many of the Timmon couldn't see a reason for us to be here, especially using their resources. They couldn't see the potential for trade. And … hold it, Teresa. We need to get that spot again. I can see fibers still sticking out there. Umm, opening their world to the greater universe was a concept so strange to them. We still struggle with that. Timmistria is a harsh and dangerous planet, and those who explore it often don't return. So exploring the sky, traveling away from Timmistria and her protection, seemed insane to them. More there, Teresa. Thank you. At best, this colony was folly, and at worst, we were a serious drain on their resources.

"How are you, Paul?"

Cara had stopped working, removed the cloth pads from his eyes, and was now bent over examining his eyes and face. Her features were foggy, and he wondered if she was feeling unwell.

"Fine."

"No, I don't think you are. Helen, I need the lotus brew now. Give me the larger cup. There, thanks. Paul, I need you to drink this, as much as you can right now. This is to fight the fever. No, don't move, I'll hold it for you."

The warm liquid was bitter but somewhat soothing. His throat was tight, and swallowing was difficult.

"Stay with me, Paul. We're nearly done, but we need to finish on your shoulder and back. Then we can let you rest, OK?"

"Sure."

"Let's hurry, Teresa. Forget the darden oil for now. Let's get the last fibers and clear his skin. Good. Good. That spot, too. Mr. Saarinen? Paul? You still with us?"

The room was very cold, and Paul could feel his muscles twitch in tiny shivers. One good thing, the cold was extinguishing the fire on his back. His mouth was feeling a little dry and numb, though.

"Sure. So where did you and Shawn build your camp?"

"I'm sorry, I couldn't understand you. Save your strength, Paul. Just a little more to go, one more spot on your shoulder. Good. Teresa, I think that's it. Helen, can you hand the towels over? We'll wipe the rest of the pitch off."

Paul was disappointed. He wanted to hear more of the story of Cara and Shawn and the settlers. Did they ever fight any of those big cat things?

"Paul, can I get you to drink more of this broth? His skin's on fire, Helen. Please go get a hospital room ready. We'll need blankets and water, of course, as cool as we can get. And send the guys in here with the litter.

Teresa, I think that's as good as we can do with the fibers. Thanks. Paul? Paul? Please drink, honey, the last of this glass."

The warm liquid was nice. He would have liked to try it again when his throat would swallow. Some of it ran down his chin, and someone patted it dry with a cloth. He was hot. What he really wanted was a cold beer. Helwin always liked a beer. Did Cara like beer? He tried to ask her, but she had slipped behind a cloud, and he could barely make out if the pretty woman holding his shoulders was Cara or not. He remembered saying something to her a long time ago that she didn't like, and he was sorry about it. After his nap, he would ask her if she wanted to have a beer sometime. Maybe she would like him again.

#

The fever was a bad one. The thermometer dot Cara had stuck on Paul's forehead had hit the 104 degrees Fahrenheit mark several times over the last 48 hours, and Cara and the three women working with her had fought it back down with cool compresses. Cara had known when she'd looked in his eyes the second time that she'd waited too long to give him the lotus brew. The reaction to the fibers had already begun, and it was just a matter of time before the fever kicked in. When it did, it kicked very hard, frightening all of them.

Paul rested peacefully now, and the thermometer showed a comforting "99 F." She was exhausted. She'd stayed up the whole time, while the other three women had spelled each other in eight-hour shifts. As the fever had ebbed, he'd become verbal. It was mostly nonsensical babbling through lips swollen by the toxins, but at times he was lucid and clear. At those times, she had asked the other women to leave the room. The things he talked about were not things to be shared. She'd felt guilty about hearing it all, but there was nothing to be done. He couldn't be left alone.

A light tap came at the door. She rose and cracked it open to reveal Shawn, shaved and dressed in clean field clothing, holding a tray of something that steamed and a glass of something that didn't. There were also three slices of what looked like fresh bread.

She slipped out and eased the door closed.

"How's he doing?"

She nodded. "He'll make it."

"Good. Now take this to the lounge and eat. Fresh chicken and vegetable soup. I picked the tubers and greens myself. Then a warm bath and bed. You're shot."

The soup's incredible aroma made her mouth water. She nibbled a slice of bread and chased it with a sip from the glass — cool fruit juice. Her stomach whined.

Between nibbles, she said, "I almost killed him, Shawn." She felt warm wetness at the corners of her eyes.

"How?"

"I waited too long to give him the fever med."

"Hey, can you hold this tray so I can have both hands free to kick your butt?"

"I deserve it."

"No, I mean to kick your butt for being too hard on yourself. Cara, you didn't nearly kill him. You saved his life. You made a minor mistake in timing while you treated him, but without you slaving over him, he would have died. Great suffering Timmistria, you're going to make a nervous mother."

"Huh?"

"If you worry so much about a guy you barely know, you'll be an obsessed hen over your children. Now here, take this tray — careful with that, it's hot — and please go eat. Get a bath. Get some rest. You're needed back at the office."

"Oh. I'll stop over there now…"

He took her shoulder in his hand, gently but firmly. "Later. Eat. Bathe. Sleep. Please. Work will wait."

She nodded toward the closed door. "What about him?"

"I'll sit with him until one of the ladies returns."

She sighed. "Yes, Father."

"Don't say that. It's creepy."

"Sorry."

She stood up on her tiptoes and kissed him on the cheek, thinking he was beginning to look like her memory of Father more and more. Then she walked off down the dimly lit hall, carrying the tray in one hand and nibbling at a piece of bread from the other.

#

Shawn watched Cara until she pushed her way out the outer door. She was far too thin, and she looked almost like a child against the door's heavy planks.

Inside the room, Paul lay quietly, motionless now that the fever had broken for good. He'd been restless, mumbling things whenever Shawn had stopped by during the last two days. He'd said some things about the Thinkers, at times sounding like he was barking commands, and random words or names — "staple," "sharp," and a woman's name, "Helwin." It was all just more to add to the mystery about this man.

Cara was falling in love with him. It was obvious from the way she tended to him in his fever. It didn't surprise Shawn, but it did concern him. She was no fool, but they both knew so little about him.

Lonin accepted him; maybe that was enough?

"You better treat my sister right, pal, or there will be hell … to … pay."

Paul's eyes opened then, slowly, like those of a jalerin, the giant crocodilian reptile that inhabited large bodies of water at the southern end of the Timmon lands.

"Morning, stranger. Or I should say, good afternoon."

Paul licked his lips, still swollen and cracked from the fever and the blood toxins from the tharnon's tail spikes.

"Here." Shawn held the small glass of water close to Paul's mouth.

He took a weak sip from the reed straw, coughed once, twice, and then spoke in a small croaking voice that Shawn could hardly hear. "How long have I been out?"

"About two days."

"That all? Feels like a week."

"How do you feel?"

"Fine." He coughed again and lifted his hand weakly for the glass. Shawn held it close, and Paul drank without coughing this time. His voice was clearer and a little stronger. "Actually, I feel like hell."

"You'll feel better. Hungry?"

"Umm … maybe." He lifted his head, glanced around the dim room, lit only by the sunlight that sneaked in around the drab linen curtain. "Head hurts. I remember people…"

"The nurses worked shifts around the clock. You were pretty bad off."

"I'm sorry I took up so much of their time."

"No sweat. It's their job."

"So who's doing my job?"

"Well, luckily, you're kind of between jobs at the moment, so there was nothing to cover. The Timmon are taking care of your camp."

"The Timmon?"

"Yes. They think that by crippling the tharnon, you prevented the deaths of several in their hunting party. You're a hero."

"Pfft."

"It's true! They even gave you a nickname. Jiltharin Bifin. Very catchy."

"What's that mean?"

"Literally, 'He Who Attacks the Tharnon from the Rear.'"

"Great. Ugh."

Shawn chuckled. "No disrespect intended. They're poking fun a bit, but they really do appreciate what you did. You're the first human ever to receive a Timmon name. You should feel honored."

Paul made a face and reached for the water glass. Shawn gave it to him. He drained it and handed it back.

"Well, I've got to get back to the field. Got to help repair a couple harvester sleds. I'll stop by the kitchen and ask them to get some food coming. Broth at first, but you should want something more solid later today."

"I don't know. Still feeling nauseous."

"I think some food will help. We need your help on some things anyway. Do you think you can just lie around all week? Just because you killed a horrible deadly monster, that doesn't give you the right to take it easy."

"Thanks for the sympathy."

"My pleasure. And that flyer is waiting. The weather is going to be best in the next few weeks, with warm air and light winds."

Paul nodded. "The fuel production is going slower than I'd hoped, too. I need to spend time on the process."

"Exactly. Well, check you later, Jiltharin Bifin!"

"Pfft."

Shawn chuckled again as he left the room, but the humor evaporated as he walked toward the kitchen. The harvest was going extremely well, and fears of starvation and disease had eased, but like their lives on Principia, it seemed they moved from one near disaster to another here. Kearnin had told him of the growing unrest of the Timmon and Delerin, and the only solution seemed to be to ship Dench off the planet and find ways to show the opportunities that the human colony could offer. Yet, Dench was one of the people they were counting on to bring commercial value to the colony.

While Cara was tied up with Paul, Shawn had received an unfavorable transmittal from the colony's sponsoring organization that available resources were becoming scarcer and that they couldn't count on continued support. The war with the Thinkers was escalating, and the military command was drafting more and more space resources into the fight. Shawn took that to mean they were essentially on their own. The sense of isolation was familiar, but that didn't make it any more comforting.

Welcome to Timmistria, land of opportunity and adventure.

Well, they knew it wasn't going to be easy.

Shawn stepped out into daylight and toward the kitchen.

Chapter 19

Cara examined the tired faces gathering around the council table and thought of all the work they'd done, all the work that lay ahead. The stifling heat of summer had given way to the tolerable heat of "autumn." The cremin migration was behind them, and the harvest was in full swing. The colonists were busy to the point of exhaustion.

Despite the challenges, it was all better than Principia. So much better.

Shawn sat at her right, head down, breathing quietly. He'd slept perhaps less than she had over the last week.

"What's your plan for the day?"

"Huh? Oh, working with the grain storage team this morning. Then we think we have a stray dragon singled out. Kearnin plans to bring a hunting party in, and we'll see if we can take it down."

"Be careful, brother. You're very tired."

"If we kill it, of course, we'll be up all night cleaning and skinning it."

As the remaining council members took their seats, 15 in all, Cara noticed Lonin was not in his customary seat, opposite hers. But he entered the room then, with his cousin Kinin in tow as usual, and with Paul Saarinen. Lonin went to his chair and motioned for Paul to take the seat next to his. Kinin took an observer's seat along the back wall. The remaining observers' seats were empty, as all village hands were busy either harvesting crops or repairing equipment.

Cara asked Shawn in a whisper, "Is Mr. Saarinen going on the hunt?"

"Wouldn't miss it."

"Remind him to take better care of himself."

Shawn chuckled. "A cremin isn't a tharnon, but I will remind him. I think he'll be more careful."

Cara tapped her egg-sized manager's stone on the wooden block. The quiet conversations hissed into a buzz and then stopped.

"Good morning, council members. I know we're all overworked and underpaid this time of year, so we'll keep this meeting short. I truly appreciate your time. I must say that this fatigue is a blessing. The hours are long because the harvest is a good one, the best in four years from all reports, and by the gifts of Timmistria, it will sustain us through the winter."

Weary faces nodded, and their relieved smiles touched Cara so deeply that her throat tightened.

"With your approval, we can dispense with the reading of the minutes from the last meeting. Pao, would you please bring the council up to speed on the village issues?"

"Certainly, Manager. The harvest progresses without incident. Stores are now 40% full and by all accounts should reach our target of 65% by the end of the harvest. This compares to total silage of about 35% last year. Primary constraints have been delays in reaping and transport because of increased security concerns. These were instituted as a result of the crellil attack and the additional possible sightings, along with the heavy cremin traffic, and increased incursions by perin flocks. Six draft jarin have been hobbled by perin bites, reducing transportation capability, and we've lost 12 field workers to jenil rash and fungal infections. The infections are not life-threatening."

Cara winced. A jenil rash was not pleasant.

"With the exception of the crellil presence, all other incidents have been fairly typical."

"How is the equipment holding out? Are repairs still high?"

"Equipment is now holding its own, Manager, with 81% uptime so far. We had the problem with bearing failure on the grain harvesters, but the lubrication correction implemented by Mr. Saarinen…"

The secretary gestured toward Paul as he said his name, but Paul didn't look up from his hands laid together on the table. "…seems to have stemmed the problem and resolved the repair overload in the shop."

"Very good. Thank you, Pao. And deepest thanks to you, Mr. Saarinen, for your timely contribution."

Paul raised his head then, his wide yellow eyes large and startled, like a cat's. His face was red from sunburn. "You're welcome, Manager."

"Any other news, Pao?"

"Nothing of note, Manager."

"Speaker Lonin, you have the floor. Are there any Timmon issues for the council?"

"Yes, Manager, but not the full council. I must call for a leadership meeting right after the council adjourns."

This was both unusual and discomforting. He usually warned her beforehand when there were urgent private matters.

"Of course, Speaker. Let's open the floor to the full council. Does anyone have an issue we need to discuss?"

Usually there were minor requests or grievances from one or more villagers, but today no one raised their hand.

"No? Very good. Let's adjourn, then. Good day to you all. Today and all days, live quietly on the land, and urge your constituents to do likewise. We are guests on

Timmistria, appreciative guests, and we need to show that every day.

"Shawn, Pao, please remain."

The other council members, free to go, exchanged smiles and left quickly. Two men stopped to talk with Paul and shake his hand, with slightly concerned looks at Lonin.

Cara smiled at the departing council members. "Pull the door closed on your way out, please, Mikela. And thank Cassa and Mella for the snacks."

She waited as the last of the full council stepped out, pulling the heavy wooden door closed behind them but looking back through the narrowing crack.

"You have the floor, Lonin. I have a good idea what this is about."

"The message is the same, Manager, but the voice is louder. There is a transport to land soon. As the Timmonilin Sentil, I ask that you put the red one on it."

"And as the Humanilin Sentil, I must respond that the answer has not changed, although it may be stronger by resolve. By human law, the leadership cannot punish someone when he has done nothing wrong, especially after all these months. I can't deport … the one you speak of."

"We both know what your answer will be, Manager, but it is my duty to continue to ask. I am here to let the council know that this failure to act has led to increasing anger and fear among the Timmon. The opposing groups gain influence."

"I understand, Lonin. And we both know that won't change our position."

"Agreed. A great fear at one time was how Timmistria would choose to address the red one. It seems she will take no action and will let matters take their course. The bigger fear now is what actions the Delerin will take, and I assure you they have much less patience than Timmistria. We have news that their anger is now a danger. They are closer to war."

"That is heavy news, Lonin, and I would do whatever is needed to help resolve the conflict between the Timmon and the Delerin. But by human law, I still cannot do what you ask."

"In my mind, I see that human law should change, but only you can do that. I have brought one of your people, Paul Saarinen, to make a request."

"Greetings, Mr. Saarinen."

"Greetings to you and the council, Manager."

"Please, how can we help you?"

"You're aware we've been working on the two-man flyer that was placed in storage."

"Shawn has kept us informed of your progress. In fact, it seems to be the only thing he cares to talk about lately." She tossed her brother a little smile.

"We'd hoped to use it to track the cremin, but we didn't have it assembled in time. We're now almost ready for our first flight."

"That is very exciting. How can we help?"

"We need a sizable fuel source. The flyer can run on ethyl alcohol, so we'd like permission and resources to set up a series of stills."

"Shawn told me about your plan. I discussed it with the council, and there were no major objections. Besides the obvious need for control of an addictive substance, Mr. Saarinen, the bigger problem is timing. All our resources, including the shops, are currently committed to the harvest. We really can't spare the parts or manpower right now. Another problem is storage. Our storage space is being filled with food products as soon as we are able to move the bulk materials out. And you would need very secure storage in an easily patrolled area. I don't think we can accommodate the request at this time."

"There is a strategic use that may raise the priority. We can use the flyer to patrol the borders and track any large movement of the Delerin. We can warn you if there is a buildup of manpower, which could signal an attack."

Shawn met her eyes. He hadn't told her about this idea.

"I thought the flyer was built for petrofuel. Why not process more of that?"

Shawn spoke up. "The little distillation unit is running full-out now to supply the field equipment that can't run on alcohol. We can't rob those users, and the unit doesn't produce enough for our needs anyway."

"Can you expand it?"

"Yes, and we plan to, but that will take much more time and shop work. Too late for the immediate need. Four or five fermentation systems will be much quicker to set up, and we can produce the liters we need fairly quickly."

Cara looked around at the council leadership and read their mood. "Pao, please coordinate with Mr. Saarinen to get him the people and the shop time he needs. Make it happen quickly, so those resources can return to the field."

"Cara, that will push us further behind on the harvest schedule and will result in a reduction in equipment uptime. We will not reach our goal of 65% full storage."

"Even if we don't, we'll be OK. We survived on half that last year, and our population has increased by only 15 adults and two infants. I know you, and I know you have a few tricks up your sleeves. You'll work something out. Maybe the folks with the infection who can't go back to the field can help with the stills, with proper precautions. Besides, Mr. Saarinen seems to be able to work minor miracles during his 'downtime,' so we can expect additional help from him. Does that cover your concerns, Pao?"

"I'll see what I can do, Manager."

"Great. You're the best. Mr. Saarinen, when can we expect the flyer to begin making regular scouting flights?"

"Ten days after the stills are running continuously, Manager."

"Very good. Don't be surprised if I hold you to that."

"I would expect nothing less."

"And I still haven't seen my plates."

"Working on them, ma'am."

#

Shawn looked around the shop and whistled. "Pao really is a miracle worker. I understand why Cara puts up with his micromanagement. Where did he find all these people?"

Paul said, "The four men wearing masks and bending steel tubing for the condensers were pulled from the field with fungal infections. The two women welding the fermentation tanks had caught up with repairing harvester blades and were looking for something to do. We'll lose them soon if critical field repairs build up."

Shawn's eyes darted about the shop. "Ten days. Are you sure you can meet that?"

"Yes."

"We have a lot of assembly work on the flyer yet."

"We'll get it done."

"And clearing the launchpad."

Paul nodded.

"But I guess you have to stay and supervise the construction of the stills?"

"No. Some of these people have done this type of work before, and the others have learned quickly. This ain't their first rodeo, as the saying goes. James can supervise."

"So, are you planning to work on the flyer today?"

"Yes."

"What are you waiting on?"

"I'm enjoying watching you hop from foot to foot in impatience."

"You're a zirg."

Paul enjoyed the laugh.

When Shawn and Paul arrived at the work shed, they found Lonin working there. If he had been conducting normal Timmon business over the last few weeks, it had to have been at night, because all his days were spent in the outside work area they'd set up. He'd already made progress pre-assembling the blades for attachment to the main rotor shaft. The cabin of the flyer was complete, except for the final wiring test and control power-up. With any luck, the solar panels had charged the small super-density battery. There were 60 assembly steps, and they had reached Step 54. With the exception of mounting and balancing the blades, all the tedious work and laborious heavy assembly were complete. The remaining steps were mostly system checks and start-up sequences.

It was the time they'd all been working toward, and Paul could feel his own excitement building.

He had planned to build tall wooden stands to set the blades on while they were bolted into place, but when they'd discussed setting the first blade, Lonin had taken the bull by the horns. He'd bent down and gripped one of the long flat turbines in his plate-sized hands and had lifted it over his head, holding it in place.

"Install the bolts."

They had done it, and that's how the three remaining blades were attached by early afternoon.

They spent the remainder of the afternoon going over the entire machine, tightening bolts, checking blade angles, cycling elevators and blade pitch controllers. At last, with Shawn and Lonin standing at the ready, Paul could find nothing else that needed checking. He leafed one last time through the assembly checklist, then folded it and tucked it into the waistband of his trousers.

"We are ready."

Neither Lonin nor Shawn said anything. Lonin nodded at last. Shawn only looked stunned.

"Let's call it a day. Be back here at 8 a.m."

"I will be here." With that, Lonin was gone.

"You all right, Shawn?"

Shawn snapped out of his trance. "Yeah, yeah. Great. It's just — I've been looking forward to riding in this thing for so long. I guess I'm in shock. I'd begun to give up hope I'd ever get the chance."

"What do you hope to see the first time you fly?"

He shook his head slowly, eyes focused on something distant. "I'm not sure. Mountains, rivers, lakes. Oceans, maybe. Oh, and more green spaces."

"Did you fly much on Principia?"

"Only when I was very young. And later, on the transport that we rode off-planet. The lifter had a small observation deck, so we were able to watch as we took off. You would think the deck would have been crowded, but none of the other passengers came up, only Cara and me. And to tell the truth, I was almost afraid to be there myself, like if I looked out the window, the planet would draw me back in, or the dream would be over and I'd wake up in that gray dormitory room at the school."

"What were you able to see from the deck?"

"Gray buildings at first. I tried to pick out our apartments. They weren't far from the port. We lived with the sound of aircraft, mostly military, coming and going at all hours. But it was impossible to tell one apartment from another, and the streets were all alike. Then the river. The Thims. We were taught in school it was a misspelling of an Old-Earth river in a country called Ingland. I always imagined that Ingland was much better than Principia. The river was thick with boats grinding their way through the heavy weeds and algae.

"Then off in the distance we could see the ocean. I'd been there once on a bike trip a couple years before. The sky was gray and gloomy both times. The beach and water were littered with the wreckage of flyers and ships from the last battle between the Six Houses, which was never cleaned up. You couldn't go in the water for all the twisted metal and contamination, so there was really nothing to do but ride up and down the causeway and take pictures of other people and a few sickly diving birds.

"On the lifter, after our one brief glimpse of the sea, we climbed into the smog layer and couldn't see anything for a long time. We finally cleared the clouds and burst into the bright sunlight, and we were almost blinded before the window tinting kicked on. At that point, there wasn't much to look at, just a sea of gray clouds endlessly spread out in all directions. But the scene was fascinating. I'd seen sunlight maybe ten times in my life after the Collapse. Now I can see more sun every single day here on Timmistria.

"When we broke out of the clouds, Cara cried. Quiet little sobs. I guess I did too. When we docked with the transport, walking through the air lock was like stepping into a different universe. I knew then, finally, that we were never going back."

Shawn looked at Paul, then at the flyer and back, as if waking from a dream. "Wow, sorry. I didn't mean to go on like that."

"That's OK. You realize this flyer has a very limited range. My guess is we'll never be able to go more than twenty kilometers from here. We'll have to stay within the settlement for several flights and won't be able to venture very far from a landing pad."

"Yes, I know. I'd like to fly all over this planet. But even if we can only fly in our own backyard, it will still be amazing."

Paul patted Shawn on the shoulder. "And I would like to fly to Shill Wellin. But I'm afraid we'd have to set up a fueling station there, and possibly one midway. That is an incredible place, and probably doubly so from the air."

"You've done a lot of flying, haven't you? In small craft, I mean."

Paul paused. The talk was getting personal, and he needed to be careful. "Yes, on Ceti Five, I worked for a mineral company and took puddle jumpers from camp to camp."

"Puddle jumpers?"

"That's a short-distance flyer that carries people and very little cargo. I saw some interesting country. I've ridden in commercial craft on a couple other worlds."

"Yes, Crest, and Cambiana."

"You read my profile."

"You brought an engineering background, so you were someone the council was very interested in. We snooped."

"Hmm."

"Don't worry. We didn't find any dirt."

"Were you looking for some?"

"Yes. But you're clean. Go back to talking about flying."

"Not much else. I have traveled some."

"Your file said you were a widower. I hope it won't offend if I ask about your wife."

"No offense taken. She was an engineer also, who died in an industrial accident. Really, there isn't much to talk about beyond that."

"What impresses you the most about flying?"

Paul paused, remembering countless flights, Helwin's warm leg against his, their hands clasped together in her lap. "How the clouds resemble the sea, sometimes flat and featureless, sometimes rising and falling in waves. I sometimes imagined riding the clouds in a sailing ship, being tossed by updrafts."

"That sounds pretty poetic for an engineer."

"Honestly, flying can be a little spiritual, if you're so inclined. Cruising above the clouds, there's a disconnect from the day-to-day activity below, like all the people on the plane are being given a look at a world above."

"Are you spiritual?"

"No."

"Do you think flying is like Heaven?"

"Hmph." Paul began stacking all his construction notes in order. He wouldn't need them anymore. "Heaven? No. But flying always made me feel above the world, untouchable. It gave me a chance to think about where I was going and what my purpose was.

Unfortunately the plane always comes down, and then you see the cars and roads and buildings, and you have to admit that you haven't really reached a higher plane. It was just a temporary escape."

"I'd like to do that again someday." Shawn walked away from the workbench and around the flyer. "I guess this little bird will be doing good to clear the trees, let alone the clouds. But … that will be good enough for now."

Paul nodded. "Yes." He thought it might have to be good enough for a very long time.

Shawn rubbed his chin in thought for a moment, muttered a curse, and said, "We can't fly tomorrow. The transport is landing. How did I forget about that?"

Paul chuckled. "It's OK, Shawn. You waited this long. Another day won't kill you. Will it?"

The expression on his face said the answer might be yes.

Chapter 20

"The people are like a jungle or a child: when they are quiet, it is time to raise your guard."
— Deminin Lajin

The room was dark and swirled in a light-dimming mist, save the bright light illuminating the padded table, where Cara's body was bound. There were others there in the shadows, many others. Even in her drugged state, she sensed them, whispering just outside the circle of light. They would begin soon. She dreaded it. There would be pain and sometimes pleasure, but mostly an overwhelming dullness. She would be touched, but somehow not touched, because of the narcotics and her ability to detach herself.

The throbbing music grew louder, and shapes swayed closer to her out of the fog. She tried to close her eyes, but they refused, and she watched as the faceless dancers swirled around and over her. The hidden audience had grown quiet as the dancers swayed and gyrated. She was surprised at how little pain there was, though she knew hands and bodies were being laid upon her. Her dazed attention was drawn to a small table near the front that was gradually illuminated by the stage light. At the table sat a heavy man, round and red of face, sipping from a short glass of brown liquid. His face was childlike and uncomfortably familiar, but his eyes burned at her where she lay, hiding within herself from the physical violation. The heavy man laughed then, and it struck her cruelly where she hid in her smallness.

She awoke, lying on her back, hands pinned beneath her, feet wrapped in the bedsheet, her body hot and damp. Her arms ached. Shuddering, she began unwinding herself from the sheet. She freed her legs and curled up on her side.

The dream had been bad, more vivid than it had been in a long time. How much was based in reality? Had she relived it so many times that it was now nothing more than a dark fantasy?

The knock startled her. Still groggy, she remembered the scheduled transport arrival and her busy day.

"Cara?"

"Yes, Helen."

"You said to wake you at seven."

"Thanks, I'll be ready in 20 minutes."

"Yes, Cara. I'll meet you at the Square."

"See you there."

Cara folded the sheet down and swung her legs over the side of the bed. The wood plank floor was cool on her feet, and she limped on her right foot from a slow-healing stone bruise. The air was cool now, at least by Timmistria standards, but still thick with humidity. Even this late in the autumn, when the harvest was nearly completed, the day would be uncomfortably warm. What the colonists called "winter" was really a long spell of mild heat, little rain, and shorter days, where native and human crops refused to grow. Their biologists were still not sure why the mild days would not produce food, and some had suggested that the strongly yellow sunlight might taper off to a point where it wouldn't support adequate photosynthesis. But neither the biologists nor Cara really believed that theory.

She thought back to the dream and shivered despite the warmth. The sense of dread would be hard to shake.

She lifted the jug of filtered water near her nightstand and poured some into the empty washbasin.

She pulled her short nightshirt off over her head, rubbed the large half-used bar of lye soap on a wash rag, and began bathing. Another knock came, and she answered while continuing to wash.

"Who is it?"

"Me. Do you need me at the landing today? If not, I want to scout more emergency landing sites for the flyer. We hope to fly it tomorrow."

"No, go ahead. I'd rather someone else was going to fly it, but if I told you not to, you'd do it anyway."

"Yes, I would. I'll come back to find out about the landing."

"OK. Hey, Shawn?"

"Yeah?"

"Do you think there's any chance Mr. Dench spent time on Principia?"

He paused. "He's never mentioned it. Why do you ask?"

"Just a hunch. Can you try to check on that? Keep it legal."

"We did a thorough background check before. It would have shown up."

"OK. Never mind. Be careful today."

"Yes'm."

Cara dipped and soaped and washed, feeling the need to be cleansed. She watched herself appear and disappear in the small mirror that hung behind the basin as she washed her arms and underarms, washing and splashing water on her face. The face looking back at her from the mirrored glass was simple, with no adornment, cosmetics, covering of lines, or added color. The face of a frontier woman? She looked healthy, if a bit plain. She hadn't worn real cosmetics in a long time, but she did try to keep her skin soft by applying oils when she had time to collect and crush the nuts herself to extract their precious juices.

She spoke words without realizing her own thoughts. "Good thing you're not trying to impress a man."

And then, as if to challenge her resolve, a man's face came to her, with strong features, pale yellow hair cut short, and a serious look entrenched in his yellow eyes.

Does he think I'm attractive?

The thought stung her, a poisoned dart to her self-esteem and another reminder of how fragile she could be.

The tunic she wore to the landings was an unflattering piece of formless cloth for a reason, to present a benign and professional image to new settlers. She could also hide behind it. But here in her cabin, behind a locked door, she refused to hide herself. She stood naked, save her underwear. At the thought, she pushed those to the floor and stepped out, now unhidden and not hiding, bare to the mirror that did not lie.

She was not a beautiful woman, at least not like some of the full-lipped and full-bodied women who had come to Timmistria. But she no longer showed the skeletal gauntness she had as a young girl on Principia.

What would a man like Paul Saarinen find attractive?

Her romantic experiences with men were few and awkward, the stuff of troubling memories. Her time had been devoted to raising her brothers, and then the single-minded quest of getting Shawn and herself off that world. She'd had no time to even consider a relationship. And now she wasn't sure what that was supposed to be.

The muscles of her legs and arms were wiry and hard, and her chest and stomach were flat and firm. She didn't think those were things a man would like in a woman. But her body was a mirror of who she was, who she had become on this world. Life was never easy here, and she didn't like the callouses on her hands or the roughness of the bottoms of her feet, but these things were honest. She had earned the right to wear the badges of this, her life, like all the villagers had. The woman in the mirror was at least authentic.

There were scars on her body, also honestly earned. Mostly small, faded, and light-colored, she could ignore them. Lonin had never asked or guessed their nature. If she ever fell in love with a man, would he be so discreet?

Paul's skin had been blemished as well. Tiny, dark scars of some pox-like disease dotted his back and neck in a few places, which was not unusual for someone who had traveled. But his body was also marked by deeper gouges and cuts, old but still angry. These weren't usual, and she couldn't imagine the life of a technical person being prone to such injuries. As she had tended to his poison-burned skin, the mystery of Paul Saarinen had deepened. His skills, knowledge, and ability to contribute in so many areas didn't add up to the person in his profile. She was thrilled to have him as a village member. She was also afraid of him.

Perhaps she should just ask him. Would he tell her the truth?

And how honest was your *profile, Cara "Harvestmoon"?*

You're wasting time. Get your ass moving.

She dressed quickly, but her mind went elsewhere into disturbing memories: Shawn's graduation, held underground to avoid arrest; a day spent at the mines in the aftermath of yet another accident, with a large crowd of other family members of miners missing and feared dead; working quickly but methodically to save Paul's life from the tharnon poison. The days all seemed to run together in her head. She was overwhelmed by it all.

Why did she still feel at times like the same small girl who had not lived her life but merely endured it from the beginning, never growing up, never getting smarter, never becoming a real woman? Her insecurity angered her.

After dressing, she left her cabin and walked briskly to the meeting place in the Square, from which the greeting party would walk the two kilometers to the shuttle landing pad. The bright star of the incoming lander was descending as she approached the waiting group. She followed its slow fall down to the tree line, and then her eyes were drawn to a row of small apartments there, lined up like tan paperboard boxes.

In one doorway stood a man. Juan was his name, and he looked to be leaving for his day's duties. Cara couldn't remember if he worked in the fields or the storage bins. As he made to leave, he was stopped by the hands of a woman, his wife, and spun around into her arms. Mariela was barefoot and barely covered by a thin nightshirt, and the vehemence of her lips on Juan's and the grip of her arms around him made him linger. Cara tried not to stare, but the image prompted her to try to remember the last time she had so willingly kissed a man with even half as much passion. A memory would not come.

I have never kissed someone like that. Not even Lonin.

Lonin, her friend, her lover, her rock. How easily she had fallen back into his arms after that afternoon at Paul's camp. So like the first time, years earlier and only weeks after she and Shawn had reached Timmistria. At that time, she had taken on more responsibility within the village, and as a result found herself interacting more and more with the Timmon liaison. No human male ever showed her the respect and consideration he did — save Shawn and her other brothers, of course, and that only begrudgingly. She began to crave time with Lonin, and finally after a long and difficult week of negotiating settler issues relating to Timmon restrictions and assistance, she seduced him. It wasn't difficult. He proved to be an amazingly careful and considerate lover, if somewhat distant.

She'd cried afterward, and he'd been puzzled and concerned.

Even now, she found it hard to define their relationship; they were more than friends, less than lovers, joined by common goals but divided by light-years of race. Could she call it love? Certainly a type of love. She had talked about her feelings with him more than once, in the warm, quiet hours before dawn. It hadn't gone well. The more she talked about how human men and women related to each other (as if she'd ever experienced that), the more puzzled he became and the more frustrated she became. After much prying, she came to understand that the Timmon didn't take mates, didn't form long-term partnerships, and didn't talk about it. There wasn't some social stigma against discussing feelings; it just wasn't important enough to talk about.

"Crap."

She'd forgotten her tunic at the office. She turned and trotted back quickly. The road was now crowded with convoys of farm wagons, pulled by dribbling draft beasts, wagons heavily laden with grains and fruits creaking along into town, and empty wagons rolling much faster back out to the fields and orchards.

"Hey, Jones! Hey, Hawn! Get them wagons unloaded so we can fill 'em up again!"

"Hold your jarins, Scotty; we can empty 'em a damn sight faster 'n you'uns can fill 'em!"

The farm workers were smiling and clapping each other on their backs as they passed.

"Hey, Cara! Tell them laggers to move their bats before those pears turn to cider!"

She turned back, cupping her hands at her mouth. "Move your bats, boys and girls!"

"Haw haw haw!"

The scene was remarkable and would have been totally unexpected just months before. Her mind went back to that day in the maintenance shop, with Shawn, bless him, bobbing and babbling about the new irrigation pipe "fabrication techniques." Paul had been standing quietly to the side, not sharing Shawn's excitement. He'd been sullen, really, nodding occasionally, his odd yellow eyes darting about the shop as if afraid to look at her. When he had finally met her eyes, the intensity of his gaze was like a laser beam into her brain.

Stop it, sister. You can't do this now.

Helen was waiting for her at the office door in her tan tunic. She followed Cara in and helped her with her own, tan this time and not the white one, and they headed out quickly. The busy street outside was still a bustle. Her own chiding words echoed from the mouths of others.

"Hey, move your bats, boys and girls!"

"Move yours, pudding head, ha-ha!"

"Move your bats! Move your bats!"

She didn't remember the harvest being as brash and joyful in any of her six years here. There were good harvests before, but those had been the result of unusually cool and wet summers, where the hybrid off-world seeds had survived. But this year, the days had been hot and brutally dry, and yet the fields had been made to produce.

At last, after so many years, the humans weren't so much at the mercy of Timmistria.

Lonin would have been angered by that thought. According to the Timmon, everything was always at the mercy of Timmistria.

Cara fell into a steady walking rhythm beside Helen, a quiet woman from Gliese, one of the first systems to be settled by humans. Here was a woman so unlike Cara. She was always under control, despite crises and hardship, the one person Cara could go to for just talk. With a few words, she would drain Cara of the drama that seemed to always fill her head. Was Helen's ease a discipline learned, or was she by nature just a calm-minded person?

It really mattered little. Cara didn't picture herself ever having that kind of peace of mind, no matter how much discipline or training she sought. But the steady rhythm of walking was doing much to calm her nerves, and she allowed some of the doubts to fly. Shawn was right; she could be such a worrier. Food to last the winter, so important just weeks before, was now a worry set aside. So she'd followed her habit of picking up new things to worry about. What was the wisdom in that?

Walking, walking, trying not to think, she let herself be led to the landing area by the quiet, easy woman next to her. Despite the energizing atmosphere in the village, she'd never felt so unready for a transport arrival. Her thoughts wouldn't obey her, finding their way back to the yellow-eyed man who'd become so important to the community and to her in so short a time, as unexpected as the good harvest.

She knew so little about him, save the effect he had on her. The mystery of him was frustrating, nearly intolerable.

"Miss Cara, we're here."

"Oh."

Helen had led them to their usual position at the landing area, waiting for the lander to lower the gangway. Where was Lonin? Right, he'd warned her he'd be late for the landing. He was working with Shawn and Paul on final preparations for the flyer.

How incredible! She wished she were there, helping them. Maybe Shawn was right. Maybe it was time for her to step down and let someone else run things. The manager job was too hard if you could no longer focus yourself or had lost your enthusiasm. Maybe it had finally worn her down. Maybe she needed a recharge.

The warning siren sounded, and soon after, in a soft whoosh of escaping air pressure, the gangway began to descend. She forced a smile and began reciting the first lines of her opening speech in her head.

#

Dench waited until the new immigrants were settled into their temporary quarters before approaching his man. At the welcome dinner, he made a point of talking to several of the new people, as if recruiting, asking them about their interest in and knowledge of mining and geology, before singling out Johanson, his fourth-in-command, a tall, blond Old-Earth Scandinavian, smart, powerful as an ox, and unflappable in a tight spot. Without Johanson's cool head and quick action, Dench may not have escaped the debacle on Sarena.

"Greetings, settler. Welcome to Timmistria."

"Are you Mr. Dench?"

"Yes, I am. Pleased to meet you, Mister…" Dench glanced around, but no one seemed to be looking in their direction. There were a couple of young females among the new settlers, and they were getting all the attention. "You can drop it. We're out of earshot."

"Hello, Mr. Dench. It looks like you've lost some weight."

"We're not exactly eating caviar and sipping champagne here, Joho. You'll need that extra body fat I told you to put on. I heard about the gazer spotter. Did everything else make it through all right?"

"As far as I can tell, boss. I haven't had a chance to power up the electronic stuff."

"No hassles from transport customs about my devices?"

"We got everything on board. One of the customs supervisors decided we were an easy mark and tried to push up the usual bribes. They won't find a body. The new inspector accepted a 20% premium."

Dench nodded. Johanson, his trusted associate, was effective and efficient in his duties, which made him a significant threat to Dench's leadership. Dench had him monitored continuously.

"Settle into your temporary quarters. Attend all the meetings. When they ask about your occupation, tell them you have geology experience and would like to work in mining. They'll point you to my group. I have your campsite selected. It's near mine, but not conspicuously so. Get acclimated. You know the basic plan and most of the details. I'll seek you when I need you, and we'll discuss the rest."

"Yes, Mr. Dench."

"Now, on the other matter. Did you bring the information I requested on our Mr. Saarinen?"

"Yes, sir. I have a data dot in my pocket."

"Great. Pass it to me when we shake hands in a moment. Is he an agent, as I suspect?"

"Not that we found. He's bigger. Military special ops. We think they shipped him here for safekeeping. He went rogue and ran a mission off the books, but he cleared the Thinkers from a key system in the process. It caused a PR stink, so they put him on ice here. The webbers couldn't find any connection to our work. Total coincidence."

"You know better than to use that word around me. There *are* no coincidences. Hmm. Interesting, though. I think I'll bid you a good evening, Mr. Johanson, and I look forward to working with you in our mining group."

Johanson pressed his meaty mitt to Dench's hand and then withdrew it, leaving behind a warm spot that lingered in Dench's palm.

"Good evening, Mr. Dench."

"And to you, my good fellow."

As Dench walked from the room, he held his middle finger against the warm place. It was a pointless gesture, since the data dot was now held firmly to his skin by atomic forces and would require a special tool to remove it. Paul Saarinen had become very interesting. Perhaps he was the first rare gem that Dench had discovered on this oversized asteroid.

Chapter 21

"A drawn ratan will be swung. To speak of war is to begin war."
— Delerin proverb

A Delerin tribal council was as different from a Timmon council as a pack of vikin from a herd of jarin. A Timmon council was reserved and relatively respectful, with members speaking only in turn. A Delerin council was an open forum, with several members shouting over each other at any given time. Members and observers came and went at random, and side conversations provided a background roar.

Larilin had been to both his own people's councils and those of the Timmon … and enjoyed neither. He worked better in small groups of two or three, where emotions would not stampede like some wild herd of banshinil.

But even in a Delerin council, there was a sense of order, a veil of process and procedure. The main topic of discussion was a dynamic, shifting thing that did not move along linear thought processes. The results were the same as those of the more orderly Timmon council; decisions were made, and plans were developed and set in motion. In fact, the Delerin legislative process, more closely modeled after the sometimes chaotic processes of the mind, was often very efficient. Timmon councils were plodding, and the human council even more so, or so Lonin often complained. Larilin would see for himself one day.

The Delerin ruling council met as seldom as possible, both because of the great distances many of them had to travel and because they didn't enjoy each other's company very much. Twenty members, "four hands full" as was often said, were in attendance, one from each of the territories, plus their retinues, meaning the room teemed with hundreds. Many had traveled 1,000 kikkin or more across the three Delerin continents.

The Shig Shirrin, leader from far-off Shir, had spent weeks crossing nearly 2,000 kikkin on storil-back with his retinue of rangers. From Shir, the westernmost continent, one must cross a lengthy, storm-wracked land bridge between the northern sea Esterin Tegir, and the southern sea, Estin Tegir. The ribbon of land was only a few tens of kikkin wide in places and was hunted by large sea reptiles. That none of the Shig's party had perished en route was viewed as a sign that their cause was worthy and that Timmistria guided them.

As was customary, this meeting was never formally brought to order. Talks began as soon as two members arrived and continued as long as two members remained. Members rested as they pleased, took food and drink, listened to or performed music, danced, engaged in recreation or sex, slept and meditated, or did none of these, purely at their immediate whim. The entire event could last for hours or weeks.

This council promised to be a long one.

Unusual by most standards, there was a particularly strong focus here, a need and an energy that had brought them all to one place without formal invitation, without provocation, without intimidation, without coercion, as was usually needed. The problem that drew them was the aliens from space, the humans, who had been allowed to occupy a section of the Timmon lands. The Delerin concerns when this permission was crafted had proved correct: the humans had brought unwanted things to Timmistria, and the Timmon hadn't fulfilled their responsibility to police them. It was obvious that the time for action was at hand.

Larilin was known as a diplomat in a land lacking diplomacy, and through many years of service had become the de facto communication liaison between the tribes. He was a busy officer, traveling constantly between territories and ignoring the many dangers that came with the travel. Many questioned his motives, but none doubted his work ethic. He drove himself tirelessly to keep the territories communicating and cooperating, his trails like the strands of a senil's web, knitting the lands together. He was also known to be a friend of the Timmon, or as near to one as there was among the Delerin.

Larilin, as second-ranked councilman, had strongly supported the human settlement. He longed to serve as the Delerin liaison with the humans, when his own people became wise enough to realize they needed one, but he expressed this desire to no one. Having secretly observed the arrival of one human transport, and the disembarking of the settlers, he dreamed of rising up in the craft and departing for worlds unknown. He kept that dream quiet in his mind for fear that Timmistria would be angered.

On that night years earlier, he'd stayed late near the Timmon village with his cousin Tellinin and their escort of two guards, watching the human space machine rise into the sky on a tail of bright light and a sound like a thousand jarin exhaling. The four of them had spent the entire night sitting awake, staring dumbstruck into the cloudless, star-filled sky. Deep in the night, with Dreyaten glaring down at them in hatred, Larilin had followed a small, dull star as it crossed from horizon to horizon. He guessed correctly that it was that same machine winding its way up into whatever lay beyond their world. He was so awestruck, he couldn't sleep for days afterward, drawn to an open hill near his kithin and entranced by the stars slowly traversing the sky above him. These lights were actually suns like their own Semeril Terl, at distances that he couldn't imagine, so that they appeared as the lights of distant campfires.

When Larilin arrived at the great hall, it was already a boiling cauldron of voices. He found a seat near one side of the chamber, surveying the crowd as he threaded his way through. The furniture was a jumble of chairs and small tables, spread around in no particular pattern. Members and observers moved them noisily at will to leave one discussion group and join another. He let his ears move about the room, focusing on the words of one group, then another, then another, gauging the subjects. Typically, the discussion was like a piece of meat being consumed by a group of jerellin, bitten and pulled back and forth, torn between related or unrelated subjects. Today was like few other meetings, in that the entire room seemed to be on a single theme — the humans and their "red beast," and what the Delerin were going to do about it.

Larilin chose a brief lull in the debate to begin. He turned and spoke loudly to a person sitting next to him, Tirrilin, from the eastern territory of Gillin. He addressed the man as if they were chewing the flesh with all the others.

"The humans may stay, but the red beast must go!"

The roar that erupted from the assembly was both ugly and unexpectedly vicious. The general feeling was summed up by the blowhard Shremin, from the Trell Wellin territory, he of small brain and large mouth. Shremin climbed on top of his chair, his neck indecently blaring at them all and his timeril glowing a distasteful roasted orange, and spat out, "Throw them all off the land! Better yet, kill them all and let Timmistria damn them to Dreyaten!"

The general tone of agreement in the chamber shocked Larilin. This was of great concern. He'd grossly underestimated the intensity of the negative sentiment against the humans. This "red beast" issue was out of control — superstitious hokum, he suspected — but nevertheless dangerous and emotionally powerful. He stood up on his own chair.

"Shremin is right, friends! The humans must all be killed!"

The roar was deafening, and Larilin was surrounded by faces framed in red. They would have stormed the human village immediately if asked.

He let them carry on awhile. Their voices seemed to rise as one, a rant as unified as any he'd heard in this chamber in many seasons. It brought sadness and shame to his hearts that this council, which rarely agreed on anything, could be so easily united by hatred.

At last, the energy of the incipient riot began to wane. Larilin, still standing on his chair, raised his arm with his hand open. At this request to speak, the council members and visitors quieted.

"Now, before we form a war party, we will need many volunteers. The humans number about two hundred. We will need that many Delerin to kill them all. So which of you will volunteer your people to kill one of the humans?"

Shremin yelled from where he stood, his face red as a lemin slug, "Why would we need so many? I can kill a hundred of them myself!"

Larilin paused to let the uproar die again, this time briefer than the last. "I doubt that not, Shremin. But you have only one life to give in payment for a human life. We will need two hundred more."

The responses were groans, curses, and denials. Shremin's voice could be heard above the others': "We owe the human sellil nothing. They are not Timmistrian!"

Larilin let the noise level drop, and then raised his open hand again. "Cousins! A word. Allow me a word. Thank you. Shremin raises a point. Are the humans 'men'? And as men, are their lives protected by the honor of Tironin? Shremin is right, they are not born of Timmistria, and they are very different from us. Most of you have never seen one of the humans, and that makes it easy for you to dismiss them as animals or savages. Fellows, I have seen the human leaders, and I have observed them secretly from a distance. I have seen their tools and their dwellings. And it is my opinion, humble as it is, that the humans are 'men' in every sense that we are. If we kill a human, we owe our life, just as we would if we killed one of our own or one of our cousins the Timmon."

"Jarin dung! They are not Timmistrian, and we are not bound by the honor. They and their red beast will kill us all if they can, and they will not abide by the honor as you would have us do. We must strike now while we are still masters of Timmistria, before they can defeat us by numbers or treachery. Larilin, I think you have already fallen prey to their tricks."

"Perhaps, Shremin. Perhaps you are correct, as you are so many times. I look at the humans and see men — smaller, weaker, slower, hardly a match for the Delerin — and perhaps my eyes are clouded by a promise of great things, or by mere sorcery, like the death spell of a coiled letin. But before you draw ratan-i, string bows, and shed human blood, think on this — what if my thoughts are true? What if these ... humans ... are men in the eyes of Timmistria? They are not of Timmistria, I agree, but perhaps they are born of Timmistria's sister.

And perhaps in Timmistria's eyes, they are not her children but are children nonetheless, here for a purpose that only she knows. If you slaughter the humans — and if we attack them, friends, it will be a slaughter, for they cannot stand before us — and Timmistria weeps over their bodies like she would our own, imagine her anger at those who drenched the ground in the blood of 200 children.

"Brothers, sisters, if you decide to go to war against the humans, I will go with you. But I will not return to my village and my people. My blood will stain the land just as the humans' will."

The council room was unnaturally quiet. Seldom did a discussion focus all attention, draining the energy from all side conversations, arguments, or joke-telling. Their attention, at least, Larilin had won.

Shremin broke the silence. "You bind us with your words, Larilin, like a whip vine wrapping us in its deadly ropes."

"I am only one man, Shremin. The council is many. The council must decide, as always."

"And now I curse your words. You keep us from the only action that will save our people. You'd use our own laws to destroy us, laws that our enemies will not obey."

"Is it better to disobey Timmistria, to turn our backs on her that she should turn her back on us? Or to live in her way and face this new universe with her leading us?" Larilin looked from face to face around the room. "If it is our time to die, then Timmistria will make that decision in her time. But I have faith that this is not that time, that she will not allow us to be destroyed."

Shremin shook his head and got down from his chair. "You win this round, Larilin. May Timmistria burn you on Dreyaten if you are wrong."

#

Larilin slashed at the snares that tossed their coiled nooses across the trail in front of him. They were a minor annoyance, but the perelin and raree in these woods were particularly vicious and dangerous. Tellinin, his aide and cousin, swung blades behind him. This path was little used and the meeting place it led to little known.

The two Delerin cut through the last barrier of heavy brush and stepped into the small clearing. It was a flat ring about 30 feet across, clear of the choking brush that carpeted this part of the woods and kept that way by a virulent circular fungus that poisoned the soil for other plants. Lonin and his cousin Kinin were already there, standing by the head-high malack posts that Lonin and Larilin had driven into the ground here together when they were young.

"Greetings, Lonin."

"Greetings to you, Larilin. How go your travels?"

"Through deep woods and under dark skies, I'm afraid. Events gain speed, Lonin. Our ability to shape them lessens."

"That is the way of things, Larilin."

"The Ah-Hilin were ready to go to war against the humans, cousin. I was barely able to restrain them this time. I hold little doubt that within weeks, the Delerin will march for the first time in 100 generations. What is the news on the humans exiling the 'red one'?"

Lonin shook his head. "They will not act to throw him out until they see his crimes. By then, his net will be cast and it will be too late."

"What of this red one, Lonin? What of his nature? Is he a demon, as the scouts claim?"

Lonin shook his head slowly again. "Not in my eyes. His red light burns as cruelly as Dreyaten on clear, dustless winter nights, but in him I see only a human man. An evil one, surely, but a man. He would die on the end of a ratan just as you or I would."

"The humans know they draw the full wrath of the Delerin by harboring this one?"

"Yes. Their leaders have been told. By their law, they have no grounds to act."

"Perhaps the Delerin do not either, but we will march all the same, and soon. And if the Delerin march, Lonin, I will have to march with them."

"And I will have to stand between your people and the humans, cousin."

"As I said, events move fast now, and I believe they rule us rather than the other way. We set all this in motion when we allowed the humans to stay here."

"The humans may have opened Timmistria to the universe, Larilin, but had we denied them, the universe would have come all the same."

"Your light shines brightly. I hope the humans gain from your wisdom and cast the red one out. If the Delerin march, you and I will not return from the battlefield."

"We have always been willing to die for our people. That has not changed."

"True, but I'd rather this were not the time or the reason. I'd prefer to die in the arms of a warm Delerin woman after fathering my twentieth child."

Lonin chuckled, a deep rumble that filled the glade. "Knowing you, I trust you are well on your way. If you hurry to your home tonight, you might complete the job. I believe Timmistria has generations of work for both of us, and our destiny does not lie soon. But if our deaths would serve her now, then it will be so."

"Timmistria is wise, cousin. Perhaps there is time left to persuade your human friends to act, but I fear you will see war-painted Delerin at the border very soon if the humans choose to stall."

"Hold tight as long as you can, Larilin. I feel the wind of change on the horizon, and Timmistria may open our eyes to a new vision."

"Shik. We should go now. Walk quietly. You may be correct. You and I have much work to do, too much work ahead of us, and our lifelines do not cross the ratan yet. Ah-hil, Lonin!"

"Shik. Ah-hil, Larilin. Ah-hil, Tellinin. Keep your heads high, your feet firm, and your ratan-i ready. Our people will find that they need us all greatly in the days ahead."

Lonin and Kinin left the clearing first, kicking up a flock of screeching shiggin birds. Large and armed with sharp claws and teeth, the shiggin were nonetheless excellent dining fare when grilled on a spit and served with peppery tallow.

Larilin turned to his cousin, who stood motionless beside him. "Come, Tellinin. The bountiful Carmarin has invited me to bathe this night, and I have a strong need to not keep her waiting."

Chapter 22

The Story of the Last Battle of the Timmistrians, as related to Shawna Harvestmoon-Serak by Lonin

In the time of the second of the three great droughts, the peoples fought over land rights, which in reality meant access to water. In those days, the Delerin did not yet control the vast majority of the land but had gained strategic advantage through persistence. Timmistria and good fortune had granted the Delerin more favorable weather and less ravage by pestilence and disease. With stronger and better-fed troops, they pressed the Timmon forces back against the bleakness of the Serinon Mountains. Each side prepared for a final deadly battle.

Seers on both sides were grave, predicting great loss of life for both armies. The Delerin had the stronger force, but the Timmon were fierce and, like any beast, fiercest when cornered. Messengers from Tironin, leader of the Delerin, were seen approaching the Timmon scouting line, carrying aloft a white and yellow flag, the traditional signal for a requested parlay. The messengers, two young female Delerin, were taken without incident directly to the Timmon encampment. They were led to a tent and asked to sit at a small table, to which soon came Teiron, the Timmon leader. They silently shared food, with the messengers being served the meat of game birds and fine fruits and breads, even though supplies were short. Teiron limited himself to one small piece of bread and challon cheese, and two cups of water, which was all he allowed himself each day. The messengers ate all that was offered despite their misgivings, since to not partake of all that was offered would have been considered an insult to the Timmon, and this meeting was not about insult.

Teiron ate slowly so as not to finish well before his guests. When they had both consumed all before them, Teiron waited. At last, the one chosen to speak began.

"Thank you, leader. Your offering was too generous."

"Despite our lot, we respect those who come in peace. You have words for me now. Please say that which you have carried to us."

"Greetings to Teiron, leader of the Timmon, from Tironin, leader of the Delerin."

"Greetings accepted and rightly returned."

"Tironin sees a fierce battle soon at hand, and great death."

"Teiron sees likewise."

"Tironin offers a second choice."

"Teiron listens."

"Tironin offers to decide the battle in the way of the ancestors, by filin, one-on-one conflict between the leaders. Tironin will offer to fight for all Delerin against Teiron, who will represent all Timmon. The victor's people will gain rights over eight out of ten parts of the disputed territories, and the fallen leader's people will willfully cede those same lands. The remaining two of ten will go to the defeated people."

"It is honorable. Teiron accepts."

If the messengers were surprised by Teiron's quick assent, they did not show it.

"A party will return at one hour past first light tomorrow. Teiron is requested to limit his party to a squire and two witnesses. The others' well-being will be protected."

"It will be as requested."

The messengers rose, were escorted out of the camp to the spot where they had been intercepted, and disappeared silently into the brush.

One hour after first light the next day, another party of two messengers appeared at that same place, and Teiron's party was there to meet them. There were no words at this meeting, and no mystery. No seer was needed to look into the future on this day. Teiron was going to his death. He was a bold and certain leader, and in his prime had been an unmatched warrior. But time lay heavy upon him, and he would fall before the younger, equally bold Tironin. The Timmon would be forced by agreement to surrender the disputed lands — the Capinon River, the Florinon Forest, the fields, the hills, and the water. But no more Timmon would die. In defeat and sacrifice, Teiron would at least give them that. All were thus honored.

The story of the fight between Teiron and Tironin was told by the squire and witnesses upon returning. Even in the sunset of his years, Teiron was one of the fiercest warriors, and it was to Tironin's credit that he did not take this fight lightly. The two warriors faced each other, each with the tellin and the sarillion, the traditional battle blades. Upon a nod of readiness from each leader, Teiron's squire dropped a stone and they came together in a violent rush.

A lesser fighter would have fallen before the mighty blows and strikes that Teiron delivered, but Tironin was not a lesser fighter and stood his ground. The fighting rage of a young warrior came over Teiron at the thought of ceding the lands he loved so much, or so the witnesses felt, and he pressed the attack. But the younger Tironin was still the greater of the two on this day.

After minutes that seemed like hours, Teiron's rage fell into fatigue, and Tironin dealt the killing blows, a hard slash to the shoulder and a thrust that pierced Tciron's breast and hearts, killing him instantly, and, evident to all who watched, mercifully.

The story as told to this point was solemn but predictable. But soon after, the events of that day became unexpected and historic.

Tironin, standing over the fallen body of Teiron, bowed his head in respect to the great Timmon leader. From the words of those Delerin who knew Tironin, he held no one in higher regard than the leader of the Timmon and no doubt felt the loss as much as Teiron's own people did. Inspired by the greatness of the world's loss — or perhaps it had been his plan all along — Tironin held one last act in the presence of the witnesses and squires of both parties.

"Bow your heads now, Timmon and Delerin, in respect to this great one fallen. It is the world's sorrow that his time was to come, and I hold it ponderous and regretful on my hearts that there was no other way. But it is for me to offer payment for this loss. From this day onward, to the honor of Teiron, let no Timmistrian, Timmon or Delerin, take the life of another without taking his own. The people will thus always understand the cost of violence, the cost of conflict, the cost of war.

"The cost of Teiron's life shall be my own, and by paying this cost I bind all of you, and your daughters and sons, and their daughters and sons, to the same fate. May no one fall by the hand of another without all people of Timmistria judging the horrible price of that loss."

Only the witnesses could know if those were Tironin's exact words, but those were the words related back to the Timmon and Delerin people, and they were taken as the truth, and those witnesses took any doubt to their graves. Having spoken, Tironin laid his tellin against his neck and pulled it across the skin and muscle and veins there, spilling his red blood in a torrent upon the ground.

It is said he fell as lightly as a feather, and his brilliant soul-light, his timeril, golden as the snow upon the Cainons, flew as a great bird from his body into the yellow sky. There he joined the blinding timeril of Teiron, and it is said that together they made the journey to the final resting place, circling the dark star Deleria at the center of all things.

And as it became an unwritten but binding covenant on that painful day, no Timmon or Delerin ever fell by the hand of another without the killer taking his own life. And war between the two races was never seen again.

Chapter 23

"God did not give Women and Men wings, because She did not want to cripple us."
— Pope Mary Louise, circa 2350, Old Earth Standard

Paul had insisted that Shawn begin his flight training as soon as the flyer was operational, but he was beginning to question that decision. The young man had an aptitude for many things, but piloting the little two-seated flyer wasn't one of them. Seated behind Shawn in the flyer, Paul thumped him firmly on the shoulder and yelled into his ear over the noise of the spinning rotor.

"Time's up! Set it down!"

Shawn nodded but fought the controls to level the craft while trying to land it on the hard-packed dirt of the landing pad. When he started drifting toward the nearby tree grove, Paul flipped the override switch on the rear control panel and brought the craft to a steadily level altitude. He then guided it slowly back over the large black "X" they'd marked in the center of the pad, set it easily on the ground, and cut the engine. The blades slowed from a steady throbbing *flup-flup-flup* to a jerky halt. He held Shawn's shoulder down until the blades had completely stopped, then released him and climbed from the small rear cockpit.

"I almost had it that time. I'm starting to get a feel."

Paul stripped off his tight-fitting leather hat and jacket, and then set them on the rear seat. He began a mental checklist of preventive maintenance items and adjustments he wanted to make before trying to take the flyer up again.

Shawn continued, with no less excitement, "Once we start flying regularly, I think we'll find all kinds of uses for flyers. Spotting cremin and large predators. Driving herd animals. Crop dusting. The possibilities are endless."

But the fuel source was a major worry. Paul had felt the engine dragging a bit whenever Shawn increased the RPM. The distilled alcohol might be too low in heat value for the flyer's small, high-output engine, especially with the high torques needed to accelerate the huge blades at low speeds.

"When we find the large iron deposits we need and can set up a large-scale smelter, we'll be able to fab our own parts and produce our own flyers," Shawn said. "I'm sure the first one would take months. But with your product-development methods, we should be able to cut that down to only a few weeks. I'm sure we can design a better flyer as well, one with a larger compartment for carrying a Timmon."

It was possible the problem was in the feed system. Paul and Lonin would have to disassemble the unit and make sure they hadn't screwed something up. He grumbled. In reality, there was little chance they'd made a critical error in the assembly. They would overhaul it anyway, checking for deposits or corrosion, but Paul was sure they'd made no mistakes. The problem was with the fuel itself, and that wasn't going to be an easy fix. Their crude distillation and filtering equipment could do only so much. The quality just wasn't good enough.

"We'll build a whole flock of flyers, and with my experience here, I can become an instructor. You know, on Principia, before the collapse, flyers carried injured people to hospitals. Do you think we'll be able to set up an air ambulance service here?"

"Quite likely."

"And another important application is aerial surveying. We can locate geological structures, fault lines, domes, and uplift areas that could hold petroleum products and natural gas."

Natural gas. That was a real possibility, if the parts locker held the right fuel parts. A good, lean source of natural gas would require minimal processing and would burn clean with little maintenance required. But compressing the gas was a problem. Paul wasn't sure that could be done with any of the equipment in the village. They should table that idea until they had advanced far enough to ship in a compressor station, high-pressure tanks, and a vaporizer.

"Eventually we'll have to build an actual airport, and then a real spaceport landing, with a suborbital elevator line, to save the costs of propulsion landing and lifting — too energy-wasting."

Paul said, "Before we start designing the Timmon space program, can we figure out how to improve our fuel so this thing doesn't crash in the middle of the forest?"

Shawn stood with his mouth wide open. "Sorry. Is there a problem?"

"Nothing serious. It's just that our ethanol fuel snarks, and if we don't make it cleaner and reduce the water content, we're very likely to lose the engine at a really bad time."

"What can we do?"

They spent the next three days setting up a carbon and desiccant filtration system, and then processing all the fuel they had in inventory. What they really needed was a selective membrane system, but the nearest one was several tens of light-years away. They were fortunate to be able to convert a small air-drying system, but as with most of the processes, they had to improvise. The work was slow, tedious, and labor-intensive, which was the norm for everything new they'd tried.

Shawn rounded up the "Pipers Team" and set them in motion, which freed him to maintain his village duties and allowed Paul and Lonin to overhaul the fuel system on the flyer. Everything was in order with the fuel controller, confirming Paul's belief that the fuel was the issue. While they waited for all their fuel to be filtered, Paul and Lonin went through every system on the flyer, adjusting and checking everything from the rotor connections and balance to the electrical-generation system.

Paul wasn't impressed by the appearance of the filtered fuel. It looked the same, and their crude lab equipment could detect only a slight decrease in water. To test it, Paul devised an engine stress test: tether the flyer to large eyebolts firmly anchored in the ground, and then try to take off. The added torque would strain the engine, and any fuel problem would cause it to falter right there on the pad, at a safe elevation.

With Paul tweaking the filtering system, and Shawn driving the work team — he was becoming a more effective leader all the time — they had the fuel they needed, about 500 liters, in two days. It was time to put the stress test to work.

"Clear."

A small crowd stood in a semicircle around the flyer, well clear of the blade circle. Present were Shawn and Lonin, of course, the seven members of the Pipers Team, a handful of other men and women, and five other Timmon — Lonin's cousin Kinin, Shawn's friend Kearnin, Crellin, the archer Paul had stood beside during the crellil attack, and the two Timmon who had escorted Paul back to Fairdawn after the tharnon incident. Paul had to be reminded that their names were Tarron and Maggon. Cara wasn't in the group, and Paul was annoyed with himself for feeling disappointed.

"Clear!"

He passed his fingers over the start sensor, and the little flyer shuddered to life as the long, thin copter blades began turning around him. The material was light micro-carbon fibers, and when at rest the blades bent downward, with their tips almost dragging in the yellow dirt. As the small engine's voice rose from a low gargle, the blades lifted as the pressure gradient of the air rushed along the blade surfaces. The *whiff-whiff* sound passing his ears gradually increased in frequency. He increased the throttle.

At half speed, Paul could already feel the difference. The little engine had handled the kick-off and low-RPM acceleration without a whimper. At ¾ speed, it was yawning. Paul centered the flight controls and raised the throttle to 90%.

"Show me what you can do."

The blades blurred into an inverted elliptical cone, tips pointing upward dramatically. Paul touched the controls again and felt the skids lift from the ground. He brought the flyer up evenly between the anchor points, with the heavy tethers of steel cable rising from the dirt, straightening, and then pulling taut.

"Fly or die, little bird."

Paul eased the craft upward still more. The cables strained but held the flyer in place, four feet above the ground. The engine hummed sweetly, with none of the shuddering he'd felt during the previous trials. The thrumming blades kicked up a circular cloud of dust that began to obscure the observers, who moved back quickly.

At 100% throttle, the flyer strained upward against the tethers, gaining an inch. The cables pulled tighter and moaned with tension, but they held. The engine was serious now, the happy singsong hum now an angry roar. But there was no give-in this time, not a stutter, a cough, or even a blink. Paul had the illusion that the machine was not trapped in its place by the tethers but was instead pulling the ground upward.

He let the copter strain against the cables for another two minutes, running through the flight checklist in his head, checking all the instrument readings, confirming by the numbers what his senses had already told him. Satisfied, he reduced the throttle, set her down between the pegs, and hit the power sensor to kill the engine. The control program powered the flyer down slowly. The blades bent sadly downward like wilting flower petals, and the engine died with one last sputter.

Paul unsnapped himself from the harness, giving a thumbs-up to Shawn and the Pipers. He was stunned when they clapped and then celebrated with a few loud whoops. All the Timmon, including Lonin, stood silently, in their same places, apparently having never moved. They were totally unaffected, as if they saw impromptu flight tests all the time.

He shook his head.

"What's wrong?" Shawn had stepped forward to shake Paul's hand.

"Nothing. Let's give her a good inspection. Check for leaks and loose bolts again. Then it's your turn."

"What? Me?"

"Yes, you. You take her up and do exactly what I did."

"I thought you were happy with the way she flew."

"I am. She proved herself. But so far, you haven't. This is the second phase of your training. Full stress test."

Shawn nodded, but his face didn't show affirmation.

"When you can lift her straight up and hold her there at full throttle, we'll lengthen the cables. When you can maneuver her smoothly around this clearing — up, down, back, forth, turning — you'll be ready for your first real flight."

Lonin and the other Timmon had moved forward to join them. "Shik, Paul Saarinen, will you be making a longer flight soon?" Lonin asked.

"I plan to, yes."

"Good. If I must wait for young Shawn Harvestmoon to learn to fly before I can ride in this machine, I fear I may not live long enough and my grand-children will be the first."

He smiled in his Timmon way. "I made a joke."

#

The treetops formed a moving floor of amber beneath them, swept in waves by the gusty late-morning wind and tossed further by the down-wash off the copter's blades. Pellin, penderin, and other flying creatures scattered before the craft like schools of leaping fish. Paul moved his fingers over the control screen, and the flyer rose smoothly to 25 meters above the trees. From that altitude, the oddly flat and level canopy of trees seemed a rugged wheat field or an inland sea choked with yellow seaweed, and the flying animals looked even more like brown and yellow fish.

Paul glanced back at Lonin, who was sitting folded up and stone-still in the center of the passenger seat. His face was expressionless as he turned only his head side to side to look around them. Paul had warned him not to lean, since his oversized body could tip the flyer dangerously. Lonin was predictably compliant.

Paul turned back to the controls. He scrolled through each screen again and was satisfied. There was one non-critical alarm signal, a redundant high-exhaust temperature alarm, that had come on early in the last flight. But that alarm could be addressed later, and there were no others. They were flying level at about half-throttle, and the engine droned easily, with no hesitation or revving. It was a good sign.

Before ever taking the first flight, the three of them had cleared off two emergency landing pads, one east and one west, each a kilometer from the main base. Even with these safe locations, any hint of trouble would have led Paul to abort and return home. When a bladed copter lost power, it didn't glide; it plummeted. If they were flying fast, the side wedge-wings would provide a small amount of lift for a few seconds, but not enough for them to glide to safety. In these brutally thick forests, a crash landing would leave no survivors.

Paul's initial heading for their second outward flight was due east, to the first emergency pad. Having traveled only by foot or by storil-back for months, he was surprised at how quickly they reached it. He actually flew past the pad and had to brake and turn around. Back over the clearing, he brought the flyer to a hover and slowly descended.

They had finished clearing out the 20-meter circle only days before, but already the trees bordering the edge had begun to retake the newly opened air space. Pellin darted across the spaces between new branches, expertly avoiding catcher vines, before disappearing into the foliage. The flat floor of the clearing was already growing in with scrub brush in spotty brown clumps.

With the landing pad located, and the engine relaxed and smooth, Paul felt confident to explore a bit, and he looked around for other features that might be interesting to observe from the air. Farther east ran a sizable creek that he had heard about but never seen. It reportedly crossed this wooded plain from north to south.

He lifted the flyer back to the 25-meter height, rotated it to face due east, and then turned back to Lonin and pointed emphatically toward their next objective, the creek. Lonin nodded and squeezed the handgrips tighter, until his fingers and thumbs turned red. Paul allowed himself a slight sense of delight at Lonin's discomfort.

Time to lay this hawk's feathers back a little.

He touched the throttle and inclined the rotor, and the flyer responded with a satisfying acceleration. He let her accelerate until the airspeed read 100 kilometers per hour. At this speed, they would cover the distance to the creek in no more than five minutes. He used the time to look for openings in the tree cover, which might indicate good places for future landing sites. A few openings dotted the tree-scape, and he saved their coordinates in the ship's memory as they passed, making mental notes on which were the most promising.

He'd really missed this, the acceleration of a powered machine, the rush of air over his face and arms, the sense of speed. He thought about trying some maneuvers but then remembered his passenger. Lonin, who'd never flown or traveled at even half this speed before, was a pale yellow statue, an ancient giant kneeling in the cockpit, hunkered down as small as he could be (which was not small) in the back seat. He was motionless, except for his ginger-colored eyes sweeping from side to side.

Paul backed the throttle down to half speed again. He enjoyed tweaking the Timmon a little, but he didn't want him vomiting or passing out. When he gave Lonin a questioning thumbs-up, Lonin slowly unlocked one hand from the handgrip and returned it two thumbs up. Laughing, Paul turned back to the controls and scouted the trees ahead for signs of the creek line.

At 50 klicks per hour, they reached the creek in 12 minutes. From half a klick away, it was a thin, dark line cutting across the carpet of trees ahead, then a meandering shadow. Then they were upon it, a rapidly flowing, rocky flume of water, a river snaking its way between thick seas of trees.

At about 20 meters wide, the creek was just able to keep the trees on one bank separated from those on the other. Farther upstream, the trees would be able to join arms, and the stream would be enshrouded, held captive, hidden from the sun in a fly-trapper's grip. But here, the churning rapids and pools were the victor, and an echo of the bright sun rebounded from the water. Where the sun didn't reflect blindingly, Paul could make out dark shapes moving slowly beneath the creek's surface. He pointed them out to Lonin, who had apparently recovered from his complete immobility. Lonin nodded and yelled above the noise of the rotors.

"Marinil. Big swimmer. 'River father.'"

As Paul watched, one of the shapes charged a school of smaller swimming shapes. Its large jaws broke the water's surface in a cascade of leaping shiny things. The marinil rolled, exposing a thick, mottled flank of brown and yellow, and sank back into the shadows of a nearby depth. The smaller fish coalesced into a school again and moved upstream to safer waters.

"Poisonous bite. Bad temper."

A poisonous bite seemed to be a common trait on Timmistria. Lonin was probably poisonous too.

Paul took this time to run another thorough check of sensor readings and noted the fuel level was at about 2/3 tank. They would head back now, with plenty of fuel to spare and two very successful flights under their belts. He spun the craft slowly, pointing the nose directly back toward the base. Before he turned to warn Lonin that they were about to accelerate again, he felt the Timmon's large hand on his shoulder. He looked down to where Lonin pointed, at the edge of the trees on the bank just to their left.

"Delerin."

Paul set the controls to auto-hover and then peered into the honey-gold shadows beneath the hay-colored trees. He saw nothing at first, and then at last a subtle movement there, then again, just farther left. But even after letting his eyes adjust, he didn't get a clean look at any of Lonin's biological cousins. Even so, by the telltales, Paul guessed it to be a small hunting party, perhaps only 10 to 12 individuals. He couldn't begin to guess their reaction to what they were observing above them.

A quiet alarm sounded from the control screen — a 60% fuel-level alarm Paul had programmed. He glanced one last time down into the trees again, and then leaned back to Lonin.

"Time's up. Gotta go."

Lonin nodded, centered his bent body, and gripped the handles. Paul eased into the acceleration this time, bringing the flyer gradually up to an efficient half-throttle. The little engine hummed; with no problems, they would arrive back at the base with fuel to spare. He decided to try the autopilot and set about tapping in a target destination, speed, and altitude, then tapped the "ENGAGE" icon on the screen. The controller seemed to hesitate before adjusting the angle and course, and Paul imagined the AI thinking about how it wanted to fly. But she steadied herself and flew true, and Paul used the time to work the auxiliary apps, initiating automatic digital mapping and photography, locating and tracking the emergency landing pad, and setting the flight mode to "MAXIMIZE FUEL EFFICIENCY."

In this mode, the craft adjusted altitude, speed, and course based on infrared and UV atmospheric readings, to take advantage of favorable winds and air densities, much like birds could "read" air currents and thermals to preserve energy as they migrated. After playing with the controls, Paul sat back and just enjoyed the ride. When he saw something particularly interesting, he took manual control of the onboard cameras and took photos.

About halfway back, Lonin tapped his shoulder again, and another alarm sounded immediately. Paul was surprised to read "CODE ORANGE AERIAL THREAT WARNING." Lonin pointed to their right rear quadrant, where higher up several dark winged shapes flew. As Paul watched, the dark flyers fell steadily toward them, easily surpassing their speed. He was reminded of the giant flying reptiles of Shill Wellin, but these creatures were smaller and more hawklike, with long, straight tails folded narrowly. The mottled patterns of feathers were soon visible on their undersides.

He checked the Taser charge and set it to auto-track. At the flight controller's urging, he touched an icon that would allow evasive action if any of the birds posed an imminent threat. He followed the approaching creatures with some concern, since he had no idea how effective the evasion controls were, how effective the Taser would be, or how fast it could recharge.

Lonin's voice in his right ear reached him over the flapping of the rotors. "They are pantellil. Sky robbers. They steal food from others and hunt smaller things. They are curious only. We are not carrying food, so they will grow bored and leave."

True to Lonin's words, the pantellil flattened their descent and glided behind the flyer, maintaining a distance of about 10 meters. They wheeled and dove at each other like drone flies, dodging easily, until something in the forest drew their attention. They curled their wings one after another into steep power-dives of impressive tightness and speed, and soon disappeared into the trees below the flyer.

"They are always five. The Delerin call them the Five Sisters. The males do not fly, instead tending their kithin."

Paul nodded, checking the sky for other unknown threats and then the controls. The threat alarm had cleared, and the navigator informed him they were approaching the main pad. He was tempted to let the autopilot land the copter but decided to bring it in once more on manual control. He disengaged the auto and gradually reduced airspeed, noting the forest opening now visible ahead of them and matching it to the approaching target on the visual flight map. As his hands worked the controls, the flyer slowed to a dead hover directly over the center of the pad and descended smoothly, settling in the dust with a barely discernible bump. He made one last survey of the system readings and cut the engine.

"Stay seated."

He had told Shawn and Lonin of the rule that no one disembarked until the rotor had come to a complete halt, but he still felt compelled to remind them. The rotor spin-down took about 30 seconds. Once the blades halted with a final lurch, he unstrapped and climbed out, and then turned to help Lonin unstrap and unwind himself from the tiny back seat. Shawn came over from the bench seat they'd placed at the main entrance to the clearing.

"Smooth landing. I can't wait until I can do that."

"Keep practicing. You're getting better. If you keep at it, we'll be cutting you loose from the tethers in a couple weeks."

"Solid news. See anything interesting?"

"We saw plenty. We've got some things to talk about. Further precautions I'd like to implement."

"What did you think of the ride, Lonin?"

The Timmon was slowly straightening his long body, stretching his neck, and flexing his hands. He still looked a bit washed-out, with a faint pink glow about his hairline and eyes. Able to stand tall at last, and gazing skyward, he shook himself erect, like a baby stork just from the shell. He planted himself in the dirt, hands on hips, feet set widely as if holding his body firmly to the soil. At last, he nodded and smiled wanly.

"Shik. Ex-cellent. When may I fly again?"

Chapter 24

"Humans tell us their gods are all-seeing and all-knowing. We Timmon do not say this of Timmistria. But I have never known of a thing to escape her eyes."
— Lonin, to Shawna Harvestmoon-Serak

Shawn and Cara found Paul at his usual haunt, the maintenance shops. He was standing in front of one of the fermentation systems, arms crossed, staring pensively at the apparatus as if it were a disobedient child. His yellow eyes never rested. Cara wasn't sure he was aware of her and Shawn, as intensely as he seemed focused on the machine. But as they approached, he turned to them and nodded. Shawn broke the silence.

"How's the yield?"

"Fair. Five percent over last week. I expected better."

"They should have the sixth tank ready in less than two days."

"We need it. I think we've tweaked the process about as far as we can go, unless you can conjure bacteria that's more active."

"Dr. Tom's working on it, but I'm not expecting a breakthrough."

"Thousands of years of brewing booze, and we still haven't improved this process much. Greetings, Manager. I'm guessing you didn't come to hear about process yields. Shawn's kept you updated on our progress?"

"Yes. He's very enthusiastic."

Shawn rolled his eyes.

Cara said, "I came to talk about capabilities. Of the flyer, I mean, not this process."

"We're ready to begin reconnaissance flights along the Delerin boundary land."

"Shawn told me that. What I'm interested in is another idea you brought up, dropping chemicals from the flyer to drive off migrating cremin. If we're attacked by the Delerin, couldn't we use the same strategy?"

"We agreed to fly recon only."

"This would be used only in defense, and only as a last resort. We'd have no intention of harming anyone."

Paul's face took on a hard edge. "Even with all good intentions, Manager, if the flyer is used on the offensive, Delerin will likely die." He shook his head, eyes closing for a moment as if he were reliving an unpleasant memory. "You might win one battle, but your war would be lost. The Delerin are not a few lumbering reptiles. There are too many of them, and your border is too long and porous for one flyer to defend."

"But perhaps we could slow them down and reduce their numbers."

"If it comes to war with the Delerin, and you use this machine to attack them directly, the Timmon will abandon you and may rise against you as well. Fairdawn would fall in a day."

Cara felt tension knotting the space between her eyes and tried to rub it away. "You're right, of course. Not sure what I was thinking. The news from the Timmon envoy is worsening: the Delerin are closer to war and could march at any time. We keep trying diplomatic solutions. I've asked the Timmon to call for a negotiation, but they tell me the Delerin refuse. I thought if we showed that we could defend ourselves, they might reconsider."

"I don't think that would work with the Delerin. They're technologically limited, but they aren't naïve. They know you have only one flying machine. They'll know they need only attack on two or three fronts. I'm not so sure they wouldn't figure out how to down the flyer anyway. Even with its built-in defenses, it's not a military helicopter. It's just a hobby craft. A flock of pellin could bring it down."

Cara felt herself nodding stupidly, and then stopped. "I'm sorry, Paul. It seems I've come to depend on you unfairly to solve our most difficult problems. Unfortunately, this problem with the Delerin is a cultural one that's been brewing since we first arrived. I'm sure engineering and science won't solve it. Diplomacy must. Shawn, I'm going to meet with the Timmon again. Keep working with Paul. Let's at least start the flyovers. Make them think a little bit. We've heard rumors that the Delerin believe we have a storehouse of weapons and evil things hidden in the catacombs of the Common House. If they really believe that, perhaps it will slow them down a little and give us more time."

Paul nodded again. "We'll be in the air again tomorrow morning."

"Good. Oh, and Paul: When you talk about Fairdawn's problems, you still say things like 'You have only one flyer,' and 'You might win the battle but lose the war.' I like to think of you as part of this community, but when will you begin to think of yourself that way? When will you refer to this colony as 'we'?"

Paul's face turned a little red around the cheeks and neck, and Cara was reminded of the Timmon emotional reflex. "I'm sorry," he said. "I guess it's a matter of time."

"Time's up."

Cara left, leaving the men in her wake. She tried all day not to think about Paul, but the burning memory of his eyes would not give her rest, and she caught herself daydreaming in more than one meeting.

#

Paul was exhausted, with little sleep over the last few days. Cara's more frequent visits to the shops weren't helping. Thinking of her felt like a betrayal.

He took a late dinner and carried it down to an empty trestle table in a corner of the small park across the street from the shops. The sun lingered just below the treetops, and deep amber shadows set a somber mood for the street. A few field hands led jarin-drawn carts into town, headed toward the storage area, which was now reportedly at three-quarters capacity. With the dangerous night approaching, no one would be heading back out to the fields.

Even the mumbling draft beasts seemed weary, heads hanging. Dreyaten was nowhere in the sky, but Timmistria's other two satellites, Thoran and Dartan, three-quarters full, chased each other from the east. The nights would be brighter for the next ten days, as the celestial twins both waxed. The numbers of night bugs and other flying pests would increase as well.

The food was fresh and well-prepared, steamed cabbages and greens with a hint of tallow, boiled grains with huge egg-shaped kernels, and jarin cheese, small but very strong. It was a better-than-average meal on Timmistria and complemented the beer nicely. But Paul didn't seem to have an appetite. He forced himself to eat anyway.

There was little pedestrian traffic here, barely enough to keep him interested. But he was surprised to see the large figure of Julius Dench on the footpath on the opposite side of the street. Dench rarely came to town, at least as far as Paul could tell from the man's limited trips to the maintenance area. It became evident from his furtive glances and his general direction that he was coming to meet Paul. The suspicions were confirmed when the large, pink-faced man crossed the street directly toward the table where Paul sat. Paul continued eating casually, suspecting Dench's visit meant nothing good. He wouldn't be proven wrong.

"Good evening, Mr. Saarinen. Mind if I join you?"

Paul minded, but he nodded toward the seat opposite him anyway. He hadn't cared much for Dench on the flight in, and even less so now. He knew from Shawn a little of the problem that Dench seemed to be causing with the Timmon, but none of that made sense to Paul. The whole life-light thing smelled of religion, superstition, or worse.

Dench stepped neatly around the bench and settled himself on the wooden seat, which creaked a little under his weight. He was large and tended to wipe sweat from his brow, which would lead most people to underestimate how well he could move. Paul wasn't most people. Most people also wouldn't have realized that Dench was not alone, that one of his lackeys had moved into the shadows farther up the street.

"I have a letter you'll find interesting, Mr. Saarinen. Or should I say 'Commander Sharren'?"

Paul stabbed the last bite of cheese with his fork. "Go on."

Dench waited an instant for a further reaction, then shrugged. "It's an e-note transmitted from the Co-Op joint chiefs to the commander of the Wee'en theater of operations. Where you were stationed, of course."

He slid the note across, a half-page memo printed neatly in cryptic military font on a sheet of printer paper, an imported sheet, oddly crisp and rectangular and white. It looked out of place sitting on the primitive wooden table. Paul set his fork on the plate, one that he'd made, pushed it all to the side, and drew the note to him.

> *11.9.5.2544*
> *Col. Z'Zyr Sentapa*
> *Urgency: 1*
> *Classification: 1*
> *Col. Sentapa: Confirming trans 11.9.3.2544. You are directed to order BU R7514 immediate offensive on _____ _____. Objective serious collateral damage to hostile _____ _____ and aid in supply support. After mission failure and loss of Cmdr. Christin-Dottir, Cmdr. Sharren will rethink his opposition and carry out his assigned duties.*
> *From: Cmdr. 2.2 John Q. Glenn*

Paul felt a deep hole where his dinner had gone.

"I can assure you that memo is genuine, Commander Sharren. Your superiors knowingly sent your wife to her death, in order to convince you to lead the next attack. These are the kind of men you work for."

Paul slid the paper back across the table. "Nothing there I didn't already know."

"Maybe not. Maybe while working out there in your garden, you realized long ago you'd been played. So this e-note is only confirmation of your suspicions. I think it still coalesces the anger, doesn't it? To know that your leaders so casually sent your wife to die?"

"We both signed the papers."

"Hmm. I hardly think disregard for your well-being was in your contract. That's just how *they* choose to look at things. I have another set of papers for you to sign, Commander Sharren, something more to offer you. One part of my offer is the chance to pay back these … men, these 'leaders of men,' I should say, who chose to kill your wife and use you for their own needs. And then to rub salt in the wounds, they cast you like a spent fusion canister onto this rock, to rot here to the end of your days. How would it feel, Commander Sharren, to hold those bastards accountable?"

Dench sat back, arms folded over his paunch. His face was like a pouting child's, but his eyes were purely serpentine. "I can understand feeling like that, Commander Sharren, because we have that in common. Soon I will have them all right here." He held out his pink, puffy hand, palm up. "And I will squeeze them until their bones snap and the blood runs down like the juice from berries."

His hand closed into a fleshy fist, tightening until the pale skin around his fingers grew white.

"That's a little dramatic, don't you think?"

"Is it? What these men, all the men like them that came before and will follow, have done to you and me is beyond reprehensible. It's inexcusable. It cannot go unavenged. And I will have vengeance."

He opened his fist and wiped his hands together, as if ridding them of the imaginary human carcasses. "Commander Sharren, you've heard of me, perhaps, or at least some of my businesses. Quark Limited? Planetary Financial Services? Stel-7 Media?"

They were familiar names. All large, multi-planetary companies. Controversial corporate raiders. Highly profitable. All led by a shadowy absentee chairman.

"Anton Demovich."

"Exactly. At least, that's the name I've used most often."

Paul nodded. "You're in exile too."

"I call it 'vacation with prejudice.' Makes it sound like I had more control over my departure. Sticky business on Sarena. A study in chaos theory, really, a few minor events cascading into a tide of unexpected non-constructive results."

"Meaning the emir discovered your plan to kill him and tried to beat you to the punch."

Dench smiled. "Does my identity surprise you?"

Paul shook his head. "I never bought that you were just a geologist."

"Oh, but I am, just a simple geologist. I have the diploma to prove it. And that's exactly what my line of work has always been. I mine for treasures, and then I own them. Discovery and ownership. It's a simple business model."

"What do you want from me?"

"Oh, come now. You know what I want. Your help! Men like you don't grow on malack trees. You're one in a million. A billion! A man like me needs men like you, and vice versa. I define the objective. You make it happen."

"And what is the objective, besides your vague inclination to get revenge on someone in the Co-Op leadership?"

Dench, or Demovich, leaned forward, his face now tight and dark. "I've got my own scores to settle. I want you to help me settle them."

"Such as…"

"I could tell you about my early life on Gliese Five, and a camping trip that gave us a very good view overlooking the city of Barren Harbor, from well up the nearby coastal mountains. I could tell you about watching from our safe campsite as waves of Co-Op ships passed over the mountains and laid waste to the city. I could tell you about my parents and sister among the dead. The commander who ordered the strikes, who'd decided to make an example of that growing planet, was none other than Vlad Shostovish, whose name you no doubt recognize as head of Co-Op security. There are others.

"But none of that really matters, does it? *We* are both men who matter, Commander Sharren."

"Do you plan to rule Timmistria?"

"Rule? This little yellow pea? I don't rule planets, Commander Sharren. I own them. I leave the ruling to men like you. That's what you do. Your destiny, perhaps. But that's a destiny you'll never realize without my resources. With men like me supporting them, men like you become rulers … caesars … kings! Without men like me…" Dench looked behind him and gestured at two workers leading a cart down the darkening street. "…farmers."

Turning back now, laying his hands flat on the table, meeting Paul's eyes and studying him, Dench seemed a pink-faced python eyeing a rat. Paul could almost see a red glow about him. He tried to imagine the reptile-eyed man as a child dressed in outdoor gear, watching a firestorm of nuclear rage destroy his city and family. The Gliese campaign was common history, a fledgling rebellion crushed with overkill. Dench, who by appearance was in his mid-50s in Galactic Standard years, would have been about the correct age, taking five years or so of relativistic time losses from interstellar travel.

"These generals of yours, whom you scrved loyally, used you. They cashed in your wife's life like a common coin and dumped you to rot on this distant uncivilized island, probably hoping you'd be killed by some random predator or disease. Join me, Commander Sharren. I offer you the chance to avenge your loss, to cast the unworthy bastards out, and to take your rightful place. No one else can offer you that, not the people in this colony, not the yellow natives, not the officers you reported to, even if they planned to bring you back from purgatory after the heat died down."

"And what do you want in exchange?"

"The means to an end. You rule; I own. You help me bring this planet under control and prove your commitment to my cause. Then you lead my forces directly into the capital and stage a takeover before the station guard can react. You can fashion that attack as brutally as you like. I don't really care. But at the end of the day, we shall see you installed as head of state."

"And you as emperor?"

"No, no! I told you, I have no desire to rule anything. I will control the commerce — banks, trade groups, transport. You will rule the people, Commander Sharren. I will rule everything else. We will be legendary."

"Once in power, what's to prevent me from naming you an enemy of the state and taking you down?"

Dench sneered. "Don't insult me. You know I have secure systems in place. And associates. Besides, your trying to throw me over wouldn't serve either of us. I would take the liberty of having a remote kill module planted on you. I have nothing to fear. And neither do you, if you don't cross me."

Paul held Dench's piercing stare for a few seconds longer, then allowed his eyes to wander to a lone field hand walking home, tools over his shoulder. The man, colored in dusk's monotone grays, glanced in their direction and then walked on quickly.

"Time's up. Are you with me?"

Paul looked farther up the street. Dench's lackey moved uneasily in the shadows.

"No."

After a lengthy pause, Dench nodded. "That doesn't surprise me. Loyal to the end. Foolish. A pity, really. You are the extraordinary man I have been seeking for quite some time, and I can't help thinking that our arriving here together was more than coincidence. Don't close the door on this opportunity. If you change your mind in the next few days, you know where to find me. But don't wait too long and miss your calling. My presence here has apparently caused a problem with the hostile natives, which will force me to move more quickly than I had planned. No matter. Things are shaping up nicely, but your help will make them much tidier."

Dench stood, now a dull gray hulk in what remained of the evening's pale glow. Paul caught a brief red glint from the man's eyes, and he didn't know if it was a reflection from the distant streetlight or just his imagination. Dench studied their surroundings, as if he could see more clearly now that the day's light was failing.

"By the way, out of respect for your capabilities, I took a risk talking with you tonight. I ask that you return that respect and keep our conversation to yourself. I hold no grudges against those who choose not to join me, as long as they remain neutral. I have little patience for those who choose to stand in my way. Good night, Commander Sharren."

He moved off then, with silent footsteps, crossing the deserted dirt street. The night creatures and insects were now audible, rattles and croaks and hushed buzzes as they talked to each other tentatively across the gloom. Full darkness lay in wait, and Dench became a ghost moving through shadows down the street, soon joined by another man taller than he was, probably the new goon who had joined Dench's mining group. Like bad memories, the two conspirators moved from shadow to darkness.

Paul sat in the deepening gloom, his appetite now completely gone. He let the darkness envelop him.

Chapter 25

DELOS RED SYSTEM

"We are but grains of sand, brushed along the beach by the breeze, battered by the surf, abraded and burnished and fractured by the passage."
— Jahhn Stin-Ell, "The Impurity of Awareness," 2466 GSD

Their shared living quarters on the command vessel CS Unification were a bad place to haggle over strategy, but that's where Helwin and Paul usually grappled, most often over breakfast, more by default than by intention. Helwin's eyes, teal and azure and other colors Paul couldn't name, darted about the steel and white cubicle, alive with preoccupation. Her face was a fortress against his arguments.

Between bites of synthetic toast, he said, "The strategy team can't generate a viable exit strategy. In every simulation, The Thinkers fence you in."

"Nonsense. At the first sign of it going negative, we'll fan-cast all the ordnance and bust tail."

She nibbled a bite of her eggs. After six years, she still didn't trust his cooking. He slid the sperillium spice tri-grinder across to her, the one they'd bought during their three-day marriage leave on Caladis. The precious ultra-dense metal emitted low levels of large-particle radiation, advertised to "intensify the seasonings and transmogrify the taste buds." If nothing else, the grinder was startlingly heavy.

"They won't give you the chance. There's no element of surprise."

She left her seat and squeezed around him to get something from the condiment cabinet. She smelled aggressively clean, as if she'd scoured and atomized every molecule of sweat or pheromone away. One evening the week before, she'd dabbed on a hint of perfume, the fragrance they'd picked out together at Caladis, and then applied some of their fruit compote strategically on her body. He'd savored that four-course meal.

She returned to her seat with a small squeeze bottle of neon blue gelatin.

"I know that, Paul. But the Wee'en have been more successful lately at blocking the Thinker ingress routes. With the Wee'en support we've gotten, the Thinkers haven't been able to bring their full firepower. We're in a much better formation."

Paul shook his head. "The same Wee'en that gave way for months while the Thinkers pushed us all around the asteroid belts. C'mon, Hel. You know we can't trust them to hold their positions. Stop rationalizing."

She brushed pellet-sized globs of the flavoring onto her scone, then clunked the jar on the tabletop.

"OK, you're right, Paul. It's a suicide run. Soon as we level off, the Wee'en are going to run, and Thinker drones are going to drop out and flak us before we get anywhere near the objective. But you know what? It's my job. And yours. I can't believe you're bailing on this mission." She bit her scone, and a tear of neon blue slid from the corner of her mouth. She brushed it off with the back of her hand. "I'd rather face the Thinkers than a court-martial."

She met his eyes briefly, hers red and wet around the edges, symptoms of too many narco-med nights and not enough natural sleep. But the hard set of her eyes couldn't hide the fear.

"Don't go, Hel. Regional command has pushed us too far this time. The system's lost. Let it go."

She continued eating, her head down. "Got to, Paul. It's my command."

They finished their breakfast in silence, save the gurgles and grunts of the ship operation around them and the hiss of the grinder as she seasoned her eggs. He imagined a life without her, and then braced for the inevitable pang of guilt that followed those thoughts, every time he so clinically considered losing her, every time they went to battle. But he trusted she did the same, with good reason. He probed the inside of his own head and found no resentment there at the thought. His own regret was just foolishness.

They had three days until she led the strike force to disable the Thinker command center. They spent the days doing three things: planning the assault, briefing the strike force, and making love frantically and desperately. On the morning of the third day they lay in bed, sweating, the smells and heat of sex clinging to their sheets.

The murmurs and growls of the ship came through the walls, artifacts that escaped the noise cancellation system, reminders of the world beyond that would call them away. After their breakfast argument, words were sparse between them, but he chose to speak to her then, his cause feeling as hopeless as hers.

"Let me run it, Hel. I'll take the team in. You lay down the screen and have the fleet ready to clean up."

She sniffed, breathing quietly for a moment, and then pulled the sheet back from her naked body. She rolled out to sit on the edge of the bed, leaving a cool line on his side where her skin had been pressed to his.

"No. Our plan is sound. You lay down the screen; we'll fall in from the belt and punch them hard and fast. They'll react, but not fast enough. You know I'm the one to lead the run — you're too much the berserker sometimes — and you're better at applying the long-range stuff anyway. You're a surgeon, and that's what I need. We have the roles correct."

"Zark the roles, Hel. The idiots at Command don't know what they're sending you into, or they don't care. Don't run this mission, or let me run it."

"We stick with the plan. I run it."

"This is over your head. You'll fail it. I'm the one who has to go."

She slammed her hand on the bed, which made only a dull thumping sound. "Enough! Let's get this straight — *Major*! I'm the ranking officer here, and we will follow the plan as laid out. Have you forgotten that you initially refused this mission? This is your command too, Paul."

"I rescind my refusal."

"Too late. I can't accept it, and I can't trust this mission to an executive officer who doesn't believe in it. That'd be suicide for you and for everyone under your command."

"I'm the only one who can pull this off, Hel. You know that."

"Your heart's not in it."

"Neither is yours. You're scared shitless."

She shook her head and lifted herself from the bed. "At this point, I'm the only one I've got. I can't trust you to run it."

"Let me, Hel. Please."

Her face muscles flexed, giving her a lean, angular expression. But the softness returned, and it was that image of her small smile that would haunt him constantly for weeks to follow, and after that always at night when his mind wouldn't rest.

"I'd be lying if I said I wasn't nervous. But I've got the best backup commander in the business, and I think I can count on him to have his heart in running the support. It's going to be fine. Now get up and join me in the shower. We have 60 liters of water credits saved up, and we have time for a foam bath before I get some shut-eye and prep for the final briefing."

#

They shared a final meal before the boarding. He didn't try again to change her mind, but he couldn't meet her eyes either. She finally spoke, her voice remarkably light and earnest.

"After this, we've got a month of leave. Let's return to Gliese."

"A little expensive, don't you think?"

As the first system explored by humans, Gliese had become an overdeveloped tourist destination, with satellite cities, engineered ecosystems on every planet and orbiting piece of rock, and high-speed shuttles connecting all of it.

"Maybe. But by the time we get back there, we'll have skipped six or eight years. We'll have some compounded interest built up on our savings there."

"Hmm. You forget I refused a mission. I'll probably go right to the brig."

"No. I documented your change of heart, with confirmation that no charges will be filed."

"They can ignore the e-con."

"Yes. But they won't. Especially after we win this system."

Paul nodded. "I love you, Hel. You know that, don't you?"

"Stop. We have a good plan, and Thinker activity has been low for weeks now. They think we're packing and leaving."

"Tell me you love me."

She slapped his arm with the back of her hand. "Of course I love you, you dumb Crestite. Didn't all the crazy things we did this week prove that?"

His face felt warm; when he looked up, her smile was devilish and devastating. He'd faced down a score of Thinkers in mech-suits without flinching, but that smile always fluttered his heart.

She purred, "And when I get back, I'll prove it some more. So remember what you're fighting for, airman."

#

"Copy that, leader. Initiating target focus at 9-0. Captain Ferelli, light up the sky for those zarkers."

Thin blue fire stabbed out from the laser cannons. The beams were invisible in a pure vacuum but visible for several hundred meters out from the muzzles as they lit up thinly spread ions and propulsion decomposition products near the gunboats. Had the beams been visible the whole distance, they would have traced narrow lines to the space behind the assault team, which had begun hard acceleration.

The Thinkers responded to Helwin's attack almost before it was initiated, peeling off from positions directly behind her squadron. New lights flicked on in her path, hidden spacecraft and drones now coming to life. More troubling were the Wee'en forces, which abandoned their defensive positions and joined in firing on Helwin's squadron.

Paul laid his hand on the text panel to send an encrypted text directly to Helwin's display. "Pick an exit corridor. We'll keep it open."

Her text reply: "Nuts to that. Blast one to the base."

"Too dense. Can't cover it."

"Going in. No choice. Do what you can."

Paul opened a channel to his gunnery lead. "Tom. Terminate your sweep and focus on an exit hole opposite the strike team's inbound vector. Open an escape route."

"Copy that. Let's burn 'em a peephole, guys."

Helwin's force of 16 was now taking heavy fire from base batteries, drifting drone craft, and the turncoat Wee'en fighters. Paul focused his laser fire on craft pursuing the strikers. He watched the numbers and could do no better than a 25% knockout rate. There were just too many of them, and more and more slipped past his containment.

"Can't keep them all off your 6, Commander."

"You're doing fine, base. Keep it up. Unit Six, bear in! You're outside my cover."

Almost immediately, the pale blue icon that was the No. 6 attack ship flared red, and the icon disassembled. Soon after, No. 9 came apart as well and veered out of the formation.

Helwin's voice roared over the open command channel. "Dammit, team, hold tight together. We need all the firepower we have. When we reach the targets, unload heavy arsenal, and then gun it for the escape hole. Base, copy my exit coordinates."

"Got 'em, lead."

Paul adjusted the heavy guns to match the coordinates Helwin had sent him. A text came in, yellow letters on the dull gray screen.

"Not going to make it. Sorry, baby."

Paul's fingers found the screen. He sent: "Don't give up, Hel. We'll get you out."

Long seconds later, her response came. "Always the optimist. Lead our people out, Paul. Don't do anything stupid."

Paul's fingers hovered over the touch pad. "Will do. By the book."

"Who you kidding? Promise me."

Two more of the icons flared red and disintegrated. The remaining 12 attack ships were still minutes from the Thinker command center and an ocean of space away from the escape corridor Paul's main gunner was trying in vain to keep open. Thinker and Wee'en fighters had now converged from all directions, overwhelming the large cannon defense. When the predicted survival rate from his ship's AI fell to 0.5%, Paul killed the readout.

He laid his fingers lightly on the pad again: "Promise. I'll get them out, Hel."

"Will fry as many as we can. Ain't gonna be no Thinker's dinner."

Paul's guns tracked a point ten seconds ahead of Helwin's vector. Two more icons flared out. The remainder tightened further.

He keyed, "Follow the hot spot I'm painting. We'll lead you out."

"Save the fire. You'll need it to make the jump point. Thinkers will have more sleepers staged. Get started on simulations. You may not have much time."

"Negative, Commander. Feed us a course, and we'll lead it."

"No point. Probability nil."

"Sorry, Hel."

Helwin's voice came over the comm. "Pull tight, dames. Let's pass so close they can count our ass hairs."

Text: "Lead them out, Paul. That's an order."

"Aye." Then: "I love you, Hel. I always will."

"Of course. Be waiting for you at the last jump point, Lover."

Two more icons flared and fell. The remaining eight, including Hel's green lead ship, closed ranks. White pips of enemy craft were a cloud of gnats spiraling around them. Another icon flared, then another. Six left.

Text: "Ggrlx. Shield down. CU. LY."

He texted "LY2," but a yellow "Link Down" blip flashed. The icon that was Hel's ship turned amber and fell into a loose collection of fractured arcs. Four others soon followed. One last pale blue cone managed to maneuver through the cloud of gnats and bury its nose into one of the two Wee'en control bases.

Paul identified the vessel and its pilot, Trent Fleming.

He whispered to himself, "Way to go, Trent. Coming right behind you."

To the general communication channel, he said, "Cease all fire. Initiate Plan E5. Be ready to scramble for the jump point in … ten minutes. Captain Ferelli, continuous scan. Anything comes within 20K of one of our ships — toast it."

"Copy that."

His new second's voice came over the private channel, the hard edge no longer there. "You all right, Chief? You need a moment?"

"No time. Let's pull all our people together and make the jump out. Keep it tight. No more losses."

"Copy that. Looks like the T's are letting us go."

Paul's holograph told the same story. The Wee'en and Thinker ships did not pursue the retreating fleet and remained in the vicinity of their command bases. The AI showed low probability of counter-assault formation.

"Don't trust them, Sharp. They may have a surprise for us at the jump point as well."

The chaos that had been the Co-Op point of attack was now an orderly assemblage of white pips in tracking orbit around the Wee'en command bases. The bastards had planned this all along. The damaged base blinked yellow on Paul's display.

An unencrypted message came across from the largest of the Thinker command ships, in crisp Galactic Standard.

"Pleased to have made your acquaintance. Please exit our system at your earliest convenience. Re-admittance will not be allowed. Have a good day."

Yeah. "Get out and stay out." I'm not done with you sarcastic zarkers yet.

Paul keyed the command-channel-only comm. "Stand down on the expedite order. Jump ETD — 51 hours. Command meeting here in 10. Rest until then. That's an order. Acknowledge, please."

"Copy here, sir."

"Copy, Commander."

Six more confirmations of the stand-down came in, all professionally unemotional.

He keyed the private line. "Sharp, take your break. I'll take first watch."

"Copy, Chief. Permission to come up?"

Paul let his eyes close and rubbed the tense spot between them. "Granted." He blanked the comm line and turned to his two assisting officers, Lts. Sharon Smith and Sharon Alvarado.

"Lieutenants, you are relieved. Get some rest. I'll hold the command until your reliefs arrive."

He could tell they weren't happy about leaving, but Lt. Smith just nodded toward the door. They could get a little intense sometimes, but he was grateful they were looking out for him. On their way out of the cramped command booth, they gave Sharp a warning look. Sharp outranked them, but rank wouldn't prevent a good ass-chewing from the lieutenants if you neglected your airmen or yourself.

Captain Sharp Ferelli, nicknamed for both his military skill and his prominent nose, took the seat vacated by Lt. Alvarado and said nothing.

"What?"

Sharp eyed him hawklike before responding. "You know why I'm here. To see how you're doing."

"I'm fine."

"You'd say that no matter what. Remember, evaluating my commanding officer is part of my job."

"Consider me evaluated. I look fine, right? I appreciate your concern."

"Don't give me the hard-boiled attitude. I can read you like a book. You're thinking you and me should have led the mission."

"Not my call. We all knew it was high-risk at best."

Sharp nodded. "Fair enough. Your shitty attitude is probably a good sign. How about you knock off, and I'll take the first shift?"

"No, thanks. Too geared up to go back to quarters. I want to get started on the jump sims anyway. Need to be ready in case the T's change tactics."

"I can run those sims better than you, but suit yourself. Relieve you in four?"

"Yeah. No, make it six."

Sharp nodded again. "Chief?"

"Yeah?"

Sharp met his eyes, then took a deep breath and looked away. "Nothing. Never mind. See you at 0200."

The six hours passed slowly. Paul let his junior officer monitor the Wee'en and Thinker movements. Nothing changed there. The T's were satisfied to let them jump out. Paul took the time to write and send the battle

post-assessment back to Central, including the formal
report, all vid and AI analyses, and confirmation of their
current mission, the pre-arranged order to withdraw from
the system should the mission fail. He received no
response other than a cryptic "Transmission Received."

Despite what Helwin had said about striking a
deal, there was a better-than-even chance Paul would face
a court-martial or at least a board inquiry resulting in
serious sanctions. In any case, his career was toast. Not
that he cared much, but with a mission refusal in his file,
he'd never command anything larger than a tanker.

The night shift was an eternity of countless sim
runs and creeping minutes until Sharp came back in and
shoved him out. Paul wasn't tired, but he was completely
without energy. On the way back to quarters, the
corridors of the "mother ship" were too quiet, and he
passed very few people.

And then he stood before the entry door to their
quarters — his quarters now. He passed his fingers over
the sensor, the doors slid open, and he stepped into a
foreign place, where everything was exactly where they'd
left it; orderly, spotless, personal items and decorations
laid out and hung exactly by the book.

On the small counter were the two things not
allowed by military regs. The first was a framed
holograph player resting against the wall by the comm
controls. The device, wafer-thin and as large as two
hands, held over a hundred hours of their time on Caladis.
The screen was frozen on the default image — Paul and
Hel standing side by side knee-deep in pale pink
seawater, both naked from the waist up, clutching the
famous red crustaceans they'd snatched from the pink-
sanded flats where the five-kilo creatures gathered to
mate. The flesh of the horned beasts was bright red,
mildly narcotic, and strongly aphrodisiac. The resort was

normally crowded with wealthy tourists with lips dyed rosy from the meat, framing exhausted smiles.

The other non-spec item in the room was the spice grinder.

Paul powered down the holo frame, vacuum-sealed the grinder, and placed them both in his small personal pack. The pack went below the bunk, which he and Hel had dressed out in new linens before she left on the mission.

He took a brief atomized wash and found his pack of synth-sleep modules. He normally disdained them, but he needed to be alert and sharp in six hours, and natural sleep was not remotely possible. He pressed one of the small flat discs against his temple and initiated the 60-second count. He was pulling the sheet back when the first alarm beep sounded and was lying safely at the second alarm. The third alarm sounded, and there was blackness.

He came awake, vaguely aware of a mild mental annoyance — the beeping again, persistent and escalating. The disc detected he was awake and went silent. He slid his fingernail down his temple and peeled the sleep module away, rolled it between his fingers, and then flicked the tiny ball toward the catch field of the compactor. A quiet sizzle told him he'd connected.

Sitting now, he felt not tired. Not rested, just not tired. The deep regeneration had cleansed his mind of built-up toxins and metabolic by-products, and it had allowed his synapses to cycle and repair themselves. Still, natural sleep was better.

He shaved and dressed, and with his clothing and personal items in hand, he took one last look at the boxy, sterile, metal and plastic cubicle that he and Helwin had shared for the last eight months, identical to others they'd shared, military standard. The only difference was that he was leaving this cubicle alone.

Before going to the briefing, he commandeered an unoccupied pod berth on the flight deck level and stored his personal items there.

At the meeting, Sharp presented the jump sims he had finished for Paul. One deviation from standard practice was Paul's location in the formation. Standard practice called for the commanding officer's vessel to exit just ahead of the big guns. But Paul would command the departure from a midsize gunboat and would be the last to jump. This was unusual but not unheard of, and Paul had followed this protocol in the past. The plan raised few eyebrows.

After the meeting adjourned, Sharp remained behind and let everyone else leave the small conference room. He seemed to be looking through the sim reports, but Paul caught him exchanging glances with Tom and Ellen. Once the conference room cleared, Sharp wasted no time in confronting Paul, who was biding his time mentally running through the list of personnel and making notes. Sharp's opening was a statement, not a question.

"You're not jumping out."

Paul met his eyes and shook his head.

"Excellent. Count me in."

"I won't be going home from this one, Sharp."

"No, but neither will a whole crapload of Thinkers. And you can't do it alone."

"Actually, I can. And I will if needed."

"But there's no need. I'm in. I'm pretty sure we can go in with a full ship. Most of the staff are unhappy about leaving this system to the zarking T's."

Paul nodded. "I'd order you all out, but I could use the help."

"I wouldn't jump out anyway, so you can forget that idea. And your sims for this assault suck, so you do need help. I got the success rate up to 35%."

"You hacked my account?"

"About six months ago. It gets boring on the deck late at night."

"Zarker."

Sharp chuckled.

"You kept that to yourself."

"Loose lips, Chief."

"So, who would join us in this suicidal insanity?"

"Suicidal? Zark that, we had less than 15% odds at Densei-Cha, and we never lost a boat. Don't write this one off. As for who would join us — everyone in the command group, especially Tom and Ellen. Since Tom got pulsed by the T's on Cha, he never passes up an opportunity to get even."

"We can't pull the whole command team. Someone's got to lead the jump outbound and the voyage back to Central. And we need to make sure they can deny any knowledge."

"Check. I'll have us a crew, Chief."

"After all these years, all the campaigns, I still don't know how to choose who will die."

"Leave that to me. I have no conscience. And stop being such a pessimist. I'll have the success rate up to 50% before the first admin ship hits the jump horizon."

In the end, word passed through the squadron, and all refused to jump out of the system. They stayed in honor of Commander Helwin Christin-Dottir. Paul could hardly blame them, although he threatened to kick Sharp's ass and then confine him to quarters for waiting to tell him until the first vessels aborted their jump runs.

It would just be more blood on Paul's hands.

#

Paul pulled his team in tight and launched the final all-out charge on the two bases, now avoiding engagement with any enemy craft in their path. Two more of his comrades fell, and it became obvious that they weren't going to make it close enough to the bases to effectively attack. If they fired their ordnance from their current distance, few would find the target and the damage would be minimal.

On a desperate whim, Paul played the holograph video of Trent Fleming's craft as it successfully dodged through the enemy net and pierced the carrier. There was a pattern to his movement, complementary to the formations of the Wee'en and Thinkers. Paul set his vessel on avoidance mode and set up a video to overlay the current patterns of Thinker craft over the earlier formations. There was a commonality that he was missing.

His own voice filled his earpieces. "Look at the patterns, Sharren. Trent saw something there. What the hell was it?"

The Thinkers moved almost as a series of connected vessels, no doubt a product of their telepathic powers. It was mass behavior, too quick and uniform to be planned or choreographed. It must be natural for them, a hive mentality.

As he watched the formations, the vessels moved back and forth in shimmering waves, and the sunlight swept over the surface of each vessel like a shade being opened.

Like a school of herring.

Paul brought up Trent's flight pattern again and saw what he'd missed before. Trent had stopped going against the flow of the Thinker vessels and had begun moving with them, becoming one of them. Joining the school.

Paul keyed his communicator. "D'dar Squad, all listen. I have a new analysis of the Thinker formations I'm sending ... now. Discontinue the counterflow attack and initiate concurrent flow. We can't beat 'em, so we gotta join 'em. Engage with those groups flowing inbound, and tag along."

Colby, his left winger, asked, "If we're traveling with them, won't we be easier targets?"

"Maybe. But they'll risk shooting their own if we're in close proximity. Disengage if you find yourself singled out. Otherwise, keep tight and stay part of the school."

Paul instructed the two d'Dar closest to him to pull closer, and then led them into the thick of a shifting school of Thinker craft that had threatened to overwhelm them. Initially, they seemed to have dropped from the Thinker notice and had become invisible. But soon the enemy moved to isolate them, and Paul shifted their track to join another "school" of Thinker craft moving opposite but still inward, like tacking a sailing ship against an unfavorable wind.

Paul and his two companions found the school they were looking for, a large group of Thinker craft flowing inward to the command bases. They fell in. Paul ordered the gunships behind him to hem the enemy vessels in, force them to close ranks and form a gyrating ball. He guided his other strikers to close in, allowing the outer ships to defend their flanks.

From what seemed like a hopeless scenario, Paul found himself staring at the twin Wee'en command bases. The few enemy ships between him and the bases couldn't stop him. His hands quivered on the control pads. His mind became very calm.

Sharp's voice came across calmly and clearly. "Don't play the hero, Paul. Drop your load and swing back around to help clean up."

Paul hesitated before responding. "Absolutely."

Helwin's voice came into his head then, as if she were sitting there with Sharp, monitoring the progress of Paul's team. She spoke the text message she'd sent just before she died.

"Lead them out, Paul."

If he rammed the base, the others would follow. But they'd followed him into this battle, even after he'd ordered them to leave the system.

The red darkness crept inward from the outer edges of his eyes.

Helwin's voice came again, insistent. "Promise me."

He cursed under his breath and lifted his hands from the controls for an instant. Then he re-engaged and began a tight bombing run.

"Follow me, lads. This one's for Commander Christin-Dottir."

With a roar of approval in his headset, the remaining strikers, over half of the squadron, followed his ship and launched their main arsenal, quivers of dirty nukes designed to wreak havoc on communications and life support. Paul wasn't able to watch the light show as he and the others pulled out of their run in a narrow band under full power, avoiding the barrage of the Co-Op's main gunboats settling into place behind them. On recordings later, he would see the two wagon wheel bases of the Wee'en blossoming with vibrating masses of orange fire, which simmered and then burst from the surfaces of the huge stations like plasma geysers.

Under heavy fire and now fighting alone, the Thinkers acted slowly, as if stunned. They balled up in capsule shapes like prickly blood cells and slowly gyrated toward their jump out points. Co-Op gunboats and medium cruisers pursued, leaving them no space to coagulate into a dangerous mass. The remaining Wee'en forces panicked and scattered, to be hunted down and destroyed almost to a ship. By the time Paul's squad made their turn around the Wee'en's base planet and decelerated, the battle had degenerated into disjointed skirmishes. The large Co-Op guns had pounded what remained of the two bases into cinders. Within hours, the system was secured. Most of the Thinker vessels were destroyed or had jumped off-system.

Back in the command vessel, Paul sent the mission report in a drone ship. In it, he detailed the heroics of those involved, both the survivors and the many fallen, and the commendations he requested. He closed the brief with an admission of his own earlier insubordination and his resignation. He then turned command over to Sharp and confined himself to his pod quarters.

Unbeknownst to Paul, hours after the dart jumped out, Co-Op ships began dropping in, including three cruisers and a destroyer bearing the markings and electronic insignia of the regional commander. Two of the cruisers took up patrol positions around the important jump points, and the third took up a command position in stationary orbit near the Wee'en command centers.

In time, Paul was summoned to the regional commander's vessel, where he was escorted by a nervous young sailor in pale fatigues to a meeting room. The sailor asked him to sit at the large rectangular table made of real wood surrounded by upholstered chairs. One entire wall was a holograph screen, and to one side was a serving cart with an elaborate layout of food and drinks.

Technically, the regional command could court-martial him on the spot, but he expected a full tribunal, probably on the nearest regional seat at Hyperion. While waiting, he fiddled with the video controls, found a broadcast on public ansible media, and viewed a bit of current news, something he hadn't been able to do for months. It was mostly planetary stuff, but there was some coverage of the Thinker conflict. He searched further and found three unregistered pirate media broadcasts. On one there was mention of the Wee'en people, and he stayed on that channel. The network had cracked the military's blackout, and the story of the Delos Red assault broke. Within minutes of the pirates breaking the story, the commercial media had also picked it up.

The report was that a "rogue commander" had needlessly slaughtered countless natives. Paul's personal profile was hacked and aired, along with his name and 3-D's of him in some obscure briefing he barely remembered, and then a wedding shot of him and Helwin on Gliese. His mind swung from boredom to anger.

Public and commercial opinion pieces scrolled along both edges of the program, mostly unfavorable, although the private opinion seemed almost evenly split, if no less emotional and irrational. On these bands, he was either a hero or a pariah. He wasn't surprised by the reactions, just surprised that the media had bothered to pick up the story and that there was any reaction at all.

He quickly tired of it and turned it off.

Soon after, the door opened and a man walked in, perfect medium-large military size and clean-cut to the point of parody, wearing the dress uniform of a Co-Operative executive officer. He moved too precisely for a lifelong desk jock, and Paul pegged him as a former CEAL, probably the covert-ops wing. He nodded at Paul as he entered and sat across the table from him. They locked eyes for a moment before the spook spoke in a voice like a muffled bassoon.

"Commander Sharren, your mission statistics are as follows: 450 enemy vessels destroyed; two enemy military space depots rendered ineffective; objective one, Jump Point B-10.5 cleared and objective two, Delos star system secured. By these measures, a successful mission. Losses: 127 friendly craft, including three J-class destroyers and an M-class administration vessel. Co-Operative casualties totaled 467, with another 57 wounded."

The agent paused as if shuffling papers in his head, although he had brought none with him. He didn't need them. CEAL agents, among others in the corps, endured direct neural memory enhancement.

The spook continued, "You've done the Co-Operative a great service. Ordinarily, we would be free to forgive your refusal of command. Unfortunately, as you've seen in the knowledge sphere" — he nodded toward the screen — "the unrestrained nature of your field execution has created a political problem for the organizational regime. Command has decided that it is in your best interest and the Co-Operative's to place you at a secure discretionary location."

"Wherever."

"You will be given alternate identification. You are ordered to remain incognito until the media attention ceases and you are recalled."

"'Don't call us; we'll call you.'"

The spook frowned but began talking *to* him and not *at* him. "Hardly, Commander. Your services will be needed very soon. You have a unique understanding of your capabilities and your role. Too many in the upper levels believe the other sentient races can be reliable allies against the Thinkers, but you and I and others we serve recognize this as liberal foolishness bordering on negligent dereliction of duty."

Paul sniffed and said nothing. The spook continued.

"Along those lines, there is an assignment involved with this deployment, Major Sharren, one that requires a keen observation that is unbiased and not myopic with misplaced sentiment. The Co-Op has an interest in the indigenous tribes in this system, and we'd like you to evaluate them for development into military applications. Their size, intelligence, and lack of technical sophistication make them perfect candidates."

"I thought we agreed we can't trust the natives."

"We have a great need for front-line divisions where the losses are likely to be high, Major, and this species fits our needs well."

"And what if I decide they're no more trustworthy than the Wee'en?"

The agent's eyes narrowed, but he said nothing more. He rose, nodded, and left silently.

Minutes later, a young ensign with burnished buttons and razor creases in his uniform appeared at the door and requested that Paul follow him to a "reassignment briefing."

Paul had nothing better to do. He followed.

Chapter 26

"If a hunter cannot tell the call of the succulent larrin from that of the deadly lefferin, the hunter should go hungry."
— Timmistrian proverb

Cara realized she'd read the same paragraph three times without comprehending it. Light streaming through her office window faded in and out as scattered autumn clouds crossed the sky. With the window open, the late morning breeze was cool. She kept her woolen sweater on, the real sheep's wool sweater, one of the few garments that remained of the small number she had brought from Principia.

She sighed and began reading the weekly report again.

The sharp knock startled her, and her surprise deepened when she found Paul Saarinen peeking in. Then she remembered he was there only because she'd sent for him.

"You wanted to see me, Manager?"

"Yes. Please have a seat."

His movements were as effortless and silent as a cat's. She doubted she would have heard him enter had her back been turned.

"Ms. Harvestmoon, I owe you an apology."

"Really? For what?"

"My judgment of your relationship with Lonin. It was insensitive, hypocritical, and out of line. I apologize." His expression seemed sincere, and his eyes betrayed no hint of condescension.

"I'll accept your apology, on one condition. No, two conditions."

His sand-colored eyebrows lifted. "Two?"

"Yes. First, that we dispense with the formalities permanently and return to a first-name basis."

The corners of his mouth turned up, crinkling the sunburned skin around his eyes.

"I can do that. What's the second condition?"

"My plates. I still want them for the formal dining room."

"We delivered them to the kitchens this morning."

"Very good. Paul, the reason I asked you to come is that the situation with the Delerin has darkened."

"Shawn's kept me informed."

"According to Lonin's scouts, they're moving closer to war. I'm still struggling to understand their motives."

"Trying to make sense of an alien race is usually futile."

"Maybe, but the Delerin are so like the Timmon. They think alike on many issues — traditions, tribal structure. And they're not so different from us. I really think they're just xenophobic. They fear us and want us off the planet."

Paul frowned with thoughts he didn't share. "Could be. We've already upset the political balance, and that's not a good thing for them."

"Except they would also benefit from our friendship."

"Really? Would they?"

"Of course. Just our technology in transportation and medicine would improve their standard of living."

"Maybe for the short term, but for the long term, who knows? They've enjoyed a stable social system for hundreds of generations. It's hard to argue with success. My experience tells me that the cost of human friendship is usually too high."

"Do you believe we have the right to defend ourselves against a Delerin attack?"

He took a deep breath and looked around her office before meeting her eyes again. "Yes."

"But you won't help?"

"I will help. But I won't fight."

"Perhaps it's none of my business, but are you a pacifist?"

Paul's yellow eyes narrowed, and the small smile returned, this time an unreadable smirk. "No. But I won't fight the Delerin."

She opened her mouth twice in question, but the finality of his denial stopped her. "Very well. You have your reasons. I do request that you increase surveillance flights. And if you have no objections, work with James and Gregor on our defenses."

"We've already extended the flight radius, and we will continue with the defense program."

"Very good. I have nothing else, unless you have other ideas about how to placate the Delerin and prevent this conflict."

He didn't seem in a hurry to leave. His face grew grave, the smile now gone. "I'm afraid I don't. I've always failed at understanding native psychology." He smiled again, this time sheepishly. "I'm not very proficient at human psychology either."

His eyes trapped her despite her efforts not to let them draw her in, amber stones with golden starbursts. She switched her gaze from one to the other. She caught herself absently pulling at the wisps of hair at her temple, and broke the spell.

"Well, if you think of anything in your discussions with Shawn and Lonin, please let me know. What we need is nothing short of a miracle, I'm afraid. Thank you, and have a good day."

"Thank you." He nodded once, rose, and slid the empty chair quietly up to her desk.

"You know, Paul, since we seem to have settled our differences, there is something I'd like to tell you. I'm pleased that you feel comfortable becoming a member of this community, even if you have objections to fighting for us. You no longer act like an outsider. You live among us, work with us, sweat with us, and have laid your life on the line for some of us. Is it possible you won't be leaving us soon?"

He met her eyes, but it was a mechanical gesture, like he was hiding something but trying not to let her see that. "I have no plans to leave."

"Good. I need you. I mean, we need your help here. Things look bad, but we've had hard times before and made it through. We'll get through this and be stronger for it. And the Delerin will realize that we have no intention of taking over or driving them from their lands. We'll make them understand."

"If anyone can do that, you can."

Cara felt her breath catch in her throat, and she forced herself to breathe. "I'm doing my best."

"I believe that will be good enough. Good day."

He took his leave and padded out as silently as he'd entered, leaving behind an echo of his presence, an afterimage of his brooding face, an image that seemed to linger in her mind, like that of an unsmiling Cheshire Cat.

It frightened her how much his presence disturbed her. Her longing disturbed her. There was something perilous about him, something dangerous about what she didn't know. Even so, she couldn't deny she longed for him to disturb her more deeply.

She cleared her mind and began the report for the fifth time.

\#

Johanson waved at a large black fly circling his head. Annoyed, Dench handed him the swatter. It looked like a foolish toy in the man's big hands, but he deftly slapped the buzzing creature to the floor. He said, "The four vessels departed Veran and should be set to make the jump in two days. Then another day in sub-r transit. They should be in orbit around this planet in about 75 hours."

"Screw the 'about' crap, Johan. I want exact times. Just because things are progressing smoothly doesn't mean we can afford sloppiness. I want those ships in position in *exactly* 75 hours from … now. Mark that."

"Got it, Mr. Dench."

"My understanding is that a confrontation between the two tribes may come to a head soon. With one missile strike, we will chop off the heads of both of these snakes and minimize any serious opposition. Now feed the rest of the plan back to me again."

"A strike team of 30 lands in two drop boats and secures the village center, then locks down all communication systems."

"Yes."

"The city manager, her brother, and the administrative staff are to be sequestered in the admin building. Daily functions of the village are to be enforced as needed."

"I don't expect any resistance, and I think they'll continue to perform their functions to maintain order, but don't be afraid to break some bones if you need to."

"Once the comm systems are secure, we set up a 500-meter secure radius around the building and city hub."

"Maintain food distribution to the colonists. Their cooperation may prove strategic. Maintain all normal functions and services, with city management at gunpoint if necessary. And don't underestimate the indigenous tribes. They're primitive, but they're fully sentient."

"Should we minimize casualties if the natives mount a resistance?"

"No; the opposite. Hit them hard and fast, and crush any foolishness as quickly as possible. They need to see our power firsthand. I don't think they'll agree to fight for me because of casual threats. It's going to take some persuasion."

"Right. Once the village is secure, we impose a communication blackout and set up a blockade on the registered jump points. Fleet movements into the Timmistria system will begin in 20 standard days."

"Fine. What risks have you considered?"

"The usual matrix. Mechanical breakdowns. Crew illnesses. Solar events in the vicinity of the jump points. All scenarios proved insignificant."

"Really? No significant risk scenarios? Well, I suggest you tighten the risk tolerances and run the simulations again until the AI spits something out, Johan. Have I taught you nothing in the last five years? There is *always* significant risk. Either your assumptions are wrong or your parameters are too loose. As you'll recall, there were no significant risks at Sarena either. This whole operation looks too zarking easy. That makes me nervous."

"We took the limit down to 0.01%, Mr. Dench."

"I don't care. This isn't a hostile takeover, Johan. We're occupying an entire star system and moving a good portion of my fleet here. The risks are there. Find them and identify them! Then change all your assumptions and find more. Complacency will down us."

"Yes, Mr. Dench. We'll rerun immediately."

"Damn right you will. It's all falling into place too well. That means we've missed the real hazards. And you need to keep an eye on our friend Commander Sharren until the place is secure. I'd give him another chance, but he's already tipped his hand and is far too dangerous. We can't take any chances on him trying to play the hero, and we can't risk his opposition. If he shows up in the village, zap him hard with the stunner, and we'll cool him in a solitary room in the admin building."

"Yes, sir."

"On second thought, we won't have time to isolate him properly. You'll just have to eliminate him."

"Yes, sir."

"Trap him at the shops. If he manages to break past you and makes a run at me, I'll have a couple surprises for him, but I'd rather you take care of him unobserved. Imagine this, Johan. An army of these big yellow bastards in mech suits under our command. We'll crush any uprising, whether rebels or shards of the fractured hegemony. And our 'friends' will think twice before trying a coup against me."

"You're still against a robot militia?"

"Absolutely. Since the Perumian Disaster, no one's willing to go down that road again. If I did, I'd lose all support from my associates, and I don't wield enough power to go it alone. Yet. Mech suits are dangerous enough, but if they're hacked, at least only the wearer dies."

"Are you sure the Timmistrians will cooperate?"

"They won't have a choice. With a squadron of military vessels circling this rock ready to incinerate it, they'll play."

Dench heard a soft crackle outside the bungalow window. Johanson had heard it too and met Dench's eyes, waiting for a command. Dench touched a finger to his lips and motioned to the back door. The big Swede moved silently and slipped out beneath the shadows. Dench kept talking.

"Make sure all the comm equipment is in place and fully operational before the drop-in. We can't afford a breakdown during the flyover. You know, Johan, this colony holds a lot of promise. We've only begun to scratch the surface in our mining work. We've got the foundation of a great crew in place, and I feel our first big discovery is imminent. With a real find under our belts, we'll be able to finance new equipment and technologies. Not just for our own work, but for other areas of development, particularly transportation. Four-wheel cycles and low-altitude flyers will make us much more efficient, and they'll provide better protection from dangerous flora and fauna. I believe the native populations will begin to see the benefits of a close relationship with our colony, which will spark a whole new era of…"

There was a violent rustling in the brush outside Dench's window, a gasp, and then two sharp thudding sounds, like leather mallets striking a synth-gel drum. The rustling ceased, replaced by the sounds of something being dragged around to the rear door.

"…cooperation."

It was Denny Dennison, the laborer who'd been doing much of Dench's lawn care and gardening. Dench motioned for Johanson to sit him up in the chair opposite Dench's. The right side of the man's face was red and swelling.

"I hope you didn't hit him too hard, Johan. I don't want him to die before I can question him."

"Shouldn't do, Mr. Dench. I hit him flat-handed."

"Your flat hand would kill most men."

Dench rose and pulled a clean cloth from the small basket by the sink, and then dipped it into the fresh water jug one of the miners had filled earlier that afternoon. Johanson was fanning Dennison with one of Dench's reed table fans.

"Out of the way."

Dench pulled his chair up and laid the cool cloth on Dennison's forehead. He lifted the man's limp hand, which was bony and heavily calloused, and patted it.

"Dennison! Dennison! Wake up, man. Are you all right, Dennison? Soak a couple more of those rags, Johan, and bring them."

Johanson did as told. Dench laid one along his unconscious helper's neck and wiped the man's sweaty, dirty arm with the other.

"Dennison, wake up!"

The man's breathing caught, and he inhaled deeply. His eyes opened slowly. Neither of his pupils was dilated, which could have indicated a concussion.

"Oh, thank god, Dennison. I feared you were dead. What were you doing outside the window, my friend? We thought you were a dangerous animal. A cup of water, please, Johan. There, don't get up. You're still woozy. Ah, thank you, my good fellow. Here, Dennison, sip a little of this, slowly. How's the head?"

When he saw Johanson approaching with the water, Dennison jerked back in the chair.

"Easy now. We know you're not a dangerous animal now. Does your head hurt?"

"A little." He continued to eye Johanson suspiciously.

"Sorry about that, Dennison. What were you doing out there?"

"I came to finish the weeding. I heard voices, so I came to your cabin to let you know I was here. But I could na' believe what you were sayin'. You're gonna take over Fairdawn!"

"Take over Fairdawn? My goodness, Dennison, how absurd. How could I possibly do that? And why would I?"

"You got ships comin' in. You're gonna bomb the Timmon!"

"Our friends, the Timmon? Ridiculous. I'm afraid that bump on the head has knocked you a bit loony. Here, more water? Have you listened outside my window before?"

"Never. And maybe I'm wishin' I hadn't heard this time."

"I share that wish, my good friend, but I assure you I have no intention of taking over the village. Perhaps you dreamed that while you were unconscious."

Dennison kept his eyes on the hulking form of Johanson, who'd backed away to stand near the far wall of the small kitchen. "Umm, you're right, Mr. Dench. I musta heard wrong. I, uh, got some work in town I need to get back to. I'm guessing I'm late for dinner, and my friends will be worryin'."

"Of course. I'm worried about your head, though. Are you sure you can walk back all right? Can you stand? Here, let me help you."

"Uh, thanks, Mr. Dench. I'll be going now."

"Of course, and don't forget your blades there on the table. Mr. Johanson picked them up from where you dropped them."

"Uh, yeah." Dennison slid the green knives into his belt and backed awkwardly toward the door. "See you in the morning?"

"Exactly, Dennison. 8 a.m. Please be prompt."

Out the door now, Dennison staggered down the walk and out the lone trail from Dench's property, kicking up a cloud of dust behind him and sending small flocks of birds screaming off into the brush.

"Should I chase him, Mr. Dench?"

"No need, Johan. He won't get far. I slipped a neuro into his water. It'll hit him in five minutes. When you find him, make it look like he crossed paths with something large and carnivorous. Take the cell disruptor, and make it messy. But don't be sloppy. The Timmon won't be easily fooled, and neither will our Commander Sharren. We need three more days without interference from the locals before we draw the strings on this net, and I don't want to waste time in the village center answering questions."

Chapter 27

"I'm getting tired of these meetings, Shawn. I never thought I'd say that about sitting down with the Timmon."

Shawn opened the administration building door and followed Cara into the renewed brightness of the hall. The smell of paint still lingered from a week earlier. Lonin hadn't told him about the meeting either, so he could offer nothing. But he was looking forward to sitting for a few minutes.

She continued, "It would be different if it was about new business."

There were only three other colonists when they reached the council room. Cara had made the decision not to call a full session. Pao Shing-Shing was there. He would have pouted for days if Cara hadn't asked him to come along. Stan Salbeh, the current head of "Security," was present as well, looking rather bored and a little preoccupied. The third colonist was Erin McLachlan, Cara's village-relations person. She was as alert as a perlid, already trying to read the atmosphere in the room. Erin was a little older than he was, very personable and very attractive, with fair, clear skin, pale green eyes the size of large coins, and deep mahogany hair. He always felt she was reading his mind.

Cara and Shawn found their seats between Stan and Erin. Erin winked at Shawn as he sat, and he felt his face heat up.

"Well, Lonin said he has new information," Shawn mumbled to Cara. "I hope so, or this is going to be a very short meeting."

There was a light tap at the door, and the guard ushered in a party led by Lonin. He was followed by his cousin Kinin and an oddly dressed Timmon whom Shawn had never met before. This native's facial features were unusual, sharper and more angular, his skin more deeply amber. With a mental shock, Shawn realized he was looking at one of the Delerin, and probably an important leader, judging by his long, white tunic. The Timmistrian looked not at all uncomfortable, as if he belonged there, but his eyes moved about the room, resting on each of the colonists. Another Delerin, dressed less formally in drab hiking clothing and looking very ill at ease, entered last and stood at the wall behind the others, eyes alive also, and his hand jittery over the hilt of his blade. Shawn was already pushing his chair back when Cara motioned for all of them to rise.

He whispered, "I hope you ordered lunch."

Lonin spread his hands and spoke quietly. "Friends, please be seated. My Delerin companion is Larilin, esteemed speaker for the general tribal council at Dlith Welkin. He comes to your council not on official business but on his own, and at some personal risk. His news is heavy and grave."

Cara remained standing, and the others followed her lead. "Greetings, our friend Lonin, and Speaker Larilin, and other guests. Welcome to our council. May we offer food and drink or other of our humble comforts?"

Lonin conversed with Larilin briefly. "No, Manager Cara. A brief audience is all we seek. Better to talk quickly and not put the Speaker at greater risk." He again motioned for the villagers to sit.

"As you wish, Lonin. We will respect your haste, and we hope to share food and drink with you and the Speaker another time."

The council allowed the Timmistrians to sit, and then they took their own seats. Lonin gestured to Larilin, and the Delerin leader spoke in the Timmistrian language. His dialect was strong and angular like his features. He spoke so quickly that Shawn couldn't keep up, catching only snippets of words and sentences — "anger," "unwise," "serious." The Delerin's voice was smooth and pleasantly compelling, with the practiced cadence of a politician, and it was jarring coming from such a large and aggressively imposing person. At the end of his speech, he nodded at Lonin, who translated.

"There is growing anger in my people. Some regret the coming of the 'alien' people to Timmistria, and recent events make these feelings stronger. The Delerin have … required the Timmon to watch the alien village. But now we believe the aliens are too powerful for the Timmon to watch. Many of us believe the aliens have become the dangerous foe we feared all along. There is talk of war, and I, Larilin, fear this will happen very soon."

After Lonin finished, Cara sat motionless, chin resting on her fingertips. Erin held an identical pose, her eyes moving back and forth between Lonin's and Larilin's faces, just as Cara's were. At last Cara sat back, hands clasped together on the table.

"Speaker Larilin, I deeply appreciate your coming to visit us today and bringing us your concerns. Can you tell us why the Delerin feel as they do?"

Lonin translated, his voice deeper than Larilin's but not as melodic. The two exchanged words several times. During the exchange, Larilin spread his hands in a large circle at one point, and then passed one hand over the other, palms facing downward. Lonin nodded at Larilin at last, and then paused as if gathering his words before interpreting.

"The Delerin are concerned that the aliens are growing in numbers, and that they build kithin well out into the forest. The alien farms are wide and far, and your plants spread outside of the settlement fields.

"And now the aliens have brought a thing that flies over the Delerin lands. Aliens fly over and look down on us. This thing was never part of the agreement. There is anger."

Larilin spoke again, but his voice now held an edge, a genuine tone of unguarded emotion. His words were less songlike and more powerful, with a layer of diplomatic control removed. Shawn knew the subject of his speech even before Larilin spoke the words "kahl melok." Lonin's calm and measured translation did not dilute the tension.

"Now the aliens have among them one like the Delerin have never seen. Our fear and doubt are strong with your flying machines and your space machines, and now you bring a human of blood-red light, like we are blind and cannot see its presence. Lonin tells me that this dangerous one offends the Timmon as strongly, yet you aliens refuse to remove this one as the Timmon ask. The Delerin people do not understand, and in this lies more anger.

"As diplomatic leader, I have used every way I have to hold back my people's anger and to prevent them from marching on your land. But the time of that holding has come to an end. Unless the aliens take action, this is a tide that will not be held back. Even if you act now, it may already be too late."

Cara looked exhausted as she responded to Larilin's speech. "Esteemed Speaker Larilin. We hear your grave words. If the Delerin march to war against our village, there is little doubt we will not survive. We thank you for your difficult and unrewarded efforts to prevent a war. And yet we must ask that you help us. I have nothing to offer you in return except the promise of a better future. Things like the flying machines will one day be tools that the Delerin will have for their own use. There are so many beneficial uses — protection from disease, eradication of dangerous predators, better control of the weather and your food supply ... and even travel to the stars. The Delerin will have a chance to join the galactic community and will take their rightful place among other peoples. But none of this will happen if we are attacked and our village destroyed."

Cara paused while Lonin translated. Larilin sat quietly unimpressed, until near the end of the translation. When Lonin used the word "kisil," Timmistrian for "star," a glint came to Larilin's amber eyes. When Lonin stopped talking, Cara immediately began again.

"Our village has existed on Timmistria for over five full seasons. Most of us have been here nearly that long. Some of us were born here, and this is the only world those young ones have known. For everyone in our village, this is our home, the place where we choose to live and die. We nurture the land, and in turn it nurtures us.

"As we hold this small piece of land as our own, so we must follow the agreement with the Timmon and Delerin, but we must also live by our own laws. This man you speak of is a member of our community, a human being like all of us, and he is guaranteed all of the rights that we give everyone. He has committed no crimes, and therefore it would be unjust for us to send him away. We have made this clear to the Timmon from when they first raised their concerns.

"We respect the laws and concerns of the Timmon and Delerin peoples, and we greatly appreciate your hospitality in letting us live on your world. One day we will pay our great debt many times over, and we will bring opportunities you may have never realized without our cooperation.

"But as a just people, we must respect our own laws. Nothing has changed in this situation. We cannot fairly force our fellow colonist to leave Timmistria."

Lonin's face crinkled up, and he turned his head in that odd canine expression of puzzlement.

"But things have changed."

"How so?"

"You don't know."

"I'm afraid I don't, Speaker Lonin."

"I warned you when the red one arrived that Death would soon follow. He has been slow, but Death has come to your people at last."

Chapter 28

Paul walked out his front door early in the morning on his way to the shops, and he was startled to find Kearnin and another young Timmon standing motionless as statues in his front yard. As he was deciding whether he should greet them or reach for his blade, Kearnin spoke.

"Please follow. You are needed."

Without waiting for a response, he sprinted off over the bridge and down the main trail. The other Timmon, who Paul learned later was Kearnin's cousin Chitin, motioned for Paul to follow. And so he had, rapidly, with the second Timmon guarding the rear. After five minutes on the main trail, they took a more rugged side path, and Paul was kept busy watching his steps and swinging his blades. They worked their way northeast toward the northern side of Fairdawn and eventually came to a larger trail running roughly northwest from the village. They'd followed it for a quarter kilometer, meeting there an older Timmon standing in the path. Paul recognized him as Lonin's cousin, Kinin, which meant Lonin was not far away.

They followed Kinin's direction and stepped through tall brush to reach a group of settlers and Timmon at the top of a sharp, tree-covered ravine. The brush was heavy but had been trampled down into a flat depression. Shawn was there, and he came over immediately.

"It's one of the villagers, Denny Dennison. It looks like a crellil got him."

Having planned a day of shop work and routine maintenance on the flyer, Paul now found himself examining the body of one of the colonists, a medium-sized man, or what remained of him, lying in a circle of smashed-down bushes. Blood was everywhere, in brown pockets and splatters. He'd died violently at that spot and hadn't been moved there after death.

"Any idea what he was doing out here?"

"Not really. He was a shop worker. Came in alone on the transport one trip ahead of yours. Nice enough guy and had made some friends. Worked general labor, field work sometimes. I think he was working with Mr. Dench in the mining group too."

"Hmm."

"Yeah. Coincidence?"

Paul didn't answer. He had very little experience with forensics, but he started looking over the scene, systematically, trying to make a mental list of what might be important.

"Has Cara seen this?"

"Yes. She's pretty broken up, I could tell, but she tried not to show it much. She left me to investigate while she went back to calm the villagers."

"Has Lonin offered any opinions?"

"No. Said he wanted you to look it over first. Of course, the Timmon will say Dench had something to do with it. They think he's drawing the crellil here by some otherworldly magic."

Paul looked over the blood patterns and reaffirmed his belief that the man had died on this spot, a swift and violent death. It would have been difficult to create this mess if he'd been killed elsewhere and brought here. Blood had exploded out in random patterns, as one might expect from severe lacerations and severed arteries.

He knelt down and began examining the body. The victim lay on his back with his legs bent to the side and his left arm trapped under him. Savage wounds covered his neck and shoulders, and a portion of his abdomen had been eaten away. His face was largely untouched but frozen in a mask of horror, wide eyes blank and cloudy. Paul had seen the facial expressions of people killed by large predators, and this victim's face looked like theirs.

Soon Lonin joined them, and Paul stood. Lonin's eyes betrayed his opinion. "What is your thought?"

Paul sighed and rubbed his chin. "Well, a large predator, a crellil or something smaller, could have done this. I'm no expert, but nothing specific here makes me suspicious. Was he traveling alone? Is anyone else missing?"

Shawn shook his head. "Pao's people are still doing a head count, but it looks like everyone else is accounted for. We don't know why he was out here, unless he was doing some work for Mr. Dench. My next stop is to interview him."

"Why don't you go do that, and I'll keep looking for … whatever it is I should be looking for."

"OK. The coroner is on his way, but that's really just a formality. He won't know any more than we do. We also stepped up patrols again, and leadership is passing word that no one leaves Fairdawn in groups of less than four."

Lonin said, "We search this area also."

Shawn said, "All right. I'll head to Dench's. Catch up with you two back at Fairdawn in about two hours?"

"Yes."

Lonin stopped him. "Shawn Harvestmoon, Kearnin and Chitin will travel with you, for your safety."

"Good, I'll gladly let them."

Shawn stepped over the tall grass, leaving Lonin and Paul alone with the body. They moved several feet away to get out of the cloud of flies hovering over it and the larger insects chasing them.

Lonin's voice rumbled. "No beast killed this human."

Paul shook his head in agreement. "No. Good job of staging it, though."

"These cuts" — Lonin pointed at his own neck — "were made by sharp things, but not by the claws of a crellil. And those parts of his body were removed by a tool, not eaten."

"Probably a disruptor. It uses a high-energy ultrasonic beam to remove tissue. Some of that wound looks like it was burned, almost cauterized. That's a giveaway."

"This dis-rup-tor. Is it used to kill like this?"

"Normally it's used for micro-surgery and fine industrial materials etching — cutting very precise channels or symbols into the surface of a super-hard material. But widen the beam, and you can peel off layers of flesh."

"Another of the wonders your people bring us. How would such a thing come to Timmistria? Human weapons are not allowed."

"It could have been smuggled."

"Smuggled?"

"Sneaked aboard a ship in someone's luggage. This thing could be the size of a writing stylus. About that long and that big around." He indicated the length and width with his fingers.

"The new ones' luggage is searched. How would this — 'smuggle'?"

"A bribe. Someone pays the inspectors to look the other way. They pay someone to let the luggage pass through with no inspection."

"Bribe. Another human word, like 'pay' and 'money.' You pay your people to do their jobs, then you bribe them to do their jobs not. Very interesting. Your society has many interesting customs. I look forward to you educating us more."

"You're the ones who let us stay here. I would have told you to kick our asses off the planet as soon as we showed up."

"So, there is a disruptor. What else has been smuggled?"

"I don't know. There are a lot of possibilities." Paul couldn't remember ever having a headache like this before.

"Paul Saarinen, what is our action?"

"I don't know that either."

"Do you not think the red one did this?"

"No, I'm pretty sure he's responsible."

"But you cannot take action?"

"Unless we can prove he did this, no, we can't. In a normal human court, we'd have to prove it to a jury of his peers. Here, a panel of judges would probably be convened. Either way, we'd have to prove this was murder, and then prove he did it. That's not going to happen. Any layman would see this as the work of a crellil. We don't have the sophisticated machines needed to prove otherwise."

Lonin shook his head. "You humans make no sense to me. You would let all the good people in the colony perish to protect one who deserves death. So bound by law, and yet your language is filled with words like 'bribe' and 'smuggle,' words that cannot be translated into Timmistrian. I envy you your flying machines, and your shelters and your farming. But I would not be like you. You talk of peace and justice and law, yet so much of what you have was gained by the ways of war."

"You are wise, Lonin. We humans are learned but unwise. But I think you would do well to protect this colony. When the Thinkers come — and they will — humans will be the Timmistrians' only hope to preserve your freedom. By the way, when did you become so cynical?"

"Cynical. I do not know that word."

"It means looking at the bad in everything, rather than the good."

Paul's words struck Lonin like a blow. His whole aggressive posture softened, and his face and body sagged. "You are right, unwise human. I have let these dangers control me and darken my mind when calm and strength are needed. Timmistria is ashamed of me. I am sorry."

Paul gestured dismissively. "No apologies, friend. We're all on edge."

"I have forgotten a lesson Timmistria has taught us many times in our history. No great change comes without great difficulty and great sacrifice. I will remember this lesson."

"And so will I."

"To stop the Delerin, the red one must leave."

"I know."

"And we cannot make him leave unless we can prove he has made this crime."

"Yes."

"Then what is our action?"

"I don't know, Lonin." Paul rubbed his temple, trying to relieve the pounding there. "I don't know yet."

Chapter 29

Shawn and Paul flew over Delerin land, places no human had ever seen. The lands were beautiful, but there was little time to enjoy them.

Despite his increasingly antagonistic attitude, Lonin had instructed Paul and Shawn on what to look for to identify a gathering of Delerin warriors, mostly very subtle movement in the forest's shadows and changes in activity of the flying creatures. These were all pretty standard observations for forest recon, and worthless from a loud, fast-moving aerial platform.

They flew along the western edge of the Timmon land, identified by landmarks Lonin had provided. Seeing no sign of Delerin movement, they moved farther west, encroaching in a slow sweep across the eastern edge of the Delerin lands. Although Lonin had no more experience than they did at searching the Timmistrian forests from above, he was still the obvious choice for this work.

Unfortunately, squeezing into the small passenger cockpit cramped his legs and back, and as much as he loved to fly now, he could tolerate no more than an hour at a time. He'd excused himself to take care of Timmon business that day.

The forest passed by about 50 feet below them, a sea of yellow and rich amber. Perelin and other flyers plied the air immediately above the trees, swimming through the heavy foliage in their fish-like dives and leaps. Occasionally a quintet of pantellil, the Five Sisters, dropped out of the infinite sky to follow the mechanical flyer. They didn't approach any closer than a few hundred yards away, and the ship's alarm never sounded.

A line appeared on the horizon in front of them, a feature darker than the treetops, as they flew through a large flock of greenish-yellow birds that shifted right and left like a school of baitfish, fleeing several larger predatory creatures. One of the predators, in its intense focus on a potential meal, clipped one of the flyer's whirling blades and fluttered downward.

As the flock cleared his field of vision, Paul identified the dark line on the horizon as a rising swell of rocky slopes. He slowed their forward airspeed, then prodded the throttle and asked the controls for more elevation. The craft complied, slowly rising to clear the first of a series of stair-step hills, rocky bubbles of granite-like stone almost devoid of vegetation. Paul continued to climb, now a hundred feet above the level of the trees behind them and not yet at the level of the rocky scarp ahead.

It was an interesting landscape, and Paul was inclined to explore it, but it was also without cover. He slowed the craft to a complete stop, then turned it 180 degrees in a clockwise spin and accelerated back toward the north. He felt a tap on his shoulder, and Shawn's voice came through the headset.

"What's up? Why are we turning around?"

"Too open. No attack from here."

"But it's interesting-looking, and there might be some worthwhile places beyond. Can't we take a quick look?"

Paul shook his head. "Not today. Have to conserve fuel."

"But we'll go there another time?"

"Yeah."

Paul guided the flyer back down off the rock and initiated another sweep, about 300 meters farther out than their last one. The rugged yellow forest was broken by spines of rock and arteries of flowing water, some clear and white with spray, some slow and brown and tannic. They traversed back along their path about a kilometer when the flight AI sounded an alarm in Paul's headset — 30 minutes of fuel remaining. Shawn would have heard it too. Paul reduced their speed until they were hovering motionless above the trees.

"Help me pick some landmarks. I'll plug them into the guidance system."

"I think we have company."

Paul looked down where Shawn pointed. The forest was thinner there and seemed oddly quiet. Then he saw a flicker in the shadows under the trees, small movements here and there. Perelin scattered nearby, spooked by the flyer or perhaps by those who hid and observed the hovering machine. Paul tried to gain a sense of the size of the hunting party based on movement and the subtle silence in the trees. They would never have detected the Delerin had he not stopped to locate landmarks.

Simultaneously, an alarm sounded and a long arrow flashed past Paul's head. His hands reacted, and the craft veered up and to the side.

"Holy crap!" Shawn shouted.

Two more arrows whizzed by before Paul could guide the flyer up and out of range, but he was able to avoid the larger salvo that followed. Safely aloft, he held position, set their radio-transponder coordinates, and then keyed the flyer into a flight vector toward the home base. They'd already cut their fuel margin too close. He set the mode to minimal fuel usage and let the autopilot take over.

"They shot at us!"

"Yes."

"I can't believe they did that."

"I would've been surprised if they hadn't, once they knew we'd spotted them. I should have pulled us up sooner."

"But for all they know, we could have weapons too. They risked a counter-attack."

"It only takes one gun to start a firefight. Once the first shot is fired, an army's committed."

"Hmph."

"The Delerin are very different from humans, Shawn, but don't be disappointed if they suffer from mob action, just as we do."

They flew in silence for the next ten minutes. Near the landing area, Paul had to focus on flying and maneuvering through flocks of small creatures that swarmed around the flyer when it came in. Paul wasn't sure if the pigeon-sized bird things would damage the blades if struck, but he didn't want to find out. He brought the craft in slowly, ignoring the second low-fuel alarm, giving the darting creatures time to clear the way. The landing skids settled into the dirt with almost no dust kicking up. Paul cut the engine power. The fuel level was below 10%.

James was there to secure the flyer. With their more frequent flight schedule, Paul had asked the journeyman shop steward to move over from the pipe shop and take care of the flyer full time. As an incentive, Paul had been teaching him to fly.

"No problems, James. We'll need to go up again this afternoon. How's the fuel supply?"

"Coming along."

"Do I need to spend some time in the production area?"

"Wouldn't hurt."

James began running a system check. They left him and headed toward the village center, stopping for a brief wash-up at the public dorm bath. The next stop was the kitchen to grab a couple sandwiches and skins of juice to wash down the dust. They were at Cara's office within 30 minutes of landing.

She was meeting with two women Paul didn't know. When she saw them, she stood slowly, nodding, and eased toward the door. The women apparently picked up on the cue and let themselves be escorted out. Cara's auburn hair was pulled back into a tight bun, revealing the clear tanned skin of her face, the strength of her shoulders and neck, and her delicate ears. She motioned for them to come in and sit, and the scent of flowers and soap followed her.

"You don't look very happy. More problems with the flyer?"

"No, Sis. We located a large Delerin party, and they shot arrows at us."

Cara's eyes opened wide, and she looked at Paul. "How many? Where? Moving this direction?"

Paul said, "Hard to say, but I think we should assume so."

"So you were able to spot them from the air. That's an advantage."

He shook his head. "Only because we'd stopped to get our bearings. At any reasonable search speed, we'd have passed right over them. Even stationary, I'm not sure I would have spotted them if Shawn hadn't. But we have an infrared signature, which may help. On the next run, I'll see if I can get a hit on that same party from higher altitudes and speeds. If we're going to cover the entire perimeter, we have to be able to fly higher and faster."

"Larilin was right. They're moving. If they attack, can we defend ourselves?"

"We can't. A couple hundred mediocre swordsmen against an unknown number of seasoned bow hunters and woodsmen? No. As larger numbers of Delerin approach, pull the people in from the outlying areas. Barricade all civilians in the admin building, and defend as small a space as possible. Put the few archers we have on the roof. Make the Delerin cost as high as we can. And then negotiate. It's the only real chance."

"If I could get the Delerin to meet with us again, take them on a tour of Fairdawn, introduce them to our people, let them see some of the children playing, show them the progress we've made, they would have to see us as being like them and not 'aliens.' We could show them our value."

"I agree. But have the archers practice. Deal from a position of power. We have plenty of defensible food stores now. Store more water and sanitary supplies, and we can hold out for weeks."

"Why is this necessary? Such madness. We've been great citizens here. We've tried to live lightly on the land."

"Yes. That's to our advantage when you negotiate, but now's the time to circle the wagons."

"Circle the wagons?"

"Old Earth reference. Prepare for a siege. Draw everybody in. Do it now. Store more water. Get the shops making arrows and bows. Sharpen the blades. In the meantime, I can get James to fly recon for me. Hopefully, we can buy you some time and warning."

#

Paul rose and rushed out, as if he'd left a fire unattended for too long.

Cara felt a lift from his energy, how easily he pushed her into action, as if she'd been stalled in a sailboat on a windless sea, only to have him blow up a much-needed breeze. Shawn was looking off out the window and spoke from light-years away.

"I'll get with the shop stewards and get them focused on weapons production. That's at least one area where we can kick some Delerin butt. I'll get Mark to start filling barrels with water and then ask him to build more."

"Ask Gregor to look over the building, where it needs to be fortified."

"And I'll make a list and ask one more time for volunteers to trained as archers."

"Thanks, Shawn. I'll call a planning meeting to be held at dinner hour. But let's get things in motion now. I'll ask Pao to start moving our people into town. We'll need linens and beds and extra clothes. Cripes, there's a lot to do, and not much time to do it."

"I better get moving."

"I have something else to talk about. I did some research, and I think I know who our Mr. Dench is."

She briefed him on her web search, including the links she'd found between their pudgy geologist and a certain enigmatic corporate raider.

At the end, he asked, "Why would he be here?"

"There were rumors of his being involved in an attempted coup, so he may be laying low. I don't know. But why here, of all the settled planets? It's so unlikely, but the evidence is there."

"Should we lock him up, just in case you're right?"

She thought a moment, then shook her head. "He's not going anywhere, and since he's moved into town, we can keep an eye on him. Let's not clue him in to our suspicions. Just ask a few of your most trusted people to watch him, and report anything funny."

Shawn agreed and then bolted from the room, off to tend his own fires. Motes of blond dust swirled after him.

She felt a weariness in her chest and tried to sigh it away. With an excellent harvest and their other advancing programs, it seemed they were going to build their goods above the bare minimum this year, perhaps for the first time, before the difficult dark months. They would all have a brief, well-deserved break, and maybe even a thanks-giving festival, before the work began in earnest in the spring.

And now there was so much to do again, and so little time. She had her own personal fires to attend to, such as instructions for Pao and Helen and Chrisof. The medical staff needed to move all their patients and supplies into secure locations in the admin building.

And yet she felt another burning need, a mystery growing within, one that kept her awake at night and full of daydreams, one that would no longer be denied. There may never be another time to solve it. She would spend a little more of her precious ansible time on another private investigation nearer to her heart.

Who are you, Paul Saarinen? Who are you, and why are you here?

#

Lonin and Kinin were the first to arrive at the Two Spires. Kinin, never one for idleness, used the time to clear brush and root out rodents and lizards that had burrowed around the bases of the wooden posts. Lonin joined him, pulling down insect webs and nests, mindful of the stings. Working this small plot of land allowed him a temporary purpose and helped uncoil the maelstrom in his mind. Kinin never seemed to suffer the restlessness that Lonin often felt. He envied his cousin's tranquility and serenity.

Larilin was late, which meant the Delerin council meeting was running on. They often did. Lonin took this to mean nothing. He and Kinin had nearly completed their work when Larilin and Tellinin entered. Larilin's look was grave as he and Lonin clasped hands.

"So the council went badly?"

Larilin nodded. "It is done. For the first time in generations, the Delerin go to war with a people other than ourselves. I am sorry. I could not stop it."

"Timmistria cries. Once the red one came, events fell like rain."

"And onward into the sea. I am ashamed of my people, Lonin. I cannot join this campaign."

"Our hearts will guide us, Larilin. Timmistria may be angry, but she will not abandon us. And you cannot abandon the Delerin, even in this folly."

"I suppose you are right. At times, one must follow one's people into the darkness in order to lead them back to the light. But I fear this anger born under a red moon will find no end, Lonin. This curse the humans have brought will bring bloodshed to your people and mine. Will you stand before the humans, as you said before?"

"Yes."

Larilin nodded. "I pray Timmistria will help us, cousin. And I wish the humans and their red one had never come."

"Our time of seclusion and isolation had come to an end in any case, Larilin. The humans speak of their enemy, the Thinkers, who would have found us in time. If the humans I love bear witness, these 'Thinkers' are less like us and more dangerous, so the human friendship may yet be a blessing."

"May you and I live to enjoy that. I have much work to do before my journey to the center of all things."

"And I. Let Timmistria guide us, cousin. I feel her strength more than ever."

They stood then, three feet and 127 generations apart. The forest was hushed, as if sensing the agitation and despair in Timmistria's heart. Larilin held out his hand, and Lonin grasped it, as Timmistrians often did, and then they hugged tightly, as Timmistrians seldom did. They stepped apart afterward, embarrassed. Not looking at the others again, Larilin and Tellinin walked from the circle. Lonin watched them go until the aggressive brush had sealed the path behind them.

"Come, Kinin. The winds of change blow from all directions. It is for us to guide them. We have much to prepare."

"The Timmon have spoken. They will not stand against the Delerin."

"No, but I must. We are few, and we may fall. You need not follow this path with me, Kinin. I likely go to my death."

"Do not insult me, cousin. We are as one. Timmistria tells me this cause is just. Our lots are cast together."

Lonin smiled. "Such passion, Kinin. I trust you like no other. You hear our Mother as few others can. Come. Let's step lightly and quickly. Time is short."

Chapter 30

The low-pitched thumping of the flyer's blades was hard to locate at first, a vibration that was felt more than heard. But as it grew closer, Shawn was able to place it almost directly from the north. The large flock of feather-tipped birds rose up and began circling the clearing again, filling the air with hoots and the hiss of their wings. It was odd how they'd begun gathering in larger and larger numbers, coursing around the landing area in a synchronized ribbon of yellow and orange and gray, like large bat-winged parakeets, swirling up and swarming the flyer when it appeared, as if guiding it to the landing pad. So far, the creatures had become only a minor annoyance and not a danger, so the men hadn't taken any measures to shoo them away.

The whir of the copter's blades and the whine of the engine joined the chorus of hissing wings, and the shiny white flyer appeared from over the trees, the blades a blurry circle above. It found the center of the open circle of sky and slowly dropped to tree level, then to 50 feet, then 10 feet, then down onto the hard-packed dirt. The frequent flights had kept loose dust from collecting on the landing pad, which was now as hard as pavement.

James was sitting in the front compartment, the pilot's, with Paul behind. Shawn felt a twinge of jealousy that James had progressed more quickly than he had, but he checked the thought and reshaped it into an appreciation that he and Paul now had a third pilot if needed. He waited until the blades had stopped turning completely before approaching the flyer. When he reached it, he patted James on the shoulder.

"Hey, Captain! Nice landing!"

James smiled. "Thanks. It was turbulent today." He pointed his thumb over his shoulder. "He made me take it out of autopilot and fight it myself. Thought I was going to lose it a couple times."

Paul took off his headset and climbed out. "Because you needed to fight it yourself. I'm not turning this thing over to you two until I'm sure you'll get back home every time. The autopilot could fail."

He walked away toward the supply locker at the east entrance of the clearing. James stayed in the cockpit, his hands moving across the controls.

Shawn said in a low voice, "He hasn't said anything to me about turning the flyer over to us."

James responded without looking up. "He just started talking about that a couple days ago, and he pushed me to finish reading the manual. He's been testing me on my flying skills, too. He said the program was up and running and he was getting bored with it."

"Hmm. Did you spot any Delerin?"

James nodded, still not taking his eyes from the screen. "Two small hunting parties, six to eight Delerin each. Hiking through some low rocky areas. When we approached, they moved away from Fairdawn. We think they were acting as diversions, drawing our attention from larger forces. We got a hit on a group moving in the deep forest northeast of here, but as we got closer, the infrared signature got vague and wouldn't resolve. Paul thinks they've found a way to hide from the IR."

"See anything else interesting?"

"Yes, a gnarly ridge covered with tall reedlike plants. When we passed over, they pointed themselves at us and fired darts. Luckily, we were high enough they couldn't reach us. We also saw a dark swampy lake filled with bright yellow and white fish. Some of them were eight feet long, and they jumped completely out of the water chasing birds. I want to set up a landing pad near there so I can fly in with my fishing equipment."

"Maybe next spring, we'll have time to do that."

"Yeah, if there *is* a next spring."

The screen beeped loudly, and James moved his hands over it, at last nodding in satisfaction.

"I'm going to catch Paul," Shawn said. "I need to update him on some of the preparations."

"OK." James pulled his face out of the flyer's screen and met Shawn's eyes. "Hey, I didn't mean what I said about there not being a next spring. We've got good people in charge — you and your sister, Paul, and Mr. Lonin. You'll get this trouble with the Delerin sorted out."

The rest of the village no doubt expected them to solve it as well. Shawn wished he shared their confidence. "You're right. It's just another challenge. Timmistria knows we've seen our way through worse. Listen, I'll check you this afternoon, James."

"Right on, friend."

Paul was storing his flight gear, consisting mainly of a jarin-skin vest, a set of goggles that had shipped with the craft, and a mini-headset. He had a large roll of parchment under his arm, probably the area map he'd drawn to mark Delerin locations. When he turned to Shawn, he had his all-business face on. He asked, "You headed back to town?"

"I was planning to. I actually came out to meet you when you landed so we could talk about the preparations."

"Good. Let's walk and talk. Where are you on moving everyone inside Fairdawn's boundaries?"

"Nearly finished. Some field people are bringing in the last of the wagons and animals, but all the outlying residents who wanted to move have been relocated into the barracks. A few decided to take their chances. I assume you won't abandon your camp?"

"No. What about Dench? His camp is well outside Fairdawn's fence."

"He agreed to move into one of the miner's apartments, near the village center. I thought he would stay put."

Paul pursed his lips, leaving any thoughts on Dench unspoken. "Shop works?"

"Full staff, started early this morning. They're building a nice inventory of weapons."

"Not much use to us if there's no one to use them. How's the practice going?"

"Quite a few volunteers. I wish I could say we had more skill. Some of the early settlers can handle a bow and ratan, but the more recent immigrants can barely fend off a perelin. I don't think they'd have much chance against a Delerin."

Paul nodded, eyes distant for a moment, lost somewhere. "OK. I'll spend the afternoon working with the archers. Hopefully there are a few with some decent skills. Blades will be less effective in a Delerin attack."

"Do you think archers can make a difference?"

"I don't think we can predict what'll prove valuable, Shawn. More skills certainly won't hurt."

They'd been walking steadily as they conversed and were now well along the trail, a few minutes from Fairdawn. There was no one on the trail within earshot. Shawn took a deep breath and let it out before speaking.

"She's in love with you, you know."

"Pardon?"

"Cara. She's in love with you. And I think you're in love with her."

They walked a ways in silence, Paul with his head down, looking at the trail just in front of him.

"I wanted you to know it was OK with me."

Paul walked on, head still bent as if he hadn't heard Shawn's last statement. They'd walked another 20 meters down the trail before he lifted himself with a sigh and spoke without meeting Shawn's eyes.

"It wouldn't work, Shawn. I wouldn't be good for her. Too much history. Another time, another place, maybe."

"We all have history, Paul. That doesn't mean anything."

"She's a special person. She deserves someone who can live up to that."

Shawn let that thought hang, as two workers pulling small handcarts passed them. They would soon be on a busier section of the trail.

"I don't know what that means. I think she deserves a chance at lasting happiness. I think she deserves a good man. I don't care about your history. I think you're a good man. Lonin thinks the world of you, and that confirms my feelings."

They were met with sounds of greater activity, and two large jarin-drawn wagons carrying barrels marked "WATER" in hand-painted letters came out in front of them. They stopped and let the crew working the teams get clear onto the trail before they walked quickly past. Shawn knew all the workers, and nearly everyone knew of Paul now, the man with the yellow eyes who could fix things. The faces of the men and women were more serious than they'd been during the harvest, but they were far from grim. Shawn waited until they were well ahead of the wagons to continue.

"If you don't love Cara, truly don't love her, then I'll understand. But if you do, then I think you should let her know. Very soon."

"It's not that easy, Shawn. I'm afraid of who I can be. I wouldn't want to hurt her." He touched a place on his neck where he'd cut himself weeks earlier.

"I think you underestimate her. Everybody does. And why not? She's the first to do that. But she can take care of herself."

Paul grunted, a choked-back chuckle, and then changed the subject. "If you'll check on the fortification work on the main building, I'll spend some time with the archers. Have the Timmon given you any indication of when the Delerin may make their move and what their plan may be?"

"No. Most of the Timmon have pulled out of our territory. A good number of them don't want us here either. Lonin thinks things will come to a head in the next few days."

Paul shook his head. "A week would be better. But a day or two is better than nothing. Maybe we should turn spiritual and ask Timmistria to help us. We're going to need all the help we can get."

They'd reached the village center where they would part, and Paul finally met Shawn's eyes. His face was hard, but it eased into a small smile. His eyes were still pinched and tight, but they sparked with the light of determination.

"We'll get through this crisis, Shawn. We won't let anything happen to your sister."

"I believe you."

Paul held out his hand, and Shawn shook it firmly, with an earnest man-hug just before they let go. Then Paul turned and walked away quickly, leaving Shawn to watch his retreating form as he stepped between wagons and disappeared in the bustle.

#

The ansible view screen bristled in lines of static before resolving itself into a cohesive image: a face, very human save the bluish cast, a little wide and effeminate, which was partly a result of the oval shape and large wet eyes, and partly a result of the cosmetics. It was Tapol, Dench's second-in-command. The Serfan race were extremely attractive and therefore sought after for visual advertising and prostitution. Dench trusted Tapol, to a degree, trusted him to wait until Dench was dead before ruthlessly taking over the organization. He might not ever try to have Dench killed, but he wouldn't ask many questions if it happened.

"Lose the pink shirt, Tapol. It doesn't become you."

"Good morning, Meetah Dench!"

"It's late evening here. Can you see me all right?"

"Yeth, Meetah Dench. The definition is acceptable."

"Good. Sorry I'm late. The village manager was using the ansible, and I had to wait for her to clear out. Have the vessels made drop-in?"

"Yeth. They are in full deceleration from jump speed. On schedule within 1.7 minutes."

"So we should hear from them in two days."

"Correct, Meetah Dench."

"Good. No suspicious activity with the crews?"

"No! Your most trusted captains. Crews were handpicked."

"And you tracked them all to the jump to make sure they weren't followed out of Veran?"

"Yeth, Meetah Dench. We tracked all Co-Op vessels in the area as well. We searched for Thinker activity. We detected none."

Tapol seemed earnestly offended that Dench had questioned the crews' loyalty at this late hour, even though said loyalty was enforced within his organization by surgically implanted death caps in all of his people's shoulder joints. But there were ways around them, and true loyalty was always more effective.

"Very well. Things are evolving rapidly here, and the ships will be needed immediately when they arrive. Send them a message to be ready to drop the landing crews as soon as they make orbit. So far, I foresee no deviation from the plan. We should have this village secure within a few hours. How are the preps at your end?"

"Generally very smooth. There were a few minor issues, closing accounts quietly, arranging clan-destine transport. All of your key control personnel will be prepared to depart for the new command center upon your orders."

"Maintain strict observation, Tapol. This is where things get sticky. If one of the Families gets word too early that your office is vacating, they'll flip on the warning lights and our window will slam closed. If we have to abort, we may not have this opportunity again, and I might have to make another unscheduled relocation. That would make me very unhappy."

"Yeth, Meetah Dench."

"This is just step one, Tapol. Like we've planned, if this falls apart, there are five bastards in the Co-Op council that still pay the piper whether I'm around to enjoy it or not. I have your pledge to see that through."

Tapol's face was impassive and serene as ever.

He was an interesting person, a true emotionless assassin. Not without feelings, no doubt — he had numerous spouses and myriad children. Yet he could implement the deaths of others without batting an eye. His pleasant face was as chilling as his blue skin.

"Well, Tapol, this is our last conversation before the action starts. Anything else we need to discuss before all hell breaks loose?"

Tapol shook his head in that mechanical side-to-side movement that was an attempt to imitate the human gesture. "No, Meetah Dench. Best wishes on a perfect mission."

"Godspeed, Tapol. My next call will be after your team arrives. Signing off."

Dench sat, watching the image on the screen collapse into a pip of light, like an ancient 22nd-century vid screen. The light faded out, and the screen was now an undefined gray blankness with no reflection, with only an occasional tic of color as the receiver tried to read stray a-wave pulses.

There was a moment coming that he'd imagined often through the years, since he'd lost his childhood; the small camping party, Anton and three other boys about his age and the two fathers who brought them into the dark woods, sitting on the soft ground, ignoring the moisture soaking up through his pant seat and the insects sucking his blood, watching the smoke from the city's burning embers rising into the glowing sky. The others wept, but he remained dry-eyed, almost hollow, cold. In those hours, he began to feel an insane anger take him. Later that night, in fitful sleep, he dreamed of those same orange-red sparks rising from the torched bodies of his family, and in the hours lying awake over the next week, as the campers moved further into the woods and learned to survive there in secret, he resolved he would kill the ones responsible.

Or so he remembered it now.

In the years that followed, as he pursued his personal objectives, he began to imagine this time of inactivity just before his plans blossomed to fruition.

The time was closer, despite the setback at Sarena, and he held these moments like sparks drifting upward on a hot breeze, up and up, above the dirt and the sweat and the pain; sparks of almost infinitely short life. He was the only one to guide them, to light the pyre for those responsible.

He'd often wondered what it would feel like, this time of calm before the storm. Would there be great satisfaction? Excitement? Anger? Fear?

He was disappointed. He felt very little except perhaps a small hint of anticipation. He'd tortured and killed these men so many times in his daydreams that the real act might seem anticlimactic.

So there was nothing now but to see it through.

Even so, for this moment, he would sit alone in silence, letting whatever human feelings that remained within him wash over and through, to touch the embers of his soul for a few minutes more.

Chapter 31

"Without the darkness, the light has no meaning."
— Timmistrian proverb

She sought him in the places he was usually to be found: the shops, of course, in his coarse brown workman's clothes, bent over a misbehaving still or in front of one of the shop machines, hands spinning gold from shards of wood or metal; the weapons practice yard, collecting arrows with the volunteer archers before the dark set in, teaching these unskilled warriors more in days than Fairdawn's usual instructors could in weeks; Pao's office, patiently requesting resources. Most of the colonists gave Pao only grudging respect, but there was nothing grudging from this man; his respect for Pao was genuine, with no intimidation (Pao wasn't easily intimidated anyway, not even by Cara). But now, all the offices were vacant and her footsteps fell quietly in the empty hall.

He wasn't here, anywhere in the village. He'd gone back to his camp for the night. The resolve that had carried her to look for him would have to wait until morning, when it would be contaminated and eroded by shaming dreams and cast aside by the new day's urgencies. Now that she'd mustered the strength to speak, she was to be thwarted; she would recede like a tide of promise ebbing in the night; the moment would pass; he would never know.

She felt her teeth digging into her lip. Nothing to do here in Fairdawn. She could only hope Lonin could arrange a last-ditch meeting with the Delerin, and she had to be ready.

She moved down the street, which was emptying as it did every evening, as Fairdawn gave the land back to

Timmistria. They were squatters here, really, welcome for hours a day but reminded nightly that they were here by the grace of Timmistria and her children.

How did she feel? Did she dare let it come? So much at stake in the next few hours; could she afford time for her own heart? *Damn, love is such a trial.*

Tender shock, she'd spoken the word to herself, dared to think of the thing as if it could be for her and not just some phantom concept, alien to the point of being superstition.

"Love."

She spoke the word aloud then, and it tasted of licorice on her lips, rich like chocolate, bitter and sticky like blood. But it didn't sound like a foreign language. Here she was, ready to bare her soul on the chance of feeling again that stirring within that she'd felt with her hand in his, even just shaking his hand. Everything about him captivated her. His masculine smell, the way he'd taken Shawn under his wing, the look in his eyes when he'd apologized to her, haunting her, keeping her awake at night. And now…

Timmistria, help me.

She'd reached her cabin. There, impossibly, sitting by her door on a small stool with his knees near his chin, head down and hands crossed in front of him, was the man she'd been seeking.

He's here.

And again…

He's here.

He looked up from the dirt between his feet — she should have swept the porch that morning — and his look was unlike any she'd ever seen from him, and it scared her. Her heart betrayed her and began to pound in her chest, threatening to burst out. She fought to breathe.

He swallowed and pushed himself to his feet. "Hi."

And that was all, but he spoke a lifetime of hope in one word.

"Hi."

He took a deep breath, trying to find something. "I need to talk. To you."

Her body found strength she didn't feel, and against her will, it strode up and stood before him. "I know about you."

He frowned. Was there regret in his eyes? Pain?

Stop, Cara. Don't push him away now.

"What do you know?"

"I know what's on the G-net, what I could find in the public domain."

He nodded, smiled a little. "So? Now you know I'm a monster."

"No, you're not. But … I can't lie. I know more than that."

He raised his eyebrows. "Yes?"

"Helwin. You said things when you were feverish. I had to stay in the room with you, you were burning. I was afraid. So much … It was wrong for me to hear. But I couldn't not listen."

He closed his eyes, night shuttering the yellow suns. He was going away, back inside himself. She'd said too much.

His eyes opened, and that gleam was still there, the one that had fired her heart when she'd walked up. Weariness, despair, fearful expectation.

She spoke before he could. "You're going to break my heart, aren't you?"

He nodded. "Yes."

She shook her head, felt her tortured lip between her teeth again. "I don't care."

He breathed, his lungs a bellows for fires within, hidden from her so far. He reached to grasp her shoulders gently, heavy as gravity.

"After … I didn't think I could … ever feel … like this."

"How does it feel? Is it…?"

Less? she thought, afraid to speak it. His hands on her were like the poles of a powerful magnet, aligning all her cells in invisible lines of force. If he let her go, the energy would drain from her and she would collapse.

"It's … different. Confusing." He shook his head slowly, eyes tired as if he were watching the sunrise after staying awake all night. He seemed weak, more vulnerable than she'd ever seen him, but not giving up or giving in.

"I can't … keep you out of my mind. I've given up trying. But I'm afraid of who I am. I'll hurt you in the end."

"I don't care. I didn't know how empty I was until I sat next to you. Didn't know how numb I was until I touched your skin and felt your heart beating on my hands. I've been blind, and I want to see. I don't care if you hurt me. I need to feel what I feel whenever I'm with you. I love you, Paul Saarinen, and I don't even know what that means."

And there, in a rush, it was out.

It was a long time before he spoke again. Words, at least, for his eyes never left hers. And even in her uncertainty, what they said was obvious.

"I love you, Cara Harvestmoon. And I don't know what to do about it."

"I don't have much experience, but I think this is where you kiss me."

He pulled her gently against his body and laid his lips on hers, and she saw their timeril alight around them, swirling in a dance of pure white light.

Chapter 32

Paul lay and listened to the night passing, like a long story told in the voices of the wind. He clung to every minute as if it were something precious, like the moments a child may cling to his mother's dress uniform before she must pull herself away and board the inevitable military transport.

Memories came of a day past, yellow sky visible in a nearby window and Claire walking stiffly away toward the exit gate with all the other mothers and fathers. He could still feel the texture of her shirttail on his fingertips as he fell back against his grandfather's legs, trying to remember then the feeling of his father's shirt only days earlier as he too had departed for assignment. She passed through the door, looking back at him at last, with a brief, unprofessional hesitation in her step, then turned her head away and walked beyond his view. There was an undeniable finality in that moment, a closure too immense and ominous for a seven-year-old. He remembered the heat of a tear stinging his eye and cheek, perhaps the last tear he ever allowed himself. When she'd returned from duty months later, he was not the same child.

Minutes and hours passed while he lay awake, daring not to sleep, gleaning as much awareness from each fragment of the night as his mind could capture. He could see the room quite well in the pinkish light of two moons. Later, staccato flashes of lightning wounded his retinas, and passing clouds dimmed the shadows. The storm passed to the south, with the thunder distant and dull. Subtle shades of gray flowed over like waves, fascinating him with their nuances of color and light.

There were the sensations of heat and pressure where Cara's hard-yet-soft body pressed against his, and scents filled the air near her, of natural Timmon soap and Cara's feminine muskiness and his own sweat. He willed time to stop, to freeze them both as they were here, all yesterdays becoming forgotten history and all tomorrows just fantasies. His metronomic heartbeat measured the continuous flow of time, heedless of his silently desperate command to cease counting.

Earlier in the day, he'd reported in to the foreign ministry. Blackburn had demanded his final assessment of the Timmistrians, baiting Paul with a promise of rapid withdrawal from assignment if he was prepared to confirm the suitability of the Timmon for their needs. Paul had stalled.

Cara stirred against him, and he felt her lips kissing his chest, his stomach, then further. When his body responded, she moved upward again, kissing as she went until she laid her soft lips on his and moved upon him so that they made love again, intimate and easy, as if they had been lovers for ages and not for just the last few hours. In their passion, Paul feared time would race ahead, and he silently bade her to grip the moment like her body gripped his, to rein in the racing horses of time and hide there forever.

But her gentle rocking became more insistent, and they thrust together in a mutual release of fire and desperation. At last, she collapsed on his chest, clinging to him like ivy. He forced his heart to slow and pressed sleep away from him again, focusing again for the remaining dark hours to sense only this woman, her smells, her sounds, the warmth and softness of her skin. He couldn't help but think of Helwin, and he ached at this double-edged betrayal. Time ran on and ignored his despair.

He had apparently dozed, for the yellow sun through the blinds touched his eyelids. Sleep had robbed him. Even so, Cara lay just as she had fallen asleep, directly on his chest, her body gently pressing him to the bed, in her own way keeping him here, away from the world, away from the advancing Delerin. Her hands cupped her mouth as if to catch each precious breath. Paul had instinctively wrapped his arms around her as they'd slept.

He pulled her body more tightly into his, and she stirred, her hands opening on his chest and releasing her captured breaths. Her eyes opened, and she tilted her head to find his. She brushed stray hairs from her face with two fingers.

"Hi." Her voice was a dry whisper.

"Morning."

She held his gaze for a few seconds, an eternity, then sighed and smiled. Her look was a question, and he answered her by touching her cheek lightly with his fingertips. She reached up and squeezed his fingers, then pulled from him.

"I need to get moving. Emergency council meeting this morning."

He watched her as she slid to the edge of the bed, lifted herself slowly, and padded silently about the room, naked at first, but gradually dressing as she gathered her things. His mind ached with the new memories of having removed all her garments slowly and methodically, the taste of her skin still maddeningly on his lips.

At last he turned his legs to the side and pushed himself from the bed. He found his underclothes laid on the chair at the bedside and pulled them on. He poured a pottery cup half full of water, and then handed it to her. She was now fully clothed, save for the items in a small pile at the foot of the bed: her hair comb; a silver Timmon bracelet; a small pouch of brown lizard skin stitched with cords of twisted talil feathers, like fine tan wire.

She smiled at him as she reached for the cup. He caught her fingers in his free hand and held her gently captive, suspended in time for a final instant of peace. Her look was no longer a question, but perhaps his was. She kissed his fingers and smiled again, this time as if there were no concerns in their world. She sipped from the cup, letting him hold her fingers.

The water seemed to revive her optimism.

"We've sent another Timmon emissary to the Delerin, requesting an audience. I think they have to talk at least once. We'll find resolution."

He released her fingers and took the cup, then watched as she gathered the last of her things. His heart began to pound, and an unpleasant tension drew a line from between his eyes along the top of his head. She must have seen something in his eyes, for she came to him and kissed him, deeply, intensely. She pulled away far too quickly.

"It's going to be OK, Paul. I can feel it. Timmistria wouldn't let us get to this point just to see it all crash down. We have purpose here, and we're going to see it through."

"I believe you."

With a confident wink, she left the cabin.

For the space of ten breaths, Paul allowed himself to assimilate the minute, the hour, the night. Then he performed the ritual of putting it away, folding it inward into a packet of mental encapsulation, until it was only a small white hum of comfort.

The time for reflection was soon over, and the time to act was upon him. Preparations were required, and he went about them quickly. He gathered his clothes, dressed, and hurried back to his cabin. Once there, he put his house in order, literally. Dishes were washed; the bed was completely torn apart and remade with fresh linens. Garbage was taken out to the compost pile.

Next, he selected clothing and weaponry. He chose nothing that had been brought to Timmistria by humans, only clothing woven in the village and a belt and shoes of Timmon leather. He gathered his weapons, the two cremin-tooth blades, one slightly longer than 25 inches, the other about 12 inches long, so familiar in his hands now, the glassy material worn smooth along the edge from frequent use. Dench and his goons had a disruptor, perhaps a stun gun and a laser, and possibly more. Paul didn't have the luxury of a fair fight or a duel. He would have to strike quickly.

Killing Dench would be an assassination. And Paul would then take his own life. Following the Timmon tradition was the only way to make them understand.

He checked the cabin to make sure all was in order, then tucked the short blade into its scabbard at his waist and lifted the longer one from the table. He chose the hidden back trail, not wanting to meet anyone. There was always a chance Dench would send his goon to kill Paul. At the trail opening, he paused to listen and heard nothing but the usual sounds of the forest life.

He took one last look at the campsite and the home he'd built from wood and rocks. It was only a way station, a temporary dwelling like every place he'd ever lived, nothing more, but he hoped someone else would enjoy his craftwork. For one painful moment he thought of Helwin, and then even more painfully, Cara. And then he eased into the brush and followed the trail around the site to the north, then took the first cut to the right and headed toward Fairdawn.

Chapter 33

The Delerin party, twenty strong, flowed through the forest in a silent lope that covered miles without startling animals. They were close to the meeting place where they would attack the human village. Terelin led them, having taken the lead from his cousin several kikkin back. He was honored that their council leader, Sherilin, had chosen to come with his party.

The others were all good in the forest, but they couldn't drive the trail as skillfully as he or his cousin could, and speed was of the essence. The humans had taken to scouting them from the air in their damned flying machine, and the party needed to move swiftly to escape detection. Other parties of Delerin were advancing with great noise, acting as decoys, but Terelin's group would strike the first blow.

They came through one final stand of black aspril trees, and Terelin pulled the group up to a halt, suddenly, so that the last nearly ran over those in front of them. Ahead was a small clearing in the trail, and in that clearing stood a group of Timmon. They were dressed as the Delerin were, in tan leather war garments. Terelin counted 16 of them. They wore red face paint as the Delerin did, although the patterns were foreign and said nothing, only gibberish.

Terelin recognized the group's leader and wasn't surprised. He stepped forward into the clearing and motioned for his party to follow.

"Lonin, stand aside."

Lonin shook his head slowly. "Not during my time, Terelin. Take your people back to your lands, and call an end to this."

"You know I cannot."

"You can. But you will not. And we will not let you and your party pass."

Sherilin, dressed not as a warrior but as a councilman, stepped forward. "Lonin. What folly is this? You would spill Timmon blood to save the humans?"

"And you, Sherilin, would spill the blood of innocent men? Would you take your own lives then? Leave your families with sorrow because of what you fear?"

"It's not for me to say, Lonin. The Council has spoken, and we go to war."

"Then your war will be with me, Sherilin."

"Your group is small. You will lose."

"I challenge your warrior to filin. Settle this one on one. The rest need not die."

"Filin?"

"Yes. A duel such as our leaders fought generations ago. Terelin is the greatest warrior of the Delerin. Some believe I am the greatest of the Timmon. Let us decide this conflict and save bloodshed on both sides."

"You dishonor the long-dead leaders. You defy Timmistria."

"I honor them by seeing when their time to rule us has ended. We will have a new filin."

Terelin stepped forward. "You cannot stand against me."

"Perhaps. Agree to the contest, and then draw your ratan, Terelin."

Sherilin, thinking this an easy victory, agreed. "Have it your way, Lonin. When you are defeated, the Timmon will be forced to cede more land to the Delerin. Your lands will be smaller than the humans' were."

Terelin added, "When I defeat you, the humans will follow you in death, and no Delerin lives will be sacrificed."

"Draw your blade, Terelin, and not your tongue."

With that, Terelin drew, and without pause the two warriors came together with a loud clang. They were evenly matched, each thrust and blow dodged or turned away. The ground beneath their feet was tossed up as they battled. Lonin drew blood first, a small cut on Terelin's shoulder. The Delerin warrior responded with a strong thrust that nearly pierced Lonin's belt and left a wet red mark in the fabric at his waist. As they fought, Lonin's movements became faster and harder to follow, but Terelin matched his speed.

Then, in unison, the Delerin and Timmon warriors circling the fight raised their voices in surprise. Lonin and Terelin ceased and pulled back. They'd all sensed the same thing, as a note blown from a distant horn. The scarlet red light had been extinguished: The red beast was dead.

Terelin took several steps back and put his blades in their sheaths.

Lonin growled, "Why are you sheathing your blades, Terelin? This fight isn't over."

"There's nothing to fight over now. Stand down, and let us proceed. With the red one dead, we may spare your precious humans … if they leave our lands."

"This filin has nothing to do with the red one. This is about our freedom. The Timmon will no longer be held captive by the Delerin."

Sherilin stepped forward again from the ring of observers. "What are you talking about, Lonin? The Timmon are free within your own lands. The Delerin don't cage you."

"Call it what you will, Sherilin, but the Timmon are made to stay in our pens like jarin. We will not abide by the borders any longer. We will have our freedom to move about the world."

"That was decided long ago. You have your land, and we have ours."

"Then we will decide it again, right on this field. Draw your ratan-i, Terelin. This filin has not been decided."

Terelin eyed Lonin darkly and began pulling his blades from their leather homes. But Sherilin stopped him with a hand on his chest.

"Hold back, Terelin. Lonin, are you truly mad? This peace has lasted more than taylil generations, and you would end it now? Would you have all the Delerin and Timmon at war with each other?"

"The Timmon will have their freedom, Sherilin. WE WILL NO LONGER BE CONTAINED!"

With that, the entire Timmon party roared and drew their blades. The Delerin, who'd stepped back defensively at the outburst, drew their own. The sound of ratan-i singing filled the clearing. Again, Sherilin stepped between the groups.

"HOLD! All of you! We will not let generations of peace die on this trail. Lonin, call your people off. Let us postpone this fight until cooler heads can talk. We must go to the human village and see what has become of this red beast."

Lonin took a deep breath and backed up a step. "Stand down. This fight will wait. But the cause will not, Sherilin."

"I see that. Let us talk later. For now, lead us to the village."

"Lead on, Kearnin. And quickly."

Chapter 34

Cara and those with her stood in front of the wooden sawhorses they'd set across the trail leading into Fairdawn. Tarron and Maggon were among the group, and they had guided Cara and the others to this place. She wasn't surprised when the large fighting group of Timmistrians ran down the path and pulled up in front of them. She was surprised to see Kearnin, Lonin, and several other Timmon leading the team, and her heart leaped in her chest. She was shocked by a freak fear that Lonin and the Timmon had joined the Delerin, which she tossed aside immediately. She remained puzzled.

Lonin spoke first and said only one word. His stricken tone renewed her fear.

"Cara."

"Lonin, what … we expected the Delerin, but what are your people doing here?"

"I may ask the same. Why are you here? And with Timmon among you?"

Behind Cara stood a contingent of over fifty of the women colonists, all dressed in heavy field clothing, with improvised dragon skin and leather coverings on their arms, chests, and legs, blades holstered but ready. Some carried long spears normally used for herding raree, others bows.

"We came to meet the Delerin. They would not come to us, so we came to them." She spoke up, so the Delerin rangers in the group would hear her voice. "We are here to talk about our rights, and to make them see us not as aliens but as people just as they are."

For a moment, there was a soundless standoff, and Cara was unsure what that foreboded. At last, Lonin spoke to her as one soothing a wounded animal.

"There is news, Cara. Dench, the red one, is dead."

"What?!" She turned to Tarron and Maggon, who had stepped up to flank her on each side. They nodded in confirmation. "But how?"

Lonin said, "We go to the village now to learn of this."

"What about them?" She gestured toward the Delerin, whose triangular faces were grim and regarded her with a look somewhere between suspicion and wonder.

"They agree there will be no action until we know the way of this story. They will not harm you, at least until we all have answers."

"They cannot enter our village unless they agree to talk."

Lonin spoke roughly at the Delerin behind him, hissing and clicking. One of them, shorter than the others, and older with white streaks in his hair and a thin face, nodded at Lonin's words.

"They will talk, but we must go. There is another, Cara, one very close to you, who is hurt. We must go."

Cara's mind jumped from fear for herself to another kind of fear.

"Tarron, Maggon, lead us! Hurry please!"

#

The forest passed beneath Paul's feet. The normally harrowing beasts and plants laid off, as if they knew he was on urgent business. He soon passed the outbuildings of Fairdawn, entirely vacated now, with no sign of human activity. The guard outposts were manned, and there were patrols along the inner village streets. They would all fall back when the attack came. Even if

Paul succeeded in killing Dench, there were no guarantees that the Delerin wouldn't continue the war, but their resolve might weaken.

The streets weren't as busy as they had been the previous day, but there were still a few villagers gathering supplies. He slipped past two wagons loaded with hay and found the main road to the village center. He began the mind preparation for battle as he moved, clearing out all distractions, focusing on the business at hand. When he found Dench, he would have to be ready to act without hesitation.

He came to the corner opposite the village center and was surprised at the number of people gathered and milling about. One group of about 20 stood near the entrance to the community building, and he could see the heads of several Timmon rising above the shorter villagers. Lonin was among them, dressed as he had been the day he attacked Paul at the camp. The crowd seemed agitated.

Paul pushed his way through them, seeking the puffy face of his adversary. He found several people crouched around a prone figure, a soft man with pasty skin and a large, bulbous body. Dench.

"He is dead." Upon seeing Paul, Lonin had walked over quickly. His voice was flat, mechanical, devoid of expression. It matched his face.

Paul examined the body. Dench's chest didn't rise and fall. "Did you kill him?"

"No, but it appears that was your intention. You are too late."

Lonin nodded to Paul's left, where another man sat on the ground with his back against a tree. Other people were crouched around him, including a young Timmon male. Paul's heart sank. It was Shawn, dressed in Timmon linens. Cara knelt on one side of Shawn, and Kearnin crouched on the other.

Paul couldn't feel his body moving, but he was soon next to Shawn. The young man's skin was ashen. As Paul knelt, Kearnin moved aside to give him space. Shawn looked up with waxy eyes and a little smile. "The Delerin … called off … the attack." He coughed weakly. "It had to be done. You under … under … stand."

He coughed again, this time more forcefully. Tiny blood drops formed on his lips. Cara pushed the long, dark hair from his face. Paul reached down to feel his forehead. There was a burning heat on his skin.

"You're hot."

Shawn nodded weakly and his glassy eyes gazed up at Lonin, who knelt down beside him on the side opposite Paul and Cara. The tall Timmon placed the back of his hand on Shawn's forehead and bent over awkwardly to look into his eyes. When he straightened up, he caught Paul's eye, his face dark. His voice was a deep whisper.

"Jin."

Shawn swallowed hard and nodded weakly, eyes glazing more. Paul took Shawn's hand from where it lay on the ground. It was like a hot game bird freshly shot.

"I had … to follow the ritual. So the Delerin … would understand. We belong … here." He coughed again, harder then, and this time blood coated the insides of his lips. He winced.

Tears streamed down Cara's cheeks when she lifted her face. "Shawn, why? Why did you…?" Her words stopped as she ran out of breath.

"It was the only way." He coughed, more weakly. "The Delerin had to know … we belong … here. Our home." He groaned, his head rolled to the side, and his eyes closed. He shuddered.

Cara panicked and looked around frantically. "Shik! Take him to the medical center. Helen! Get the doctor! Help me!"

She tried to lift Shawn and urged the others to help her. His eyes opened again, unfocused.

"Stop, Cara. Just stop."

Lonin's voice was as quiet as Paul had ever heard it, and incredibly steady. "He is truly of Timmistria, Cara. He has followed the old rituals and takes his own life. It is the way."

Her expression was one of total confusion at first, but then realization came as a mask of horror to her face. "No! Paul! Help me lift him!"

"Stop, Sis. You can't save me. It … was … uh, the only way."

"No…!"

She fell into Shawn's lap, and he raised his hand to her head, patting it lightly. His voice was little more than a whisper now. "We … Kearnin and me, we went back to where … Mr. Dennison was. Dench had him killed. There were … large footprints. Kearnin tracked them the day after he was found … footsteps coming from Dench's camp. His assistant…"

Shawn's eyes rolled over and met Kearnin's. The young Timmon's face was a conflict of misery and pride. Shawn then noticed Paul's clothing.

"I knew you would … try to kill him. He … had men looking for you. But he trusted me."

He coughed again and spoke between gasps. "I went to him. He … smiled. Then I stuck him with a quill." He turned his hand to show an angry red pockmark on the underside of his arm. "Then me."

He closed his eyes, and tears slipped down his cheek. "I didn't want to kill him, Paul. But I didn't see any other way. We owe the Timmon." He sniffed, then gasped. His voice was barely a breath. "Did I do the right thing?"

There was heartache, and then there was another pain that words could not name. Paul felt that pain, for the second time, as he had on Delos Red.

"Yes, Shawn. You did the right thing."

Cara sobbed, crumpled in Shawn's lap, and Paul could do nothing but kneel there, wishing he hadn't obsessed over cleaning the cabin, wishing he had left the damn place minutes earlier. Shawn's hand soon went limp on Cara's head, and his breathing slowed and then stopped. More people gathered, but the only sound was Cara's muffled crying.

Paul might have knelt there until the end of days, but events took place quickly from that point, and he was pulled from his desolate reverie. Word of Dench's death had spread like wildfire. Kinin came to speak in Lonin's ear. He rose and motioned for Paul to follow. Once aside, he spoke in his quiet voice, which was the sound of tree limbs groaning in the wind.

"The Delerin leaders wait nearby. They have stopped their attack, but they must see the red one dead, and they must hear from the 'White Lady.' We need Cara to council with them. I know it is hard, but this may be her only chance to save the village."

"Zark 'em."

"Paul."

The contingent of Delerin fighters stood to themselves, a forest of strange yellow men, like young malack trees growing suddenly on the small plot of ground in the village square. He felt the rage rising, and he ached to draw his blades. His vision turned red.

"Paul."

"Let me talk to her."

He went back to Cara. She had stopped sobbing, but she still lay with her face in Shawn's lap, motionless. He squeezed her shoulder. She was limp, as if all life had left her as well.

"Cara. We need you. You have to meet with the Delerin. They want to talk. It may be our only chance."

Paul was afraid of how this would be for them. She would hate him for inspiring Shawn to kill Dench, for not stopping him, for arriving too late. If he'd been the one dead on the ground, perhaps she would have cried in his lap, and Shawn would have been there to support her. He felt his light, the color of things burned.

"Cara."

He stroked her back as softly as Lonin's voice had spoken, feeling her body stiffen as she began to move. Her voice was a hoarse whisper.

"Can you get me some water?"

She began to slowly pull herself up, still not looking at him. He stood and reluctantly left her. He walked past Dench's body, expecting to feel something — hatred, disgust, *something* — but there was nothing there, just an empty grayness.

James and Gregor were talking together near the body. When they saw Paul, they waved him down and came to him.

Gregor said, "Mr. Paul, do you need us to do anything?"

He thought a moment, looking back at the group of Delerin who had joined Lonin's party. "Yes. Where are your archers?"

"Still practicing at the range we set up behind the shops."

"Good. I want everyone you have on that roof in two minutes. Tell them this is *not* a drill. If any of those

Delerin bastards makes a move, I want to see arrows in their necks. Am I clear?"

"Yes, sir."

"Do it now. Go."

Gregor looked once at James, then turned on his heel and dashed from the square. Paul turned to James. "How many of the chemical bombs were you able to make up?"

"Fourteen. I have some extra chemicals left, but I need more of the coverings."

"Fueled up?"

"Always."

"Good. Load the bombs in the flyer, and get in the air above this clearing as soon as you can. Same instructions, James. If the Delerin act, let 'em have it. Focus on the leaders — you see them over there. Don't worry about bystanders. The chemicals probably won't kill anyone, but they'll wish they were dead. Any questions?"

"Nope."

"Good. Move out."

James ran off toward the air pad.

As Paul approached the administration building, he noticed the tall dark figure of Dench's goon standing in the shadows. He drew his blade and walked toward him. The rage came again and he picked up the pace, breaking into a run. The man held something dark and shiny in his hand and raised it, but he took a step back. He must have seen the death in Paul's eyes, because he spun on his heel and ran up the street. Paul bellowed and chased him, but the responsibility for those behind him grabbed him back, and he stopped.

When he was sure the goon had fled completely from the square, he returned to the town building, found a large clay flask and cup in Cara's office, filled them from the public water faucet, and took them back to her. She was alone, kneeling by Shawn's side, her hands holding his limp one. Tears had formed dirty smudges down both of her cheeks.

"Cara. Here's the water."

She laid her brother's hand gently in his lap and took the mug from Paul. Her eyes didn't leave Shawn's fallen face. She drank, a sip only, then handed the mug back.

"Thank you."

She lifted herself from the dirt onto her hands and knees and pushed to her feet, brushing the dust from her trousers and hands. She looked at him then, and there was nothing bad there for him, just the resigned look that he'd seen when things were not going well.

"I'm ready."

Chapter 35

"In the hearts of the smallest, there live giants."
— Lonin

When Cara rolled to her hands and knees, and then pushed herself to her feet, it was a lift of a thousand pounds.

Shawn lay where his head had collapsed onto his chest; it was a small movement, but it felt like the felling of a great tree for her. Part of her willed him to stir, to move, to rise, to deny the truth that was eating away at the inside of her heart. He was gone, like all her other brothers and her parents before them, and he was not coming back.

It seemed her whole life had been to see one dream through. There was only one goal that drove her to carry on, to keep driving, to keep living — to save him.

She had failed.

There were people all around, pressing in on her, but none of them mattered now. Only she and the empty vessel that had held him, the person she loved most. The bubble she'd built around him over the bleak years hadn't been strong enough to hold his soul. He had slipped away.

She had deceived herself all along. The shield that protected them and kept everyone else out had never been strong enough to keep him. Inevitably, he grew too vast, too fast. He was a giant now, a towering malack that no vessel she could ever have forged could have contained. She'd known he would come to great things. And he'd proven her correct; he reached the sky.

Now when she had nothing left to give, these people outside the bubble, these outsiders, wanted more from her. Couldn't they see she'd given everything she valued, everything she loved? What else now? What more?

"Cara, we need you."

Paul.

Of all those here, he'd lost all he loved as well. She understood a bit about how he must have felt when he arrived. If she'd had the ability to feel anything at this moment, she would have felt the pain that had been in his heart when he stepped off the shuttle months earlier. But she could feel nothing. Nothing but a dark empty space. Little wonder he'd been so distant, so aloof. Even she couldn't feel more disengaged from this place now, from these people. How had she dared to chastise him for his distance? What inner strength he must have drawn on to refrain from setting her straight.

She felt shame. She had sent him away to get her water. She was thirsty, but more than that, she could hardly bear to look at him.

All these people around her … she could feel their energy, their need. They needed her. To do something. What was it? Here were Helen and Gregor and Teresa. She could name them, all of them. She could name all 200 of them. They needed her. She thought she'd needed them, but really, the only one she'd needed lay dead at her feet. He'd given all, all he had. And yet it wasn't enough. Why did they think she could give enough where Shawn could not?

She should be angry, not just at the Delerin people but at all of them. The giving was all she and Shawn had ever meant to them, and now when they'd taken all there was to give, they wanted more.

But just as she could feel none of Paul's pain, she could feel no anger. There was only a blank space where her feelings lived, no definition, no commitment.

She could choose not to feel.

Or she could choose anger and its child, hatred.

Pao was there suddenly, pushing through the bodies to reach her. He took in the scene in one long look, then studied her face. He wanted to speak, it seemed, but something in her expression must have told him words were pointless. He stepped away and began giving instructions to the others. The Delerin stood as a group, watching. Watching the gathered colonists, whose numbers were growing, watching Lonin, watching her. She realized they were all watching her. All expecting.

The Timmon were there as well — Lonin of course, with Kinin standing near, arms crossed. Maggon and Tarron, the two women who'd helped Paul home after the tharnon attack and who'd agreed to lead her to where the Delerin would approach the village, and then they'd followed her. Other Timmon women were there as well, some she had never met before this day, before the confrontation.

Couldn't they see she was empty? Her timeril was a tiny flicker, threatening to go out.

Kearnin knelt by Shawn's side, his hand resting on her brother's chest. He didn't look up at her, didn't look at her longingly like the others. He expected nothing. Of all of them, perhaps he knew how much Shawn had given, how much he had loved this place and how much he gave to defend it.

And then he did meet her eyes, and a shock of understanding passed between them. His thoughts were as if he whispered them in her head: *Don't let Shawn's death mean nothing. Don't let this moment escape.*

Suddenly, she wanted to scream, "I have nothing left! I have nothing to give you!"

But Kearnin's look was unforgiving.

She sent back her own thoughts then, hoping he would hear them. *I have nothing. But I will give you everything I have.*

She tightened her belt. Paul was there. The look in his eyes was so concerned, it was tragic.

She said again, after reading the uncertainty in his usually steady eyes, "I'm ready."

She took his hand and led him to where the six Delerin rangers stood, as still as giant chessmen. Larilin had come as well, and stood to the side, and as Cara and Paul approached the group, Lonin joined them and moved to stand by his Delerin counterpart.

The villagers were very quiet, but she could feel them moving up behind her.

Could she save them?

She let her gaze wander one last time to where Shawn's body lay. Kearnin was there as he'd been before, on one knee, hand on Shawn's heart. Did he still see Shawn's timeril? Was it like a light that leaped away when the person died, or did it fade? Or did it bleed?

Il Ne-Hilin Sil Gon Arin. One Death Leads to Many.

Not today. Not on my watch.

She let her eyes choose among the Delerin. Their warrior was there, big even for his people and towering over her. And yet she was not intimidated. They had taken all from her; what could this one do now? Another was among them, dressed not in field clothing but in something more colorful and formal. A leader of some kind. The deminin.

She stepped forward alone, signaling Paul not to follow. His part was done. Bless the man, he had done all she had asked, despite his own pain. Of all of them, he was one she owed something to. If she'd turned to search his face, his look would have been the same as Kearnin's, the thoughts the same. As deeply as she had lost, her work was not yet finished.

"Liaison Lonin, you wished to speak with me?"

"Yes, Manager Cara. May I introduce Sherilin, Deminin for the Delerin people, from Dlith Welkin, and Terelin, chief of the Delerin militia."

The deminin, the one named Sherilin, spoke to Lonin in the clipped Delerin accent. As he spoke, the military leader, slightly taller but less robust than Lonin, stood with feet wide and arms crossed in front of his chest. He was dressed in field armor, heavy woven trousers and a heavy leather vest with metal slats interlaced. His face, pinched by what could only be smug arrogance, was painted in crossed patterns of red and orange, dress and paint similar to but distinct from that worn by the Timmon. His twin thumbs were tucked into his belt, and he touched the scabbards where his blades hung.

There were five other Delerin in the group, standing in a semicircle around the deminin. The leader spoke in a tongue similar to that of the Timmon, in the tone of one accustomed to command. His words were abbreviated and angular, like the shape of his head and ears. He stopped speaking abruptly, and Lonin translated.

"Deminin Sherilin has long heard of the 'White Lady,' the queen of the aliens, and is pleased to meet her at last."

Cara stood quietly, as if she hadn't heard a word. Lonin watched her, concern building on his face. As the pause stretched on, the Delerin leader cocked his head in puzzlement and glanced at Lonin. Out of the corner of her eye, Cara could see people moving into position on the admin building roof. At the same time, she became aware of the dull throb of the flyer's blades approaching from behind him. The sound rapidly grew closer.

"Manager Cara?"

At last she spoke, only to Lonin. She'd always counted him as her friend, and sometimes her lover, but how did she feel about him now? "Yes, I heard you, Lonin. Before this moment, your words would have been excellent news. Today, things are different." She took a deep breath and gathered herself, raising herself as tall as she could and pulling her shoulders back. "You may tell the Deminin Sherilin that we have long requested a chance to meet and talk with the Delerin, but they have always refused. For many years, we have worked to be good citizens of this planet, so that one day we could call the Delerin our friends. Now their aggressive behavior has caused the Co-Op village a great deal of trouble."

She nodded at Lonin, who looked at her with concern but then translated. The Delerin leader's face knitted. When Lonin stopped, Cara spoke again.

"I no longer have a need — or a desire — to speak with the Delerin. I will let them know when I may be ready to talk. If things were different, I would ask them to leave our territory as soon as possible. I would ask Timmistria to withhold her anger, because I cannot, and would ask that she guide the Delerin safely back to their place of council."

She nodded for Lonin to translate. He hesitated, his eyes searching her face, but then he spoke, and his words began to take on the anger that she was beginning to feel, to allow herself to feel. As he spoke, the faces of the Delerin grew harder and darker, and red flared around their ears and eyes.

When Lonin finished, Cara continued, "I would ask you to leave, but I trust you will not go, despite all the hardship you have caused us. I have given all I have, and I have nothing more to give you.

"But I offer you another way, another way for you to get what you came here for. Your warrior is here. And I am here. You are all of this world, and despite the desires of the Delerin in this matter, so am I. This is my home, and I would rather die than leave her.

"So, in honor of the covenant between your peoples, I call upon you to honor your own traditions and grant my people our last rites of freedom. I speak to you as an equal in the eyes of Timmistria. I invoke the way of filin."

Chapter 36

Cara Faces the Delerin
— As told to Shawna Harvestmoon-Serak by Administrator Pao Shing-Shing

To see wonders that you never imagined, how profound do you think that would be? Things so incredible that you think you might be going mad?

We villagers seldom speak of that day, and only then in intimate groups with quiet tones. Many of them will not speak of it at all, as if acknowledging the events would steal their magic.

But I was there. I know what I experienced. And I was changed forever.

I left the craft offices as quietly as I could, having left instructions with the medical guild attendant for the disposition of Master Shawn's body. Poor Cara, her last surviving brother was gone now, by his own hand, in the strange tragic gesture to save the colony. So brave, but so wasteful. If only he had learned to trust me as his sister did, his sorrowful death could have been avoided. But to him, I'd always been just Pao Shing-Shing, Cara's rather unconventional assistant. He was a clever and genial young man, but his lack of respect was very frustrating, so much so that I nearly confronted him about it on several occasions.

When I returned to Fairdawn's square, the scene seemed to have slowed to a stasis of almost imperceptible motion. Opposing each other were the two native entourages, one from the friendly Timmon and one from the hostile Delerin, and then the villagers standing in small groups, not sure what to do. Paul Saarinen, de facto leader of the fledgling militia and the man I knew even then that Cara loved, stood near her side, his right hand twitching just above his belt, where his cruel cremin-tooth blade was holstered. To my observation, Mr. Saarinen has always seemed like a keg of something explosive. I've never seen him lose his composure, but with him violence has always lurked just beneath the surface. At that moment, with his dear friend dead as a result of the Delerin aggression, I was concerned I would witness the power of his bottled anger for the first time, and I feared it.

To one side stood the small band of Timmon, the tall, stately but ethereal guardians of our colony, with our liaison, Lonin, among them. They are capable of anger and mirth just as we humans are, but in dire times such as this, they are impassive as stone statues. Cara liked to tease Lonin about that very thing, and his response was likely to be the following phrase: "My face is not my timeril." I could only guess that the timeril, the soul lights, of these few Timmon, trapped between the human colony and their own aggressive and unreasonable cousins the Delerin, were burning as brightly and hotly as crystal-blue gas flames.

The group of Delerin stood in the center of the crossroads that defined the southwest corner of the village square. Perhaps I compliment our village by giving it more significance than it deserves, this extraterrestrial abode for 218 adventurers and refugees. Fairdawn is modest, of course, humble, just a small ragged green square of Earth set in the golden forest of Timmistria. But for all of us who came here, it's an emerald, a forested jewel in a field of amber and straw. This garden has its thorns, but we have made this hostile but beautiful land our home, and most of us would rather die than leave here. Therein lay the real crux of the problem with the Delerin. We tried to preserve their land and treat it well, but it is our nature to bring our own worlds with us, and perhaps we had in effect taken a patch of Earth and dropped it into the Timmistrian forest, thus angering the Delerin people and their gods.

The Delerin stood in the center of the crossroads, six impossibly tall beings, faces as impassive as those of the Timmon, dressed for war in tan leather cloaks and red battle markings over their skin and clothing, their incredible physiques clearly visible in the hot sun of the late-summer afternoon. Looking at them, nine feet tall and three wide, wraiths and phantoms, one would not be mistaken to think these six warriors could have slaughtered the entire village of mere humans with only the strength of their bulging arms and the edges of their blades. And before this army of six stood just two of our people, bold and formidable by human standards but diminutive against the sky-rubbing backdrop of yellow Delerin warriors. Cara Harvestmoon, my leader, and Paul Saarinen.

The breath of all the villagers seemed to catch in that moment. I didn't know what I thought would happen. Nothing stirred, no bird called nor perelin screed nor raree snorted nor cleft-footed jarin grumbled. I imagined that in that instant, all life on the entire planet paused in anticipation and fear, but also perhaps excitement. Not one person in that square doubted that when our hearts began to beat again, the world would be changed forever.

As I watched, frozen like a fool, my feet leaden, Cara seemed to rise as an osprey in the morning sun and stepped forward, now paces ahead of the large group of armed villagers gathered behind her. Mr. Saarinen moved to join her, but she pressed him back with a subtle turn of her small hand, and she advanced alone. She stopped two paces from the Delerin and pulled her jade green field blade from its scabbard. She seemed to weigh it in her hands, as if judging its value like a jeweler might a large gemstone. The Delerin eyed her warily, still emotionless as domestic robots. I had never feared for Cara so much in my life. But there was also a part of me that wanted my leader to confront those ruffians, to bring them down. I am a peaceable person, but so intense was the anger in my torso and abdomen for the death of Master Shawn and all the strife caused at the hands of the Delerin that even I, Pao the administrator, Pao the manager's annoying assistant, Pao the campfire joke of weak masculinity, twitched with rage at them, wanted to see them taken to task for their arrogance and intolerance. But then my heart kicked madly at the thought of Cara dying at their hands, and I was thoroughly ashamed of myself.

She spoke then of discord with the Delerin, chastised them for their actions, and then she spoke the words that will forever be burned into my memory: "I invoke the way of filin."

All of our people present were aware of the Timmistrian legend, and certainly all the natives were. The collective gasp nearly cleared the village center of oxygen.

As I stood watching, rigid with fear and loathing but shaking with rage, Cara stepped forward and set her ratan on the ground at the feet of the Delerin.

And then she continued, "Your covenant with Timmistria calls for you to take your own life if you find you must kill another of your own. As your proverb says, 'One Death Leads to Many.' I offer you another choice. Take my life in exchange for the lives of all of my people, and take not one life of your own people in exchange for mine. If you believe that we threaten you, that we have not loved and nurtured the land you have allowed us to occupy, and that we have not honored and respected Timmistria in all her ways and forms, then kill me, but allow the rest of my people to live on your world to the end of their days. We will see to it that no others come and that no others are born. And then the time of my people on Timmistria will come to an end.

"Know that no matter how our ends may come, we all will die of broken hearts."

She then stood before them, arms held loosely crossed at her waist, head held high, as Lonin translated her words in a quiet whisper.

No one breathed. I swear not a single heart beat.

And then Paul Saarinen, our Co-Op warrior, former military commander, drew his own blade and stepped forward. I knew about his background long before Cara did. He was a well-placed commander in the special forces before being exiled on Timmistria. He'd led a suicidal operation on a pro-Thinker system many light-years away. If any of the villagers could have competed with a Delerin in hand combat, it would have been Commander Saarinen.

He stepped forward and calmly laid his blade next to Cara's, then returned to her side for a moment, before moving to stand just behind her, arms crossed like hers and head high. And then all the others followed, villagers all, men and women, surrendering their weapons. They formed a growing and silent blockade of humanity before the Delerin, a solidarity, a singularity, perhaps. But this was not like a black hole where no light could escape; it was one of whiteness, where all light was captured and amplified to shine out in all directions, radiating and illuminating all things near. At some point, our Timmon friends joined the procession, Lonin leading them, and the younger one, Kearnin, Shawn's great friend and field companion, Lonin's cousin Kinin, and the two Timmon women who'd escorted Paul back to Fairdawn after his injury by the massive tharnon cat. All of our Timmon friends and benefactors stood with us at that critical moment.

I was completely overcome by emotion, and even though I bore no weapon, I stepped forward. Immediately, an exhilarating presence and an uplifting rush filled my head and chest, as one might feel if one were to leap from a cliff and find that one could fly. I walked to within a few feet of the still-unmoving Delerin host and lay my electronic writing stylus among the huge pile of blades and bows and staffs, the emerald glow of the ratan-i almost blinding now in the punishing yellow sunlight. And then I returned to the group of villagers standing with heads high and eyes forward, looking to the distance. The taller figures of the Timmon rose above the heads of my people, my brave, wonderful people. Pride filled me then, even more touching than the exhilaration I'd felt a moment before.

I made to pass around the group to stand at the rear, but Commander Saarinen reached out and pulled me to his side, and held me with him, his arm clasping me firmly about the shoulders. And then I wept, standing next to him. I wept not for the fear that still gripped me, but for the beauty, the brotherhood. There was never a time in my life when I felt such intense belonging.

And then the most incredible thing happened, something that my words will never do justice, something I would never believe myself if I hadn't been there to see it and feel it and be nearly consumed by it.

The air around Cara came to life.

It began with a faint glow that blossomed about her head and shoulders, at first a wavering in the air like the vapors from a vessel of light oil. Then the vapors pulled light from her skin and hair and body. She glowed. And the air about her began to hum.

I glanced at Paul, and the light of wonder was in his eyes as it was no doubt in mine, and in all the others around us. My thoughts were probably those of the others — are we seeing her timeril? Is her sorrow so strong that her vessel has cracked and her soul light is spilling out? If I was afraid for her before, I was now terrified. I thought she was dying.

The Timmon and Delerin delegation stepped back, their faces frozen in awe. This was not just a revealing of her timeril, for they claimed to see those all along. Cara's light was described as strong and white, earning her the title of "White Lady." This new thing, this was something different, strange, wondrous. The creatures in the village were now silent.

Cara raised her hands in a gesture of openness, of welcome, and the air about her swelled and spun. A whirlwind sprang from the earth, raising dust from the street. The dust whirled up and away in yellow veils and ribbons, but none touched her. The light grew around her until it began to hurt my eyes.

Cara lowered her hands, and from my angle I could just barely see her gesture; open hands held in front of her, offering her palms and forearms to the Delerin, offering her veins, her blood, her life. At least that was my interpretation.

For an instant, the warrior Delerin, who was shielding his own eyes as I was, gripped his blade handle with one hand. But his grip gave way, and he shrank back, disarmed by his marvel. Even the hardest among the Delerin host could not help but be moved.

And then I heard a whirring noise, rising from the forest in the east, first soft as a whisper and then louder, louder, like a thousand tiny drones rising, and I feared some trap set up by the villain Dench. But what came was a flock of small birds, gray and yellow and pearl, the little ones we called Timmistrian parakeets, swirling up like a great school of fish, and then swirling down into the square, a living, breathing cyclone, spinning on an axis that was Cara. Their chirping cries came to me in waves, in a multidimensional rhythm that pulsed in my ears just as their flashes of color and light pulsed in my eyes. The other villagers gasped, and their hands flew to their faces in astonishment.

And then the birds flew from the square, and the light from Cara faded, and I wept again, willing it to return. And then we were as we were before, a group of 218 unarmed villagers, a family. No, we were more than that now. We were a "kithin," one such as Timmistria had never known. And I belonged.

Chapter 37

After the Delerin left the square, the other villagers and the Timmon stepped back, leaving Paul there with Cara. She was once again a small woman, body sagging as a balloon figure whose air was slowly leaking away. He found he couldn't move, couldn't make himself step forward the three paces that separated them. He couldn't deny what he'd seen and heard and felt, and yet he couldn't believe it either. Emotions flooded him from reservoirs too long hidden in shadows. He wanted to laugh, cry, praise god, run away. But he could do nothing except stand and wait.

At last she turned to him and took his hand. When their eyes met, she was not different; she was the same small but powerful woman he'd met his first day on Timmistria. But he would never be the same.

She led him back to Shawn's body, now slumped back against the tree, as if asleep. She knelt by her brother, her hands in her lap. Paul could barely hear her words over the sound of the flyer, which was now hovering over the town square. The Timmistrians had all vanished, but Paul suspected tense discussions were in progress somewhere nearby.

"Oh, Shawn. I failed you. I failed all of us."

"You didn't fail him, Cara. I did."

"You were planning to kill Dench, weren't you?"

"Yes."

She shook her head and didn't look at him. "It always comes down to killing in the end, doesn't it? Even the Timmon, with their high-flung moral code, their eye-for-an-eye trade-off, dressed in war paint. Like children. No, less than children. Children don't kill each other. And for what? I'm disgusted with all of you."

There was nothing he could say, so he said it silently.

"Mr. Saarinen?"

Paul turned to find a dark-haired bookish fellow approaching; he didn't know him but had seen him a few times near the admin building. The man looked highly agitated.

"Yes?"

"We have a situation."

"Tell me about it."

"About an hour ago, the satellite radar picked up four vessels approaching Timmistria from the direction of the jump point. Then we lost contact with the satellite. This all happened within a few minutes."

"Thinker ships?"

"I don't think so. The sensors showed Co-Op spectrum. We think they're terrestrial. Our tracking system isn't very sophisticated, but the AI indicates they may be decelerating into an orbit around Timmistria."

"Terrestrial? I haven't heard that word in a while. What's your name and duty? Quickly, please."

"Uh, Sidney Shell, sir. I'm a chef by trade, but they made me the communications leader because I studied electronics as a hobby."

"From Old Earth?"

"Yes, sir."

"Very good. Have you received any transmissions or chatter from these vessels?"

"Nothing so far. Should I attempt to contact?"

"Yes. Find out who they are. But do it tactfully. If they're hostile, we're in no position to do anything about it."

"Yes, sir. I'll go do that now."

"Good, Sidney. I'll join you in a minute."

Shell took off like a scalded dog, leaving a trail of dust-blown footprints in his wake.

"I have to go, Cara. We have company."

"I heard. I'll come with you."

She made to rise again, looking weary. He offered his hand and helped her to her feet. The Timmistrians were still out of sight.

She asked, "Why unscheduled ships? Who could they be if not Thinkers?"

"I don't know. Unlicensed salvage? Rebels? We'll know soon enough."

They were nearly at the communications room before she spoke again. "Thank you, Paul."

"For what?"

"For everything. For being here."

"I wish I'd come an hour sooner. Or a day."

Cara's grip on his arm tightened. Her body moved closer to his, and he could smell her sweetness. When they reached the comm center, she said, "I'll come in for a minute, and then I need to get the coroner to look after Shawn."

"Go now, if you need to. You may be leading all the women and young ones into hiding in the forest if these ships are pirates."

She nodded. "I'll go soon. Let's see who they are."

Shell and a tall Asian woman with spiked hair were hunched over the direct digital sets, like a scene from an old war hologram. When Cara entered behind Paul, Shell stood clumsily.

"Sidney, pull up the spectrals on these ships."

Shell's fingers played on a hand pad, and the small view screen above him lit up in vertical lines of color, with tiny gray text below. Paul leaned in to study the display.

"Any warning from the satellite before it went silent?"

"I just played it back. The satellite reported an impending impact alarm."

Cara said, "It was shot down? Are you sure they're not Thinkers?"

Paul shook his head. "The signature is definitely terrestrial, but it's not military. I'm guessing pirates or slavers, but they've got…" Then he remembered his evening conversation with Dench. "They're not pirates. They're Dench's private militia. Sidney, what range does the ground-based radar have?"

"Sir?"

"When an inbound shuttle comes in, at what altitude does the ground radar pick it up?"

Shell frowned and pulled at his chin. "About ten thousand feet. Maybe 15. We're almost blind without the satellite."

"That won't give us much time if they drop down in a shuttle. Probably less than two hours. Even less if they use individual drop capsules. They've had plenty of time to make orbit, so we have to assume they're on the way."

As if on cue, a soft tone sounded from the console, followed by a second. The spiky-haired woman played the panel this time and shifted her gaze between screens. Her first words since they'd entered revealed a deep voice and an accent very close to that of Paul's home region.

"Two vessels incoming. Shuttle-sized. The AI's working the flight path now."

Paul said, "They won't land. The ground party will jump directly over the village."

Another tone sounded, and the main screen lit up with a red border. Shell said, "We're being hailed!"

He worked his touch pad and leaned forward so his nose touched his display screen. "They sent us a message. Text only. A 'Captain Seven' wants to speak to Manager Cara and a 'Commander Sharren.' Do you know anyone by that name, Manager?"

Cara met Paul's eyes, her brow creased.

Paul said, "Maybe. Sidney, send a response. We'd like to know the nature of the visit."

As Shell entered the code, the comm screen hissed on, displaying only a spattering of dots. He and his colleague continued to pore over their own small displays.

"They ask to speak only to Manager Cara and Commander Sharren."

"Tell them we're here. Request visual."

Shell gave him a dubious look as he typed. The screen came to life and resolved, and Paul found himself looking at a weasel-like face, nearly hairless, with small eyes and a knobby brow. It took him a moment to realize he was staring into the face of one of the carrier folk. Its lips moved in the bizarre rippling motion characteristic of their speech.

"Captain Seven here. May I please speak to Manager Cara and Commander Sharren?"

"We're here. Are you receiving our visual?"

There was a brief pause, and then the mouth opened in a possum's grin. "Yes, we see you now, Commander. Bright and clear."

"OK. Now who the hell are you, and why are you here?"

"Pardon, Commander. We are a private flotilla outbound from Veran, bound for Timmistria. We were formerly under registration by X-Thellin Corporation."

"Formerly?" He whispered to Cara, "X-Thellin is one of Dench's companies."

"Yes, Commander. We no longer fly for that entity."

Paul waited for more, but the carrier fellow sat placidly silent.

"You are carrier folk. You were not in command when you departed Veran."

"No, sir."

"Who was?"

"Captain Embrov."

"So, where is Captain Embrov now?"

"He is resting, Commander Sharren."

"Resting. Captain Seven, did you mutiny?"

"Yes, Commander. We waited for the warriors to leave, then we asked the captain to rest."

"Why?"

"The mission was bad."

"What was the mission?"

"As we understand, to take control of this colony and to bring more warriors to Timmistria."

Cara and Paul exchanged looks.

"Are you leading the regular crew, Captain Seven? Where is the crew?"

"Resting."

"So, who's running the ships?"

"We are."

"You? Just the carrier folk?"

"Yes, sir, the vzenkkl."

"How many of you are there?"

"Seven."

"Seven. You're operating a jump-capable vessel with seven personnel?"

"Yes, Commander."

"The other three vessels are also under your command?"

"Yes."

"Seven crew on each of them as well?"

"No, sir. The Vladivostok has eleven. The Moscow has thirteen. The Chernobyl also eleven."

"And the regular crews on those vessels are also 'resting'?"

"Yes, sir."

"Captain Seven, I'd be lying if I said I wasn't intrigued. What can we do for you? Surrender?"

"No, Commander. We request orders."

"Orders?"

"Yes. You are the closest Co-Operative League commander, so we are reporting for duty and await orders from you."

Cara shrugged. Her eyes were sunken wells. Paul turned back to the screen. "Captain Seven, I assume the ships are in orbit around Timmistria. Can you continue ship's operations?"

"Yes, sir."

He wanted badly to ask how they'd learned, but he'd worry about that later. "Can you call back the two shuttles that were launched?"

"No, sir. They are too far away now. But they will return to orbit once the warriors depart."

"OK. Stop all radio contact with them and block all global positioning data. Let them fly blind. We will stay in contact with you. I will get back to you in less than six hours. If you don't hear from me by then, assume we've been taken, and you will surrender to Captain Embrov. Any questions, Captain … Seven?"

"No, Commander."

"Good. Sharren out."

The comm specialists regarded him.

"I'll explain it all later. Meanwhile, Sidney, keep this all under your hat. The other villagers don't need to know what's going on here until we have time to sort it out. Can you do that for me?"

"Sure."

"Thanks. Keep someone on that digital set around the clock. Anything comes in, get me immediately. No exceptions."

"Yes, sir."

"Excellent."

Cara was leaning on him heavily now.

"Cara, let me get you home." The others' regard deepened. He could hear the rumors already. He said, "Let me help you up, Manager."

She rose limply, like one tied to strings. As they pushed through the door, she whispered, "We can't leave him there. Or Dench either."

"We'll see them taken care of, Cara, but we've no time to grieve right now. I need you to get all our non-fighting people out of sight and secured. I need the streets empty when these mercenaries land."

"You're going to fight?"

"Yes. If Dench's people were still in control of those ships, we wouldn't have a chance. But with the carrier folk holding them, we've got a shot."

Her hand was warm, but her eyes were rimmed in red. He asked, "Are you fit to lead the non-fighters out?"

She nodded. "Yes. No. Does it matter? Just win this fight."

"If we fail, you'll have to surrender."

Her face hardened. "We'll see."

"Promise me. Don't try anything rash."

"I'm not promising anything. I guess you'd better not fail."

He almost smiled then, at the hardness suddenly in her eyes and the fire in her voice. The White Lady,

Lonin had called her. Even now, after another devastating loss, her light shone brightly.

Before he could protest again, James and Gregor spotted them walking into the square and came for orders. James had parked the flyer on the wide street in front of the admin building, which would have been a real trick in strong wind. Paul briefed them on the situation. A plan took shape in his mind, and he gave it to them as quickly as it formed. He closed with a sobering thought.

"No mercy, guys. Shoot first and ask questions later. We have no diplomatic restraint here."

Cara interrupted, her face suddenly stricken. "Many are going to die, aren't they?"

Paul hesitated. "If we fight, some of us will die, maybe some of the Timmon."

She moaned. "Always the killing. Why? What does it ever get us?"

"They mean to take over the system and enslave the Timmistrians. It's fight and die now, or fight and die forever after. We have to make our stand now."

She said, "This is not how it's supposed to be. This is not why we're here. Think of something else, Paul. There's got to be another way."

Paul felt the insides of his head being tugged apart. Another way.

There was a chance. He wouldn't want to run the AI simulation on it, but it was something. If it didn't work, the shooting would be their fallback.

He barked rapid orders to James and Gregor. After a few quick questions and reassurance that they were up to the task, they ran to their stations, as if they were accustomed to combat.

To Cara he said, "I have to find Kearnin or Lonin. We're going to need help from the Timmistrians. And I need to find out what weapons Dench was carrying."

Cara looked at him, then suddenly seized his face and kissed him deeply, taking them back for a moment to that eternal quiet place in her cabin where time seemed to stop. And then she released him and was gone.

He stood for an instant, his lips tingling and heart racing, then ran in search of Kearnin.

Chapter 38

The first sign of trouble came when the shuttle pulled out of its entry dive and leveled off just above the thin cloud layer. Through the clouds they could just make out patches of yellow and brown, with a few other colors speckled in. The bridge crew was unable to reestablish communications with any of the orbiting strike vessels. Nick opened a channel to the other shuttle and inquired about their luck.

"Negative, chief."

"Alright. Continue hailing, but we're still a go here. We bail out in ten minutes."

His orders had been clear: make the drop; secure the target encampment and make contact with Dench, clear any members of the two indigenous tribes, then hold the encampment until further orders.

Nick yawned, ran a final system check on his gear, and confirmed that the others in his team were doing the same. The only interesting part of this mission would be descending in the "bat man" flight suits. His people were going to get bored quickly, and he'd have a tough time keeping them from amusing themselves with the captive villagers.

At five minutes to drop, he ordered them all to the tube station, where they suited up. They were ten strong here, seasoned men and women, all human save the lone Halite. Ten more reported "suited and ready" from the other shuttle. The plan was to drop separately on the north and south borders of the village square, and then they would converge on the main buildings in the village center. Each of them was given a data blurb with a list of the colony's leaders, names and roles, beginning with one Village Manager Cara Harvestmoon.

Nick checked with the comm guy one last time. There was still no contact with the orbital ships, probably the result of an EM resonance in the atmosphere, but it was odd that they hadn't detected it earlier. He shrugged. When they returned to the ship, he'd put a kink in someone's shorts.

"Shut up and line it up, people. Keep your distance on the drop, and no zarking around! I don't want anyone hanging from a tree. Adams — you're on spot. Baker on deck. Ten seconds … and go!"

The first trooper entered the tube and was gone in a whoosh of air, followed in short order by the other eight. Before entering the tube, he confirmed with the pilot to return to the strike ship and send down an ansible comm pod as soon as possible, then he stepped into the tube launch. He was sucked from the belly of the plane into the bright sunlight, plummeting headfirst through the mottled clouds.

He spread the membrane between his legs to maintain his head-down orientation. Wind friction slowed his airspeed. He extended the flaps at his sides and arms to add lift and drag. It all had to be done methodically and patiently or he could be thrown into an uncontrolled tumble, which would likely kill him.

As he soared and shed speed, the wind noise that leaked through his membrane helmet abated, and his steep dive flattened. The target appeared as a red bull's-eye on the heads-up display inside his flight goggles. When he was directly over it, he banked into a wide spiral, corkscrewing downward to the straw-colored lands below. Without the holo display inside his faceplate, he would have struggled to spot the village from this height. The colonists had hidden it well and created an obscure visual footprint.

The others were below him, curving around and down, descending more like vultures than bats. The first, Adams, made touch-down and scurried to cover. There was little to fear here in the way of resistance. The pre-mission reports indicated these people didn't have even a decent-sized blaster.

Two minutes later, Nick flared his airfoils and settled to a running landing that brought him into the circle of his people, assembled now with weapons drawn. The dirt was framed by single-story structures made of stone and wood spaced sporadically along each side. There were no people in the street or visible through windows.

"Team B, are you landed and in place?"

"Yeah, Nick. The street's clear."

"Same here. Proceed to the meeting point. Full alert. Guess they saw us coming."

Nick signaled, and his front line led the team forward.

The deserted streets made him uneasy, but he knew how to deal with games. He'd start busting down doors soon.

They reached the main street in front of the only two-story building, with numerous windows of foggy glass. It was drab like the other structures, if slightly more robust. This would be the administration building, as described in the mission brief. Team B entered the street from the opposite side of the town square, using buildings and trees on each side of the street for cover, converging into a single flowing entity, much like an amoeba.

At last a resident appeared, a man dressed in drab tan clothing like a farmer, pulling a small handcart into the square from a side path. He seemed oblivious to Nick's people until he was surrounded by them.

Nick cleared his throat, and the man looked up in surprise. His face was sunburned and unshaven, as one might expect a colonist's to be, but his eyes were an odd yellow color, which seemed to fit with everything else. Maybe the water did that to you.

The farmer said, "Oh! Who are you?"

"I'll ask the questions here. Where are all the people?"

"They're hiding. The natives went on a warpath, and everybody's left town. Are you from the Co-Op? I don't think we were expecting a transport."

"Yes, we're from the Co-Op, and we're here to see someone. Mr. Dench. Where can we find him?"

"Oh. Sad news. He died."

Nick traded looks with his second, Fin.

"How? He was alive yesterday."

"A spider bit him. They're really bad this time of year. The cool weather drives them indoors."

The sound of a throbbing machine crept into Nick's awareness, like an old-style jet-turbine engine running in the distance.

The yellow-eyed man backed away with his cart, looking a little anxious, like he'd realized they weren't from the Co-Op. "Well, time for me to go. I'm supposed to pick up some pipe fittings from the shop and take them to the water station. We've got a field down without irrigation. The plants are already starting to wither."

"You're not going anywhere, except to Mr. Dench and then the village manager. Shiv, frisk him."

The man stood still, hands on the cart handles, a bit flummoxed. "But … I've got to get seals for the water pumps."

The sound of the engine grew closer, and Nick pegged it as a thopter. He was becoming more uneasy. Things were odd and out of place here.

Shiv drew his blaster, and the villager slowly raised his hands like some befuddled idiot at one of the retail stores Nick robbed as a teenager.

"Clark, Simmons — check the main building. I'm guessing this manager is hiding in there somewhere. Don't break any bones, if you can help it. We don't have medical support."

"Uhhh…"

With a breathy sigh, Shiv collapsed into the farmer's arms. The man took the blaster from Shiv's hand and leveled it at Nick's head. He used the soldier's limp body as a shield.

"Hold it. Glad you all could drop in. No quick movements, or Wonder Boy has a real bad day."

Nick shook his head. "Fancy. You must be Sharren."

"I am."

"Did the Co-Op send you here to intercept us?"

"No, but I'm here to do that anyway."

"What are you, a Space Ranger? One man, one planet?"

"No, I'm going to make you an offer."

Nick tapped at his wrist and stalled. "I'm not sure what you have to offer, except maybe giving me that piece before we fry the head off your neck. Dench really dead?"

Sharren nodded. "I can show you the body."

"So … what, we're just going to stand here? You're not going anywhere."

"And that's my offer. I have your ships, and I'll give you one of them back and grant you free passage from the system."

"Wow, generous." Nick hit the final code and checked his wrist. He could see the active light on Shiv's blaster cut out.

"Game's up, you're weapon's offline. Fin, Clark, get the weapon and put some binders on him." To Sharren, he said, "We were told to kill you on sight, but I'm going to let you show us Dench's body first. I'm guessing it's still vertical and walking around."

Sharren said, "I wondered if you had a master kill system. That will make things easier." He reached into his pocket and pulled out a shiny ebony disk, rounded on all edges, and held it above his shoulder. Red lights blinked on the thing's side, and it emitted a faint whistle.

He said, "This is Dench's disruptor, set on overload. My thumb slips off this kill switch, kablooie. You're right, you should have shot me on sight."

Nick felt red anger boil up his backbone into his scalp. He wished he had shot the zarker. But Johanson said he'd take care of the guy and Nick wouldn't have to worry about it. Sharren's eyes were just wild enough to stick a little needle of fear into Nick's brain. The "rogue commander" story must have been accurate.

Sharren let Shiv's body slide from his grasp and to the ground, not worried about getting shot.

Nick said, "So here we are again. We just going to stare at each other all night?"

"No, I made you an offer. You give me the master panel, and I have a shuttle come down and take you happy vacationers back to the yacht so you can head back to where you came from."

"You know I can't do that. And I'm not sure you're willing to die here."

A patently sad expression came to Sharren's face. "I had planned on dying today anyway."

He whistled loudly, and from nowhere, yellow-skinned giants stepped from the shadows and formed a cordon around the entire square. Archers — both native and human — leaned over the roof edge, with arrows nocked but not drawn. Many of the natives on the ground brandished wicked green scimitars, with no expression Nick could read, not grim or stoic but completely blank. The engine noise he'd heard earlier ratcheted up to a throaty roar, and the shadow of a small thopter skirted the trees around the perimeter.

Sharren said, "If I twitch my thumb, this thing will kill me, you, and at least ten of these fine people. My friends and that L-10 hovering nearby will finish off the rest. The other option is safe passage out of the system."

Nick smirked. "Why should I trust you, rogue?"

Sharren pursed his lips. "Maybe you shouldn't, but I have nothing to gain by killing you or locking you up, and you're like me, too dangerous to keep around. These Timmistrians don't like to kill people, so it's just better to send you on your way."

Nick said, "Well, there is still the matter of Mr. Dench. I need to see him."

"Just as soon as you power down the rest of the weapons and give me the master control."

"Let me think about it. I'm still not sure you're not bluffing."

Sharren's face darkened. "Think quick. If I have to start a countdown, I probably won't stop it."

Nick's duty to his employer was to never back down in a hostage situation, and his people, now all standing dead quiet around him, knew that. Normally, he would just walk up to the man and take the disruptor from his hand, but his gut told him this was no bluff. Sharren was wild-eyed and up on his toes, like a merc on an adrenaline high, as if relishing the moment he could move his thumb. Nick could usually smell a bluff from a kilometer away, and he concluded this wasn't one.

He said, "How do I know you have the ships?"

"Call them."

"The comm went down, some kind of EM interference."

"No, I told my people to block you. Try them now."

Nick touched his wrist again and said, "Stark to Moscow, come in."

The clipped sing-song voice of a carrier folk responded from Nick's wrist. "Captain Eleven here."

"What the zark?"

Sharren shrugged. "Yeah, I'm shocked too." He filled Nick in on the carrier folk take-over, with enough details of the ship's processes to prove to Nick that the folk did hold the ships and were reporting to him. Nick had to suck his jaw up at one point in the explanation.

Nick said, "This is insane."

"Yes. But in a few seconds I start a countdown, and letting me bomb half of this village would be more insane. Power down."

At last, Nick nodded. "Show me Dench's body, and we'll take the deal."

#

Dench's mercs were disarmed and led to one of the storage units, where they were given food and water. Paul oversaw their confinement personally, stationing himself outside the holding area while using a hand radio to make arrangements with the carrier folk for one of the shuttles to land. Lonin returned to the square after dispatching most of his people, and then guided a group of eight rangers to stand guard. Without weapons, the mercs were no match for a few Timmon.

During a lull in the radio transmittals, Lonin said, "You knew the Timmon would not kill these men, but you told them differently."

Paul sensed a test. "It was a bluff. But keep that to yourself. Dench's goal was to enslave your people and force you to fight in his army. Death for him and his people seems appropriate."

"Timmistria must decide what is appropriate. But I think killing these people would not have been a good thing. Timmistria might have assisted us, but she would have punished our lack of mercy. They are the instruments of Dench's evil but not the source."

"You'll find out how worthy of your mercy they are if we screw up and they escape. They are killers just like Dench, and their vision is fogged by testosterone and esprit de corps."

Lonin shook his head. "Your words puzzle me as they often do, but somehow I see the meaning. These warriors feed on pride and breathe danger, and death becomes a friend to them. Such men are hard to win over." He looked at Paul with the piercing depth of vision that would always remind him of their fight at his camp, perhaps the only eyes that had seen his timeril. Lonin's words were revealing but not accusatory. "But you are like them, and they respected you and accepted your offer."

"And you are more like us than you let on, big man."

Lonin shrugged. "There is still the matter of the Delerin. They agreed to help you, but this battle has made them as hostile as before. They fear another like Dench." His face pinched, and dark colors framed his eyes. "The Timmon also fear your people no less."

"Then it's up to you and Larilin to bring them to the table. Remind them that we now have three trans-stellar strike ships at our disposal in stationary orbit over Timmistria. We're not going anywhere."

Chapter 39

Johanson crashed through the brush, trying to hide behind the disruptor. He was a good half kilometer from Dench's cabin, where he could barricade himself. Sweat rolled down his face, and his skin burned where the damn casting vines had wrapped around his head as he ran. The dragon blade was gone, torn from his hand when he'd ducked under a flock of the cursed bat-things that were trying to land on his neck and shoulders.

Two shadows glided through the tree boughs above him, hissing down at him in regular intervals. One of the creatures screamed loud enough to rankle his eye bones and jolt his heart into spasms. The bush reached out for him like a hundred scratchy rat hands, tugging at his skin and clothing, knotting around his legs and ripping him off-balance.

He came to a fork in the trail and lunged down the path to Dench's place. The vines had grown across, and he had to swing at them with his free arm, cursing the lost blade. Only about a quarter kilometer remained, and he pushed and thrashed and ignored the injuries. Free for an instant, he sprinted, pumping his arms and trying to control his breathing and panic. He could just make out the sunny patch where Dench's cabin sat, and he prayed it would keep the beasts out.

With a violent thrashing, one of the winged tigers bounded from the brush and landed on the trail directly in his path. It raised up and spread its feathered arms. Johanson skidded to a stop and raised the disruptor, his arm shaking violently. The beast swung its paw in a golden flash. The weapon flew from Johanson's hand, and fresh blood and pain burst from his knuckles.

His muscles seized all over. He tried to back away, but the beast stalked him, craning its snake head so it was eight feet tall. It hissed loudly enough to jangle his teeth, and the smell of putrid rot assailed his nose.

He heard loud rustling behind him, and something settled onto the trail, something that hissed at his back. He thought for a moment about diving into the brush. He heard Dench's voice calling him a fool for getting himself there in the first place.

Chapter 40

A New Filin

"Kearnin is outmatched. He may be killed." Lonin could feel the heat rising from his neck to his temples and scalp, the heat of frustration and fear. "This filin was to be *my* contest. Only my life should be at risk."

Lonin stood with Deminin Lajin and three others in the Dlith Wellinin, a large natural bowl near the Timmon-Delerin border. A similar group of Delerin rangers and aides stood at the far side of the bowl, beyond the area set out for the fight. The Delerin glanced over at Lonin's group occasionally, faces as blank as rocks.

Lajin offered no consolation. "You should have considered this possibility when you pressed for a new filin, Lonin. When you battled Terelin in the wood, on that day of sorrow and triumph, you did so without the full backing of the Timmon people. And now our council has met and by a large margin approved this filin. But you will not be our champion."

Lonin's role as liaison with the humans had become more important for his people, and so he was disqualified from fighting in the filin unless no others volunteered. But more than ten of tens of strong Timmon men and women had stepped forward. Lonin persuaded most of them to stand down, but many refused — Kearnin among them and the most adamant. To Lonin's regret, Kearnin was selected and could not be dissuaded. No words from Lonin could move the stubborn young man.

Lajin continued, "I think you judge him weakly. He reminds me of a younger me. His light is nearly as bright as yours, and I sense a hidden strength of which even he is not aware. Perhaps he learned this trick from this human friend of yours."

Lonin said, "I do not fear any lack of strength or drive. My fear is that he is too young, and too much of his work still lies before him. I think he chooses to die for his people, just as Shawn Harvestmoon chose."

"If that is Timmistria's need, then it will be. But I trust, like you, that his work is just beginning."

Lonin felt the need to argue further, but it was clear that the deminin's resolve would not be diminished.

#

Kearnin settled the vest and pads over his shoulders, and pulled the leather straps tight enough to pinch. The smell of tanning oils and herbs was strong from these items. His mother and father had cut and stitched the garments as they'd all shared meals in the ten days since he'd been selected. His parents had been Timmon-calm on the outside, but their timeril pulsed with anxiety. They were torn, his mother's brother had explained to him, between fear for him and pride in his courage. Kearnin trusted that his own timeril was like a storm-tossed sea.

Kinin, his official squire, handed him his blade belt, and he wrapped it firmly against his hips. They were alone in a small lean-to built just for this purpose. It was made of bare wooden boards, with only a small table and a backless stool inside.

He needed calmness of mind and centeredness to the task, and few among the Timmon could match Kinin for these traits. The elder had changed very little since Kearnin was a young boy; he remembered listening to Kinin's wisdom with all the others his age, following the old ranger's hands as they shaped bows and arrows and blade handles. Kinin met Kearnin's eyes now with a look that held no emotion other than warmth.

Kearnin said, "I am happy that you do not try to talk me from this challenge."

Kinin said, "That isn't my way, or yours. You are no longer the young child you were when you first grasped my hand, even then with the firm grip of a leader. You chose this path with your eyes open. And Timmistria has granted you the honor. It is not my place to question. Nor is it Lonin's, even though he would see himself enter the circle today."

"Perhaps the Timmon people would be better served by Lonin, and I fool myself. Perhaps I doom our people's needs with my arrogance."

A brief red flash played over Kinin's craggy countenance and was gone.

"Ne, young warrior. Such thoughts are not those of a champion. You chose the place, and Timmistria has judged you worthy, and now it is your duty to seize the moment and let Timmistria guide the future." Kinin stood to straighten Kearnin's garments. He nodded in satisfaction and placed his iron hand on Kearnin's shoulder. "Kearnin, you chose this. Your people chose you. And Timmistria has chosen you. The time for questions has passed."

Kearnin drew in a deep breath, feeling the warm air fill his chest. He exhaled slowly and nodded his readiness.

#

Lonin joined Paul, who stood alone with a clear view of the combat area. The colony's new warrior chief was the only human allowed at the filin. As usual, the man's timeril was hidden, and his expression told Lonin nothing.

Lonin said, "I am to blame for this. I have let my desires bring danger to my people and to Kearnin. Timmistria's anger at me is smaller only than my own."

Surprise came to Paul's eyes. Lonin had been told years earlier that human domestic cats were not allowed to come to Timmistria because they would kill everything they came upon. He imagined them fearsome beasts. Shawn had said Paul's eyes were very much like those of a cat.

"You sound like Cara when she doubts herself. God help the universe when you two stop second-guessing everything you do and just carry on."

Lonin gestured toward the Delerin warrior, who stood frozen while others adjusted his protective garments. Terelin pushed their hands away and shrugged his arms outward and upward. His chest expanded and rippled. "Terelin is my equal, or nearly so. I fear Kearnin will fall to him quickly. His anger over Shawn's death drives him to this trial, and I fear he seeks to join his friend. I can only hope his end is merciful if it comes."

Paul frowned as he watched Terelin make one final adjustment. The man seemed to be appraising the Delerin warrior and looked like he wished he were entering the ring. "Don't sell him short. He might have a few tricks up his sleeve. And don't misjudge his love for life."

Lonin searched Paul's face, but the human would reveal nothing more.

#

Kinin left Kearnin with a firm pat on the shoulder, and the young Timmon stepped forward toward the filin circle. Three Timmistrians stood there: two judges, one from each race, and Terelin. Kearnin regretted his own arrogance at accepting the challenge, but this one wore his power like flashes of calarantin over his brilliant amber light. Kearnin could smell the smoldering fire within his opponent.

Words Lonin had spoken the day before came to him. He had shared them only when he had conceded that Kearnin could not be deterred.

"Anger is a tool, Kearnin, to be wielded when the need arises. But it must be measured and reined in, so that it lends physical strength but does not weaken your judgment."

Other words followed in Kearnin's head, from the human warrior, Paul Saarinen. The man had spent the better parts of several days teaching Kearnin all he could of his warrior's ways. The human could never match a Timmon in physical prowess, but Kearnin learned that Paul's skills were far superior.

"The magic angle of defense is 45 degrees," Paul had said, demonstrating by angling one flat hand against the other. "Don't meet your opponent's strikes straight on. Deflect them with glancing blows that turn the energy away. Allow the momentum to pull your opponent off-balance."

His words were often strange, but he demonstrated everything. There were other teachings. How to move one's feet, to lead with the outer foot and never cross them. How to feign and fake one's direction with the movement of one's eyes. The spin kick and the scissor blade. Kearnin's mind filled with the advice, jumping from stance to form to rhythm, moves and positions jumbling together in a confusing tangle.

He reached the circle before he realized it, and nearly stepped within it before he caught himself. Paul's last piece of advice came then, drowning out the others. "Before the fight starts, clear your mind of all technique. Relax your body and just feel it. Feel your opponent's movements with all your senses, and feel your own. And then refuse to follow the dance; lead it."

His head buzzed with the energy left behind as the words faded in slowly tapering echoes. He could feel the resonance of the collective timeril of the ten people present, like the songs of the forest, until the voice of the Timmon judge drew him from the enormous space that was the inside of his head to the small place that was the filin circle. When he focused, he saw Terelin's eyes burning at him. The Delerin warrior's timeril was a tight aura around him and revealed nothing except readiness.

"Young warrior Kearnin, please take your place." The judge who had spoken, an old Delerin with bright orange hair thinned to ribbons on his scalp and deep pools of honey for eyes, motioned toward Kearnin's place on the circle, which was nothing more than a ring of dark sand 20 feet across, poured carefully into a shallow dish in the yellow dirt.

Terelin took this moment to speak from a place of icy coldness. "You seek things that your people cannot have, young Timmon. I understand your desire, but I am the instrument of your denial."

Kearnin said nothing. His opponent's words spread through his thoughts like fire through a grove of dead malacks.

"Your friend is dead. For this you should blame the humans, not my people. Your anger is a weakness that will be your undoing."

Kearnin's head now felt like the torch that lights the trees, and he knew his feelings were revealed. Terelin nodded in satisfaction.

Kearnin reached across his body with both arms and drew his battle blades, the tellin and the sarillion, from their scabbards. Normally the handles of his ratan-i were so familiar he could hardly feel them, as if the blades had become part of him, long green claws, fang-sharp and gleaming. But the rough cloth and resin wrappings of these ceremonial blades pressed uncomfortably against the skin of his palms and fingers. He squeezed until his fingers reddened and his grip brought pain, and then relaxed his hands and savored the relief that came after.

Terelin pulled his ratan-i and clanged them together, the translucent teeth ringing like metal bells throughout the arena.

The two warriors circled for the space of three breaths, and then Terelin lunged in a blur, intent on ending the fight quickly. In two steps, he cut off Kearnin's path and brought his sarillion down at an angle aimed at the Timmon's legs.

Kearnin stepped to one side and deflected the deadly blow with a downward strike, swinging high with his tellin to block any high following stroke from Terelin. Then he turned on his toes and sent a round kick toward Terelin's neck. The Delerin stepped away from it and countered with his own tellin, shearing the cloth at Kearnin's ankle and nearly finding flesh. Kearnin's momentum pulled him around, and he staggered. He was able to find his feet and ready his blades, but not before he'd wasted one of the surprise tricks Paul had taught him.

Terelin paused just long enough to mutter, "Clumsy of you," and then pressed forward again. This time he feigned a high backhand slash and then swept his sarillion upward in a jab designed to pierce Kearnin's belly.

Kearnin leaped back too late. He managed to block the uppercut so the tip just grazed the inside of his thigh, but Terelin's second blade came in high and sliced Kearnin's upper arm. Kearnin began a swing kick but held off, and wisely so. Terelin's ratan-i were poised to trap and remove his foot in a scissor cut of their own.

Terelin grimaced in disappointment that Kearnin had not tried the kick again, then he launched into a wide-stepping straight assault of arms and blades and feet that pressed Kearnin back to the defensive. The older Delerin was more muscled and stronger than Kearnin, although not faster, but the weight and speed of his weaving swordplay kept Kearnin leaning away. When Kearnin evaded sideways to deflect the attack, Terelin deftly followed, as if he could read Kearnin's next moves in his timeril. Kearnin made a turning parry and caught a glimpse of Paul standing with arms crossed next to the statue that was Lonin, and Paul's words repeated in his head: "Refuse to follow the dance; lead it."

But he couldn't break Terelin's advance to mount his own offensive. The Delerin pressed forward and covered the ground side to side as easily as a yar-cat. Kearnin's odd thought was to tell Paul that Timmistrians did not dance, and he suddenly regretted his lack of experience. So far, Terelin seemed intent on wearing him down, driving him around the circle of the open arena. The warrior's blade lashed out, catching Kearnin in the hip, like a burning ember driven into his flesh at mid-thigh. Another bold stab cut along his ear in an unexpected thrust that he deflected at the last instant, a stroke that nearly severed vital vessels in his neck and ended the fight right there.

Neither of his blades had touched the Delerin yet.

The battle went on like this for many agonizing minutes. The only sounds in the circle were the swish and ring of blades, the thud of feet, and the grunts of the warriors. Kinin had reminded Kearnin he had the endurance of a mountain wolf, but the young Timmon could feel the heat rising in his body, and his lungs ached. Terelin seemed unaffected. His timeril was no less focused than it had been when the contest started.

The Delerin suddenly stopped his attack long enough to speak. "I give you one chance to bow, young fool, before I end this. If you drop your ratan-i now, I will not take your life." Kearnin used the pause to cool himself. Even Terelin's skin glowed in the blush of heat. His efforts had begun to take a toll as well.

Terelin continued, "The cost to your people will be half of your lands, and none of your people shall let their shadows fall on Shill Wellin for ten generations." He paused and shook his head. "No, that is not punishment enough for this foolishness. We will make it 100 generations."

In their fight, they had moved around the open clearing so that Kearnin could, with a slight turn of his head, see Lonin. The Timmon leader had no doubt heard Terelin's offer, and the hearing of it had brought a change to Lonin's countenance. His shoulders curled forward and his brow followed, hands moving to the handles of his blades. A darkness fell over him, a cloud over his light, and the red of rage framed his face. Kearnin feared Lonin would step into the circle and dishonor the filin.

Kearnin dropped back into a defensive stance. "Ne, Terelin. You insult the Timmon now and dishonor Tironin, the champion saint of your people. I will die rather than give you more of the lands that are not yours to own."

Terelin sneered. "Timmistria deems you lacking. Even your cowardly leader Lonin was unworthy of this filin."

With a snarl, Kearnin launched himself forth, throwing arms and blades at the Delerin, and caution to the wind. For an instant, the Delerin ranger was on the defensive, but he soon turned Kearnin's blades away and again gained the advantage. He spoke through clenched teeth as he pressed forward, wounding Kearnin on the arm and bruising him with a savage punch of his blade hilt. "You Timmon and your human friends ... your masters ... have soiled the hallowed grounds ... of Shill Wellin for the last time. The humans ... must leave ... now!"

He swung his blades like shining fish darting back and forth in clear water, and Kearnin was always an instant too slow to stave off the injuries that were drawing away his life's power. His mind filled with despair. He'd volunteered for this fight to honor Shawn, and to die, either in battle or by his own hand afterward. But his own death wasn't a true loss for him, only a keeping of Timmistria's works.

As they spun around the circle, he saw Lonin again. The darkness and anger had left him, and he stood as one chanting a tribal ritual, his hands open in front of his body, his light as golden and pure as Kearnin had ever seen it. Images of faces and timeril came to him then: Lonin's, smiling as he'd led Kearnin's first party of rangers through the waving green grass of the Valley of Birth; Kearnin's parents, quiet but nurturing, firm but patient as they tried to harness and guide his unfettered flame; his siblings and cousins and friends jostling and challenging each other to master their lessons, the ones they were given by their Timmon instructors and the ones that Timmistria herself provided, almost as an afterthought.

These people he could not let down, despite his arrogance.

And then, the face of his human brother came to him. Shawn, glowing pink in the afternoon sun, as they traipsed through the woods, delighting in all they discovered together. The face that had radiated with puzzlement and questions and wonder, even when they were just sitting and talking about their lives.

And then he saw Shawn lying poisoned by his own hand. The young man's face was pained by what he had just done, this killing of the one called Dench. His timeril twisted and roiled with the colors of self-hatred and fear, and yet he'd found a small smile amidst the poison's pain. "I had to do it, Kearnin. We owe your people this much, to police our own."

And then the kernel of anger that had been nipping at Kearnin's insides swelled, anger at the humans for putting Shawn in the place he found himself, anger at the Delerin for their pointless aggression, and even anger at the Timmon for their distrust. But mostly anger at himself for not acting, for failing his dear friend.

Terelin caught Kearnin with a spinning kick in the right temple, which Kearnin partially blocked with his arm. The blow stunned him and sent him tumbling. Red crept in like a shadow ring around his vision, and he felt as if his timeril, his being, came loose from his body for an instant before clawing its way back. He tumbled in an acrobatic roll the human children called a "cartwheel" and then came to rest on his feet, blades still firm in his fists.

Terelin paused.

Kearnin said to no one in particular, or to everyone, "I will not let you down."

The last fighting move Paul taught him awakened in his brain, and he let it loose, a body-spinning dance from foot to foot, blades circling him in an unyielding shield of green light, rising and falling. He spun at Terelin like a tight whirlwind, his blades singing in twin arcs around him. Terelin stepped away, avoiding the blades, striking only if Kearnin got too close. The Delerin was letting him drain the last of his strength.

Kearnin had no idea how much strength remained within him, but it didn't matter; it would all leave his body as this fight drew to its bitter close.

He spun, and the blades spun with him as Paul had taught, high and low, keeping Terelin's viper-bite stabs at bay. But soon Terelin saw the pattern and exploited it, finding the flow in the spaces between Kearnin's arcing ratan-i in which to thrust his own deadly weapons. The points stuck Kearnin in the ribs, the arms, the shoulder. But to reach Kearnin, Terelin had to move close.

Kearnin feigned weakness and slowed slightly, and Terelin took the bait, his head dipping just to one side, the "tell" that Paul had taught Kearnin to look for. Kearnin changed his path immediately and spun in the opposite direction to flank his opponent.

But Terelin spun back the opposite way! It was a "head fake," a deception, another sign that Paul had warned him of. It placed Terelin directly in Kearnin's path, waiting with blades poised for the fatal strike.

It was then that Kearnin played his final trick, a move he had imagined but never spoke of to Paul — he was naïve for thinking his fighting mind could conjure something the human warriors had not practiced in all their wars.

He kicked his feet in the soil and turned his body so that he now spun at the magic angle of 45 degrees from the ground. He let his blades hug his body tightly, like a pair of fangs rising from his flesh, tracing the sacred lines.

Terelin was startled and adjusted his angle of attack, but Kearnin was expecting this and countered, swinging his arms at odd angles, striking the Delerin's blades so the ring of stone on stone hurt the ears and green sparks danced in the yellow grass and earth.

Kearnin let himself go. He didn't track Terelin's desperate dodging with his eyes, but he felt the warrior's movements even before they happened. His own limbs and the cylinder of his torso moved almost on their own, feeling, feeling the dirt beneath his toes, the air flowing over his skin, the positions of his blades. And then time and space seemed to slow to a near stop before resuming slowly, as if the two warriors were caught in amber.

And then he saw the vision of what Paul Saarinen had tried to impress. What had Paul called it? The magic angle of defense. But it wasn't always 45 degrees as Paul had said. It was different each time, sometimes wide, sometimes narrow. The vision filled with a visible energy that Kearnin could see, like the slopes and peaks of the landscape model he had created for the hunting party, the one Lonin had scolded him about. Kearnin realized at once why Lonin had grown angry and had forbidden him from continuing. His vision was the being of the world, the timeril of dimensions. In that place lay almost unspeakable power, best kept hidden away, before it could be used against the Timmon.

Terelin lashed out with his short blade directly at Kearnin's hip, and Kearnin set his own tellin deeply into it, turning it away just enough to slide by his garment and absorbing most of Terelin's effort into a rebound strike that grazed the larger Delerin along the side of his cheek. Terelin's eyes widened and his neck flashed red. He stepped forward with a high thrust intended to pierce Kearnin's shoulder.

Kearnin could see at once the lines and paths of the sarillion like the lines of Timmistria's dust in bright sunshine, and the smaller tellin coming around low, point first, into his other side. Without thinking, he raised his blades like the spiked jaws of the pantin bird, trapped the long sarillion from each side, and pulled it past his shoulder, while his knee rose to deflect the knife hand. He was now inside Terelin's guard circle. It was a simple thing to drive his elbow under Terelin's jaw and his knee firmly into the center of his body.

Before Terelin could even gasp, Kearnin set the magic angle of his feet, slashed outward with his blades, driving both of Terelin's weapons uselessly to his sides, and then lifted his body forward, pushing Terelin off-balance. His opponent seemed to rise up as if on a cushion of air before crashing onto his back. He tried to roll to the side, but Kearnin landed on him and pinned him with his knees, laying the edge of his sarillion across Terelin's throat. His tellin pierced the leather covering Terelin's belly but stopped before plunging past the skin.

Time stepped back into its normal tempo, in the rhythm of the beating of Kearnin's hearts. He heard the complete silence of the filin circle.

Terelin's timeril roiled in red, the bright crimson of rage, but with no fear.

He said, "You've beaten me, young Timmon. Finish it, then. If Shill Wellin and the lands you seek mean so much to you, then kill me and yourself, and dishonor our patriarchs, Teiron and Tironin."

Kearnin felt a great surge of force pressing in on his body, so hard that his breath stopped and his hearts paused. All the energy leaked from him like water from an urn. Terelin could have pushed him aside and lunged for his blade, and he would have been powerless to prevent it. His mind had fallen to only one thought; how much Shawn Harvestmoon had loved Timmistria and Shill Wellin, that he would take his own life to preserve them for the Timmon. How much Shawn had loved the Timmon people, and especially him, Kearnin. Terelin had been correct; Kearnin was not worthy.

Kearnin's hearts beat again, and his lungs drew breath. He rose off Terelin then and stepped backward. If Terelin's hand had sprung up and killed him, he would not have cared. But the Delerin didn't move from the ground. Kearnin backed out of the fight circle and laid the edge of his long blade across the side of his neck.

Before he could pull it across the flesh and spill his blood, hands seized his arm, and Lonin's voice spoke in his ear. "Do not do this, Kearnin. This will not bring your friend back."

Kearnin flexed his arm, but Lonin's grip tightened, stopping him again.

"This is not the way. One Death Leads to Many, and one death is too many. If you do this, Timmistria will be angry. Your people will mourn. And Shawn will weep. Do not … do this."

Kearnin pressed against Lonin's grip. The blade bit into his skin. His death lay a small distance away. If he pushed outward, he could sever the lines of blood in his throat before Lonin could stop him.

Lonin said, "Our people need you. There is too much work ahead. Timmistria calls, as do your people. You must answer that call and take your place, Kearnin. Your sacrifice for the loss of Shawn will be the pain in your hearts, but it cannot be your life."

They struggled, strength on strength. If Lonin eased his pressure at all, the blade would sever veins. The pain that gripped Kearnin was like a mountain of rocks pressing on his chest. The swell of anguish in his head threatened to burst his skull.

Lonin said, "Please."

Kearnin opened his hand and let the blade fall, where it struck the sand with a dull thud. The pain did not ease. It remained, undiminished.

Lonin said, "You have become our greatest warrior. I could not stand against you. But I see the battles before you, and they will be fought with your soul and your being and not your blades. Timmistria calls, Kearnin. You must follow."

Lonin released his arm at last, to pat his shoulder.

Before Lonin could grasp his arm again, Kearnin raised the short blade in his other hand, laid it against the wrist of his dominant hand, and sliced off his outer thumb. The blade parted the muscle and bone like the petals of a flower. Sharp pain shot up his arm like fire, and for an instant the anguish in his heart lessened, but the physical pain soon faded and his heartache returned. Then a puff of breeze brushed the open wound, and the nerves bristled.

Lonin stared at him in horror for an instant, his timeril flashing shocked orange, but then his expression softened with the light of understanding.

Kearnin said, "I am no longer our greatest warrior."

Lonin said, "Ne, you are mistaken, Kearnin. Your timeril brightens by the moment. 'The mighty grow as they serve, until they tower above the malack.'"

Kearnin looked down at his hand, blood flowing from the pulsing wound. He lifted the hand for Lonin to see.

"I am like him now."

Lonin said, "And he was a true Timmon leader, like you."

"If I am so mighty, then why must I weep now?" He laid his head on Lonin's shoulder, letting the sobs wrack his body.

Lonin's great hands touched him gently. "To weep like a human is not shameful."

Chapter 41

"Timmistria's tears wash away our own."
— From "Sonnet No. 7," *Poetry from a Yellow Heart* by Larilin

Paul hand joined with Cara's was firm but gentle, and his restless energy seemed to pass to her. The village square dazzled with blossoms and buds, and throbbed with energy and an air of anticipation that Cara could almost taste. Gentle showers during the night had scrubbed the air until it was playfully cool and damp. It was as if Timmistria herself had chosen to freshen her face for the special day ahead.

The frequent rains had saturated the fields, and Pao was concerned the farm workers wouldn't be able to get the spring crops planted. Cara wasn't worried. The magician walking next to her would figure something out.

She'd sent James out early to check out the shuttle landing area. The pad was set on a high area and usually drained very well, but she didn't want Lonin's space taxi buried three feet deep in mud and unable to take off. James, thorough as ever when it came to his beloved flying machines, had drilled core samples down ten feet to confirm the ground remained firm and compacted. He'd been pushing Cara to get him the materials he needed to pave a larger landing area in flexi-crete.

"Commander?"

The voice from Paul's handheld radio seemed to come from around them, the ghostly disembodied voice of one of the Sharons, two newly minted officers who had chosen to join Paul's forces in the Timmistria system. Cara could never tell their voices apart. The woman sounded slightly annoyed, which Cara had learned meant things were right on schedule.

Paul pulled the palm-sized disk from his belt. The communicators had been included in one of the shipments of goods they'd received in the months following the Delerin crisis. These items had been sent directly from the Co-Op Central Command, part of the program she and Paul had negotiated.

The negotiations had been contentious from the beginning, and at one point, the Co-Op threatened military action against the system. Paul's response was: "Bring it." The regional command had backed off. Things went more smoothly after that.

Paul said, "Go ahead."

"The shuttle has separated from the transport and is dropping into the outer bands."

"10-4. How's the weather looking for the return flight?"

"Satellite's showing clear skies for 400 klicks west. The weather geek says storms may kick up this afternoon, but the shuttle should be able to dodge them."

"Has Sharp reported any activity at the jump point?"

"Negative."

"Very good. Keep an eye on the transport. Trust, but verify. Out."

Paul rolled the disk into a small cylinder and stuck it back on his belt. "It's good to have friends in high places."

Suddenly, a weaving flock of penderin invaded their space, forcing Paul and Cara to drop their hands and draw blades. The flock dove at the gathering crowd but then veered off and disappeared as quickly as it had appeared.

Farther down the road, they came upon Shawn's grave and memorial, a large but simple stone block set upright at the back of the plot, as if to hold the creeping forest back. It gave the dates and read simply, "Shawn McElroy Harvestmoon — Rest with Timmistria."

Next to the gravestone stood a larger-than-life stone statue of Shawn. The figure was Timmon-sized, carved by an anonymous sculptor and set secretly next to the grave marker weeks after he was buried. For the eyes, the sculptor had inset large multifaceted yellow crystals. When the morning sun fell on them, as it did now, they glowed with an eerie golden fire.

The statue and stone were draped with ribbons and talismans, in yellows, reds, and oranges, some feathered or knotted with brown and copper hair, all characteristic of the new Timmistrian art that had sprung up since the crisis. The ground was sprinkled with bright stones and small teacup flowers of a kind Cara had never seen before, all nestled in the fine spring grass. Either birds or people or both had dropped the seeds there at the statue's feet.

She stood before the memorial, feeling everything all at once, breathing deeply to ease the tightening in her chest. She visited often. Sometimes, like this morning, she did not cry.

She said, "You know it was wrong."

She heard Paul scuff his feet behind her. "Yes."

"Sometimes it bothers me that they honor him so much for doing something that was wrong."

"They honor him because of all the things he did, not just killing Dench."

She sighed and let it drop. This was not the first time they'd had this conversation.

Dench's body had been placed by the villagers in a deep grave at his campsite. None of the Timmistrians would go near the body once they'd looked upon it and confirmed what their inner eyes had already told them. The villagers marked the grave with a flat stone marker, and few ever visited. Those who did claimed the yard had become overgrown with brush and weeds, save for the plot of ground where Dench's remains lay. It was a lifeless rectangle of earth, like a barren callous. The body of his assistant, Johanson, had been laid beside him in a similarly marked grave.

Johanson's body had been found about three kilometers outside of town, lying just off a trail, savaged by some predator. His face had been eaten away. Dench's shack, unoccupied for months, had been overwhelmed by vines and was now inhabited by all manner of creatures.

Presently, Helen and a large group of villagers joined them. Their loud banter stopped, and they fell quiet in front of the memorial. Several bowed their heads. The devotion made Cara uncomfortable. The Timmistrians had wanted Shawn's body laid by the monuments to Teiron and Tironin, their patron saints. Cara hadn't allowed it.

She was drawn from her trance by the star that was the landing shuttle. It fell from the sky, brightening as it descended under hard deceleration.

Yellow light seeped through the thickening foliage of the trees above. Soon these woods would be dense with leaves and vines and flying creatures, and they would all be busy planting crops and repairing things broken by the hard winter weather.

Oh, Cara had plans. If these villagers thought they were going to have an easy year just because of one good harvest and some new toys, they were sorely mistaken.

"Let's go, everyone. Let's greet our new friends."

She and Paul led the group down the trail, reaching the section now undergoing renovation. Workers were laying cut stones on a solid base of sand and gravel, in a design similar to that of the ancient Romans, an Appian Way of sorts. Other well-wishers hurried down the trail to join them until the group swelled to about sixty. It was the first civilian transit shuttle since Dench's foiled coup had delivered the three fighting ships into their laps, the first shuttle since the negotiations with the Co-Op had been completed. Several military craft had delivered goods and machinery, mostly communications and detection gear needed to secure the new jump points against Thinker incursion.

Dench had discovered the true treasure of this system, the strategic jump point directly to Smyth Alter, and had given them the means to exploit it. He had fulfilled his own prophecy of bringing them prosperity.

This was also to be the first transit to take people from Timmistria to other planets. When Cara's staff had offered visas for emigration, to her relief only a handful of villagers had accepted, and most of them were people who had developed serious medical issues that the colony's primitive services could not treat. She was grateful, for she had thought many more would have applied, perhaps those who had endured the worst of times or had lost loved ones here.

And then there was Lonin, the first of the Timmistrians to venture off-planet, chosen to represent the two races as their first ambassador to the Co-Operative League of Systems at Smyth Alter.

Tears stung her eyes as they entered the large clearing around the pad. Through glistening wetness, she saw the shuttle grounded. It complained about the landing with loud clunking, whining, and hissing noises. In the safe staging area were three villagers, including James, and a group of Timmistrians, about twenty in all. Lonin was there, of course, at the front; Kinin next to him, looking tragic; Kearnin and his cousin Chitin; the deminin, Lajin; Tarron and Maggon; and several others Cara recognized but could not name. Apart from them stood two of the Delerin — the diplomat Larilin and his cousin Tellinin. Larilin gazed at the shuttle in open wonder. The other Delerin eyed it suspiciously from over Larilin's shoulder.

Cara spent the next ten minutes speaking with each of the villagers who were leaving. She let the tears flow and the laughs come, hugging them all, each in turn, eight friends she would not see again. Paul was there always, letting her grip his hand when she needed, which was often.

The alarm sounded, the ramp was lowered, and a sextet of carrier folk came down in a flurry and began their work, unloading a large number of containers. These crates would contain many things Fairdawn had needed for a long time — medicines, tools, lab equipment, seeds and cultures, and at last, a new synthesizing machine.

James checked the manifest of each box the carriers set in the staging area, until he apparently found the one he sought. He walked around a crate that looked like all the others, only larger, and patted it with his hand. It would be one of the two flyers they'd been promised. He'd studied the plans for weeks and would probably have it assembled in a few days.

The first mate introduced himself and informed Cara that the passengers could begin embarking. Cara and the other villagers walked with them to the ramp, giving them each gifts and packets of food and bread.

After the last were aboard, she and Paul joined the Timmon, with Paul occasionally responding to radio transmissions. She wondered if his duties as military commander would begin to steal their time together and annoy her. She sighed. For everything they gained, there was a cost. Sometimes it was too high. But she decided she could live with a radio transmission here and there.

Lonin said, "Greetings, Demina and Commander."

She felt the pang of formality. "Stop it, Lonin. We're Cara and Paul. Always and forever."

"I have no words. It is hard to feel such excitement and such sadness at the same time."

"And I have so many words, but they can't describe how I feel." Her throat tightened, and she could say nothing more. She embraced him then, wrapping her arms as far as she could around his wide waist and burying her face in his midsection. Her eyes blurred, and she tasted the wet saltiness that dribbled to the corners of her mouth. He held her and patted her back gently. When she pulled back at last, she shamelessly wiped her eyes.

"You'll make an awesome ambassador. I'd love to be there when you enter the halls of congress for the first time. The looks you'll get. Jaws will drop."

"I wish you would be there as well."

"And you'll come back soon. You have to stay in touch with your constituents now, and attend town hall meetings, and campaign. Your friend, Larilin, will be trying to take your job."

Lonin smiled and nodded. "He may follow soon. I think the 'wanderlust,' as you call it, is in his veins."

"Come back to us, Lonin. We will need you here."

"I will return. Soon."

Paul stepped forward and held out his hand. "Take care of yourself, big man."

"And you … Paul."

"Thanks for everything."

"We lived too much together for thanks to pass between. You are my brother. I have gifts for you."

Lonin turned back and gestured to Kinin, who stepped forward carrying something long and bulky wrapped in red cloth, as well as a small pouch.

"Paul, you have become a brother Timmon, and you need a proper Timmon blade."

With that, Lonin took the larger item from Kinin and drew the wrap carefully away, revealing a green cremin-tooth blade like Cara had never seen. The handle was richly stained malack wood, inlaid with lighter woods, metal rings, and sparkling things like gemstones. The blade itself was shiny and flawless, and the color was stunning: not the pale, foggy jade of most blades but a deep emerald crystal. Its facets caught the sunlight in mirrored flashes.

"Paul, Timmon brother, please take this blade."

"I don't know what to say. Thank you, Lonin."

Paul lifted the blade from Lonin's cradling hands and tested its weight. "It almost swings itself."

"It is a ratan nap, a 'father' blade, made from the fang tooth of an ancient cremin lord. Some hold these blades to be magical and believe they will protect your people from any danger."

"I will keep it safe."

"You will wear it and use it! A blade has value only when held in your hand."

"I stand corrected. I will wear it daily, and when it finds my hand, I will think of all my Timmon friends with a proud heart."

"When you use it, we will know. May it protect you and this lady, and all you value. And now for you, Demina Cara…"

Kinin took the cloth and handed Lonin the pouch, from which he carefully withdrew a short leather band tied to an amulet of some kind. It was a necklace, with a strange white stone fragment. Lonin caught it in his large palm and held it out for her to see. The stone, attached to the leather band by a silver loop, glinted with many colors, similar to an opal that Cara had been given as a child and had long forgotten before this day.

"My lady. This is a shard of a cremin stone. They are very rare, found in the venom gland of perhaps one in one hundred cremin. They are found only in the carcasses of very old cremin, and never as a whole stone, only as a broken piece, and always only one. It is said that if one looks deeply into the shard, one may see a small part of Timmistria's being. And if one may find all the shards and piece together an entire stone, one might see Timmistria in all her light. No complete stones have ever been brought together."

"It is beautiful. Shall I wear it now?"

"If you please. It is yours to wear as best suits you."

She turned, and Lonin placed the stone on her neck, tying the cord behind her. It felt warm against her skin, like there was energy within it. "Thank you, Lonin. We have a gift for you as well — nothing as fine as you have given us, but something to remind you that you have many friends here on Timmistria who are thinking about you."

She took a small packet from her robe pocket, which she had carefully wrapped in native paper painted with colorful swirls. "Here. It's a book of photographs of all of us. We took them with a small camera we had, but we didn't have a printer or paper until recently. Open it! See, there is a picture of each of us in the council, the shop people, others you worked with, and…"

Lonin had come to a year-old photo of Shawn. Cara's mouth would not speak, so she closed it. Lonin looked at the photo for a long time, before mercifully breaking the uncomfortable silence.

"I will remember you."

Cara wondered if he was speaking to her and Paul or to the one in the photo. He looked up with a Timmon smile.

"I will look upon this and think often of all of you."

Someone coughed nervously. It was the first mate, who had joined them silently and was now standing politely to the side.

"Yes, Mr. Foster?"

"Ma'am, I regret to rush you, but the satellite images show a system moving in rapidly from the northwest. We need to lift off in less than ten minutes, or we may be delayed."

"Thank you, Mr. Foster. We will clear the area."

Cara embraced Lonin again, and then tore herself away. He shook hands then with Paul and had embraces and words for all the Timmistrians present, especially Kinin. His last goodbye was for the Delerin council leader, Larilin. They shook hands and spoke, and she heard him say something like, "You will join me soon, cousin."

With one last wave and smile, he walked in bold strides up the ramp, as if afraid it might rise without him, and then he was gone.

"Move back, everyone. Get behind the blast barriers if you want to watch the lift-off."

One of the Timmon translated for the Delerin. Larilin nodded, and as one group, they all strode silently behind one of the safety barriers. Most of the villagers had already cleared the area and were headed back to Fairdawn with the new immigrants and containers of supplies.

Two carrier folk raced down the ramp and past Cara and Paul to get two large crates, the last of the luggage and supplies for the ship and those leaving on her. As they passed, they spoke in unison.

"Good-bye,   Demina   Cara!   Good-bye, Commander Sharren!"

Paul, hands on hips, watched them hoist the last boxes, then shouted over the noise of the engines revving up.

"Saarinen! My name is Paul Saarinen!"

"Yes, Commander Saarinen. Good-bye!"

With that final chorus, the carrier folk climbed the ramp, and the alarm horn sounded.

Cara and Paul trotted behind the nearest barrier, and the ground staff gave the "all clear" confirmation signal. Immediately, the engines came to life, and the great craft lifted into the sky in a hail of dust and wind. It cleared the trees and disappeared downwind and out of sight. Soon after, the roar of the large suborbital engines kicked on, and the shiny metal mushroom came into view again, this time rising rapidly into the yellow sky on a tail of light. And then it was a distant flame, and then a bright star, and then gone.

Cara stood paralyzed, scarcely believing that Lonin had risen up into the sky. She reminded herself she had no time for the sadness in her heart.

"Come, Commander Paul Saarinen, of the Timmon Space Patrol. We have much work to do and no time to dawdle here."

She took Paul's hand and led him back to the village, while they discussed how the flyers could be used to seed the soggy fields. The mixed group of Timmon and Delerin followed, chatting energetically in their shik-shikking language, sometimes interspersed with a few words of Galactic Standard, to Cara's dismay. The sun warmed her shoulders, casting orange shadows that danced ahead of them with each step. It was a lovely day, perfect for working outdoors. And after that would come the lovely night, perfect for lying awake together and not sleeping.

Epilogue

"Winds from the stars, like the dusty gales in the spring, scatter us throughout the fertile lands. We are the Seeds of Life. Yet we are called away before the crops come to fruit, never to know the strength of the harvest. We plant, and our children reap. They in turn plant and sow, but the harvest will fall to their children. So it is, and so it must be. And the lights of all shall carry on to the end of our days."

— Sy-laril, Timmon poet. ca. 2600 G.S.D.

Read on for an excerpt from TIMMISTRIA RISING,
Yellow World Book 2!

Darkness flipping tumbling
Head snaps red sparks
Grasp for something solid stop toppling again again
Red light flashing across
Cold chair hard pad air buzzing angry like bees in
her head
Awkward too large for her Cara body
I am not Cara?
Arms head swing strike hard beaten bruised
Burnt air stink stale breathing her own exhale
Wanting vomit begging for torment to end
But tumbling tumbling powerless limp like a glove
in a whirlpool
Lungs ache ragged breaths two three
Falling deep deep pit no more

Made in the USA
Columbia, SC
28 August 2019